ONE PUCKED UP PACK

SARAH BLUE

Spotify Playlist

Snowfall – Ingrid Michaelson

cardigan – Taylor Swift

Sweater Weather – The Neighbourhood

Somewhere Only We Know – Keane

The Scientist – Coldplay

Teeth – 5 Seconds of Summer

I Don't Wanna Live Forever – ZAYN, Taylor Swift

All You Had To Do Was Stay – Taylor Swift

I Will Wait – Mumford & Sons

drivers license – Olivia Rodrigo

Easy On Me – Adele

House Of Memories – Panic! At The Disco

Evergreen – Omar Apollo

High Water – Bishop Briggs

Only Love Can Hurt Like This – Paloma Faith

Circles – Post Malone

Wish I was Better – Kina, yaeow

you broke me first – Tate McRae

Can You Feel My Heart – Bring Me The Horizon

TiO – ZAYN

Same Old Love – Selena Gomez

Lego House – Ed Sheeran

She Will Be Loved – Maroon 5

Stay – Rihanna, Mikky Ekko

What is an Omegaverse?

An Omegaverse is an alternate universe where humans have a specific designation in a hierarchy based on their biology—-**in my series they are not shifters**. You are either an Alpha, Beta or an Omega. Your designation determines specific traits of your physiology and personality.

Alphas tend to be aggressive, they're generally more dominant and hold positions of authority. Many Alphas form packs which increase their wealth and dominance. Alphas have a history of taking advantage of and abusing Omegas. Alphas who are assigned male at birth have a fleshy ring near the base of their penis that swells during intercourse called a knot. It allows them to "lock" into place with an Omega. While Omegas are the most physiologically compatible when it comes to taking an Alpha's knot, Betas (or even Alphas) can take a knot with practice. Female Alphas have a lock that clenches around the penis and holds it inside, female Alphas and male Omegas are a great fit for this. Female Alphas can lock with other designations.

Betas are the closest to everyday humans. Their scent and sense of smell are not as strong as an Alpha or Omegas. They tend to be the most level-headed out of the designations.

Omegas tend to be the softest and most gentle of the designations. Generally, they do not hold positions of power, are homemakers or have positions in lower standing. Their scents are extremely arousing to Alphas. Out of all the designations, Omegas are the most likely to be abused or treated poorly. Alphas have the most opportunity to reproduce with Omegas.

Omegas go through **heat cycles** during which they are the most fertile. At this time they're sensitive to light, noise, and scents. They require the comfort of a nest full of soft fabrics and textures. Their body requires a large amount of sexual stimulation during a heat cycle, and it can last for several days. If the Omega is with an Alpha, their Alpha or Alphas will do everything in their power to make sure they are cared for and comfortable during their heat. Going through a heat cycle as an unbonded Omega can be unsafe for their physical health and sometimes their safety.

Scent matches are basically your fated mate. No other Alpha or Omega will smell as good as your scent match. You are physiologically a perfect match for each other, in this universe this is a very rare thing to find.

Please note that my Omegaverse falls under a more sweeter category than dark. Though there are issues in the system of dominance in society my books lean on the sweeter aspects of society and not the darker side.

To my two favorite girls who love a good cry Sam & Sandra

A Note From The Author

Welcome to the world of the Pucked Up Omegaverse. If you're here for the why choose hockey romance but don't know what an Omegaverse is, please make sure to check out the 'What is an Omegaverse' page to get some context.

Please note that there are depictions of loss, grief, and depression in this book. For a full list of content warnings for One Pucked Up Pack please visit my website.

https://authorsarahblue.com/content-warnings/

CHARLOTTE

Chapter One

*T*iming *is a bitch.*

It's kinda the entire story of my life. Not just as I stand here in the doorway of my shared dorm suite, watching Harrison Daiger knot the brains out of my roommate, Olive. While this truly sucks—seeing as I slept with that Alpha two weeks ago—it's really not the worst timing in the grand scheme of my life.

I wasn't even born on time, being eight weeks premature to my parents who had me in their early fifties. I designated as an Omega four years before my other peers, which has now had an overwhelming lingering effect on my social prowess. I didn't even really like Harrison, but I'm twenty. My heat could start at any time. It could start before I finish my degree, and I'd have to leave campus. Sometimes I just need a knot and the stupid, giant-cocked jock was nearby and let me go for a ride. He let me take, so I took. That's really the only thing the Alphas at this godforsaken school seem to be able to offer me—a good time and a thick knot. And who am I to deny what my baser instincts want? So I hook up with Alphas, and nothing more has ever come of it. *It's not like it bothers me or anything.*

At this moment though, it looks like he's taking from Olive, ass cheeks clenching as he ruts her on the kitchen island.

Olive's red hair is sticking to her back, her cheeks are pink with exertion and the room smells like watermelon and patchouli. It makes me want to fucking throw up.

I clear my throat, and the two of them look at me with very little interest. My roommate, not caring at all that I've walked in on her fucking someone. Harrison doesn't even look ashamed about banging my roommate two weeks after me. Honestly, it's not uncommon at Mercy University.

You have your Omega dorms, and the Alpha and Beta dorms are mixed. Thankfully, as Omegas, we only get one roommate and private rooms that are attached to a small kitchen and living space. They even allow us to scent each other to see if there will be any hostility in the living arrangement. But after living with Olive for three years, I can say with complete honesty that I'll never eat watermelon again in my life.

"Sanitize the counter when you're done," I say as I walk to my room, shutting the wood door, locking it, and nearly yeeting myself onto my beanbag chair. I'm so sick of this place. I don't mind the school portion of college. It's the people, the atmosphere, the fact that I don't feel like I fit in. I've been here three years and still my closest friends live back home in Vermont.

I feel hopelessly homesick. I miss my mom, the smell of our house, my childhood bedroom, the cold weather. But what I miss most is our dog, Hank.

Thinking about the giant, colossal head, no brain Newfoundland waiting for me at home is what breaks me. That's what makes me cry, not the guy I hooked up with banging my roommate, not missing my mom, not feeling alone. Thinking about the massive dog who will wag his tail so hard and will probably knock me straight on my ass when I see him is what breaks me.

I'm usually not much of a crier. Tears usually flow when I'm pissed, not when I'm sad. But being homesick has me feeling lost, I need to go home and recenter myself. My biggest regret in choosing to go to Mercy University is how far away it is, being all the way in North Carolina when my home is in New England. But you can't just turn down a full ride. Most of the Omegas in the dorm are here on partial or full scholarships. All a part of an initiative to give Omegas more options—supposedly.

Personally, I think it's a load of bullshit. Guess who doesn't get full rides to Mercy University? Alphas. All of them come from extremely wealthy families. It's basically like handing these entitled douchebags an Omega on a platter. The University boasts about the Omega dorms and being so progressive about Omega rights. It's all truly in an effort to help these Alphas find their pack and an Omega while they're in school. They don't even let us attend classes after we go into heat, unless you're bonded and find pack housing off-site.

As bitter as I probably sound about the injustice of it all, I'm not an idiot. I wasn't turning down a free education. I can say with complete certainty that I've given my studies my absolute best. I plan on being a bookkeeper, which I can do virtually. Being in an office is simply not an option. You don't have to disclose your designation on applications either. It may not be my dream, but it's pragmatic.

It's not that I'm fully opposed to pack life. I've just never met a single Alpha who has made me think that they're a decent person. I just use them for their knots, get what I need, and dip. I haven't had any complaints, and the part of me that's insecure notes how none of them has ever made an attempt to get to know me better either.

I wipe at my eyes and pull out my phone, staring at the picture of Hank. He looks so stupid but so adorable with his tongue lolling out, his black long fur covered in snowflakes. Winter break can't come soon enough. I scroll through my calendar and see that I can leave in a week and a half. I just need to get through these next ten days, and then I can be home.

On a sigh, I get out of the beanbag chair, open my cabinet, and grab a fist full of Oreos and a water bottle. I turn on my heated blanket and tuck into my bed, then text the one person in this universe who has my back. Piper, my best friend since I was four. We both grew up on the same street, and Piper has always been my rock. It makes more sense now that she designated as an Alpha. Our relationship has honestly been an Omega-Alpha relationship, minus the sexual benefits. I always worry that I take advantage of Piper, but she calls me her trial Omega. She's on the path to become a surgeon and doesn't have the time to settle down and treat an Omega properly (her words, not mine). So for now, knowing how to take care of me will prepare her for the male Omega of her dreams.

It's unfortunate we couldn't just be into each other. Not that we didn't dry hump a few times during sleep overs, but we were truly meant to be best friends. Piper may not romantically be my Alpha, but she's my soulmate in one of the deepest senses I imagine people can be connected.

Winter break can't come soon enough.

Piper:

You're telling me. If this is undergrad, I have no idea how I'm going to make it through the next ten years.

Are you sure you want to be a surgeon?

Piper:

More sure than anything.

I'll be your sugar mama while you go to school, don't worry.

Piper:

You know I was serious about Boston or New Haven if it happens for me next year.

I'm thinking about it.

Piper:

You better. Hot chocolate date first thing when you get in, and bring Hank!

See you soon.

Piper:

See you soon, Charles.

I roll my eyes at her nickname for me and put down my phone, feeling more at ease having spoken to Piper. Her offer to move into her apartment in Boston and finish school online is tempting. However, if you go virtual, your scholarship goes down in funding. *Shocker.*

But I know that if I lived with Piper, she would help me with the issues I have. She would help me with my social anxiety and be there for me. Part of me doesn't want to be so dependent on her. I know she'll be busy with school, and we won't have a ton of time to be together, but anything has to be better than this.

There's a soft knock on my door, and I groan, not wanting to leave the warmth and coziness of my bed. I somehow prevail and pad my feet to the door, and when I open it, it's a red-faced Olive. My roommate is pretty and slightly taller than me, which isn't hard since I'm barely five foot.

"Sorry about Harrison. I thought you were going to be in the library till late," Olive apologizes.

"It's not a big deal. It's fine, Olive."

"I know you hooked up with him two weeks ago. He told me."

"We did," I say, not that I was trying to hide anything. It's just a little awkward to know you've both ridden the same ride. I wonder if it was as unmemorable for her as it was for me.

"I just wanted to make sure there were no hard feelings. We're going on a date before winter break."

Walking in on them fucking didn't hurt me. The fact that he wants to court her, take her on a date—that's what makes me feel like I got punched in the gut. It's just another reminder of how

I'm not good enough. It's why I hate being at Mercy so much; I'm completely whittled down to being an Omega, and I can't even seem to get that right. Nothing I do is good enough for these people or these Alphas. I'm just there for a good time and seen as nothing more than what my body can give them.

What is it about my personality or scent that makes me so unlikable to these other Alphas? I know that I'm not outwardly bubbly, and maybe I have a little resting bitch face, but none of them care to take the time to get to know me.

But he's taking the time to get to know Olive.

"That's great, Olive. Seriously, no hard feelings."

"Phew. I wouldn't want to make things uncomfortable, since he will be stopping by," she says, and I nod my head. "Of course, only during specific hours."

Alphas have to check in at the reception of our building, and then they're escorted to the dorm they are visiting. There's a strict time frame that they can be here, and the receptionist always checks in with the Omegas to make sure that the Alpha is a wanted guest. I can at least appreciate the concern for our safety. At least they aren't putting us in a lottery to see which one of these smug assholes gets to knot and bite us.

Maybe that's my problem with Mercy. Most of the Alphas here are smug athletes who think they're god's gift to women. Maybe I should make a rule: no more jocks. But it doesn't help that most Alphas hold mostly physical attributes, and they happen to be attributes I really like. There's something about abs, meaty thighs, and a firm ass.

Maybe I should give Betas another go. I'm sure they could get creative with the amount of toys that are on the market. But then again, there's truly nothing as satisfying as an Alpha knot. Or Alpha pheromones, not that I've found any Alpha scent addictive. They're nice, better than a Beta's scent, but no Alpha has me wanting to roll around in their scent like catnip at the present.

"Seriously, it's fine. Invite Harrison over. It won't bother me."

"Thanks, Charlotte. You're seriously the best roommate," Olive says as she walks over to her portion of the suite.

I shut the door and roll my eyes. Of course I'm the best roommate; I stay in my room, keep all my food in here, and basically never talk to her. I could have tried harder to get to know Olive, sure. But what's the point? Eventually, Olive and I will part ways. Olive lives here in Raleigh. Not to mention she wants a bond mark ASAP. Being friends with Omegas once they're bonded is impossible. Priorities change when you have a pack. Why set myself up to get hurt? I plan on moving back home the first chance I get. Why grow attached to someone I know won't stick around?

That thought stings, and I shove the miserable feeling down. I'm already emotional enough. Thinking about my abandonment issues is not where my mind needs to wander. I don't want to think about how my mom is turning seventy this year, or how my dad was sixty-two when we lost him. Or how I've navigated this designation alone, and I still can't help but always feel lonely. No, these aren't emotions I want to feel right now.

What I need now are some more snacks, *Gilmore Girls*, and my heating pad. That will be enough to get me through these next ten days. And probably my arsenal of sex toys, because as much as I hate to admit it, seeing Harrison wanting to actually get to know Olive makes me not want to let any of these Alphas even get a whiff of my perfume.

While I should make a promise to turn a new leaf, become someone who is more open and friendly, I decide to masturbate until I fall asleep.

There's nothing a good orgasm can't fix.

MIKAEL

Chapter Two

"**G**ood game, men," coach Kumerlee cheers as we all skate off the ice into the locker room. My nose is still fucking bleeding, and I want to go back out there and punch number twenty-one so goddamn hard he can't remember what day it is. At least I tripped the fuck and didn't get called on it—twice.

I rein it in, my temper a blessing and a curse. It's the one thing that makes me valuable. I'm nowhere near as talented of a hockey player as Eli or in as niche of a position as Anders. Shit, they flew him across the country to come here and play. He's going to be a goalie at a collegiate level for one season and then go pro. Eli will be drafted within the first couple of rounds. Sometimes I'm jealous of his talent and the fact that his parents paid for him to go to skating classes as a kid. I know Eli didn't have an easier life, but at least money made it bearable.

What I do is brawl, my sheer size making me important on the ice. The fact that I'm not afraid to take a hit, or hit someone else is one of my strengths in hockey. I'm sure if I went to therapy, they would want to talk in more detail about why I enjoy getting physical and how it stems from my childhood. But I don't plan on getting my head examined any time soon.

My only focus is to keep my grades up enough, so I can stay on this team and do whatever the fuck I can do to play pro. If I don't get on a team, I don't know what I'll do. All my eggs are in this super small basket that's so competitive and cutthroat, but I'm not sure how I can make this dream happen. I'll even take a feeder team. I just have to be playing hockey in the states. I'd even settle for a team on the Canadian West Coast. But I'd like to be as far from Quebec as possible.

"NHL is watching, Martel," coach says, clamping a hand on my shoulder. Nearly everyone in hockey uses last names or nicknames, but sometimes hearing my last name makes me sick.

"I know, coach."

"You're tough, and how fast you can move on the ice with how fucking big you are is exceptional, but you need to learn when to pull it back. It's a brutal sport, but you gotta rein that anger in," he says. It's not like he hasn't given me this speech a million times. "If you can get that under control, I think I can help you take this to the next level," he says.

"You mean it?"

"Do I look like a fuckin' liar?" he says, a mix of German and Bostonian accent in there. It's just as odd as it fucking sounds, listening to him talk. He's a hulk of a man, slightly bulkier than me and only a few inches shorter, probably around six foot three.

"No, sir."

"Great, get cleaned up, and get ready for debrief."

I walk with my skates on, entering the locker room. The last game before winter break was at home, and as badly as I want some time off, I can't afford to lose any momentum. Thank fuck Eli's parents are loaded and are letting us stay at their cabin in Vermont. There's apparently a lake right outside the cabin that freezes over in the winter. The perfect place to make sure we don't get rusty during the time off. Eli and Anders are probably going to hate me when I make them do skate drills and weight lifting with me. They can complain all they want. We need to stay focused, and now is not the time to forget about our goal. Not when recruiters and agents will choose who they want over the next couple of months. Eli and Anders already have eyes on them. I need to stand out, and that isn't going to happen by slacking off or getting distracted.

"What did coach say?" Eli asks, his sturdy shoulder bumping into mine as he passes me and sits on the bench, unlacing his skates, and starting to undress.

"Just to control the temper."

"What's new?" my best friend laughs. Eli is one of the few people I never get pissed at. It's really hard to get mad at a ginger who smiles, takes you on vacation, lets you crash at his house, and not to mention is the team captain.

"Yeah, he said if I can get that under control, he might know some teams that are interested."

Eli smiles in happiness for me before he sighs, and the smile falls. The likelihood of us all ending up on the same team is so slim; the statistics of all three of us going pro are already thin enough. The idea of not being able to see him and Anders everyday leaves a pit in my chest. They're the closest thing to a family I've ever had. The Alpha part of me knows that they're pack, but the realistic side of me knows that it's not possible with being a professional athlete.

Part of being a pack is being able to live with each other. No way that's going to happen. The other part would be finding an Omega who likes all of us. Finding an Omega is hard enough, finding one who likes all of us, that's like finding a goddamn four-leaf clover in a fucking desert. Let alone that none of us have time for one. That's something to think about in the future when we're hanging up our skates in the professional sector. It's just not heard of, packs in professional sports. You have to choose one or the other.

"Don't think too hard about it," Eli says, giving me a gentle look. I sigh and sit down. He knows how much this all means to me. It all spilled out of me on a drunken night freshman year. It's basically when Eli adopted me. His family might be loaded, but Eli needed someone too. Then Anders moved to America with his thick accent and needed some friends and, well, we all just got each other.

Not that I don't like the other guys on my team, who are all predominately Alphas as well. It's just that Anders, Eli, and I, we have a bond. We get each other, and it's a shame that if we wanted to be anything else but professional athletes, we would make that pack come true. The only thing I want almost as much as a career in hockey is a family I can be proud of. But I need to be proud of myself first. I need to prove that I'm more than my namesake before I'd ever be ready to have a pack or a family.

"I'm going to be hitting that lake hard during break," I say to Eli.

He smiles. He just got a veneer put in a few weeks ago, so he, thankfully, has all his teeth. I have a partial that I take out during playtime, so I currently look ridiculous missing an incisor right now. The price you have to pay to be the team's enforcer.

"Honestly, I can't wait to just have some time to clear my head. The cabin is great. You guys will love it."

When Eli says cabin, I'm not sure if Anders and I will be sharing a bunk bed, or if it will be a mansion and his family just calls it a cabin because it's their smallest property.

"Your family is really okay with us staying at the cabin for Christmas?" Eli rolls his eyes as he takes off padding and throws it onto the floor.

"You know very well that Jean and Edward don't give a fuck if they see me at Christmas." I nod my head and start unlacing my skates. Eli is proof that your parents can give you all the money in the world, not hit you, but you still have no idea if they really love you or not.

Anders is the only one of us with loving parents. They just also happen to live in Finland. From what I've gathered, they are considered upper middle class, and his family is extremely supportive of his hockey accomplishments. As they should be, the man has saved our asses on multiple occasions this season. He's been the best goalie that Boston University has seen in decades.

Speaking of the devil, he walks out of the showers with a towel wrapped around his waist. "Are we leaving tonight or tomorrow?" he asks. Anders' English is absolutely immaculate. The man knows the language better than I do, but he has a slight accent to most words.

"I figured tomorrow. It's been snowing further north, and driving through that shit is a nightmare," Eli replies. Anders lets out a sigh of relief and so do I. As many hits as I dolled out tonight, I took just as many. My shoulder and quads are sore, and I could use a good night's rest before a road trip.

"What is there to do in Vermont?" Anders asks.

Solid question, but as long as I'm off campus and not back home, I'm content. I don't care if there isn't running water and we have to shit in a bucket.

"Fishing, hiking, skating, relaxing. And the town is actually pretty nice, there are plenty of food options. We can't ski or snowboard, but maybe we could go tubing."

We both nod our heads. The last thing you want to do is risk a completely avoidable injury this close to finishing the season and the potential of going pro.

"We've gotta be ready to kick ass during the Desert Hockey Classic," I say.

"I do not like Arizona," Anders says in a monotone voice, and Eli laughs. We can all agree that we like being in New England. The dream would be all being drafted to teams in the area. I would even settle for anything, as long as it's cold.

Coach walks in, a big smile on his face. He chomps on his gum dramatically with his clipboard in his hands.

"This was a good game against UConn. Those are the types of scoreboards I want to see. Becky," he says, looking at Eli. His last name is Beckford, and somehow the nickname Becky caught on in his high school days. "Next time we'll get you that hat trick. Larsen," he says, looking at Anders. "Excellent goaltending. Defense, that's how you protect your goalie. I'll be sending out game footage during the break. I expect all of you to relax during winter break, but to not take this time for granted. Right after Christmas, we're back on the ice, and then we're in Arizona. You need to be stretching, lifting, and getting in skate time when possible. John will email you workout sheets, and I expect you to keep logs. Understood?"

There's a loud chant of understanding from the whole team, and Coach nods his head. We all circle each other, no matter what level of undress we're in, and put our hands in the middle. A low bark between us picks up until it's loud as fuck. It might be stupid, but it gets us riled up before we all scream, "Bulldogs!" and throw our hands in the air.

There's a ton of chatter between teammates as I get into the showers. This camaraderie is something I never want to give up. I don't know if it's the competitiveness in me or the Alpha side of me that craves this. I crave the competition, the revelry, the support of my teammates. Hockey is in my blood, and I'll do anything to hold on to this as long as possible. It's the one place I can let my anger out in a healthy way, where I can skate so fucking hard my lungs hurt. I'm sure there are more important things in life than a sport. But for me, this is it, and that includes the people that come along with it.

CHARLOTTE

Chapter Three

"Honey, can you take Hank out?" my mom hollers from her bedroom. Hank is already lying on the bed with me, so I kiss his massive head and scratch behind his thick, floppy ears.

"You wanna go outside?" I ask him, and he does that cute thing where he tilts his head, his tongue lolling out of his mouth as he rises from the bed and heads toward the backdoor. I put on my boots, hat, gloves, and jacket. As soon as I slide open the door, he barrels into the snow on the ground. Little balls of snow and ice gather into his deep black fur.

I inhale deeply, the fresh air filling my lungs, and release the breath I was holding. It smells like home here, and I'm finding it harder every day to find the will to go back to school with only three more weeks left of winter break. Being here has cleared my head. I don't want to miss time away from my mom, or my dog. I'm tired of the overwhelming scents in the Omega dorms, and the overconfident Alphas who think they run the University. I'm planning on bringing it up with my mom. I know I can't let my education go to waste, but I don't know how much longer I can stay somewhere that I clearly don't belong.

The air is so crisp and fresh; I take another deep inhale and hum, Hank trotting proudly over to me with his big Kong ball in his mouth.

"Ready?" I ask him as I take the drool-covered red ball and toss it over the snow. He chases happily after it and brings it back quickly. He might be over a hundred and fifty pounds, but he's still just a baby to me. His first birthday is coming up in February. I don't know what charged my mom to get a massive dog with no help, but she said she missed me and needed company around the house. I guess the fact that he's so big can make him feel like a human presence.

Hank drags his nose around the snow, rooting around the ground for something. The yard is completely fenced, so I feel comfortable leaving him outside. "Do you want to go in, boy? Or stay out here?" He plops down into the snow and lies on his side, giving me his answer. "All right then," I say, smiling at him and going back inside.

My mom keeps the house warm, and it smells like campfires and pine in the house. It's always smelled this way. It's one of my comfort scents. We aren't allowed to have candles in the dorms, so I use wax melts to try to recreate the scents. Our home is small but cozy. A simple ranch-style home with two bedrooms, two bathrooms, a small living room, and an eat-in kitchen. Not much has changed in the decor since I was a child. It's simple with the kitchen having pine-colored cabinets and green laminate countertops and two shaky wooden stools under the island. The living room still has wood paneling, the original fireplace works, but we don't use it often. There's family pictures everywhere. Sometimes it hurts to look at them. To see my dad happy and smiling and remembering that he isn't here.

I worry about my mom being here alone. Her health problems always make me worry, not to mention she's close to seventy. She's diabetic and tends to forget to take care of herself. Every time I'm home, I do my best to make sure she sets appointments for herself. It also feels like every time I come home, I see how much further she's slipping away from me.

I sigh, blowing warm air into my hands as I make myself a coffee. "Mom, do you want a coffee?" I shout down the hall.

"No thanks, hun," she says. I can hear a low hum of whatever show she's watching. I put my favorite hazelnut coffee into the Keurig and feel relief when it doles out the hot substance. There isn't sugar on the counter, so I tug on the first drawer under the coffee maker. It doesn't give right away. But when I tug hard enough, it opens. The drawer is stuffed with envelopes, so full that I can see that documents are even jammed behind the drawer.

Taking the first letter in my hands, addressed to my mother, it's already been read. I probably shouldn't read her mail, but something about how many letters in here is worrisome to me. I blink a few times, wetting my contacts as I read the page. The first words are diabetic retinopathy and diabetic neuropathy. I read further, seeing that her primary care is referring her to different experts in these fields and that this was sent two months ago. I pull out the next envelope. It's a payment from my dad's social security that is signed, saying she deposited it into her account. The next envelope is from

my school, stating that my tuition is still being covered until I reach
my first heat. I roll my eyes and put the envelopes back in the drawer.

I need to make sure my mom made those appointments, and as
much as I want to leave school, I can't. There's no way I can afford
to get my degree from Mercy without getting the scholarship funds.
I need to at the very least finish out this year, and then maybe I can
transfer to an online option.

I can do that, finish out this year and then come home. That way
I can have a degree, bring in money, and take care of mom. No way
am I waiting for the pack of my dreams to sweep me off my feet and
solve all these fucking problems for me. That would be nice though,
wouldn't it?

I find sugar in the pantry and add creamer to my coffee, letting the
warm liquid take off some of the chill. I'm meeting Piper tonight,
but as I scroll through my phone, I look at the weather for tomorrow.
Mostly sunny and around forty degrees. I make a plan to get Hank
up early in the morning, so I can go for an early skate. I've been going
almost every other day to the lake to skate, let out some frustration,
and get some much needed exercise. While I tend to stay in my dorm
room at school, being at home makes me feel like I have so much
more freedom.

My feet pad along the soft beige carpet that my mom is hyper
diligent about vacuuming. As I get to her door, I knock on the
frame. "Yeah, hun?" she says as she folds her laundry. I watch her fold
the shirt and wonder if that's what I'll look like in nearly fifty years.
I've seen pictures of my mom in her twenties and thirties. I might
be more petite, but we share the same face shape and bright blonde

hair. I hate to say it, but sometimes I hate my mom for having me at nearly fifty. Not that I was planned, but I'll always feel like I never got enough time with my parents. Like I'll be alone. My parents are Betas, tried to have kids for forever, and at the ages of forty-nine and fifty, they had me. It would mean more to me if she took care of herself better so that we had more time. I need more time.

"I found the letters in the drawer. Have you made those appointments?"

She huffs, irritated that I looked at the drawer, but doesn't stop folding. "Yes, it's just all the way in Burlington. Soonest I could get in is the spring," she says. I'm at least happy that she's taking this seriously.

"How are your eyes doing?"

"They're fine, honey. How about yours?"

"They're good. The new contacts work great. I just need to do better about taking them out at night and wearing my glasses."

"No headaches?"

"Only sometimes." I shrug. I've worn glasses or contacts my whole life. My vision is basically shit. I had laser surgery when I was four to try to mitigate some of the retinopathy. But luckily the new contacts help, and there are always my glasses.

"You'll let me know if that changes."

"Yes, but you'll also let me know if anything changes with you."

She stops folding her laundry and wraps me up in a warm hug. My mom might be a Beta, but she smells like home to me. It's probably a combination of our home scents and the fresh air. I cling to it, wrapping my arms around her body.

"I'm happy to have you home," she whispers against the top of my head, and I squeeze her tighter.

"I'm happy to be home."

"You're my special girl, you know that?" I nod my head against my chest and sigh, hating myself for my thoughts earlier. My mom might have been the oldest on the playground and got mistaken for a grandma, but fuck, if I didn't have the best mom anyone could have asked for. She's always protected me, always made sure I was first, and she always let me know how well loved I was. I cling against her, smelling her scent that warms my blood and makes me feel loved and whole. I don't know how I can let this go. Surely nothing else, no one else, could ever make me feel a fraction of cared for as she does.

"Don't you have plans with Piper?"

I sigh and pull away, my mom stroking my hair and the side of my jaw as we part. "Yeah, she's picking me up, and we're going to Jack's."

"Tell her I said hi."

"I will." I squeeze my mom one more time for good measure. I walk back to the kitchen and whistle for Hank to come inside. He prances toward me with snow clinging to his fur. I grab a towel and wipe down his paws, belly, face, and chin.

"That's a good boy. You wanna see Piper?" I ask, like he completely knows who Piper is. Hank may be cute, but as far as brightness goes, I would say he's on the side of big head, small brain. He lies down in the kitchen next to the heating vent as I do some finishing touches to my makeup before meeting with Piper.

Fat snowflakes fall from the sky as I open the front door, Hank nudging Piper's thigh. She dutifully pets his head and coos at him.

CHARLOTTE

Chapter Four

I groan as I wake up, blinking and seeing nothing but a blurry black blob in front of me. He decides to thoroughly lick my face by way of saying good morning. Mindlessly, I reach for my glasses on the side table and put them on my face. The sun is rising, and I stretch in bed, knowing that I'll miss the warmth, but if I don't get up now, I won't get up at all.

"Let's get ready, boy." I pat his head and let him outside as I get ready, putting in my contacts and dressing warmly. I keep my hair down, loose around my back, as I put on a wool cap. When I let Hank in, I put his vest on. It has pockets, and he carries our snacks, water, and my skates as I get my boots, jacket, and gloves on.

Say what you want about big dogs, but Hank loves being useful, and he loves the snow. We're kinda made for each other.

The lake is about a mile walk, but I don't enjoy driving, let alone in the snow and ice. My boots have spikes on them to help me not eat shit. I'm not a terribly clumsy person, but anything can happen when you're walking on snow and ice. Hank also walks close beside me, never walking too far ahead or astray. We both love these days when we get to spend most of the day outside. He gets to roll around in the snow and cool off, and I get to forget all about school. He's slightly miserable in the summer, but it could be worse.

I smile at the beautiful scenery, the trees covered in thick snow, the lake completely frozen over with a thick blanket of ice. I grab the blanket off of Hank's vest and put it on the ground as I take my boots off, storing them on the blanket and putting on my skates. They're old, nearly a decade old, but they're broken in and perfect on the ice. They were originally white, but at this point, they're more of a tan color. I lace up the pink laces, making sure they're tight enough around my ankles.

I smile down as I look at the worn skates. Nothing but good memories of my dad taking me out on this very lake and holding my hand as we skated together. Or when he would drive me into town and take me to the indoor rink for lessons. My parents didn't have a ton of disposable income, but when I told them I wanted to learn how to skate, they made it happen. I went to group classes and would go to open skates. I smile at the memories even though sometimes they hurt so fucking bad I want to crack into a million pieces.

I pet Hank and kiss his head, relieve him of all of our items, and put them on the blanket. He knows to stay nearby and not walk on the ice. He just walks around lazily and plops down on the snow now and then and uses his snout to dig. "Be a good boy," I tell him. He acknowledges me by raising his head, but continues to explore.

My arms are out by my sides, holding my balance as I walk on the skates, reaching the lake's edge. As soon as I'm on the pristine surface, I sigh as the sharp edge of my skate leads me farther out onto the ice. The air is so fresh; the surrounding sounds are so quiet as I glide over the ice. It feels like I'm floating as my feet carry me in a small circle.

I never thought I was going to be a figure skater, but I know a few tricks. Really, I just love skating, the feeling of the cold snowy air hitting my skin and the weightlessness of going too fast over the smooth surface.

Sometimes on the ice, it's like my head is clear. Skating has a deep sense of nostalgia for me, and sometimes it makes life seem simpler. Like all I have to focus on is keeping myself balanced and feeling the cold air against my skin. I'm not thinking about my issues at Mercy, or all the other overwhelming shit that can consume me if I let it. I'm just Charlotte, and I can live in the moment completely.

I just simply skate. I do a small twirl and love the dizzying feeling it gives me. With my arms close to my chest, I do another one. My cheeks are cold, and smiling makes my teeth cold, but I can't help the grin that takes over my face.

It's like I'm in my own snow globe of happiness. It's just me, and the lake, and Hank is around here somewhere. I'm so caught up in me and how light I feel I don't even notice at first the guys on the other side of the lake. I squint, seeing three large bodies holding sticks and one smaller one holding a stick as well. I shrug and just keep to my small corner of the lake, holding in this happiness for as long as I possibly can.

I do a spot check and make sure Hank is nearby. His gaze is facing the newcomers on the ice, but he doesn't make a move toward them, just observing.

My calves are feeling a little overworked, but I push past the burn, skating backwards and in a circle doing a few spins. My lungs feel like they may explode, a combination of the skating and how cold the air is. I should take a break, eat a snack, take a drink, and warm up. Reluctantly, I skate toward where my blanket is off the ice. I applaud myself for being an Omega who takes care of herself. I'm nearly to my little set up by the ice when I'm hit with such an intense force it makes me fall to the ice.

My feet in skates don't hold me up as I go down harshly, the back of my head hitting the ice. My hand clutches my chest where whatever the fuck hit me made contact. I thought my lungs hurt before, but now they're screaming. I blink my eyes and can't see shit, and I wonder how hard I hit my head.

"Mother fucking cocksucker," I mumble under my breath.

"Holy fucking shit," I hear a deep voice say.

"Kid, you can't just slap shot and not know where the puck is going." That voice is a little mean, slightly accented, but not an accent I'm unfamiliar with. Maybe French Canadian?

I'm nearly wheezing. My head is throbbing. For some reason, my nose feels wet. And don't get me started on how bad my left tit hurts. I groan and hear a bark in the distance. No doubt Hank is worrying about me. I try to sit up, but feel dizzy and lie back down instead.

"You probably really hurt that kid. You need to be more careful." That accent is different from the first,, but I can't help but like it. His voice is soft and commanding at the same time, while still having a softer edge.

The sound of skates hitting the ice fast and hard booms through my ears before there are three loud scratches against the ice.

"Hey, kid, you okay?" the one with the deep voice says. I remove my gloved hand from my face and whine. It's pathetic, but I'm hurt.

"I'm not a fucking kid," I groan.

"Clearly not," the soft voiced one says.

The mean voiced one starts spouting out a string of phrases I can't understand, and I touch my head again. Oh my god, did I hit my head so hard that I can't understand?

"Oh fuck," I groan. "I can't even understand you."

"Stop cursing in French," deep voice says to the mean one.

"Sorry," he says. I'm blinking, the sun still bright above us as I take the three men in. With the cold air, scenting is extremely difficult, but there's no doubt in my mind that they are all Alphas. I can only see blobs of them, and I blink a few more times. Great, I've hit my head so hard my vision has gotten worse. *Just fucking great.*

"Where does it hurt?" deep voice says.

"My chest and my head," I say, wincing as I touch the back of my head.

"Can you get up?" sweet voice asks. I look over at him, blinking. My vision clearly is not adjusting well to hitting my head, so I clench my eyes shut.

"If I pick you up and carry you off the ice, will your dog freak out?" deep voice asks.

"No, Hank is a good boy." I wince as soon as I say it, but I hear a few light chuckles.

"Mikael, go grab her stuff and lead the dog to the cabin. Anders, grab our stuff." I really like the deep voice guy, I've decided. The way he tells the two men what to do and they do so with no bitching at all. There's something about a man in charge that has always enthralled me. While I'm guilty of being a bit bossy, it would be nice to shut my brain off every now and then.

"If he bites me, it's on you." I know now that's Mikael's voice. *The mean one.* Once my vision isn't fucked, I'll be able to put faces to names.

"Just get the dog." He clears his throat, and there are two hands, very large hands, on my side. My lips part, and I gasp. "Can I pick you up, sweetheart? Is that okay?" he asks. I wonder if he can smell that I'm an Omega. I can't pick up his scent, but I know when I'm near his chest, he will no doubt be able to scent me. I wonder if maybe my sense of smell isn't as strong as other Omegas. Maybe that's why no Alphas have been alluring to me. Fuck, I'm just really damaged goods at this point, aren't I?

"That's fine."

His hands are gentle as he picks me up by the back of my neck, being careful of my head, and underneath my legs. He stiffens as he brings me close to his chest, and I can hear his inhale like a pin drop. He clears his throat and attempts to act cool. Meanwhile, I rest my head against his chest, getting a whiff of the richest pine scent I've ever smelled. It's not a heavy scent; it's just enough to entice me, and I wonder how I can get his scent to be thicker. I'd deny it in the future, but my first thought was that *he smells like home.*

ELI

Chapter Five

As soon as the little shit who had been following us around all morning took the shot, I knew against all odds it was going to hit the small person a distance away. What I didn't expect is how fucking hard the kid could hit the puck.

We all thought he hit a kid with how short she is, but now that she's in my arms, her white blonde hair flowing around her face and her rich pancake and syrup scent infiltrating the center of my brain, we couldn't have been more wrong.

My experience with Omegas is basically zero. Not that Omegas are rare, but they aren't common. They aren't in everyday public spaces. They certainly shouldn't be out on a frozen lake by themselves. The thought irritates me as I frown down at her.

"Why are you out skating on the ice by yourself, little Omega?" Her eyes are shut, and I wonder if her head hurts really bad or if something else is going on.

"There's usually no one here, and I love to skate," she says with a little bite. I can't help the grin that takes over my face.

"It's really dangerous to be on a frozen lake by yourself. You never know what could happen," I say gently. Something deep in the inner core of my being tells me to be gentle with her. She's small, carrying her is nothing. Skating with her bridal style in my arms is effortless. But I don't know shit about Omegas, and I don't want to come across as a domineering Alpha asshole.

Her cheeks turn pinker than they already were from the chill of the air, and she shrugs her shoulders. "You're probably right. I did bring Hank though."

"Hank?"

"My dog."

"Interesting name. That dog is fucking huge, how much does he weigh?"

"Around a hundred and fifty pounds," she says, her eyes still closed. I want to look at her, see what color her eyes are. I feel like she'll be easier to read then. I'm just pleased that she's talking, and that she didn't hit her head so hard she's confused.

"What's your name?"

"Charlotte," she says, and I smile.

"That's a beautiful name." Her cheeks redden even further, and I can't help but to squeeze her just a bit closer to my chest.

"What's your name?" she asks. Her voice is soft and the perfect pitch, almost melodic.

"I'm Eli. The one who was cursing in French is Mikael, and the Finnish one is Anders."

She nods her head, resting more of her face against my chest. I've probably been skating way slower than necessary. Her body relaxes slightly in my hold.

"Where are you taking me?"

"Our cabin is right here on the edge of the lake."

She opens her eyes then, blinking rapidly. Her left eye is completely blue, the right is blue on the top half and green on the bottom half. They're striking, but unfocused. I watch as her pupils dilate and panic takes over.

"Are your eyes bothering you?" I keep my tone calm so that she doesn't worry.

"I think my contacts somehow shifted or fell out when I fell. I can't see fuck all," she says. and I can't help the laugh that rumbles out of my throat. I even catch her smirking at the sound. "I have glasses in Hank's vest," she says, and I nod my head.

"You can rest your eyes till we get you there."

"You're not going to lock me in your basement and keep me captive?" I laugh again, and she smiles.

"Not unless you want us to. Even then, the cabin has a crawl space, and well, even though you're tiny, I don't think you'd be comfortable." I finally reach the edge where the ice meets the snow. This is going to be the tough part. I brace my ankles and walk steadily, making sure that there aren't any divots on the ground. Luckily Anders and Mikael took everything to the house and are headed outside with boots on. Anders opens his arms first, and I pass the Omega over to him. His eyes widen as he takes in the same realization as I did a few moments ago.

"Yes, I'm an Omega. Can we move on?" Anders stills but carries her into the cabin. Mikael looks at her with curiosity, but apprehension as well. While my experience with Omegas is limited, something tells me that Charlotte is a little different. More blunt with her approach than what we've been taught about Omega behavior. And I don't know if all Omegas smell that fucking amazing, but I want to bottle her scent up and carry it with me everywhere I go.

I shuck off my skates and leave them in the wet room next to Anders' and Mikael's. Anders places the Omega on the couch, grabbing a small blanket while Mikael lights the fire. Her massive beast of a dog walks up to her and nudges her hand with his snout. She pets his head without opening her eyes. "It's okay, baby. I'm fine." Her voice is soft as she calms the panicked dog. "Can one of you get Hank's vest? My glasses are in the blue pocket."

Rounding the corner, I grab the vest and dig into the pocket, grabbing the glasses case and putting it into her delicate hand.

"Thank you," she says quietly as she opens the case and puts the glasses on. She sighs as she blinks her eyes. The frames suit her face, thin black frames on the top and none on the bottom. Anders lets out a breath when he takes in her face for the first time.

"How's your head?" he asks. She blinks at him a few times, her eyesight adjusting as she gives him a smirk.

"It hurts, but I don't think I have a concussion or broken skin."

"May I?" he asks, and she nods her head, giving him permission to touch her. Anders leans over, his blond hair looking nearly brown compared to hers as he removes her hat. White blonde hair clings to the wool as he places it down on the couch. His fingers gently search through her hair, feeling for a bump. I watch as the Omega's eyes close hazily and her lips part as my Alpha teammate inspects her gently.

"You might have a bump, and your eyes?" Anders is probably the sweetest one of all of us, but the way he's speaking to the Omega now is in a tone I haven't even heard before.

"Much better," she says, nodding.

"Where did the puck hit you?" Mikael interrupts the conversation.

Charlotte closes her mouth and looks at Mikael, taking in his appearance. "My left tit, but you're not checking it," she says. Anders and I can't help the laugh that explodes out of each of us. Mikael's mouth is parted in surprise as he looks at the small Omega. "Do you have any Tylenol or a bathroom I can use?"

"I'll get it," Mikael grumbles as he heads to the kitchen.

"Let's take off your skates first," I say, and unlike Anders, I don't ask. I just get on my knees and unlace her skates, noting the wear they've taken on. No doubt from years of use and love. Something about that is endearing to me. Charlotte gapes at me as I stand back up, towering over her on the couch.

"Follow me," I say, holding out my hand. She looks down at my hand like it's offensive for a moment before shrugging and putting her much smaller hand in mine. Why do I want to touch her? I mean, from a biological standpoint I get it, and now that we're in the warmth of the cabin, it makes more sense. Her scent is heady and thick like syrup is dripping down my throat. The need to protect and do other things to this Omega is staggering.

The clicking of nails against the hardwood follows us as we reach the bathroom. I release her hand, and she pats the dog's head.

"Hank, sit," she says. He doesn't listen, and she just rolls her eyes and walks into the bathroom, shutting the door behind her.

Feeling like a loser standing outside the door, I leave Hank on Omega duty as I walk back into the open concept living room and kitchen. I might have undersold the place to the guys. While it's a cabin, it's a luxury cabin. We each have our own bedroom and bathroom, and all the furnishings are modern and new.

Taking off all the layers from outside, I shuck them onto the dining room table. It feels stifling with the fire going in here and for other reasons I'm not sure I want to explore.

"A fucking Omega?" Mikael hisses.

"What?" I ask, blinking at him.

"It's going to smell like fucking pancakes and syrup in here for weeks. We should have taken her home."

"She hurt herself, and it was partially our fault. We need to make sure she's okay."

Mikael scoffs and pours himself a scotch, and I groan. "It's ten in the morning."

"And?"

"And we have a guest, and you're being a dick."

"I'm not being a dick to her."

"Well, you're certainly not being nice," I reply. Anders hums in agreement.

"What do you want me to do, wait on her hand and foot and treat her like a princess?" Kinda, yeah, because that's what I want to do.

"No, just be fucking friendly to someone for once."

"Fine." He shoots the scotch back in one go, and I wince.

The soft turn of the door and soft footsteps being followed by paws alert us to Charlotte's arrival. She's taken off her jacket, and it's in her hand. I hold out an arm and throw it on the table next to mine. She winces, and her eyes look watery as she cups her boob. I shouldn't look at her chest, but I do. She doesn't have an overabundance, but I can't deny that I like what I see.

"Everything okay?"

"It's just bruised really bad. Do you have an ice pack?" She hardly even finishes the sentence before Anders is taking a bag of frozen pizza rolls out of the freezer.

"Come," he says, holding out his hand and tugging the Omega back to the couch. He directs her to lie down, hands her the frozen pizza rolls, and proceeds to cover her in a faux fur blanket. What in the fuck is going on here?

Mikael comes back to the room handing Anders the Tylenol and water, which Charlotte takes without a fuss.

"I'm sorry," she says.

"What the fuck are you sorry for?" Mikael says, and I want to smack him on the back of the head.

"Imposing. I'll leave just as soon as this headache goes away." I see the smugness fall off Mikael's face. Meanwhile Anders looks like he has a unibrow with how furrowed his eyebrows are.

"You're fine, *mon sucre d'érable*." After he says it, it looks like Mikael wants to slap himself as he walks away and heads to his bedroom.

"That wasn't English, right?" Charlotte asks concerned.

"It was French."

"Good, thought I was losing it." Hank gives no fucks as he jumps onto the leather coach, taking up the second half and resting his head on the Omega's thighs. "Sorry, is it okay that he's up here?"

Even if I cared, which I couldn't give a fuck, I wouldn't deny her if she wanted her dog to cuddle her.

"He's fine. Can I get you anything else?"

Her cheeks heat, and she shakes her head no. Anders clears his throat and bends down on his haunches to be at eye level with the Omega.

"What do you need, Omega?" he asks. It's so soft, if it wasn't dead silent in here, I wouldn't have heard it. Charlotte whines, and for whatever reason, it has a direct connection with my dick. I clear my throat and sit on the Lazy Boy, throwing a knitted blanket over my crotch.

"I was going to eat before I got hit in the tit with that puck," she says, and I cover my mouth, trying not to laugh. She isn't even trying to be funny, but something about the way she words things is hilarious to me.

"I'll get you something. Here's the remote," Anders says, giving her a once over before heading to the kitchen.

"I should get the shit kicked out of me more often," she whispers, and I lose it, laughing loudly and gaining a grin from the gorgeous Omega lying on my couch.

"Yes, about a mile down the road. I'm just home for winter break. Is this your place?" I've seen this huge cabin before, and I think it's usually rented out, but it's not often I see people here.

"My parents bought it a few years ago. We're here for winter break too," Eli says.

I furrow my eyebrows and wonder why none of them are spending Christmas with their family, but consider that it would be rude to ask.

"You're hockey players?"

Anders laughs. "What gave us away?" He smirks, and have I mentioned his jaw line?

"Besides the fact that you're all huge and taking a hockey puck to the chest?" I ask, and Anders winces.

"How's the bruise?" he asks, and I can't tell if he wants to see my boob or if he really cares. And then I wonder why I want him to see my boobs so badly. Not that they're anything special, but there's enough to grab onto.

I clear my throat and try to calm myself down. I can smell myself perfuming, and no doubt the Alphas next to me will pick up the scent. "It's okay."

Anders arches a brow at me, his arms crossed against his chest making his biceps bulge. "Okay, it hurts," I concede. He nods and grabs two more Tylenol and this time a bag of frozen blueberries. I wonder why he didn't give me this one first instead of the pizza rolls, but I'll take it.

"Are you sure you don't want us to take a look or take you to a doctor?" he asks. I shake my head. My head doesn't even hurt anymore, and it's just a bruise.

"I'll be okay. Promise," I say, giving the kind Alpha a smile. He blushes and sits back down on the arm of the chair.

"What college do you guys go to?"

"BU," Eli says, and I nod my head.

"My best friend goes to UMass. Well, for now. She applied to Yale for medical school." Eli scoffs, and I assume there is some rivalry there.

"You?" Eli asks, and I dare to say there's something hopeful in his voice.

"Mercy University." Eli doesn't react, but Anders does with a wince. "I know," I reply to Anders' unspoken reaction.

"Sorry, I was recruited by them as well." He doesn't elaborate, and Eli looks confused.

"That's in North Carolina, right?" Eli asks, and I nod my head.

"You got a full ride?" Anders asks, and I nod again. I'm shocked that he knows so much about the school, but if he was recruited by multiple colleges, it makes sense. Eli still looks confused.

"It's pretty much the college where the affluent send their Alpha sons to snag an Omega with a full ride," I blurt out, and Eli's eyes widen.

"What the fuck?"

"Indeed."

"Um, I guess we should have asked if you have an Alpha or a boyfriend or something. Not that I mean... just don't want to step on anyone's toes," Eli says, and it's cute. Actually, beyond endearing how his freckled cheeks redden as he speaks.

"I'm unbonded and very single."

"Okay, good," Eli sputters. "I mean, not good. Just, you're in a cabin with three Alphas you just met and it could be... Fuck, should we order food?" He changes the conversation, and I'm grateful for it.

I should ask one of them to drive me and Hank home. Deep down I know this, I shouldn't even be entertaining the idea of hanging out with these Alphas. But the other option is to go home, and what, sit in my room alone? Having someone ask me about myself is nice, and have I mentioned how good they smell?

"Food is good." I give him a smile, watching the large Alpha's cheeks darken again as he gets up and grabs a handful of menus out of the drawer.

"What's good here?"

"Jack's for coffee, Milanos for pizza, and Szechuan Garden for Chinese."

"What would you like?" he asks. I'm not sure if I'm just used to the bare minimum or Anders and Eli are just nicer and more compassionate than any other Alphas I've come across.

"Chinese, please. I'll have the Kung Pao." Eli nods his head and calls the restaurant, clearly already knowing everyone's favorites—it's impressive and cute. I wonder how long they've been friends. I realize I can just ask. "Are you guys pack?" I ask Anders. He scratches under his chin and shakes his head.

"Best friends, teammates. Not pack." When he says it, it sounds like he wishes they were.

"Why not?" I'm probably overstepping here, but I'm genuinely curious.

"We all want to play hockey. A part of that is not knowing where you're going to go after you get drafted. How can you be a pack when you're all in different states?"

The hard reality hits me, and I nod my head. I should probably leave, go home, and just be thankful I met some Alphas who are nice and restored my ideals about maybe finding a pack one day. There's no future here, and I'm the queen of not building friendships, so they can't get broken. But as I lock eyes with Anders' gray stare, all I see is warmth. I can't help but wonder what more I could learn from them. Anders, Eli, and even the mean one are hot as shit. Maybe I could handle a friendship, or even more than a friendship, for winter break. It's been weeks since I've been with anyone, and these are by far the most attractive men I've ever been around, let alone being Alphas.

It doesn't even have to get physical. I can be friends with people. Right?

I glance back at Anders. I don't know him, but I want to. Can I grapple with the idea of an expiration date? Maybe knowing when this will end will help me let loose a little, not feel so afraid to be me. It's time to truly be myself. I've got nothing to lose. After Christmas, we'll all be going back to school. I vow to myself to try to let go and have fun. That's what winter break is for, a break from the pressure of college.

With my internal struggle at ease, I smile at Anders. "Want to help me take Hank on a walk?"

"Of course," he says. We both get off the couch, disturbing Hank, who stands up. I assume Anders is going to grab his stuff and I'm going to grab mine. He takes me by surprise when he pulls my wool hat over my head and then holds out my jacket for me to put my arms through.

Yup, Charlotte, we've made the right choice. Even if I'm a princess for just a few weeks, it's better than not being one at all.

Chapter Seven

*W*e're so fucked.

So fucked, I can't even think straight as Charlotte and I walk carefully down the plowed street. I walk close enough to her to make sure she doesn't fall. Not that I think she's clumsy, but it's icy out and well, she's already hit her head today.

She's so short she barely reaches my chest. I don't know why I like it so much, but as I stare down at her, I'm in awe.

She's my fucking scent match.

I don't know how much Eli and Mikael know about scent matches or Omegas in general. Eli seems to be stumbling a bit, and Mikael ran away. I grew up in pack life, and I want pack life. I've always just assumed it would happen when my career is over. Being a goalie is a short-lived position and part of the reason I chose the position. Hockey is my life, but it isn't everything. I want a pack of my own. My scent match is just casually walking next to me, and I'm trying to keep my fucking cool.

Has she not noticed?

Thankfully, the cold air calms her scent. I'm not being drowned by vanilla pancakes and thick maple syrup. As soon as Eli put her in my arms, I knew the perfect match for me. She's my Omega, but this revelation couldn't come at a worse time. We go to different schools. We're all hopefully going to get drafted this summer.

A small hand wraps around my forearm and lightly squeezes.

"You okay?" she asks. I look down at her slight frame. She's gorgeous, her eyes are unique and something I haven't seen before. I find her glasses adorable, though I can't help the aching in my chest that she has to have glasses at all. It's fucked up, but Omegas are usually the healthiest of all the designations. Their main purpose is to be the best to mate with, have children with. So their beauty and health usually reflect that. Not that I think she's flawed, I just wish I could make it better.

"Just thinking." She smiles and loops her arm around mine. I can feel a rumble start in my chest and push it down. She'd probably go running for the hills if I started purring for her right off the bat.

So fucked. I'm so, so, so fucked.

"Penny for your thoughts?"

I sigh and take the leash from her hands. Why does such a small person have such a massive dog? I take the safe route and just talk about school stuff. Not the massive life changing epiphany happening right now. My heart sinks, and I wonder if I'm not her scent match. Would she be reacting more strongly? I mean, I've been pushing my pheromones down to not overwhelm her. Maybe she just hasn't been able to scent me completely?

I'm a coward as I change the subject completely. "This place kind of reminds me of home."

"Finland?"

"*Juu,*" I say, and she smiles.

"What about it reminds you of home?"

"It's not as cold, and you have more sun. But the snow, the village feel."

"Do you miss it?"

"I miss my family, the food, and sometimes the culture. But the United States is where you go to play hockey, and that's what I wanted."

She nods, her body leaning slightly against mine, looking for warmth. I welcome it and try to calm myself down, not pick her up and bundle her inside of my jacket, like that would even be close enough.

"So how good exactly are you guys at hockey?"

I grin down at her, kind of liking that she doesn't give a shit. To say that me and the guys don't have any problems getting girls on campus would be an understatement. As soon as I scented this Omega, though, they all fucking disappeared.

"Pretty good."

"How good is pretty good?"

"Eli and I will definitely be drafted. Mikael should be, but he is up in the air."

"Why?" I wonder how much I should divulge. It's not like she seems to know much about the sport, but I stick with an easy answer.

"His job on the ice is to enforce more than anything. He keeps me protected, but sometimes his anger gets the best of him." She hums, and we continue walking. The only sound is the jingling of the dog's collar and our footsteps as we crunch against the ice. "What about you? Do you have one more year of school?" None of the three of us are planning on graduating. If we get drafted, we're taking that opportunity.

She sighs. "Maybe. Mercy doesn't let you stay on campus on a full ride if you go into heat."

My anger spikes, and I look down at her. "That's fucked up." I want to ask her what her plans are for her heat and why she isn't on suppressants. The thought of other Alphas touching her already brings me to a level of anger and jealousy that I'm not used to. I barely know her, and I feel this way. I can't imagine what it's going to feel like if we form a real connection. I rake my hands through my hair, and she continues speaking.

"I'm getting a degree in accounting, thinking I can work from home when I graduate. But I'm considering finishing this semester and doing my last year online."

"Mercy is really that bad?"

"I'm sure for other people it isn't. But it's not for me. I've only stayed because I have a scholarship."

I nod my head, angry that they forced her into that option.

"It's not fair." I didn't mean to say the internal thought. She smiles up at me and nods.

"No, it's not." She shivers, getting even closer to me as Hank shoves his nose into the snow. "My house is actually right over there," she points to a simple but cute single level home. My heart sinks, wondering if she wants to go home. If we were too forward. She looks at me wide-eyed for a moment. "For Hank, not for me. I need to feed him. He's a big boy. He gets three meals a day."

"I understand, Hank," I joke. Charlotte and I smile at each other as she opens the front door. We both take our boots off, and it makes me smile. I've had to train the shit out of the guys to take all their shoes off in the house. Seems Charlotte has manners.

I give her space and look around the living room, seeing pictures of Charlotte as a child with what looks like her grandparents. I wonder if they took her in or if her parents were never in the picture. There's a clanging of dishes and kibble hitting stainless steel as Hank trots into the kitchen.

"Charlie, hun, are you home?"

"Just dropping off Hank," she says down the hall.

An older woman, probably in her seventies, comes down the hall, her light blonde hair short. She's wearing pajamas, and she gasps when she sees me. "Dammit, Charlie. I look a mess, and you have company?"

"Mom, this is Anders," Charlotte introduces us.

Her mom gives me a once over, and I feel like a real dick for thinking she was her grandma.

"Lovely to meet you," I say, holding out my hand. She gives me wide eyes and looks over at her daughter. After the shock settles down, she smiles.

"You too. Where is that delightful accent from?" she asks.

"He's from Finland. We have to meet the rest of our friends. They ordered food," Charlotte says as she attempts to manhandle me out the door.

"Do you want to put new contacts in?" I ask her. Charlotte's mother beams at me, like a full-blown ear-to-ear smile. Charlotte looks at me like I have two heads, but nods and walks away to go put in a fresh pair of contacts.

"Didn't think I'd see the day she brought an Alpha home, to be honest," her mom says quietly.

I want to tell this woman that I just met Charlotte, but she's changed everything. But I think that might come across a little too strong. "We just met, but I think she's lovely."

Her mother nods and smiles. "She's very special. Sometimes she doesn't realize it. I feel like if she had more than me and Piper to tell her that, she would start to believe it." I nod at the small older woman. "Where are you all staying?" she asks.

"We're at the big cabin on the lake," I say, not knowing the address. Eli drove us here.

"Ah, that big place that sits vacant most of the year?" I nod, and she rubs her hands over her arms. She seems happy, like overly excited her daughter brought a strange Alpha home, but there are clearly some maternal instincts clicking at the moment. "You mind giving me your number just in case something happens?"

"Not a problem," I say, pulling out my phone and embarrassingly putting the caller ID as 'Charlotte's Mom' since she didn't say her name and enter her number into my phone, then calling it so she has my info. What's even worse, I don't even have her daughter's number in my phone yet. I plan on changing that this evening. The fact that she wants to come back to the cabin with us is a good sign.

Charlotte comes from around the corner, her glasses gone. She looks beautiful either way, but I like being able to see her face. Hank rubs his enormous head against her thigh. "You stay here, Hank."

His face is dark, furry, and slightly squished, so I can't read his expression, but he doesn't look pleased to be left behind.

"Be careful, and let me know what time you'll be home," her mother says from the doorway as we leave the house. As soon as the door shuts, Charlotte lets out a huge exhale.

"She's nice."

Charlotte nods. "She is. She means a lot to me."

I nod, missing my mom, my dads, and siblings. But this is what I signed up for. We walk quietly for a few blocks. I'm thankful that she doesn't push me to talk, leaving space for quietness. Not everyone has that skill; some people just can't stand silence.

The cabin is in view, and Charlotte takes a step and hits black ice. My arms are wrapped around her waist before I can even think. I'm pulling her close to my body, her thick maple syrup scent making me shudder. I can wrap my arms around her and touch my biceps, I can't help but feel overwhelmed. I've dated girls, sort of. But this protectiveness, hunger, and desperation for her has me feeling feral, like I'm not the one in charge.

"Do you want me to carry you the rest of the way?" I ask, my warm breath hitting her cheek. They were already flushed because of the cold, but now they're bright pink.

"Maybe we can just hold hands instead?" she suggests, and I nod. It's not as good as having her pressed against my body, but I'll take it. I slide her down my frame till her boots hit the slush. I hold out a gloved hand, and she places her much smaller one inside my palm. I wish that it was skin on skin, but I'll take what I can get.

"Thanks for coming back with me."

She squeezes my hand lightly, looking up at me with a smile. "I'm trying a new thing where I try harder to make friends."

I squeeze her hand back and grin. I keep the thought to myself, so I don't scare the shit out of her, but there's no way she's going to be my friend. *She's going to be so much fucking more.*

When we get to the cabin, Eli has all the Chinese out on the counter and is making himself a plate. He grins as we walk in, like Charlotte was going to disappear.

"You're back."

"I'm back," she says. I help her take off her jacket, and we take our boots off by the front door, then we load up our plates. I don't know what direction tonight is going to take, but I'm eager to find out.

CHARLOTTE

Chapter Eight

B oth the Alphas keep their distances. For some reason, both of their scents are subdued. I've scented them and have the gist of what they smell like, and so far I like—really like. I want to see what their scent is like at pure strength, and to do that, I need one of them to feel in distress or turned on.

I know I should feel guilty for trying to make them feel either of those emotions. But I have to know. It's like every Omega sense I have is trying to tell me something about these Alphas, and I just can't put my finger on it.

Sure, I'd scent some Alphas back at school, and some had better scents than others. But these two, it's like I'm itching to get a strong whiff of either of them. I could hardly scent Anders outside. I might have slipped on purpose, and when he held me, the hazelnut was faint. It was like I was scratching the surface of his pheromones. It doesn't help with the cold weather outside; it makes it so hard to smell anything.

Eli makes my plate of food for me, not even thinking to let me make it myself, and I shockingly let him. This is something Piper does often, and I hate it. But with this Alpha, something about the action is comforting. Maybe I've given Piper too hard of a time when it comes to her Alpha instincts and how she treats me.

Anders keeps his distance from me but holds out his arm to have me sit on one of the wooden stools at the island. I take my seat, and Eli pushes the plate in front of me. The food smells amazing, but I'd rather be scenting something else. I give him a smile, and his cheeks redden.

"I... uh... should have asked what you wanted first," Eli says, rubbing the back of his neck. I really like how bashful he gets. It's clear he hasn't been around many Omegas. Anders seems more comfortable around my presence and scent. Mikael, who knows? He still hasn't come out of his room.

"This is perfect, thank you, Eli." He shudders as I say his name, but no deep scent comes off of him. Maybe if I get them to break a sweat? Thinking of them sweating gives me devious thoughts, so I redirect my train of thinking before this whole place smells like maple pancakes.

"You're welcome."

"I'll take up Mikael's plate," Anders says. Eli nods at him. I was hoping he would come and take the stool next to me. But he stands on the other side of the island, holding his plate with one hand and eating with the other.

"You took the big guy home?"

I nod and take a bite of my food and swallow before responding. There's nothing worse than someone who talks with their mouth full. "He needed to eat. I love having him around. I probably miss Hank more than I miss anything when I go to school."

Eli looks at me thoughtfully. "Never had a pet growing up. He seems friendly."

I furrow my brows but nod. The idea of never having had a pet makes me feel sad for Eli for some reason. "He is. He's a little stupid sometimes, but I love him with my whole heart."

"I feel that way about Mikael," Eli jokes.

"Did I say something to upset him?"

"No, don't take it personally. He's a hard guy to get to know."

"But you all are best friends?"

"We are. We all just clicked. I'm not sure how to describe it. We work well on and off the ice. We live together, work together. I guess we kind of do everything together."

"Are you guys romantically involved?" It spews out of my mouth before I even think about it, and I feel my cheeks heat.

Eli laughs and puts his plate of food on the counter. "No, nothing like that. It's more like we're family."

I nod and hum, trying to figure out exactly how I feel about that. "No girlfriends back on campus?" Clearly feeling bold as fuck tonight, aren't I?

He grins. "No. No girlfriends."

Anders walks back into the kitchen, limber and quick on his feet. I know a decent amount about hockey, haven't been to a game in person, but my dad used to watch it all the time when I was a kid.

He doesn't mention Mikael at all as he makes his own plate and puts it on the counter, standing just like Eli is. What gives? It's warm in the cabin. I want them close, so I can get a really deep whiff of what they've got going on.

"Something to drink?" Anders asks.

"Sure."

"We've got water, lemonade, beer, and tons of alcohol."

"Are you guys twenty-one?"

Anders grins and shakes his head. "We're all twenty."

"Same. I'll have a vodka lemonade," I say confidently. I haven't really spent much time drinking, but one drink might help me relax a little more around these guys. Maybe help me feel emboldened to take what I want. *What is it that I want exactly?*

"Coming right up. Eli?"

"Beer is good."

Anders makes my drink first and places it in front of me. He waits, staring at me with his intense, pretty, gray eyes. I take a sip and hold back a wince.

"Need it sweeter?" I don't want to be a bother, so I shrug. Before I can stay anything else, Anders slides the glass out of my hand and adds two drops of this pink liquid and slides it back. "Try it now."

I sip and hum, barely tasting the vodka. "Perfect." I give him a smile, and I swear his chest puffs up before he turns to the fridge and grabs two beers. His veins pop and his forearms flex when he pops the tops of the bottles. That... that is what they mean when someone says the female gaze. Because that did more for me than any Alpha who knotted me at Mercy. *What the fuck?*

The cool cocktail helps calm my nerves and I drink it a little quicker than I should. I hum and look around the extravagant house. "So what do you want to do?"

"Ever play *Catan*?" Eli asks, and I shake my head. "Well, you're in for quite the treat, little Omega."

I think I perish on the spot when he calls me little Omega. I've never liked the phrase before, but from him? I don't care if *Catan* is the worst game on the planet, having him call me little Omega is worth it.

"I should have picked more wheat! I don't think either of you explained this game properly," I say with a pout as I roll. My resources are absolutely fucked. I've got a shit ton of ore, and neither of these Alphas will trade with me.

"Seems as though someone is a sore loser," Eli jokes, and I give him a scowl, taking a sip of my second vodka lemonade, handcrafted by Anders himself.

I blink my eyes at Anders and give him the biggest puppy dog eyes I can imagine. "Please, Anders, won't you trade me for some wheat?"

Eli laughs. "Anders is the most cutthroat of all of us. He won't trade for anything."

"Anything?" I ask, fluttering my eyelashes at Anders. I watch his throat bob, his Adam's apple moving deliciously up and down his throat.

Anders clears his throat. "I could be convinced."

Eli looks at Anders like he's committed treason, and I realize that this is my moment to strike. To get his pheromones out to the surface and get the full force of what this Alpha is made of. But what can I trade to get close enough to him, turn him on, and get the wheat that I need to make a fucking settlement?

"How about I trade you two ore for two wheat, and I'll sit on your lap for the next two rounds?"

Anders swallows, and Eli blinks. "Wait, that was on the table?" Eli asks, irritated he didn't get the same deal. That pleases me.

"Unless it's against the rules?"

"No, it's not. Deal," Anders says.

I gather every ounce of confidence that I've ever felt in my life as I stand up from my seat and walk over to Anders. He moves his chair, so he is facing the side of the table, not under it anymore. His muscular thighs spread wide. I wish he were wearing sweat pants instead of khakis, but I'll take what I can get. I can tell he's tense, but his eyes read complete seriousness as he puts his cards down, one hand flat on the table, the other on his thigh. Stepping between his legs, I sit on his left thigh, so I can face the table. His hand automatically touches my lower back for support. I can't help the gasp that escapes me, or the perfume, or the slick.

Anders shuffles slightly, jostling me.

That's when it hits me. The full epic force of his scent. It's not just hazelnut, it's just like a hazelnut latte, my go-to drink, something that comforts me every time I'm down. His scent sends shivers down my spine and makes my heart beat a million miles per minute.

He's my fucking scent match. Fuck.

I've just randomly stumbled across my perfect match. I meet his eyes. He looks at me like I might shatter or crumble. *I just fucking might*. Part of me wants to straddle him and kiss his face till neither of us can breathe and this cabin smells like a perfect mix of our scents. But the bigger part of me is terrified. That part wins as I pop off his lap, embarrassingly.

I'm a runner. It's not something I'm proud of, but it's my coping mechanism for anything that happens that I'm not comfortable with. I run. It's easier than facing whatever this is.

"I'm just going to run to the bathroom."

"Charlotte," Anders pleads.

"Be right back." I'm already walking away. I hear him groan, and Eli asks what's going on. This is too much. This was supposed to be simple, a way to finally let myself get to know people without fear of abandonment.

What am I going to do?

I'm already so bent out of shape, I think I've missed the door to the bathroom. Maybe this one is it? I turn the door handle, and what I smell hits me before my eyes can make sense of what's in front of me.

Campfires.

The scent is so overwhelming my mouth waters. Mikael had to have recently touched himself in this bedroom for it to be this potent. I blink rapidly, and a whine escapes my throat. My carnal urges tell me that these two are my Alphas and that we need to act on it. My baser instincts tell me to run now before I get hurt.

I'm momentarily paralyzed by all the possibilities and thoughts running through my head. I don't know what to do. I know we should all probably talk, but the part of me that's terrified of letting someone in is telling me to run as far away as possible.

A door creaks, and Mikael walks into the room with a towel wrapped around his waist. Rivulets of water drip down his olive-toned skin, trickling between each toned muscle. His dark hair is wet and slightly curled around his face. His face looks so fucking furious that it makes me cower.

He approaches me, and it's then I recognize his full height. He's easily a foot and a half taller than me. I'm fucking weak, too afraid to look him in the eye. What will I see?

A warm finger lifts my chin and tilts my face, so I have to look up. Two deep pools bore into me. His face is blank. I can't tell if he wants me or if he despises me.

"You don't belong up here," he says. His voice is deep, and it makes my knees weak. My perfume surrounds us, and he groans. "Go downstairs. I don't want you up here," he says with authority, but he doesn't use his Alpha bark.

"You're... you're my scent match," I stumble.

"It doesn't matter. Go back downstairs."

It doesn't matter? I blink a few times, staring at him indignantly.

"What do you mean, it doesn't matter? It's so rare. How can it not matter?" I'm sure my voice sounds pathetic. Mikael's hand still hasn't left my face.

"Please go downstairs."

His voice is deep and demanding as he says it. It's clear that he means all business as he glares at me. How can he just dismiss me completely like this? He's acting like this means nothing to him, like I'm simply an inconvenience. Not like he's overwhelmed that we're scent matches, but that he's disappointed. Like I'm not a good enough Omega to be his scent match.

I know I was feeling overwhelmed and needed to get my head clear, but I wouldn't turn away from my scent matches. I, at least, wouldn't talk to them like they are undeserving of me like Mikael is right now. Even though Mikael is turning me away, his scent says something else as it assaults me with its full force. It's like campfires are now bored into my soul, and he doesn't seem to give a shit.

I open my mouth to speak, but Mikael pushes his thumb between my two lips, groaning, before he grabs me by the shoulders and pushes me just beyond the barrier of his door. The last thing I see before he shuts the door are his furrowed brows and his towel, hardly hiding his erection.

This is too much. I need to clear my head. I walk back down the hall, unable to look Eli or Anders in the eye.

"Eli, can you drive me home?" I ask while I stare down at my feet.

"Uh." Eli sounds just as confused as I feel.

"Charlotte, can we talk?" Anders' gentle voice asks.

I clear my throat, still looking down. "Is it okay if I go home for the night? I'll give Eli my phone number, and we can talk tomorrow."

"Okay," Anders says softly. "I'll grab your things."

I can hear the disappointment in his voice, and I feel it too. As badly as I want to stay here, explore this and figure it out, I need a moment to fucking breathe, to take in all this information and to just think clearly without the hazelnut or campfire scents drowning me. I look over at Eli, not fully having scented him. I'm not sure if it's a good or bad thing.

I glance up as Anders hands me my belongings and gives me a tight smile, his face full of worry, and I feel guilty for putting it there.

Eli leads the way out to the garage and opens the door before he opens the passenger door for me. I have to really climb to get into the seat. He stands sentinel, making sure I don't fall. Once I'm fully into the truck, Eli rounds the front of the vehicle, looking just as confused as Anders. I think we're all confused. At least Eli and Anders seem to want me around to figure this out. Mikael seems like he wants nothing to do with me.

Once Eli is in the driver's seat, he grabs the steering wheel, glances at me, and reverses the truck out of the garage. My house is only a few blocks away, the drive will be short. The silence is deafening, and I want to explain myself. But I don't know how to. Finding your scent match is a near miracle, and I have two! Two scent matches who live nowhere near me and are both on career paths that will keep them far away from me.

"Did I miss something? Did we do something to make you uncomfortable?"

I sigh, and point to the left for Eli to turn down my street. "My house number is 671. No, it's not that."

Eli huffs but doesn't push me any further. As soon as we're in front of the house, he pulls his phone out of his pocket and hands it to me. I put in my phone number and hand it back.

"Does it have to do with the way I'm feeling?" he asks, his voice soft.

"How do you feel?"

"Like I just met you, but you're mine. Like my sole focus is to please you and make you comfortable. Like I'm craving fucking pancakes and maple syrup."

I bang my head against the headrest and wince. Eli's hand is wrapped around the back of my head, and he gently rubs the juncture of my neck and skull.

Looking into his deep green eyes, I ask in a whisper, "Can you make your scent stronger?" Needing to know, is it even possible to have three scent matches? He looks confused, but nods as his thick pine scent fills the cab. I moan, and his eyes widen.

"We're... you're all my scent matches."

"We're what?" Eli asks, confused.

"You don't know about scent matches?" He shakes his head and sighs. His hand hasn't left my skin, and I just want him to rub harder. I want his hands on me always, his scent as strong as it is now.

"I didn't really get a lot of Alpha and Omega education. My parents are both Betas."

I lick my lips and nod. His gaze is tearing into me, and I want to curl against him but run as far away as possible at the same time.

"Alphas and Omegas are already meant to be attracted to each other physiologically. Each of our scents are alluring to each other. It's rare, but your scent match is basically your best match. It doesn't get any better than this from a physical standpoint. It's like it's meant to be."

His mouth gapes open, his eyes roaming all over my face to my mouth.

"And this scares you?"

"Doesn't it scare you?" I ask. How can it not? He shakes his head, and I furrow my brows. "We just met. This is a lot to take in."

His hand leaves my neck. I whine, and his eyes are wide. "I... I don't really know what I'm doing when it comes to an Omega. Tell me what you need?"

"Honestly, right now, I don't even know. I think I just need to lie down and take some time to decompress. I promise we can all talk tomorrow."

"Promise?"

I nod my head. Eli reaches out to touch me again but pulls back. I almost whine again, but I keep it trapped in my throat. I don't want to confuse him any further.

"Text me, so I have your number. I promise to reach out."

"Can I walk you to your door?" I nod, and he immediately gets out to let me out of the truck, holding onto my elbow as we walk to the door. The feeling is bittersweet. I know that by saying goodnight my Alpha, I mean, my scent match, will be walking away from me. But on the other side of things, I need a moment to collect my thoughts.

"Tomorrow?"

"Tomorrow." I squeeze his arm before I open the front door and walk in. I thought I could escape them, but their scents are embedded in my clothes. They're the comforting scents of my home.

Hank follows me into my room. I strip naked and crawl into my bed, wondering what the fuck I'm supposed to do and wishing I didn't run away.

Chapter Nine

*M*y fucking scent match.

She had to be beautiful, and sweet, and drop in my lap at the worst fucking possible moment. I can't afford to be distracted right now. Not to mention that if I don't go pro, I have literally nothing to offer an Omega. Hockey is what I'm good at. I don't have backup money like Eli or a family to go home to like Anders. I need this career more than I need to be thinking about starting a pack right now.

Not only do I need it financially, I need to prove to myself that I'm nothing like *them*. Nothing like the family who does what they need to scrape by, nothing like the family that throws fists instead of using words. I need to be better, and I'm not good enough to be someone's fucking Alpha right now. I wouldn't even know where to start. It's not like I've even been someone's boyfriend before. Now I'm supposed to, what? Just be mated to someone for the rest of my life?

What the fuck?

If I could go back in time, I would drown that little kid that hit Charlotte with the puck. Maybe then Charlotte wouldn't have gotten hurt, and the tiny little thing wouldn't have ended up in our cabin.

As soon as I scented her, I knew. *Mon sucre d'érable.*

Fucking embarrassing. I'm just thankful that no one speaks French, and I got out of there as soon as I could. I came up to my room, attempted to meditate, to read, to get my mind off of the girl downstairs.

I wound up jerking off three times. My knot has never been as swollen as it was when I jerked off to the memory of her scent. It's fucking pathetic.

I'm pathetic. I don't deserve to be an Omega's Alpha, especially not with who I am now. I was supposed to grow over the next few years. Prove myself in the NHL, and then maybe settle down with a Beta. This was unexpected and unwanted.

How am I supposed to tell Anders and Eli, the two Alphas who were actually decent to her, that out of all of us, I'm the one she's predestined to be with? When she came in here looking frantic and finally smelling my scent, I wanted to hold her, fuck her, make her mine. At least that's what the primal part of me wanted, the part that I push so deep down it's just like a background noise in my mind. She needs to stay the fuck away from me, with her sweet scent, big doe eyes, and long blonde hair that would be perfect for wrapping around my fist.

I hate her for interrupting my progress. I know it's not her fault, but why did she have to bulldoze her fucking way into this cabin and change everything?

She looked so dejected as I shut the door on her. She needs to keep feeling that way. Charlotte needs to understand that I'm not the Alpha for her. Scent match or not, this isn't fucking happening. It can't happen, right? How am I supposed to manage finishing school, somehow managing to go pro, and being someone's Alpha? There's no fucking way.

My temper is flared, and all I want to do is punch something as I dress, pulling on sweatpants and a Henley before I make my way downstairs to face everyone. To see if Charlotte is still here, not because I want to see her, but to see if now is a good time to talk with the guys and tell them what's happening. Eli seemed really interested in her, and I feel bad for impeding his winter time fuck. But it's not happening. She can't come back here again.

My bare feet pad across the wooden floor to find Anders' hands in his hair, elbows on the table, and a half played *Catan* board in front of him.

"You all played without me?" I try to make light of the moment, and Anders looks up at me with an irritated gaze. He is the most even keel of all of us, but right now he looks about ready to fly off the handle.

"You weren't exactly making your presence known." His tone is dark and unexpected.

"Where's Eli?"

"He's driving Charlotte home."

I nod, probably because I scared the fuck out of her. *Good.*

"About that. She can't come back here."

Anders stands up and crosses his arms across his chest. "The fuck she can't. She'll be back tomorrow."

"She can't come back here, Anders. Trust me." I've never seen Anders like this before. He doesn't lose his temper. I don't understand why he's being this way, but he doesn't fucking get it. She might seem like a fun winter time fuck to him, but I can't have my scent match prodding around this cabin, shoving her scent in my face. The fact that I know my scent match is out there is already fucked up enough. Having her rubbed in my face when I can't have her would only make it worse.

"She's my fucking scent match," Anders growls and swipes the *Catan* pieces off the table, and they clatter on to the floor dramatically.

I stare at him wide-eyed. "She's *my* scent match." This has just gotten fifty times worse. My heart is racing, and I rub the heel of my hand over my chest.

"What?" Anders growls.

"I knew when we brought her to the cabin. She figured it out when she opened the door to my room. I told her to leave."

"You fucking told her to leave?" I've never seen Anders so pissed as he walks over to me and pokes at my chest. "She looked upset. I thought it was because she realized I was her scent match. But it's because you were being a fucking asshole and scared her off."

"It's for the best, Anders. We can't afford the distraction right now."

He scoffs, pushing at my shoulder. It pisses me off, and I have to tame my temper. I love Anders, but if he thinks I won't hit him, he's mistaken. If he touches me again or pushes me further, he'll force my hand.

"Do you not realize how fucking rare this is? How honored we should fucking feel? Who cares about how we make it work? You just made our goddamn scent match run home!"

The sound of the garage opening and closing alerts us to Eli being home, and Anders sighs and paces the kitchen. Eli looks confused at our stances and sighs. He tosses the keys to his car on the countertop and puts his hands in his pockets before he speaks.

"So we're all her scent matches."

"All of us?" Anders replies in awe. I glare at him. How in the fuck can they see this as a good thing? Right now it feels like a curse, the worst obstacle that couldn't have come at a worse time. It's been so fucking hard to get to where I am today, and life is just throwing her in my face to fuck it all up.

"Apparently. I didn't even know there was such a thing until Charlotte just explained it to me. I still don't understand."

"It means that she would need to be the center of our lives. That hockey would be on the back burner. That there's no way we can make this work if we all want to go pro. How the fuck can we take care of an Omega, let alone when we're all living in different places throughout the country?"

"This is all moving fast," Eli says, rubbing his head.

"You don't fucking get it. Neither of you gets it. She will ruin our lives, everything we've fucking worked for."

"Fuck you," Anders says. His shoulder hits mine as he grabs his shoes and jacket. He slams the door as he leaves the cabin.

"This is all a lot of take in," Eli says, pouring himself a whiskey. I give him a look, and he pours me a glass as well. We clink glasses and take our seats at the island. "It sounds like it's fate. How do you dodge something like that?"

"By never seeing her again." Why don't they get that this could be so simple? We should leave now, go back to Boston, and forget this ever happened. These two are already talking like they're planning on dating her. I need to convince them otherwise.

"I don't think I can do that. How can you be so casual about this? I didn't even know scent matches were a thing, but I can already tell that I'm attached to her. The thought of never seeing her again makes me physically hurt."

I groan and stand up to pour another whiskey. "Hockey comes first."

"Mikael." He furrows his brows at me and acts like I'm the one being unreasonable. When these two are the ones letting a girl they've spent a few hours with throttle everything we've worked so hard for.

"I don't want to hear it, Eli. If you and Anders want to ruin your life over an Omega, go for it. But you're not taking me with you."

"Can't we just talk about this?"

"There's nothing to talk about. I need hockey. I need this to work out. I don't need an Omega."

The whiskey burns my throat but helps soothe the sting of my lie.

"She's coming back tomorrow," Eli mumbles, staring into his glass like it holds all the answers. Like our lives didn't get upturned by a blonde who's barely five feet tall.

"Then I'll leave."

"Mikael, it doesn't have to be like this. Maybe just spend some time with her. Like we plan to. Get to know her. I know that's what I want. Maybe we're scent matches, but we aren't really a good fit. We should at least find that out."

Eli's ignorance must be fucking bliss. He doesn't understand that now we've found our scent match, no one will ever compare. He doesn't realize that if he lets her, she will become the center of his world, not the thing he has spent his entire life striving for. The scent of maple and pancakes will be his fucking downfall.

"I'll make myself scarce."

"Mikael," he groans my name one more time, but I'm already walking to my room contemplating if there is anywhere else I can go.

I know there's not. I'm alone in this world, except for Anders and Eli. Will she try to take them away from me too? She's already threatening everything else. She might as well take the two people who give a shit about me.

I don't have a car to get back to Boston, nor the money. I'm stuck in this cabin with two blinded Alphas and the lingering scent of maple that's going to haunt my dreams.

Chapter Ten

F uck Mikael, the pessimistic, selfish asshole. Having a scent match is a gift, and to turn that gift down is unacceptable. The icy snow crunches beneath my feet. The sun went down a while ago, and I'm reminded of home. It's around four in the morning at home, so I can't even call my mom. Her excitement would be unreal over me finding my scent match.

My mother is an Omega. I understand the dynamics of things. How some things are instinctual and primal while others are true feelings. I know that I don't truly know Charlotte, haven't even scratched the surface. What I do know is that biology is telling me there isn't a better person on this planet for me than Charlotte, and I'd be a fool to let that go.

I don't even have a plan when I leave the house, just that I'm angry and don't want to get into a fight with Mikael over this. He's stubborn, and I know that I can't get him to see reason. If he feels this strongly, the only thing that will change his mind is him, or possibly Charlotte. The plain single-story house is in front of me before I even consciously thought to come here.

She asked for space, but here I am, being a fucking creep. I should go back to the cabin and keep my promise to her that we would talk tomorrow. But the deepest part of me wants to comfort her, to let her know it's okay. She shouldn't be alone right now. I sure as fuck know I don't want to be.

I feel like a goddamn stalker for looking into the window on the side of the house. Internally I'm smacking myself, but externally when I see her wrapped up in a massive bundle of blankets and her beast of a dog cuddled next to her on the bed, I feel relief. The twinkle lights in her room give off a warm glow. This is the point of no return: go home, or knock on her window like some obsessed creep.

My knuckles lightly tap against the cold glass of her window. She stirs, but doesn't investigate right away. I should let her sleep. But when she turns and I see her face, her eyes and cheeks puffy, I know I'm not going anywhere.

I tap just a bit harder. That wakes her up, and she blinks at her window, grabbing her glasses off her nightstand and squinting. Her fingers hold tightly around the purple fuzzy blanket on her bed. She tugs it close to her collarbone. It's then I realize her shoulders are bare. *Shit*. With the blanket firmly wrapped around her body, she comes to the window. Her brows furrow as she unlocks the window and slides it open.

"Anders?" Her voice is soft, and sleepy, and really fucking cute.

"I'm sorry. I shouldn't have woken you up. I wanted to make sure you're okay."

"Your cheeks are bright red. How long have you been outside?"

"Outside or outside your window?" I'm ashamed that I even have to ask. At least I haven't been outside of her window for that long.

"Uh, both, I guess."

"Walking around for a few hours and I found myself in front of your house just now."

The wind whooshes behind me, and she shivers against the cold. "Do you want to come in?"

Shock is probably written all over my features. "Really?"

"Can you fit through the window?"

"Yeah, back up."

She holds the blanket against her body tightly. I look over at her bed, and the dog hasn't even moved this entire encounter. Charlotte sits on her bed as I pull myself through her window, ass first, and then bring over my legs one by one. I shut the window quietly and turn to face Charlotte. Her eyes are wide as she looks me over.

"You're really limber," she says and smirks. She's handling me being a creep really fucking well.

"Goalies need to be."

"Hmm." She pats the bed, and I take off my shoes and leave them by the window before coming and sitting on her bed. Her room smells distinctly like her, like the scent was curated specifically for me. It's so condensed in the space I'm half hard, and I can feel my flesh pebble with excitement. Her room is deliciously feminine. Woven tapestries hang on nearly every wall, each in completely different styles. A mass of books are piled in a corner along with a massive bean bag chair. The bed is so incredibly plush and soft I feel like I've been sucked in by a cloud. "So you're here." She wrinkles her nose, and it shifts her glasses. Her collarbones are exposed again, and she catches my glance. "I obviously wasn't expecting company," she says shyly.

She sleeps naked. She's right next to me, and the only thing between us is a fucking blanket. I swallow thickly. "I know we said we would talk tomorrow. I'm a dick for coming over here, but I wanted to make sure you're okay."

Charlotte looks down, her hands still clutching the blanket, and sighs. "Learning you have three scent matches is a lot."

I clear my throat. "I thought you would be happy about finding scent matches." I don't want to presume, but it's kind of the Holy Grail for Omegas.

She gasps and reaches out, touching my forearm. "Oh, Anders. I'm not upset that it's you. I hope I didn't make you feel that way."

A little, but I don't say that. "You just didn't seem happy about it. It was a surprising reaction."

Her hand hasn't left my arm, and it's comforting. "It's more so the situation. I have three scent matches that leave in two weeks. How cruel is that? The idea of getting to know you guys and then have you leave, I don't know if I can handle it. I was thinking about if it would be a better idea to not physically be around each other and maybe get to know each other virtually." She tilts her head, trying to gauge my reaction.

"If that's what you really want." I keep it simple. If she told us that it's all we could have now, I'd accept it. I'd hate it, but I can understand where she's coming from.

She shakes her head. "As soon as I tried falling asleep, I wished I would have stayed. That I had your scents around me. I think it's too late for that."

"We can figure it all out. I'd really like to spend the time we do have getting to know each other better."

She smiles, shrugging her bare shoulders and nodding. "I think I'd like that too. I'm fucking scared, but I have scent matches." Her eyes water, but she blinks away unshed tears. "I didn't realize the feeling would be so intense."

I nod, understanding completely. It's overwhelming, this need to make her happy, know that she's safe, and to care for her. This need for her is all-consuming.

I stand up, looking down at her drowning in her fuzzy blanket. I want to pick her up and put her on my lap, but I know I should give her space. "I can pick you up in the morning."

She chews on her bottom lip, making me want to free it with my thumb. "Or you can stay."

"Stay?" She nods her head and stands.

"Let me just go get some pajamas. Make yourself comfortable." I want to tell her not to get dressed on account of me, just the opposite actually. Stay blissfully naked.

She pads across the bedroom to what appears to be her private bathroom. I remove all my cold gear, putting it on top of my boots along with my pants. I decide to keep my shirt on, unsure of what she's comfortable with. I sit on the bed and pat the sleeping dog's head. He lightly snores but doesn't move, just lies on the far end of the bed. I give him good boy pats because that means that Charlotte will be even closer to me.

Charlotte comes back into the room wearing a white camisole that I can nearly see through, if it was just a tad brighter in here, and a black pair of cotton shorts that contrast against her skin. As I glance down and see the skin of her thighs exposed, my mouth waters.

"Do you need anything?" she asks in a soft voice, and I shake my head. She nods. "Can I be in the middle?" I nod, words not able to leave my mouth, thoughts not really running through my head. All I see is my Omega—my nearly naked Omega. I've only seen her in winter gear, and now she has on next to nothing. My scent is in full force, and so is hers as she wiggles her way to the middle of the bed. I grab all the blankets and toss them over us as I lie down next to her. No skin is touching, and I really want to touch her, but I don't want to push my luck. "You can touch me," she says, her glasses still on, her unique eyes looking at me tentatively.

"How?" She picks up my hand and puts it on her hip, slightly wincing at the chill of my palm.

"Sorry."

"It's okay, you can come closer."

I move closer to her, our chests nearly touching, her body heat radiating onto mine, her sock covered feet touch my calves. Her warm breath grazes the bottom of my chin, and I shiver. Charlotte's scent hasn't been as strong as it is at this moment. I'm nearly choking on it. My dick is hard, and my only thoughts are about how she's mine. This girl I just met, where I pushed my way into her bedroom late at night, has asked me to stay. She's mine, and I'm hers. There's no turning back, there's only going forward.

Her hand starts at my collarbone and glides over my Henley as she lazily explores the ridges of my chest.

"Anders?"

"Yeah, *Kulta*?" It slips out, but it fits. She feels like a fucking prize, and her blonde hair is like strands of gold.

"Kiss me."

My fingers tuck a strand of hair behind her ear before gently taking her glasses and removing them. I turn and place them on the nightstand and turn back to Charlotte. My fingers are back on her face, starting at her hairline and slowly sliding down her perfect heart-shaped face. Her lips part when I reach her cheekbones, and I lightly grab her chin, tilting her face up to mine and bringing our lips together.

It starts off with slow, gentle, exploratory kisses. But once her tongue touches mine, I'm fucking done. Scenting her is one thing, but tasting her? She was already solidified for me. I won't just let my scent match walk away. But now that I've tasted her, she's as good as bonded to me.

She moans into my mouth, and I return the sound in hers. Her lips are soft, and her kisses are demanding. She's not shy about what she wants as she pushes her body closer to me, her hand sliding under my shirt and her thigh pushing between my legs. One of my hands is under her head and touching her back while I caress her jaw with the other. Charlotte rubs her hot center on my thigh, and I groan and fist her hair.

When she gasps, I release her hair. "Was that too much?" I ask, nearly breathless. Charlotte doesn't answer, she just slides her hand in the back of my hair and fists my hair as hard as I just grabbed hers. "Fuck." Our lips are back on one another's, the urgency increasing with every swipe of her tongue or nibble on my bottom lip.

"Please," she whines. It sends more blood down to my dick, and I groan.

I fist her hair, tilting her face up to mine. "What do you need, *Kulta*?"

"Touch me, please, Alpha."

I nearly come in my fucking boxers. I've never had a girl call me that in bed, let alone an Omega, or the one who happens to be my fucking scent match.

My eyes meet hers, and I wonder how good her vision is without her glasses. She seems to be able to track my face. I kiss her one more time before my hands glide down her sternum and over her breasts. My thumb teases one of her hard nipples. "Is this where you want me to touch you?" I knead the hard bud between two fingers, and she squirms and shakes her head. My heart is beating so fast I feel like I've just done hours of lightning drills. She looks eager and wanting, I can scent her arousal, but I need her words. "You're sure this is what you want, Charlotte?"

"Yes, I want you. Please touch me. Make this ache go away." What man can deny that? My hand goes lower, roaming over her flat stomach till I reach her shorts and cup her pussy from the outside. Her shorts are drenched.

"Holy shit." I mean, I've been educated on Omega slick, but I didn't think it would be shorts soaking wet. "All this is for me?"

"Yes, you drive me crazy. You smell so good right now. Can I touch you?" Can she touch me? I nod, because the fact that she's even allowed me in her bed at all is unreal. Her hands are warm as she rakes her nails over my abs, making me flex, before she grabs my cock from the outside of my boxers.

"Fuck." It spurs me into action, pushing her shorts to the side and touching her slick, hot pussy. "Jesus Christ, Charlotte." I wish I could see, taste, but I'll take whatever she gives me. She explores and grips my knot, making me jump and growl. Her perfume is flaring out at me as I slide a finger inside of her and rub her clit with my thumb, her cunt gripping my finger deliciously. I bring my lips down to hers.

The kiss is messy, and our hands are frantic as she touches me and I touch her. I'm so close, and she hasn't even touched me skin to skin. "You want more?" I ask, and she nods her head frantically. I put a second finger in her pussy, making her whimper. Her cunt grips my fingers tightly. She bites my lower lip and thrusts her hips toward me. I groan as she drops her hand inside of my boxers. Her skin touching my cock has my brain fried, and she strokes me slowly.

I need to make her come. "I need to see what you look like when your Alpha makes you come."

She shudders. her pussy clenching around my fingers as she moans. Her hips thrust into my hand as her eyes flutter and her mouth parts. She's quiet, but her body shivers with her pleasure. She doesn't let go of my cock and continues stroking me. Her scent is overwhelming, and when she whimpers out, "Anders," I groan and come over my stomach and her fist. I've never come this hard for this long. My mind feels at peace, and I jerk slightly when she continues stroking me throughout my release.

Once we both fall from our climaxes, we stare at each other.

"Holy fuck," I groan.

"Yeah. If that was that good, I can't imagine everything else," she says shyly. I nod. My hand is covered in her slick, so I don't touch her right away.

"Should we get cleaned up?" She nods, and I stand up, doing my best to not get my jizz on my shirt or boxers. When I stand, she eyes my cock hungrily. True Alpha satisfaction rolls through me. "You like?" I joke, trying to lighten the mood.

"Oh, I like." She smirks, grabbing me a washcloth and tossing it to me while she gets changed and comes back to the bedroom.

"Is it alright if I stay?"

"My mom sleeps late, it's fine."

"Okay." She crawls back to the center of the bed. This time comfortably wrapped in my arms. The room smells like us, and it's now my new favorite smell. "Tomorrow." She says it like the word means a million things at once. We talked a little tonight, but it was mostly carnal urges. Tomorrow, I guess, is a day of reality checks and exploring this fated connection.

"Tomorrow," I reply, kissing her hair and sighing in contentment before sleep takes us both.

CHARLOTTE

Chapter Eleven

I snuck Anders out of the house around eight in the morning. We couldn't stop kissing as I tried to push him out of the door. He's so charming, easygoing, and he makes me feel comfortable. I've never felt as safe with an Alpha as I have with Anders. Maybe I should be concerned that he knocked on my window while I was sleeping, but I was relieved. I had cried myself to sleep, thinking I'd fucked everything up. I have scent matches; I should be celebrating, enjoying this time, not worrying about how we're going to manage it.

They're my scent matches, we'll figure it out. I've honestly never heard of rejected scent matches.

I'm tugging on my boots and waiting for Anders to pick me up. I feel bad that he had to walk home this morning, but he said he didn't mind. He told me to dress warmly and bring my skates. I grin as I layer up. Hank is staring at me like I'm a crazy woman. I pack a bag of extra clothes and my glasses. Probably presumptuous, but I don't care.

My mom stops me in the hallway, looking me over with a huge smile on her face. "This have anything to do with you sneaking that

Alpha out of the house this morning?" She smirks and continues walking past me.

"Uh, you knew?"

"I might be old, honey, but I'm not stupid."

I clear my throat and tug at my collar, knowing that I need someone to confide in. "He's my scent match."

She turns on her heel and blinks at me. Her hands reach out, holding my forearms before they slide down and hold my hands. "Oh, Charlotte."

"The two guys he's at the cabin with, they're my scent matches too."

She gapes at me, her hands nearly squeezing my hands so hard that they feel numb. "Three scent matches?"

I nod my head. "Three scent matches."

"Wow. Okay. This is amazing." Her smile is radiant, and I expected her to be happy, but not this happy. She's nearly glowing. Her hands leave mine, and she strokes my hair and plays with the ends. "I'm always worried that if I was gone, what would happen? Now that I know you have scent matches... You have your Alphas, Charlotte." Tears well in her eyes, and she shakes them off. "I just didn't want to leave you alone. No one should be left alone."

My eyes fill with tears, thinking about my dad and how alone she felt. But also her morbid talk sinks deep into my heart with my greatest fears. "Mom..."

"No, honey. I didn't mean to get all depressing. This is just good news. I know none of the Alphas at school did anything for you. Who would have thought you would meet them here, at home?"

"They go to school in Boston. I'm not sure where they live during the off season. They're hockey players. I don't know what that means for the future either." My mom grabs my shoulders and looks me in the eye. Sometimes looking at my mom is like looking into my future with how similar we look.

"Don't let the fear of the future hold you back, Charlie. This is a gift. Don't let it slip through your fingers because you spend too much time worrying. Don't run away before you get the chance to see how amazing it could be." I nod, and she leans forward and kisses my forehead before wrapping me up into a hug. "I'd like to meet the other boys too." They are far from boys, they are gigantic men, but I don't correct her.

I nod, knowing that Eli won't be a problem. Mikael may be another story. She pulls away from the hug, only to pull me into another. "You deserve this, Charlie. I'm so happy for you and so proud of you."

I sniffle, but hold back tears. Moms just really know how to lay it on thick, don't they?

There's a knock at the door, and my mom pulls herself away from my arms but follows me to answer. When I open the door, Eli and Anders are both there with smiles on their faces.

"Ma'am," Eli says, holding out his hand.

My mom shakes it and laughs. "You can call me Kathy. It's nice to meet you..."

"Eli."

"Anders, Eli, and who is the third?" Mom asks.

Eli rubs the back of his neck with a gloved hand. "Mikael was busy this morning." He says it smoothly, but my mom is no dummy, she knows something's up. She nods her head and gives the guys a once over.

"I'd love to cook a meal for everyone. Maybe in a few days?"

"That would be lovely, Kathy," Anders says politely, and my mom nods her head. I go to grab my bag, but Eli grabs it first and throws it over his shoulder.

"Make sure to call if you won't be home tonight," Mom calls as I'm shutting the door. I watch as Eli's cheeks redden and I can't help but smile.

"Thanks for picking me up."

"I'm just glad you agreed to hang out today," Eli says, opening the passenger door.

"Anders, you can sit upfront. You're much taller than me."

He shakes his head and nearly pushes me up into the passenger's seat, then shuts the door and gets in the back.

"So what's the plan?"

"We were kind of hoping you were up for a skate? We need to stay in shape and, well, your time got disturbed yesterday," Eli says.

"I'd love that. It's noon on a Saturday though. The lake will be packed."

"As long as there aren't any rogue pucks, we should be fine."

I nod. The warmth of the cab feels nice, so does the comfort of Eli and Anders scents. I wonder if they are projecting more pheromones around me, or if it has to do with knowing they're around their scent match. I don't really care about the reason, I just don't want it to stop. I want to ask if Mikael will be there, but I'm not sure if there is a point.

Since their cabin is right on the lake, Eli parks in the garage. Anders gets out and grabs me by the waist and puts me on the ground. I don't miss how slowly he drags me down his body as he helps me plant my feet on solid ground. I give him a smirk, but he just leans down and kisses me lightly before Eli comes to our side of the garage with my bag looped in the crook of his arm.

We're all already dressed to go skating, except for the skates.

"Need your whole bag, or just the skates?" Eli asks.

"Just the skates." Eli opens up my bag with no care in the world, grabs my skates, and carries them alongside his own. "You aren't bringing your sticks and gear?"

"Nope, just skating drills today. Hope you're ready," Eli smirks, confidently taking my hand in his as we walk through the shoveled path of snow down to the lake.

"Should I be concerned?" I whisper over my shoulder to Anders, who just grins and shrugs his shoulders. "That doesn't make me feel any better."

"Don't worry, I'll go easy on you." Eli says, tugging my hand and pulling me closer to him, leaning down to whisper against my hair. "This time."

"Now I'm definitely worried."

Eli and Anders both laugh at my expense, but I don't feel like they are laughing at me. No, it's light, cute, and flirty. We all sit at the old bench by the lake. I feel something I can't exactly put words to when I'm between them. My perfume wafts off of me, and I feel my cheeks heat. I'm definitely not virginal or inexperienced by any means, but when it comes to more than one Alpha, that is something I definitely haven't done.

Neither of the guys says anything about my scent, and I hope the cold air helps hide my slutty, little thoughts. We all take our boots off and put our skates on. The way they lace up is like it's second nature. They both have their skates on by the time I'm almost done with my first.

Eli grunts and looks at my handy work, then shakes his head. "Not tight enough, baby," he says. I think I faint or lose consciousness for a moment as he leans forward and laces and tightens my skate till it meets his approval. He doesn't ask to do the second one, he just slides it over my foot and gives it the same attention.

"It feels too tight," I say, and Eli grins.

"I bet it does." He shakes his head and laughs, standing up. Anders follows, and they each hold a hand out to me. The lake is filled with adults and kids, but not as crowded as I thought it would be. The lake is quite large, and there are maybe two dozen people on the ice. Someone brought a speaker, so Christmas music is playing as the guys help me walk the few feet to the edge of the ice.

I can't decide if I want to continue holding both of their hands, or have them let me free so I can prove to them that I'm competent on the ice.

Anders makes the decision for me as he lets go. "Show us what you got, *Kulta*."

"What does that mean?" I ask him as he skates backwards and me forwards. Eli is still holding my hand.

"Mmm, not sure I plan on telling you."

I gape at him, and he grins. "I'll make you a deal. You catch me, I'll tell you."

"You're nearly a foot taller than me!"

"Better get to skating, Charlotte."

He takes off backwards, which is still fast as hell.

"He didn't say anything about help," Eli says. His grip on my hand is firm as we both skate. I'm skating harder and faster than I have in my life, Eli nearly tugging me behind him. I feel bad that I'm slowing him down until I realize his intention. He uses the momentum of being in front of me to sling shot me across the ice. I continue skating as hard as my legs and lungs will take me. Anders' eyes widen as I grip his shirt. I give him a grin, and he grabs me by the hips, holding on to me as he continues skating backwards, just dragging me as I keep my balance and stand still.

He leans forward to whisper to me. "It means gold. As in precious, and your pretty blonde hair." My cheeks heat as he pulls back, and I look back at him.

I'm not sure what to say. I've never been given a pet name. And one that basically means precious in Finnish, I'm not sure how to take it. I just tug on his shirt and bring him down for a light kiss. I forget that Eli's here for a moment until I hear the ice shavings from him coming to a stop next to us.

There's a moment of worry about how he may feel, but when he looks at us, he doesn't seem upset or frustrated that Anders and I have progressed further than him. I reach out my hand, and Eli takes it. We skate at a much more manageable pace around the lake.

"Did you take ice skating lessons as a kid?" Eli asks.

"I did, before I perfumed."

"So until you were what, sixteen?"

I sigh and adjust my hat tighter over my ear on the one side. "I designated at twelve."

He stops skating and gapes at me for a moment. "Twelve?" He sounds astonished. It really is unreasonably young to designate.

"Yeah, I had to stop doing a lot of things. I was homeschooled. I couldn't do skating lessons any more, didn't really leave the house. As you can imagine, being that young as an Omega was unsafe for many reasons. I've had some not great encounters with both Alphas and Betas, if I'm being honest. Everyone seems to have an opinion on my designation and what we should be doing for them."

"I'm sorry you went through that."

"Me too. I think it's why adjusting to college has been so hard. I spent so much time with just my mom and my best friend, Piper. Then college was a huge shock, being surrounded by people constantly."

"Do you think it's just your school?"

I shrug. "I don't know any different, so I'm not sure. I don't think being around a bunch of other Omegas or self-entitled Alphas helps." He growls and stops skating for a moment and shakes his head. "Eli, is everything okay?"

"I... I just don't seem to really like the idea of you going back to school with other Alphas around. Sorry. I, uh, actually haven't growled that many times." I furrow my brow and nod my head.

"Did you not have much designation education?" I ask, purely curious. For an Alpha, Eli seems a little clueless.

"My parents sent me to boarding school. It was more religion based than designation based. Most of the students wound up designating as Betas. I think I was one of three Alpha students. No Omegas. Honestly, I've hardly been around Omegas before."

I squeeze his hand tight. "I think you're doing a good job."

"Yeah?" He sounds so hopeful. I smile and nod my head.

"So where do you guys live when you're not in school?"

"Anders goes home most summers, and Mikael stays at my place in Connecticut."

My heart sinks just thinking about the distance that will eventually separate us. I shake it away and take my mom's advice. Live in the present. Enjoy this moment, take it all in, and don't let it go.

Do not run away from this, Charlotte.

Eli smiles down at me as a few thick flakes fall, collecting on his dark hat. He leans down as a loud, irritated voice sounds over the ice.

"Fucking really? We're supposed to be doing weight training." Eli pulls away, and I see Mikael's dark, frustrated gaze.

Chapter Twelve

Anders came home smelling like her, more than just smelling like her. It's clear they did something last night. I don't think they fucked, but he definitely touched her. If her scent didn't give it away, the huge smug smile he had on his face sure as fuck would have. Part of me wants to punch him in the face for being so stupid, and the other part of me feels jealous that I'm not carrying that scent. *I fucking hate this.*

They invited me to meet our scent match. I declined with some colorful words and went up to my room.

This isn't how winter break was supposed to go. The draft is this summer. This is probably the last time we will all be together for a long time. We're supposed to be practicing, staying sharp for the rest of the season. Not chasing some blonde girl who, as far as I can tell, offers nothing to the table but her looks and scent. I'm not letting myself get sucked into this Omega's vortex like Anders and Eli. They seriously can't contain their dicks over one sweet—albeit ridiculously sweet—scent that's wrapped in a pretty cute bow.

No, she's not *cute*. She's just like any girl. She's not special to me—she can't be.

I'm tossing a ball against the wall, trying to let out some frustration, but it doesn't work. With the lake right in our backyard, it's a no brainer. I'll skate off some of this anger, and then when the guys drop off their little piece, we can all weight train together.

Before I'm at the lake, I see them. Anders watching Eli and her skate with a soft expression and Eli looking at her like the world revolves around her.

She's going to fucking destroy us.

My mouth opens before my brain even contemplates not being an asshole.

"Fucking really? We're supposed to be doing weight training."

I can't help it. My eyes dart to Charlotte first, her blue and green eyes staring at me in confusion and her pink lips parted.

"We will this afternoon," Eli says in a sharp tone. It's his annoyed captain tone. I roll my eyes and skate a few laps. Letting my heart rate rise, the exercise warms my body and slowly helps me clear my head. I love how cold the air is here. It fills my lungs painfully as I push myself to keep skating and free my mind.

After a few laps, I finally slow. My heart is raging in my chest, my feet gently gliding along the ice at this point.

"Did I do something to offend you?" her soft voice says, but it startles me nonetheless.

"Jesus fuck, do you just sneak up on people?" I look down at her. Even though she's in skates too, she's still over a foot shorter than me.

"Sorry. I thought you heard me."

I shake my head and skate a little quicker. She surprisingly keeps pace. I'm happy that it's cold and she's not too close to me. Not being able to scent her helps with pushing her away.

"Are you just going to ignore me?"

"Trying to."

"Did I do something wrong?"

I slow, feeling a little guilty. I push it back as I look at her face. It's a reminder of everything that I could lose by falling into this trap. Look at Eli and Anders, they're already fucking falling over themselves, and we don't even know her.

"Yeah, existing." I watch her face fall as I say it, and I know I'm a fucking dick. I should take it back. Part of me wants to, but I don't. I skate away, toward the bench, preparing to leave the ice.

Charlotte skates over to Eli, who wraps an arm around her shoulder.

Anders looks pissed as he skates to me and fists my shirt. "You don't have to like her, talk to her, acknowledge her. And you won't treat her like fucking shit. What's wrong with you, Martel?" He throws out my last name, and I swallow. Anders usually has his temper in control, but right now, he looks even more pissed than he did last night.

"You might be okay throwing away your future for a piece of ass, but I'm not." Wrong fucking thing to say.

I don't expect his swing. So when his fist hits my cheek, I nearly fall backwards. But years of brawling on the ice has prepared me for this moment. He fists my shirt, and I fist his as we hit each other. I don't hit as hard as I can, and I don't think Anders is either, but they aren't gentle punches either. I taste the metallic tang of blood in my mouth. It spurs me to hit him harder, right beneath his left eye. He groans, and we both tumble onto the cold, hard ice.

There's a feminine sounding gasp, and then Eli is pulling us apart and cursing.

"The fuck is wrong with you two?"

Anders and I get to our feet. I spit the blood out on the ice and look to my left. Charlotte looks horrified as she takes in mine and Anders' appearance.

She coddles the blond Alpha, cradling his face and asking him if he's okay. I spit another patch of blood on the ice, staining the perfectly white and blue color. It's what I do, *I ruin things*. At least that's what I've always been told. I've always been a disappointment, never good enough. Not until I found hockey.

Eli fists me by the shirt, and I let him as he pulls me to the corner of the lake.

"Mikael, what the fuck?"

"He started it."

"Did he?" He arches an eyebrow, calling me on my bullshit. "Listen, man, if you can't handle this, I can get you a ride back to Boston."

I meet his gaze. I've been hurt a lot in my life, but Eli telling me to leave is one that cuts deep. He's better than any family I've had. He may not be seeing this all clearly for what it is. But I can't fault him.

"I don't need to go."

"You need to at least be cordial, and stop being such a fucking dick."

I nod my head, wanting to say something snarky about leaving his precious little Omega alone. "Promise me we will still take training seriously."

"I promise. But you also need to understand that Anders and I are pursuing this. We have a scent match, man. What are you doing?" He looks genuinely concerned, and I shake my head.

"Eli, you have so much natural talent, you're going to give that up for an Omega?"

"I'm not sure why you think we need to choose?"

"You're so naïve, Eli." I say, skating away, not looking back, and not making amends with Anders or speaking to Charlotte.

I've held myself in my room for a few hours, hoping that Anders has calmed down, but in my self-reflection, I've only grown more pissed off.

I mean, I get it. She's attractive and smells good. But that's all it fucking takes to keep their eyes off the prize? Everything we've worked for?

Being hungry wins out over my sulking, and I head down to the kitchen. I'm surprised by the sizzle of a griddle, and I almost think about turning back and going to my room, but it smells too fucking good.

When I enter the open concept kitchen and living room, Charlotte is in the kitchen, and Anders and Eli are fussing over her. I roll my eyes.

"You don't have to cook for us," Anders says.

"I love cooking, and it's just grilled cheese and tomato soup. Will you sit down?"

Anders and Eli comply and sit down at the island. When Anders' gaze meets mine, he gives me a glare, but looks away. There's a nice, little, purple bruise beneath his left eye. He should fucking know better. I want a grilled cheese, but I'm sure as fuck not going to ask her to make me one. So I open the fridge door and peer in, hoping that there's something easy for me to grab.

"Would you like one?" Her voice is calm, no malice or anger toward me. My initial response is to shake my head no. She doesn't let me answer as she hands me a plate with a bowl of soup and the most gourmet looking grilled cheese I've ever seen in my life.

I blink at her and hold the plate in my hand. "The polite thing to say is thank you." She adds a little sass to the end of thank you, and I hate to admit that I like it.

"Thank you." I turn on my heel and walk away. I can feel Eli and Anders staring daggers at my back. I don't get the same sensation from Charlotte, and it makes the pit of my stomach churn. Why is she being so fucking nice? If anyone should be giving me glares, it's her.

When I get back to my room and bite into the sandwich, I groan. It's really fucking good and the best thing we've eaten that isn't take-out since we got here. The bread is clearly from a bakery, and I have no clue what cheeses she put in this thing, but it's immaculate. I dip it in the soup, loathing how goddamn good this sandwich is and how fucking polite she was when she handed it to me.

My phone buzzes, and I groan, worrying that it's one of the guys telling me to stop being such an asshole, *again.*

Jenkins:

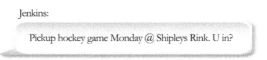

Pickup hockey game Monday @ Shipleys Rink. U in?

I really don't know how the fuck Jenkins got into college with the way he texts. I can't imagine his writing is much better. A hockey game is what I need. Even if most of the guys playing aren't at our level.

We're in.

Jenkins:

Harley will be there.

I roll my eyes and don't send him a text back. Harley is a Beta we go to school with, and we may or may not have hooked up a few times. But it wasn't anything more than that and won't ever be anything more than that. I send a text off to the guys, letting them know the plan.

Jenkins invited us to a pickup game on Monday at Shipleys.

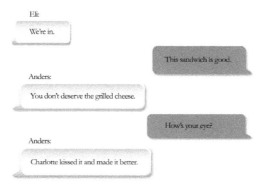

I groan and throw the phone, wondering why it makes me so angry. Is it because I think Anders is being a dumbass, or is it something else?.

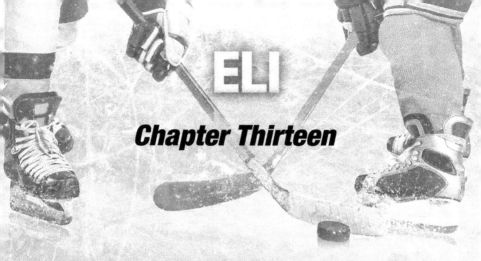

Chapter Thirteen

I t's getting late, and I'm not sure how to broach the subject of Charlotte staying the night. Not that anything needs to happen, but I just don't want this day to end. Anders and Mikael fighting aside, today has been perfect.

We did promise Mikael that we would weight train though, plus it's getting dark outside. I'm not sure how to keep her here, while also keeping my promise to Mikael. I'm not sure why he's so twisted up about this, but I don't want him to feel abandoned by us either.

We're on the sectional, with Charlotte between the two of us wrapped up in the softest blanket we have in the house.

"We need to do some weight lifting with Mikael."

"Do we, though?" Anders says, still pissed. I watched it all go down. He hit first, but I'm sure Mikael goaded him into doing it.

"We promised."

Charlotte bites her bottom lip, and I wish it were my teeth. "I could watch," she squeaks. "Or I could go home, or just wait up here. Whatever."

"You can watch."

"Where's the weight room?"

"Basement, might want to take your blanket." She nods, keeping it wrapped around herself as she shuffles to the basement. Anders is in front of her, and I'm behind, making sure she doesn't bust her ass on the stairs.

Mikael is already lifting, loud music booming in the space. Mikael glances over at us and Charlotte, thankfully holding his tongue. Charlotte just sits on the mat, wrapped up in her blanket, and quietly watches us lift. I spot Mikael, seeing as he and Anders still aren't talking. She appreciates his form and takes the time to watch him when he isn't able to scowl at her.

I kind of get Mikael's hang ups. He has the most to lose out of all of us. Don't get me wrong—playing hockey is my life goal. But if I got hurt, or it didn't work out, I'd be okay financially. Anders has a family to go back home to. Mikael has nothing. His eggs are literally in one basket, and that is the NHL. Mikael has to work harder than all of us to be good at hockey too. I'm not even being egotistical saying that—he would admit it. He wasn't born with an outstanding natural ability. He works hard every day. I'm not sure if Charlotte symbolizes him losing everything he's worked for. But I worry his negativity and being a general dick is going to ruin his chances with Charlotte and us. I can't believe he's being so pigheaded. It all makes sense now. Why we all got along from the get go. We all share the same scent match; we're supposed to be pack. I get that hockey is his dream, but does he really think we'd let a packmate flounder?

I'm sure it boils down to pride and proving himself, but it's fucking annoying. I must be scowling at him as he hefts the weight above him and puts it back on the rack.

"Ease up, Becky," he says, and I roll my eyes. My nickname causes me to forever loathe my last name, Beckford, and that it's stuck with me all these years.

I go to see Charlotte's reaction, but she's lying flat on the mat, bundled up and passed out.

"I'll carry her upstairs and text her mom," Anders says. I nod my head and look back at Mikael.

"You ease up."

"I'm fucking trying. We're good for the pickup game in two days?"

I roll my eyes, but nod. "Yeah, we're good."

"I'm really going to try," he says softly, walking out the door and turning off his music. I sigh and accept that as a win. As long as he isn't rude to Charlotte, that's all that matters.

I shower and go on the search for Charlotte. Anders took Charlotte to his room, and I can't help but feel left out. I open his door, and his voice is low. "You can take the right side." He can't see my smile in the dark, but I cuddle next to her, not touching, but close enough to feel her body warmth. I've never considered this sharing aspect, but so far, I don't feel bothered. It's like deep down, I know that Anders isn't a threat. He's my Omega's scent match, just like me. We're a team, like always.

I sleep more soundly than I care to admit.

"Oh, it's snowing pretty hard. We've got to go outside," Charlotte says, pulling on her boots.

"Aren't you sick of snow?"

Anders and Charlotte both scoff at the same time, and I hold my arms up in surrender.

Her jacket is on, and she's about to open the door for us to head out, but I tsk at her. "Forgetting something?"

She pats around her body. I tug on her wool knit hat and she smiles. Her scent comforts me as she pulls me out the door.

"You'll come out later?" she asks Anders, and he smiles and nods his head. I appreciate the fuck out of him giving us some alone time together.

She holds her arms out to her sides, her palms up as she spins and falls backwards into the snow. I'm near her in a second, and she laughs.

"Fuck, I thought you tripped."

"Despite what you think, I'm not really that clumsy."

"Good to know."

"Come on down, the weather's fine."

"What exactly is it that we're doing?"

"Snow angels."

"Snow angels?" I furrow my brow, and her boot taps at my shin.

"Fine." I lie down next to her in the cold snow and watch the white, fat flakes fall from the gray cloudy sky. It's actually pretty beautiful and peaceful in a way.

"You've never done a snow angel? Aren't you from Connecticut?"

I clear my throat and look at her. Her cheeks are pink, eyes bright, and her blonde hair is covered in flakes. "My parents weren't the playing type."

"You didn't have friends?"

"Not many, and most of the time, it was in the house. My parents thought the kids who played outside all the time were unrefined or feral. They wanted me to be a very specific way."

"What the fuck does that even mean?"

I shrug, knowing that my parents aren't the best, but I want for nothing. Maybe except acceptance, maybe a dash of love.

"I don't know. I sound stuck up."

"No, it sounds like you need to have more fun."

"I have fun," I say and furrow my brow at her as a fist full of snow smacks me in the face and melts down my cheek. I use a gloved hand to wipe the snow off and blink at the small Omega next to me. "Did you just throw snow at me?"

She's already half up on her knees before she's fully standing and runs like a bat out of hell, laughing. "Oh, you better run!" I grab a fist full of snow, packing it down and tossing it, making sure I hit her below her shoulder blades. When it hits her back, she squeals and bends down to make her own snowball. She tosses it, but it comes up short, and I run again, making quick strides in the fluffy snow. It's perfect for snowballs, not too icy, but it sticks nicely.

I don't see her pack another ball, but this time it hits my chest. "Oh, you're in for it!"

She laughs hysterically while trying to run. She doesn't stand a chance in a foot race as I finally reach her, picking her up by the waist and holding her close to my chest. "Do you yield?"

"Never!"

"Have it your way." I fall back to the ground with her on top of me, before spinning and putting her back on the ground. She smiles at me, her pretty eyes shining. I can see our breath in the cold air. I take a gloved hand and tug on a finger with my teeth, pulling the glove off. Her eyes follow the motion, and she licks her lips. My cold hand cups her cheek, and I tilt her chin toward me. "Yeah?" I ask. She bites her lower lip, and all I can think about is how I want it to be my teeth. She blinks and nods her head, and that's all the confirmation I need.

Her hands are on my chest as I lean forward, and our lips meet. It's a cold kiss at first, both of our lips freezing from being outside. Snowflakes hit my back and fall around us, and I hold her cheek and dip into her mouth with my tongue. She hums in approval, and her body shifts under mine. The kiss is no longer cold as our tongues explore one another. Her one arm is wrapped around my neck, bringing me closer to her.

She tastes unlike anything I've ever experienced, like I can't get enough, or I'll never get enough. This kiss is single-handedly changing my future, and I accept it. Scent matches are no fucking joke. I want more, need more. Her smaller body against mine. Her hands clutching against me, begging for more.

I can't help it when I grind against her, no fucks given about our thick winter layers or how cold it is outside. As we lie in the cold winter snow, the quiet wind surrounding us and snow falling down on us, all I can think is how I never want this to end.

That's when a thick and heavy packing of snow hits my back. I break our kiss, and Charlotte looks up at me like I'm special and the kiss was as revolutionary for her as it was for me. I lean forward and kiss her again. Another snowball shatters across my back.

"Oh, what the fuck?"

"Get a room!" a bunch of younger teens scream as I get pelted with icy snow. I at least shield Charlotte.

"What are you doing? We can't just take this lying down—literally," she laughs at her own joke, and I smile.

"What's the plan?"

"We need protection, and then we pelt the little fuckers hard with snow. Where's Anders?"

I text him that we need reinforcements as Charlotte pushes snow to make a shield. All the while, we're both getting pelted with snowballs. She put me in charge of throwing and snowball manufacturing.

It's looking grim for our team as Anders comes storming out of the cabin, some weird looking tongs contraption in his hands. I notice that he's using it to pack the snow and putting it in one hand, and then unmercifully beaming it at the kids. He takes his sweet ass time getting to our 'fort'.

"What kind of shield is this?" he asks, both of our frames are both exposed.

"I made the shield," Charlotte glares at him.

"It's perfect. Just a bit small." He saves himself, knowing damn well if I made it he would have given me shit.

At that moment, Anders gets taken off guard as a mound of snow meets his face. Charlotte and I laugh uncontrollably as he cleans off his face.

"Oh, those little fuckers are gonna pay." He scoops snow with his tongs and tosses them over our snow barrier. The screams of terror from children let us know that Anders meets his mark each time.

"He's crazy! Let's get out of here," one of the kids says.

"Cowards!" Anders yells behind the safety of Charlotte's snow shield.

Charlotte is in a fit of giggles, and I want to tickle her so badly, but I don't know how she'd feel about that, and she has so many layers on.

"Let's warm up now that we've been victorious," Charlotte says. I nod and lean over and kiss her. She hums and gives me a smile. As quick as it happens, Anders leans over and plants a kiss on her. Her maple and pancake scent is thick, even in this cold air. She shuffles, adjusting herself, her cheeks even pinker than they were earlier.

"Let's go." Anders hefts himself up, and I do the same. I can't help myself as I pick up the Omega and toss her over my shoulder. She doesn't protest as I make strides in the snow and walk back to the cabin. I don't miss Mikael tugging the blinds shut from his room as we walk back to this house. I wonder how much he saw.

We spend the rest of the afternoon playing games, touching constantly, and Charlotte makes the most amazing chicken parm soup.

It's getting late, and it's about that time where I want to ask her to stay.

"I really need to go spend some time with my mom and Hank," she says. She sounds disappointed, but pragmatic. I can tell Anders is just as disappointed, but he agrees. I don't want to miss any of the time we have with her when things are simple. I know that this time is a bubble, where there's nothing to worry about when it comes to distance or schedules. So I just stay in the bubble. Facing reality sounds terrible anyway.

"We're playing a kind of scrimmage game tomorrow. Would you like to come?"

She beams. "I'd love that."

"I'll drop you off, and we can pick you up at around ten?"

"Perfect," she grins, leaning forward and kissing me. She catches Anders' pout and kisses him next. I'm shocked that I feel no jealousy. It just feels so fucking right.

Chapter Fourteen

Piper texted me last night, and we have plans to meet in a few days. The guy she's seeing is here, and I don't find myself feeling negative about meeting them. Except for the fact that I haven't told my best friend that I have three scent matches. *But that's a problem for another day.*

I feel like I'm in a dream, that this isn't really my life. How did I go from hating school and not feeling content in life to having two Alphas who are dying to get to know me? Who also treat me with so much care and kindness I can't help but feel special and cherished.

I'm guessing this is what people call the honeymoon phase, but is it truly a phase when they're your scent matches? I'm not sure. I've been meaning to do more research, but I just haven't had time. I think I'm caught up in the bliss. I have to constantly remind myself that it's okay to stay in this happy, little bubble.

I maybe go a little harder with the makeup and my outfit than I have the other days that we've hung out, but I want to feel pretty. It's the first time I'll be out with my scent matches in public, and I can't help but want their approval. That's a lie. I want more than their approval. Maybe adoration and complete devotion are the better terms for it. But I feel insane thinking it.

This conviction of knowing that they're it, that I've found my scent matches, makes me feel alright with the warp speed these relationships seem to be going. Well, at least with Anders and Eli. It's not like I haven't fucked an Alpha after just meeting him. At least I haven't done that yet. But my heart, yeah, she's on the fucking line with those two. Mikael has been an asshole, but something about his brokenness calls to me. I just want him to let me make it better.

Once I have my jacket on and grab my purse, I kiss Hank on the head and wait for the guys to come and pick me up. My mom is sitting on the couch sipping on a cup of tea.

"You look beautiful, sweetie."

"Thanks, Mom." I'm nervously tapping on my thigh, and she notices.

"You have nothing to be nervous about."

"I know. It's just, you know, going out being around people." I've gotten better, less socially awkward, but large crowds can be tough. Especially because the guys will be playing hockey, and I'll be by myself.

"Well, I found this. Maybe you could put it in your purse. People will usually leave you alone if you're reading." My mom gets up and hands me the small book. It's probably five by five inches and maybe fifty pages thick. The title reads *Fate Found*. I flick to the back and sure enough, it's a book written by an Alpha who found his scent match. It's his biographical story and their personal experience.

"Thanks, Mom." She nods and wraps me in a warm hug. I squeeze her tight and slide the small book into my purse. "Did you read it?"

"I did, and I've been doing some research."

"And?"

"And you have nothing to worry about, honey," she says while pulling the curtain back. "Looks like they're here. Please let me know if you'll be coming home." I blush but nod and give good boy Hank just one more pat on the head. He looks so sad to see me leaving.

"Don't worry, buddy. I'll bring you out to play tomorrow." I lean forward and kiss his massive noggin, then open the door before Anders can even knock.

His smile is beaming, and he looks at me appreciatively before holding out his hand. "You look beautiful."

"Thanks," I say shyly and take his hand in mine. He gives me a gentle squeeze before opening the back door of the truck and helping me get in. I slide all the way behind the passenger's seat, so Anders can just climb in after me.

Mikael's scent nearly assaults me as I buckle my seat belt and stare at the headrest and his loose dark hair. He doesn't say anything, which I guess is better than him acting like a dick. Eli, however, reaches back and squeezes my thigh.

"Thanks for coming."

"Of course, I'm excited to see you guys play." There's a terse noise from the front of the truck, but I ignore it. "So who are you guys playing?"

"It's a variety of other guys who play in college or played on travel teams, but not at the collegiate level. So it's kinda a mix of guys."

"Will you play on the same team?" That makes Mikael laugh.

"No, probably not," Anders says. I furrow my brow. His hand reaches over and squeezes my thigh. "Wouldn't be fair."

"You guys are that good?"

"You wound me, Char," Eli jokes from the front seat.

"Sorry. I know the basics of hockey, most of the game rules and things like that, but I don't know what it takes to be the best."

Mikael grumbles something from the front seat, and we all ignore him.

The drive is longer than I was expecting, but I enjoy Anders' touches and listening to the guys attempt to sing some of the songs that are on Eli's playlist. It's also nice to be surrounded by their scents without Mikael saying anything negative. Part of me wishes he would speak though, at least try to hold some conversation with me. I feel like he's written me off without attempting to get to know me.

Eli pulls up to a small shop, and Mikael hops out of the car.

"We kind of guessed on what type of sub to get you," Eli says sheepishly.

"I love pretty much everything."

"Good. This place is the best."

I clear my throat. "Is Mikael okay that I came along?"

"He's fine, ignore him," Eli says simply. How do I ignore someone when every instinct in my body is saying that he belongs to me? I just nod my head, Anders' thumb rubbing soothing circles on my thigh.

Mikael comes back to the car without a word, holding two bags. Eli reverses, and we drive toward the stadium. "We'll eat at the rink. Eli is a freak about people eating in his car," Anders says.

"First of all, it's a truck. And second, listening to you fuckers eat in such a small, confined space is my personal nightmare."

"I'm fucking starving," Mikael grumbles. I feel like we all look at him, having been the first time he's spoken up the whole trip. He just faces out the window and stays silent the rest of the way.

Lunch was delicious. They ordered me a turkey BLT with avocado, and it was amazing. I grabbed a coke and a bag of M&M's before sitting in the stands. The guys went to get dressed in all their gear as I sit here waiting for the game to start.

Eli gave me a very stern look and said, "If anyone gives you any shit, you find me right away, yeah?" I nodded my head, and I'm very grateful that I thought to wear some scent-blocking panties this afternoon.

I take out the book from my mom and start reading as I wait for the game to start. The book is about an Alpha named Pearson who met his scent match, Ebony, when he was twenty-five and she was twenty-three. She had already been bonded to two other Alphas at the time. When they met, it was unlike anything he ever experienced. He describes it as falling instantly, scenting her and knowing that she was his future, that nothing would ever compare. That if he didn't make Ebony his bonded mate, he would never have a day of peace in his life.

A huge smile takes over my face when I realize Ebony is quoted in the story. She describes finding her scent match unlike anything else. She loved the Alphas she was already bound to and doesn't want to compare her partners. But her connection to Pearson is cataclysmic, like the universe destined them together. She wanted his bite nearly as soon as she met him.

I'm eager to read more when a door slams open and a bunch of hockey players take the ice. There are two teams, black and white. I have to squint and try to find mine—*damn, possessive much?* I spot Anders first, mostly because he's by the goal. He gets down on the ice and does these stretches that look like he's humping the ice. I nearly have to excuse myself. Why don't they air this portion of hockey on TV? I swear the female fan base would go up astronomically. He's covered in thick pads and stretches his legs so wide it has my jaw slacked. I know guys joke around about wanting girls to be flexible in the bedroom. I realize I'm no better than a man as I think very dirty thoughts about Anders' flexibility.

I only spot Eli because he waves at me. I grin and wave back, watching him skate around the rink. Him and Anders are both in black jerseys, so I know to look for Mikael in white. He's scowling at someone in a black jersey, and Eli skates between them. I wish I could hear their conversation. At least I can take some solace in knowing that he doesn't reserve all his scowling just for me.

There's a lot of stretching, skating, and talking before two referees take the ice and blow the whistle, starting the game. I shove the book back in my bag, excited to pick it back up when the period ends, but I'm even more enamored by watching them all play. Eli is so fast on the ice; you wouldn't think someone his size would be able to skate so quickly. I'm not sure about his position, but he seems like the guy who scores. Mikael is lethal on the ice, and it does more to me than it should. When he pushes a guy in a black jersey against the boards, I find myself liking it. Mikael doesn't seem to be around Anders, so I guess his position is more defensive.

Anders stops a puck with his stick and passes it to his defensemen, who then passes to Eli. He does some quick stick work, getting past the white team's defense, and smacks the puck right into the corner of the goal. I'm on my feet clapping and cheering before I even think. Eli's teammates hug him and clap his shoulder. But I definitely don't miss the beaming grin from him on the ice. As light as it makes my heart, it's quickly squished when I see Mikael's scowling face. I sit back down on the uncomfortable stands and tuck my hands under my thighs. I watch as Eli shoves Mikael, but Mikael just skates away.

It's a lot of back and forth during the first period. I get the impression that Eli, Mikael, and Anders aren't giving their all in this game, and I make a note to ask them about it. The referee blows the whistle, and the two teams skate off to their respective benches. I use this time to take a much needed pee break. I leave my jacket but take my purse with me. The bathrooms are right behind the stands, so I feel fine.

Just as I'm walking to the ladies, an arm reaches out, the large palm flat against the brick wall. He smells like patchouli, and I fucking hate that scent. Why do all these shit Alphas smell like patchouli?

I look up and notice it's the same guy that Mikael was scowling at earlier.

"Excuse me," I say politely.

"What's the rush, little Omega?" I furrow my brows, not liking that term from him at all. It only sounds right coming from my scent matches.

"I just need to go to the bathroom, if you could just move."

"Oh, come on. Don't be like that."

I go to bend under his arm and walk past when he grabs my arm. His grip is firm, but not enough to leave a mark. Just another intrusive Alpha who thinks he can take what he wants. I'm really contemplating kicking him in the dick, but he has all his hockey gear on.

"I'm used to Betas being the puck bunnies. No need to play hard to get, sweetheart. You came here for a knot, right?"

"Don't touch me!"

"Maybe this whole putting up a fight thing could be fun." He leans forward and smells my hair, and I push against his chest. Just as quickly as he was in my space, he suddenly has his back against the wall, a scathing Mikael in his face.

"The fuck do you think you're doing, Felix?"

"What's it to you, Martel?"

"She told you not to touch her."

"You know these puck bunnies like to play games."

"She's not a puck bunny, and even if she fucking was, no means no, you fucking dick."

Felix goes to push himself off the wall, but Mikael pushes him back against the hard surface.

"What's your fucking deal? She's not yours." Mikael just pushes him against the wall again, and Felix laughs and grins. "Martel pussy whipped. Never thought I'd see the day." Felix looks over at me. His gaze is predatory, and I feel uncomfortable and wrap my arms around myself. "Guess I can get the appeal on this one. She does smell sweet. You share?"

Mikael fists his shirt and pushes him so hard against the wall I swear I can hear Felix's bones rattle. *Tu la touches encore et je te casse les doigts, asshole.* " Mikael shoves him one more time until he comes and puts an arm around my shoulder and walks me to the bathroom. Mikael is huge when we're just standing next to each other. He's on skates while I'm in sneakers, so he's basically a giant. "Are you okay?" he asks softly once we're by the bathroom door.

"He's not the first Alpha who thinks he's god's gift to Omegas or can take what doesn't belong to him."

"You don't belong to anyone." It feels like someone's just punched me in the chest when he says the words. I nod and turn to the bathroom door. His large hand shuts it, and I startle. A sigh escapes me, and I turn to look at him. He's looking down at me, his brown eyes giving me no clue to how he's feeling. "I'll wait out here till you're done."

I nod and go into the bathroom. I'm so fucking frustrated I could scream. Is it pathetic that I was hoping maybe he would take it back? I don't know what he said to Felix in French. All I caught was asshole. But I guess he's just being a good friend to Eli and Anders.

It hits me even harder when I think back to the book. How can I have such a strong pull to Mikael, and yet he can so easily fight it? Maybe I'm not his scent match, but he's mine. I shake all the negative thinking out of my head, not wanting Mikael to have to stand there and wait for me much longer.

When I leave the bathroom, he watches as I take my seat on the stands before he's back on the rink with the team. I can feel Anders and Eli glancing over at me. The game is not as exciting as it was earlier, but I watch dutifully, even though it feels like my heart is breaking. I have two Alphas who are really giving this a shot. They are the ones I should be giving my attention to.

A pretty Beta with dark brown hair wearing a BU sweatshirt sits next to me. "Mikael Martel, really?" she asks.

"Pardon?"

"Might as well cut your losses there, sweetheart. Mikael is the kind of guy you fuck. He's not looking to settle down. I'm sure there are plenty of other Alphas who would be interested."

I eye her up and down, no idea how my face looks. Pretty sure that I can't control the irritation I'm feeling. "And who are you?"

"Harley, and you are?"

"Mikael's scent match, if you'll excuse me." She gapes at me for a moment and doesn't let me pass.

"You're setting yourself up for failure. A guy like that doesn't stay faithful once he's pro." I ignore her and grab my coat to go stand toward the ice. My gaze meets Mikael's, and the look he gives Harley is one that I'm glad I haven't been on the other side of.

My phone buzzes, and Piper's name pops up. I sigh and rub my forehead. Today has been a lot. I know immediately that we need a coffee date. If anyone can help me with this problem, it's going to be Piper.

CHARLOTTE

Chapter Fifteen

I didn't spend the night at the guys' cabin last night. Something about my interaction with Mikael just has me feeling off. The feminist part of me is screaming fuck yeah, I don't belong to anyone. The Omega part, however, is screeching that I belong to them and why in the fuck haven't they claimed me as theirs?

It seemed like they needed time to practice and do hockey things anyway. Mom dropped me off at the coffee shop; she has bingo at the VFW and it was on her way. Piper is meeting me, and I'm freaking out about how she's going to take the news. I've already preemptively gotten both of our coffees and commandeered our favorite table by the window.

When she walks through the door looking like a goddess, I give her a smile, and she unwraps her scarf as she comes and sits next to me.

"What's going on, Charles?" She arches an eyebrow, and I know I'm caught. Usually when I'm home from break, Piper and I spend every waking moment together.

"Here, I got you coffee."

"Hmm, buttering me up, are we?"

I take a sip off my coffee and sigh. "So maybe there's a little thing I haven't told you?"

"What?" She's sharp with the question, and I clear my throat.

"Ifoundmyscentmatchesandtherearethreeofthem," spews out of me like one giant word.

"Come again, Charles?"

"I found my scent matches. Three Alphas."

She blinks at me, and her mouth is wide open. "Say something."

"I'm thinking, damn. That's a lot of information to process. How long ago was this?"

"Only a couple of days. I know it's fast. Like really fast. But it's like a thread pulling us together, Piper. It's like, sure, they're basically strangers, but every fiber of me knows they're mine."

She blinks at me again and takes a sip of her coffee. Her fingertip swirls around the rim, and she opens her mouth to speak multiple times before she sighs. "How do you feel about it?"

I grimace. "Part of me is excited, the other part is terrified."

Piper nods her head, knowing probably more than anyone my fear of abandonment.

"Are they still in school? What's the plan?"

I shrug and grimace. "There is no plan."

"What do you mean? You found your scent matches, and there's no plan for when winter break is over?"

"They go to BU." I keep it short, knowing that I have to explain the whole story, but I feel embarrassed. Maybe even stupid that I've decided to live in this bubble when everything will inevitably fall to shit.

"And…" Piper arches a sharp dark eyebrow at me.

"They're hockey players."

"So?"

"Like really good hockey players. Like getting drafted before they graduate kind of good."

She just stares at me, I feel my cheeks heat. "Oh, Charles."

I want to cry, but I hold it in. I'm sure as fuck not going to cry out in public. Crying is reserved for when I'm in the shower by myself and no one can see me. "I know."

"But they all want to be with you?"

I tug on my turtle neck. "Fuck, is it hot in here?"

"Charles?"

"Eli and Anders are one hundred percent in. Mikael, not so much."

"What's his deal?"

"Well, he's probably said a total of thirty words to me, so I'm not completely sure. But from what I've gathered, he sees me as a distraction."

Piper shrugs her shoulder, and I gape at her. "What? You're a very pretty distraction."

"Piper!"

"What? I'm just saying. If I found my scent match Omega, I'm not sure I would go to medical school."

It's my turn to blink at her. "What?"

"You're not mine, and I care for you so much, Charlotte." She takes a sip of coffee. "If I found the one, I'm not sure I would feel comfortable spending all those hours away from them. That's why

I hope to fuck I don't find an Omega until I'm already stable. But finding a scent match is rare. These Alphas would be stupid to let this go."

"But they already have their futures planned."

"If they aren't willing to make it work, then they aren't worthy of you. I'm not saying they need to give up hockey. But there needs to be some give and take."

I rub my head, the feeling of a headache coming on. Maybe I need to take my contacts out and switch to glasses. "I don't know what to do, Piper."

"What do you want?"

"Them, but how the fuck is this supposed to work?"

She sighs and reaches out to hold my hand. "I don't have the answer to that. But what I do know is you're worth fighting for. So if they care about you, they will make it work. I also think you should try to enjoy your time with them while they're here. Don't go overthinking about what happens after Christmas. You guys should talk about it, but really get to know them. Make sure they are worth it." I nod my head and squeeze her hand back. "Nick and I were planning on going to Stowe tonight, maybe you and your Alphas could come."

I roll my eyes at her over-enunciated "Alphas" but nod my head anyway. "I'll text and see if they want to come. I don't think they can do any winter sports though."

"They have tubing and lift rides."

"I'll let you know."

"Need a ride home?"

"You just want to see Hank."

She grins, drinking down the rest of her coffee. "Guilty."

I feel lighter after talking to Piper. They're my scent matches, and we'll figure out a way to make this work.

Shockingly, all three guys come to Stowe's, and I'm elated. We all drove together and are at the base of the mountain as we wait for Piper and Nick to get here.

"So Piper is your best friend?" Eli asks.

"Yes, since we were little. Oh, and she's an Alpha." His eyes are large, and he opens his mouth to ask a question as Piper and Nick come into view. I wave a gloved hand at her and smile. Nick is not what I was expecting. He's about the same height as Piper, just under six feet, and has dark black hair in a man bun. His features are striking but simple. He smiles and holds out his hand. As I shake it, I can feel Anders' massive frame behind me and an arm snaking around my waist.

I shake Nick's hand briefly. "I'm Charlotte, this is Anders, Eli, and Mikael."

Nick waves at the Alphas and nods his head. "Nick, nice to meet you." I'm polite to the attractive Beta, but I hate to admit that I know he won't last. As adamant as Piper thinks male Alphas aren't for her, I know they are. As much as Piper likes being in charge and caregiving, I know that she craves to be on the receiving end as well.

One day she will come to the same conclusion. Until then I will be nice to Nick and send my condolences for when Piper rips his poor little heart out.

"And this is Piper." I hold out an arm to Piper, and she looks over each of my Alphas and nods her head.

"Nice to meet you guys. What would you like to do?"

"We can't ski or snowboard," Mikael says sharply.

"Tubing? Lifts?"

"Let's do the lifts first before the sun goes down. Tubing is more fun when it's dark anyway." Piper says.

Eli and Anders give each other a conspiratorial look, and I glare at them, neither of them giving anything off. Piper and Eli go off to buy tickets for both of the events, and we stand around awkwardly. Anders fortunately breaks the silence. "So where do you go to school?"

"UMass with Piper. You guys?"

"BU," Mikael says, and Nick nods his head.

"Thought about going there, but I got more grants to go to Mass."

"Makes sense," Anders says.

The conversation is not flowing easily, and I clear my throat. "So you and Piper?"

"Yeah," he grins. "She's funny, nice, and we kind of just hit it off."

"She's special." Anders gives me a questioning glance, and I roll my eyes.

"She is," Nick says. This poor unfortunate soul doesn't stand a chance. I give him a smile that I hope is friendly and doesn't scream that I pity him. Hopefully when Piper breaks his poor little heart, she does it softly.

Eli and Piper come crunching back in the snow with wristbands. Piper hands Nick his, and Eli puts mine around my wrist before kissing the side of my head. I may not be able to feel his lips through the material of my hat, but I feel cozy just from the gesture.

Eli takes my hand, and we all walk as a group over to the ski lifts. The lifts are set up for two people. Piper and Nick gracefully get on the lift first, neither of them stumbling or looking like idiots. Eli lets go of my hand and leans in to whisper in my ear. "Sorry, baby."

"What?"

I barely have a moment to figure out what's going on as Anders and Eli get on the next lift together. Anders glares at Mikael in a way that screams don't be a fucking asshole, while Eli gives me a look that says he's sorry.

"Looks like you're stuck with me," Mikael grumbles next to me. We walk to the waiting area, and the next chair swings around. I'm a little slow to sit, and Mikael steadies my arm, making sure I'm stable before dropping the top rail. "You good?"

I nod my head and watch as the ground gets farther and farther away from my feet. Not a great moment to remember that heights aren't my favorite thing. I scoot just a little closer to Mikael.

"I wonder how many people die from falling off of these things every year."

"That's fucked up," Mikael says.

I shrug and take in the view. A thick blanket of white surrounds the area. Massive pines are weighed down with heavy snow, and skiers glide down the mountain. But as pretty as it is up here, I can't help but look at Mikael. I thought for sure that he would take in the scenery, but nope, he's staring right at me. His deep brown gaze analyzes me, and I can't read him at all.

"Why do you hate me?" I say it so quietly I'm not even sure he hears.

"I don't hate you."

"It feels like you do." That's when his gaze breaks away and a hand goes to his face.

"I don't hate you, Charlotte."

Should I be getting wet from the Alpha who has been nothing rude to me saying my name? Probably not. But here we are. I wore special panties, but I can tell he scents me when he groans.

"Did I do something wrong?"

"No."

"Do you not like women?"

He glares at me, and he scowls. "I like women."

"Do you not find me attractive?"

"For fuck's sake. You know you're pretty, Charlotte."

"Then what is it?"

"It's either you or hockey."

I blink at him, trying to decipher his words, and I remember what Piper said earlier—that if she found her scent match, she might not continue medical school.

"I'm not asking you to pick."

He groans and looks away from me.

"Do you know how many packs there are in professional sports?"

"No."

"None. Anders and Eli are so caught up in you they aren't think-ing logically. How do we make this all work when the three of us get drafted to different teams? Huh? Pass you around like the fucking brotherhood of the traveling Omega? That's not fair to anyone."

I blink at him as his hard stare meets mine. "Hockey is all I've ever had. The one thing that's mine, what I'm good at. The only thing I know how to do. I'm not smart like Anders or well off like Eli. This is literally all I have. I have nothing to offer you if I don't make it in hockey."

I reach out and touch his arm. "Mikael."

"Don't. It's better that we don't start anything. Maybe in a few years. Maybe when I'm better." I don't even notice the lift is back at the bottom of the hill, missing most of the ride from staring at Mikael and taking in all his fears. Most of which aren't completely wrong. I mean, I have the same fear of being abandoned by them as Mikael seems to have of me.

As he walks away, it's when my temper flares, and I don't think. I just grab a wad of snow and chuck it at his back.

"What the fuck?" he says as he spins around and glares at me.

"Yeah, what the fuck? Maybe in a few years?" I say to him with irritation in my voice. What am I supposed to do? Just sit on my hands and wait patiently for him to come to me after he's done playing hockey?

"That's what I said."

"A few years of me, what? Getting fucked by other Alphas during my heat?" He growls and stomps toward me.

"That's enough." He points at my chest, and I give him one of his scowls right back.

"Oh, what? You don't like the idea of me fucking other Alphas?"

"Charlotte, don't push me." He growls my name, and it's hot. I want to toss this sexy asshole into the snow and kiss and lick him everywhere.

"No, don't push *me*. You don't even speak to me. You glare at me and grunt and tell me you don't want this right now. But you can't have it both ways, Mikael. You either want this, or you don't. Figure it the fuck out, because I'm going to get to know Anders and Eli. If we get to know each other is up to you. If you're okay running away from your scent match, that's fine. But I'm not running away from mine."

I want to crunch more snow over his perfect head, but I wouldn't be able to reach. And as mad as I am at him, I wouldn't dare to throw snow on that perfect face.

Eli and Anders are waiting for me. I'm glad they didn't interrupt.

"Tubing?" Eli asks.

"Yeah, let's go."

"Everything okay?" Anders asks. I tug at his jacket and bring him down for a kiss. I might look back at Mikael and see him sulking. But I don't really care. If he doesn't want to explore this while we can, so be it. I have two scent matches willing to put in the work, and right now that's all I can ask for.

"It will be," I say as we break the kiss, and he smiles down at me.

CHARLOTTE

Chapter Sixteen

Tubing was a blast, especially when I sat on Eli's lap, and he was super hard the whole trip down. Having that power over an Alpha is something that I never truly understood. I've had sex with Alphas, but this flirting and intimacy isn't something I've really experienced before, and I love it.

I'm proud of myself for not letting my conversation with Mikael bring me down for the rest of the night. Tonight is about me getting to know Anders and Eli more. And by more, I want to be touched, and I sure as hell want to touch them. It's been days since Anders climbed through my window, and that was just light petting. I need and want more. They've both been perfect gentlemen, but I'm totally ready to test their limits tonight.

My mom already knows to not expect me home, and we ate at the lodge before heading back to the guys' cabin. I'm still cold from being out in the snow all afternoon and shiver when we hang out in the living room.

"Cold, *Kulta*?"

"Yeah, a bit."

"Hot tub?" Eli suggests. Yes, hot tub. I don't have a bathing suit. Let's all get naked!

"It's not a sauna, but it will do. You up for it, Charlotte?"

"Sounds great."

"I'll get towels," Eli says.

"I'll be up in my room," Mikael says. Though I expected it, it's not any less disappointing.

Anders turns on the back deck, light and in complete bare feet, he turns on the hot tub and removes the cover, then comes back into the cabin.

"Drinks?" he says, arching an eyebrow, and I nod. He looks so damn good, his dark blond hair ruffled from his hat and the white T-shirt that clings to his body. Anders pours three drinks and takes them outside, putting them on the edge of the hot tub. Every time he opens the door, a cold chill rushes through. "Do you... uh... want something to wear?"

I shake my head no and keep eye contact with Anders as I unzip my jacket. His eyes shift between looking at my face and following the motions of my hands. Once the jacket is on the floor, I pull off my two shirts. Just my pale pink bra is in view. It's lacy and sheer, and it's obvious Anders likes what he sees. Anders licks his lips, and both of our scents are thicker in the room. I slowly unbutton the clasp of my pants and roll them down my thighs, kicking them off once they're at my ankles. My panties are just as sheer as my bra, and I know when I'm in the water, they'll be able to see everything.

Anders shifts himself in his pants, and I gasp, wanting and needing everything he wants to give me.

"Fuck." It startles me, and I turn around to find Eli holding towels to his chest as he takes in my body. "You look... fuck."

I grin at him and walk seductively out the back door. "Mother-fucker," I swear as my feet walk over the snow covered deck stinging my skin. As quick as possible, I rush to the hot tub, climbing the stairs and sinking into the hot water. I curse again as I feel my hair around my collarbone and grab the hair tie on my wrist, then put my hair in a messy bun. I hiss as the contrast of cold and hot confuses my brain but sink further into the water.

Anders and Eli blink at me from the door.

I crook a finger at them. "Are you guys just going to leave me out here by myself?" They both shake their heads no and comically undress quickly. Both of them are wearing tight, microfiber boxer briefs. Eli briefly turns around to pick up the towels, and I get a view of the most delicious ass I've ever seen.

Anders gets in first, followed by a shivering Eli. Anders shakes his head at him and splashes him lightly with the water. "Sorry I didn't grow up in the fucking North Pole."

"Such a wittle baby," Anders replies as he wraps his arm around my shoulders, his thumb brazenly playing with my bra strap. "Are you warm enough, Charlotte?" Eli glares at him, and I smile.

"I am."

I feel excited, but nervous. Sure, Anders and I fooled around, but Eli and I have only kissed. Plus I've never quite been in this position of having two Alphas who want me at the same time. But I'm a horny Omega mess, and I want whatever these Alphas are willing to give. Fuck waiting another moment. I need them now, even if I have to make the first move.

"What do you need?" Anders asks, always so fucking in-tune with me. I smile at him and think. Playing games has kind of become a thing between the three of us.

"Truth or Dare?"

"Oh, Char baby, I don't know if you're ready for that." Eli's tone is joking, and I know he's just trying to push me, so I push back.

"Nervous, Eli?"

"Nope, you go ahead and start us off," he says confidently.

"Eli, truth or dare?" I arch an eyebrow, already knowing he's going to choose dare.

"Dare."

"I dare you to take my bra off with your teeth." He gapes at me and blinks. His gaze alternating between Anders and me. He licks his lips and moves forward, keeping his chest half covered in the hot, bubbly water.

"Sit on Anders' lap," he says, smirking at me. I don't have to be told twice as I scooch and sit on Anders' lap. I can feel his hard cock pressed against my ass, and his arms loop around my waist. Eli's lips part as he looks at my chest, my nipples visible through the sheer pink lace. I swallow thickly, waiting for him to touch me. "You want this off, baby?" His fingers graze over the shoulder strap.

"I said with teeth." Eli and Anders both laugh at my authoritative tone.

"You did," Eli says. His lips start behind my ear and trail down my neck. His kisses are so delicate, soft, and warm. My hands hold on to Anders' thighs for support, and he joins in, kissing the other side of my neck. It feels like my brain short circuits. Having this much attention on me at once is thrilling and surreal. My skin feels sensitive and hot, and I can't help but want more. I want everything they will give me—together. Anders' hands wander mischievously. One is on top of my thigh while the other holds onto my waist. Eli has one tangled in my bun, while the other is gripped against the side of the hot tub to keep him steady.

The first drag of Eli's teeth against my collarbone nearly has me coming on the spot. I can't help the needy whine that slips from my lips, making both Alphas groan. That's my new favorite sound, I decide. Anders' grip around my waist tightens, and I eagerly grind against his crotch. He retaliates with a nip to my earlobe. My head falls back slightly against Anders' shoulder, and Eli licks a trail from my collarbone to my lace covered nipple that he sucks through the sheer material. The sensation makes me arch my back and groan. I can't control my hands as one rises from the water and clutches the nape of Eli's neck, holding his mouth just where he is.

His tongue rolls and lavishes my nipple. He takes his time in giving me attention before his teeth graze over the full flesh and snag on the cup of the bra, pulling it down, exposing me completely to him.

He groans and takes the nipple into his mouth, sucking so hard it makes my clit pulse. When his mouth leaves me, the cold air hits my skin, and I'm panting from the difference in temperature. Eli kisses his way back up to my shoulder where he grips the strap with his teeth and tugs it down my arm. He pulls back slightly to look at his handy work and grins before giving my left breast the same attention as he did the right. I'm nearly shaking by the time my bra is at my rib cage.

"Anders, give me a hand."

Suddenly, deft fingers behind me unclasp the material, and my pink bra is floating on top of the bubbles. My chest may not be large, but I gotta say, they look excellent above the warm water, and the view gets even clearer as the jets turn off.

Eli unabashedly stares at my chest, and I let him, loving presenting myself to him in this way. Anders is still hard and gripping me tightly as Eli grins and leans over.

"Truth or dare, Char?" I've never liked that shortened version of my name, but for Eli, yeah, I like it.

"Dare." Please make it something dirty. He smiles and nods.

"I dare you sit that cute, little ass on the side of the tub and let me have a taste."

Anders squeezes me tighter, and I feel his cock twitch beneath me. It's going to be fucking cold the second I get out of this hot tub, but it's going to be so worth it. I smirk at Eli and stand as his muscular hands grab my hips as he perches me on the side.

"Make sure she doesn't fall," Eli tells Anders. Anders wraps his arm around my hip and squeezes the flesh on the side. He's going to be so close to us as Eli tastes me. The visual is erotic, dirty, and all-consuming. But not even my visuals can prepare me for the real thing. Anders' face is by my waist as his other hand spreads out my leg, and Eli spreads the other. Eli's thumb trails down my wet thong that clings to my skin.

"Such a pretty pussy," he whispers before he leans forward. Pushing the thong to the side, his tongue swipes over my clit, down to my entrance.

I reflexively arch back, and Anders' brawny arm keeps me steady. I'm grateful for Eli's thoughtfulness. Eli takes his time savoring me. His tongue swiping, rolling, and flicking against my clit. I moan loudly, thankful that it's late at night and that this side of the deck is blocked off from wandering eyes.

Light snowflakes hit my skin, and I shiver. Only the bottom halves of my legs are still warm in the water. Eli's green eyes gaze up at me before inserting two fingers inside of me. This time he doesn't mess around as he curls the two fingers and sucks my clit—hard. I shake, and Anders holds my thigh open for his teammate—packmate, whatever the fuck. When I look over at Anders, his gaze is locked onto where Eli is eating me out, and I fucking lose it. My back arches, and Anders keeps me steady as my legs shake and my orgasm hits. I have one hand holding the side of the tub and the other wrapped around the back of Eli's head, keeping him at my core. He moans against my cunt, my thighs shake, and I whimper from the release.

I should feel completely satisfied and sated, but all I want is more. I want to be full. I want to kiss and taste too. Anders slides me back into the warm water, and I wince at the stinging heat against my cool skin.

Eli licks his lips, and, knowing that he's savoring my slick, has me nearly feral. "Let's go inside."

"Anders didn't get a truth or dare," Eli says incredulously.

I spin, looking into Anders' beautiful eyes. "Truth or dare?"

"Dare." We're all predictable as fuck.

"I dare you to carry me up to your bedroom and fuck my brains out."

Anders blinks at me rapidly, and Eli clears his throat. "You heard *our* Omega."

Oh, I definitely like the sound of that. "Out of the tub first, so I don't drop you," Anders says, and I smile. Standing up and grabbing my bra, I exit the tub. A movement of light catches my eye from the second floor. I watch as the blinds close from Mikael's room. I smirk to myself. *Not so unaffected, after all.*

Well, he's in for a treat, because I don't plan on being quiet when these Alphas take me up to their beds either.

Chapter Seventeen

I hold on to Charlotte's hand as she climbs down the hot tub's steps, grimacing as her feet touch the cold snow. I'm quick to grab our towels, wrapping one around my waist and bundling her up with the second before scooping her up in my arms. She giggles. Her whole body is flushed, and I definitely don't think it's because of the hot tub or the cold air.

I've never shared before—but fuck—I enjoyed it. I never thought I'd get off on watching someone touch my woman, but watching her expressions as Eli touched her, it was spectacular. But now I want to do my own touching. Charlotte doesn't seem shy with her sexuality, and I'm happy for it. The things I want to do to this Omega are borderline obscene.

"The cold seriously doesn't bother you at all?" Charlotte says, interrupting my thoughts as I continue walking back to the cabin. Eli is behind us, closing up and securing the hot tub.

"No, you get used to it." She sighs, and her two fingers squeeze my chin to look down at her. "Kiss me, Anders." I obey immediately, kissing this sweet Omega until we reach the glass sliding door. When I break our kiss, she blinks at me, licks her lips, and sighs. Eli is nearly jogging behind us, acting like the snow is hot lava, until we're all in the warmth of the house. Charlotte doesn't even wiggle out of my arms, just content being held against my chest as we figure out our next move.

"My room. The bed is bigger," Eli says, and I nod, agreeing with his strategy here. Charlotte rubs her thighs together. There's a light scent of chlorine, but it mostly smells like maple as we walk down the hall to Eli's room.

The house is quiet, and I wonder what Mikael is doing. For damn sure, he's missing the fuck out. As I put Charlotte down and she drops the towel, I can't help but stare at her body. I love how forward and confident she is. But as she bites her bottom lip and wraps an arm around her waist, I realize that maybe she's not as confident right now as I thought.

"You okay? We don't have to do anything," I assure her.

"It's not that. I've just never, you know," she says, pointing at the two of us.

"Us neither. We, uh…" I clear my throat, and Eli sighs.

"We've never been with an Omega." Eli clears the air on that front, and Charlotte's cheeks redden.

"I, um, have been with other Alphas. I just got tested a few weeks ago at the doctor's, and I'm all clear." She says it shyly, like we would blame her for being with anyone before us. It's just that her designation is rare, and she's attracted to what she's attracted to. Which, luckily for us, as her scent matches, should be us from now on.

"We are tested all the time for hockey. We're good."

"I have an IUD."

Eli and I gape at her. No working thoughts roll around in my head. Just the fact that she wants both of us, and like *that*. "I, um... I have always used a condom before, so this will be a first."

"Firsts for all of us then," Eli says, walking over to her and standing behind her. The height difference is staggering between us and Charlotte, when we're so close to each other.

"Tell us what you want, *Kulta*."

She seems nervous, and I wonder if us boxing her in like this is too much. She looks around the room, which is pretty plain. Just a simple king-sized log-framed bed with a quilted blanket on top and standard wooden furniture pieces. The cabin is devoid of personal touches, but I guess that's Eli's family in a nutshell.

"I want to make you both feel good," she says in a breathy voice.

"Well, that will be easy. Go lie on the bed, Charlotte." She follows my orders, but goes above and beyond as she sheds herself of the damp thong, before crawling on the bed and resting her head on the pillow. Her blonde hair is still in a messy bun, and I can't wait to have my fist tangled in it. I go to the right side of the bed, and Eli goes to the left, getting completely naked before we're both on the plush mattress. Being naked around each other is nothing, but I'm not sure how this dynamic is going to work, but I'm eager to make it good for her.

"What now?" she whispers.

Eli answers her first. "Kiss Anders, baby."

She turns, and Eli pushes her bare ass against his hard cock as her lips meet mine. One of my hands cup her jaw as the other tangles in her hair. She gasps against my mouth as Eli touches her. She moans into my mouth, and I break the kiss to see Eli rubbing her pussy.

"So fucking wet," he grumbles.

Charlotte grips my hair—hard—tugging my face against hers. Her tongue is frantic against mine, kissing me with a passion I've never known. The room is primarily her scent, and Eli and I are tangled in the cloud of arousal filling the room. Our kissing, light moans, and the sound of Eli fingering her wet pussy are ringing in my ears as Charlotte pulls away from our kiss. Her hands go still in my hair, and her face shrouded in half-lidded desire.

"I need a knot."

I look over at Eli, who is usually the most confident Alpha I know. But as he swallows thickly, I nod. Usually Eli is in charge. He's our captain. Fuck, I could even see him being the Alpha of this pack, if Mikael gets his head out of his ass and we figure out how to make this work. I say that, knowing that as soon as I knot her, there's no turning back. After we're locked together, she's going to be mine forever.

"I'll give you what you need, *Kulta*. You want to taste Eli?"

"Yes," she says enthusiastically. Eli relaxes and lies on his back, his legs spread wide as Charlotte crawls on top of him, kissing him hungrily. I lick my lips, liking that she'll taste like both of us, and get to my knees behind her. Her ass is perfect, and I can't help myself when I give it a light smack. She groans and pushes her ass further up to me, like the sweetest offering I've ever been given.

"Are you presenting for me, Omega?" I ask in a deep timber, and she moans. She scoots back on to the bed, kissing Eli's chest as she moves backwards, her ass getting closer to my dick every second.

She wiggles her ass at me while her chest is close to the bed. Her forearms support her as she kisses Eli's dick.

Her cunt is dripping, a sheen on the sides of her thighs. My chest purrs as the tip of my length slides against her slick pussy. "Fuck," I groan as I squeeze one of her ass cheeks, spreading her apart for my viewing pleasure. Holding my knot, I glide into her hot center.

It's unlike anything I've felt. Pussy is great, don't get me wrong. But her scent, her pussy wrapped around me... It's nirvana.

"Fuck. Fuck." Charlotte backs her ass against my cock, not giving me a moment to collect myself. I can hear her licking and sucking on Eli's dick, his gaze completely fixated on her face as he cups it gently. There's a loud slurping noise, and I thrust into her, making her gargle a moan around Eli's length.

"So fucking good, baby. You're doing so well, taking both of us. You look so pretty with my cock in your mouth," Eli praises her. Alpha instinct is really something. For a guy who's never really been around Omegas, he's doing amazing.

I smack her ass like I did earlier, and she moans. "Seems like our sweet Omega likes having her ass spanked."

"Good girl spanks," Eli says between a groan.

"That's right. Fuck, watching your cunt gripping my cock is driving me crazy. Are you ready for my knot, *Kulta*?"

"Please, Anders." She pops Eli out of her mouth just to beg, and it drives me wild. I've been with Betas, never really worrying about my knot. It's just too big and stays on the outside. I'd never dated someone long enough to even consider knot training. When I'm getting head or jerked off, it feels nice when it's squeezed. But none of that prepares me for the pressure and pleasure that fills me when I push my knot into Charlotte's pussy.

She whines, her thighs trembling, and Eli's taken over, fucking her face as I rut into her. My knot swells, and I begin to panic. I reach around her, my front pressed to her back as I toy with her clit. She squirms, hardly able to keep Eli in her mouth as she moans and shakes. Her pussy milks me, squeezing my knot like a vice. I kiss and lick her back, my teeth grazing against her delicious skin.

Eli groans and shakes, the scent of his arousal thick as he finishes. As soon as he's out of her mouth, Charlotte shouts, "Yes, yes, don't stop!" I rub her clit with more pressure, and her cunt spasms around me.

"Fuck, you feel so good."

It sends her over the edge as she falls, her face against Eli's thigh as she shakes and pants. Her moans ricochet in the room. She grips me so tight I can't hold back another second as I fill her with my cum. The sensation makes me black out for a moment. How good it feels to have my knot so deep in her, knowing there's no barrier between us.

We're both panting as I kiss her shoulder. I don't know how long we'll be locked together. But I don't want this to end.

Eli strokes her hair, his chest purring for her. "You good, baby?" She nods her head, pressing closer to his skin, no care of the mess. I can't help the grin that spreads over my face. Obviously being raised in a pack, I conceptually knew how great it could be. But actually being a part of one, cherishing this one special Omega... It's everything, and I'll be damned if we let this go.

I maneuver us so that we're both on our sides. It was difficult, but my arms were starting to shake from holding my body weight off her back.

Eli is about to get up, but Charlotte grabs his arm and tugs him to the bed. "Don't leave," she begs.

"I'm going to get something to clean you up," he says softly.

She shakes her head. "No. Come here."

He follows the bossy Omega's directions and lies back down. I hide my grin in Charlotte's hair. Eli may be team captain, the boss on the ice, but it's clear who the boss is in this situation.

"I'm here," he coos at her, cupping her face and kissing her lips, no doubt tasting himself on her.

"Let's spend tomorrow being lazy together," Charlotte says.

"We don't have to leave this bed."

"Good. Cause I need your knot too."

Eli swallows and nods his head. I'll tell him how life changing it is tomorrow, and he has nothing to be scared of.

"Do you need anything?" I ask.

"Just this," she says, snuggling up against both of us and comically falling asleep extremely fast.

Eli sighs, dragging a hand over his face and looking at me. "Anders, we need to make this work."

I nod and look down at the sleeping Omega. "She still has another year of school."

"She can do it online."

"Where, though? Who knows where we will all get drafted?"

"We can take turns. Come here during the summer, and we can all be together."

I sigh, knowing that it's not a permanent fix. She's my scent match. My career as a goalie isn't as long as Mikael or Eli. But could I give it up completely? I groan, not wanting to think about it. We've all worked so hard, and hockey is our passion. But the passion I feel for Charlotte in this short amount of time is almost as strong.

"We'll figure it out," Eli assures me. And for now, that's good enough. I'd rather enjoy the sleeping Omega in my arms instead of worrying about what we're going to do a year from now.

"Yeah, we'll figure it out." I go to sleep fooling myself.

CHARLOTTE

Chapter Eighteen

God, it's hot in here. There's a light snore to my left, and it's then I realize I'm squished between two hockey players' bodies. I smile when I think about what we did earlier.

Holy fuck.

I love sex. Well, I thought I loved sex. But last night was like a live wire to everyone of my senses. Having two Alphas' full attention on me is something I can definitely see myself getting used to. I thought I would be more nervous or timid about being with more than one person, but being with Anders and Eli is like second nature.

Their scents were cocooning me, their praise riling me on. It's almost like I never realized how reverent or significant another human's touch could be. On a base level, I knew that I would crave them more than any other person because they're my scent matches. But last night... it altered who I am. Pack life was on the back burner for me previously. I always thought I'd go on suppressants or go to a heat facility like Heat Haven to have my heats serviced. Conceptually, for me, I didn't see a pack in my future. But now... now it's all I want.

My stomach grumbles, and I gently untangle myself from Anders' hand on my hip and Eli's thigh between my legs. They both shift and groan, but don't wake up. As soon as I'm free of their delicious body warmth, I shiver and realize I have no clothes. We passed the laundry room on our way to Eli's room. I quietly turn the doorknob and tiptoe to the laundry room, then grab the first thing I find. It's a worn black hoodie, and I toss it over my head. Mikael's thick campfire scent warms me to my core. Their scents combined on my skin does something to me. It's almost like a switch flips. A tingle trickles down my spine, and I shiver and shake it off. The hoodie hits me mid-thigh, and I hold the sleeves in my fists, keeping my hands warm. My feet are freezing, but I'm just planning on getting a snack as I pad my way over to the kitchen.

Their pantry is stocked to the brim. I wonder if the guys went and bought all this food, or if someone else shopped for them. I shrug, grab a bag of popcorn, and toss it into the microwave, wincing when I push the popcorn button. It's loud as shit. I'm hopeful that they can sleep through anything. Like a stalker, I stand by the microwave, waiting until it hits two seconds, and pop it open, so it doesn't make an obscenely loud noise.

My feet are like ice cubes, so I take my bag of popcorn and perch myself on the countertop. My legs sway as I inhale the buttery deliciousness. It's dark in the kitchen, but the reflection of the moon on the piles of snow outside brings some light into the cabin. I'm bringing a fist full of popcorn to my mouth when a low voice scares the fuck out of me.

"Why are you up?" I jump, nearly dropping the popcorn bag. He reflexively catches the bag and puts it back in my hand. My mouth waters as I take in Mikael's appearance. He's shirtless with tight navy boxer briefs. I won't lie to you. I look at his bulge, and well... now I'm perfuming in the kitchen.

"Wanted a snack," I say quietly.

"That's my hoodie."

"Do you want it back?" Surely if I sat on this counter naked in front of him, he wouldn't be able to deny me. He may push me away on a consistent basis. But his scent-matched Omega, naked, wet, and willing in front of him? I know he wouldn't stand a chance. I don't want it to get that far. I want to win Mikael over with who I am as a person—it's important to me.

He clears his throat and looks at my bare legs hanging on the side of the cabinet. "Can I have some?" I hand the bag out to him, and he puts his big hand inside, taking a fist full of popcorn and shoving it in his mouth.

"I saw you."

"What?"

"I saw you watching us in the hot tub."

He clears his throat and moves to the refrigerator, then grabs a beer, popping the tab and taking a sip. "It was hard not to with the noises you were making."

"Did you like what you saw?" I put the popcorn down and place my palms on the cool kitchen counter. Mikael's face is stoic as he looks me over. He picks up his beer and takes multiple large gulps, his Adam's apple bobbing with each sip.

"Does it matter?"

"Yeah, it matters."

Mikael approaches me, and goosebumps appear all over my body. I thought his scent was thick on his hoodie, but now, fuck. The only time I've scented him this heavily was that day in his bedroom.

He places his palms on the outside of mine, so close that if I stretched my thumb, I'd be able to touch the flesh of his hand. He leans in, his face only a foot from mine. Mikael is so tall that even standing and leaning, he's still towering over me.

"Yeah, I liked what I saw."

"You could have joined."

He sighs, his breath tingling against my neck.

"Charlotte." The way he says my name makes me wet. I shift my weight on the counter, pushing my thighs together.

"Mikael, you don't have to fight this."

He groans and leans closer, his nose trailing from the tie of his hoodie up the column of my neck. "You smell like all of us," he whispers. I'm not sure what to say to that, but then he leans closer, and I feel his hard length pressed against my knee and gasp. "I don't want to."

"You don't want to what?" I'm nearly panting from his proximity. The most inner part of me is shouting to take this Alpha and put him into a rut, so he marks me and never lets me go. I shake my head, clearing that possessive thought from my mind.

"Fight this."

"So don't," I gasp. Feeling bold, I place my hand on his chest and gaze into his eyes. He's still so hard to read. But as his eyes scan mine, he sighs, and one of his hands grips my jaw.

"I don't deserve you yet."

"What?"

"I have nothing to offer you, Charlotte."

"I'm not asking for anything. I'm asking for you to give me a chance, Mikael."

He groans, and his body is so close to mine his body warmth is nearly radiating off of him. One of his hands grips my hip, and I moan, shifting my body as close to him as possible.

"Promise me you won't ruin us," he says, pulling away. His deep brown eyes assess me.

"What?"

"Promise me that you won't ask us to quit hockey. Promise me that it's all of us or nothing."

I stall, more so shocked by his request than anything. The last thing I want to do is make broken promises, and my silence has him taking his hands off of me like I'm toxic.

"Goodnight, Charlotte." His back is already to me as I stand up and follow behind him, grabbing his arm.

"Do you want me to make you a blind promise without thinking about it?" I feel like I'm stomping my foot and throwing a tantrum. He glares down at me.

"No, but I also can't act on this until I know your answer."

"I don't want you to give up what you love, Mikael. But you're my scent match, basically my destined soulmate. Are you telling me that hockey comes before that?" I don't wait for him to answer. I'm being honest, I understand that they've spent the majority of their lives working toward this goal, and I don't want them to give it up. Timing again is not on my fucking side, but it's better than me bonding a pack, and then finding my scent matches. Fate brought us together now for a reason, and the fact that he is scoffing over this gift is pissing me off.

"Charlotte," he pleads.

I spin around and point at him. "I'm going back to bed with Anders and Eli. Neither of them treat me like a burden, like I'm the fall of their hopes and dreams. I didn't choose to be your scent match, Mikael. But I am actively choosing to get to know you and see where this could go. So go back to your room and brood. Just know you're missing out on this precious time we have. I hope you don't regret it."

On that last note, I turn back down the hall and walk back to Eli's bedroom. I shuck the offensive hoodie off in the hallway and glare at it. I'm not sure what pisses me off more, the way he makes the tension so thick between us that I want what I can't have. Or that I feel so rejected to my core that it makes me want to cry.

I feel itchy and uncomfortable in my own skin. Wanting something soft, I open their hall closet and grab the softest alpaca blanket I've ever felt. I make a note to myself to grab some things from home tomorrow. The cabin feels a little stifling, and I need some of my own touches to make it feel comfortable.

With the blanket wrapped around me, I open Eli's door and crawl back into bed.

"You okay, baby?" Eli says groggily, his arm gripping my hip.

"Eli, how is this going to work when we all go back to school?"

He sighs, gripping my hip hard and scenting my hair. "I don't know. But we'll figure it out."

There's a whine that wants to rip out of my throat, but I lock it down. It's just so crazy how people who didn't even exist in my mind have become the center of my world. Maybe Mikael's fear is warranted, but there's no point in fighting the inevitable.

"I will probably need to switch to virtual for my last year anyway."

He nods. "I wish it was easier, Char, I really do. Just know I'm in this 100%. Whatever that looks like—I'm in."

"You promise?"

"I promise. I know it's fucking crazy. I didn't even know about scent matches until a few days ago. But it's like the moment I picked you up off the ice, I knew something precious was in my arms. We're not letting you go."

I nod, my nose pressed against his chest, his pine scent calming me. I try to push down all the fears of how I'll feel without them in the same place at the same time. Maybe I should just go virtual now and move to Boston. I sound crazy.

Strong arms wrap around my back, and I sigh. "I promise too," Anders says behind me.

I wish that both of their promises made me feel more secure, but the feeling of this being doomed before it really gets to start sits heavily in my stomach. I get a tingling feeling that I should leave before I get left.

Chapter Nineteen

I'm fucking this all up and the worst part is I know how bad I'm messing up, and I can't help myself. When she looked up at me with those longing, blue eyes and I had my hands on her, I wanted to give her everything. I suppose that's the problem; she has the ability to make me throw everything away. And I know if I did, I would resent her, even if she was my everything. That's no way to start a relationship. Anders and Eli are in so fucking deep that I know if I don't get on board, it will be me ruining everything, not her.

It was unfair of me to ask her that question on the spot and walk away when I didn't get an answer. But I needed an out. If I didn't walk away right then and there, I would have fucked her on the counter, given her my knot, and we would have been figuratively and literally knotted together forever.

The thing is we're scent matches. I know that nothing will compare. There's no going back to school and wanting anyone else. But how attached I get is the problem. If I could just keep her at an arm's length until I'm ready. Until our futures are secured. Nothing in our lives is a certainty right now, and that's probably what has me in shambles most of all. I've spent my life in uncertainty. I just want one fucking moment where my life makes sense—where something, anything, is clear.

And just because Charlotte and I aren't together right now doesn't mean we won't be some day. I don't want to be labeled as the pack dick, even if the title fits. That's why I'm wearing khaki pants and a sweater right now as we sit at Charlotte's dining table. The last thing I want is her mother to know what a fucking asshole I am. I didn't want to come, truly; I wanted to stay at home and sulk. But when Charlotte said her mom was making dinner and that we were invited, I knew I couldn't bail.

It doesn't hurt that her mom makes a mean ass baked ziti.

"Wow, Kathy, this is delicious," pack suck-up Eli says to Charlotte's mother.

"Oh, thank you, Eli. I made two because I didn't know how much you boys could eat."

"Thank you for having us over," Anders: pack kiss-ass number two says.

"Of course. So, Mikael, where are you from?" Kathy asks.

"I grew up in Quebec."

"Oh, how lovely." No... not really. Not that Quebec was the problem, more so the people that I was surrounded by. It's amazing how people have the ability to taint a place.

"Have you lived here your whole life?" I ask Kathy. Charlotte beams at me like I've figured out world hunger when I simply just asked her mom a question. Damn, my bar is fucking low.

"I have. After the war, my parents met and settled here. My father worked at a lumber yard for a good part of his life. Vermont will always be home to me." I realize she's talking about World War II, and I gape a little and nod my head.

"It is lovely here. We haven't used the cabin much, and I regret that now," Eli says, looking at Charlotte. Like in some other universe, he would have found her sooner. I'm jealous of how sure Eli is that we will figure out how to make this work, that he can have it all. How can he be so fucking confident? Part of it pisses me off while the other part of me yearns for that raw assuredness.

"Everything happens for a reason," Kathy says.

I hate that saying, but I nod my head. Was my father an abusive asshole for a reason? Did my brother leave the first chance he got to leave me home with them and never turn back for a reason? The idea of horrible things happening to you to teach you something leaves a bad taste in my mouth, even though I know Kathy didn't mean it like that.

In a moment of weakness, I look over at Charlotte who is frowning down at her food. She looks flushed, and I wonder what's going on in her head. Not that I have a right to her thoughts. She's made it pretty clear that she thinks I'm being a coward—maybe I am.

Kathy pulls out a photo album, and Charlotte seems embarrassed as Anders and Eli coo about how adorable she was.

"Excuse me," I say to find the bathroom. I feel so fucking out of my depth, so confused, so overwhelmed. I want to consume myself with Charlotte, but want to run as fucking far as I possibly can at the same time.

I don't find myself in the bathroom though; I find myself in Charlotte's room. Her scent is thick, so saturated in the small room that it makes my dick hard. I chastise myself mentally but sit on her bed. A journal is open, and I know I shouldn't look, that it's an invasion of her privacy, but I do it anyway.

I'm sorry I haven't written to you in a while, Dad. It's not that I don't think about you all the time, I really do. It's just I haven't had good news lately, and I know how much you loved our game of good news, bad news. Well, the good news is, I found my scent matches. The bad news is, one of them wants nothing to do with me.

I get it, Dad, I really do. I'm scared, scared that they'll leave me like you did. I know you didn't choose to leave. But I can't help feeling the effect of your absence every day of my life. What if I let them in, and they leave? I know that no day is guaranteed, and we're all going to die some day. But the pain of losing someone is the hardest thing I've ever gone through.

I'm working on it though. I know you would be so pissed to hear me talking like this. Pissed that I'm using you as an excuse to not put my heart out there. Especially when I found something so rare. Scent matches. I have fucking scent matches!

Of course Mom is thrilled. She worries about me a lot, probably just as much as I worry about her. She likes them, and I think you would too. It's funny, I think Mikael would be your favorite, even though he's the one that wants nothing to do with me. He's serious, logical, handsome, and he loves hockey.

I forgot to mention that they're all hockey players. You would love them all just because of that. I'm sure you'd be working your way into getting free tickets as soon as they play professionally.

I don't know how to make this all work. But I know you'd want me to be happy, and I think they could make me happier than I've ever been. So I'm going to take your advice and lead with my heart and not my head for a change.

I love you, Dad, and I wish you were here. I know you're here in your own way, and I think you'd be proud of me.

       Love, Charlotte♥

I put the journal down and scrape my hands through my hair.

Fuck.

As if she wasn't endearing enough, and the fact that she's putting her heart out there. She's trying, and I'm fucking hiding. Hiding behind hockey and sulking to save myself.

Could I put her before hockey? Am I being blinded by pheromones and the idea of this fated match? Or am I being a hardheaded asshole and not listening to what my body is telling me? All I know is I'm so sick and fucking tired of fighting this internal conflict.

There's a clearing of a throat, and I look up to find Anders propping his hip on the doorframe, looking at me. We've made up, got over our scuffle a while ago, but he still doesn't agree with how I'm handling things.

"You good, man?"

"No," I sigh, my elbows on my knees and my head downcast.

He comes down and sits on the bed next to me. Bumping his shoulder next to mine, he sighs before he says, "The timing is shit. I'll give you that. None of us know where we're going to end up. We have a semester to finish, and we don't live near each other. Honestly, it's a fucking cluster fuck. But can you honestly tell me that you don't look at her and see our future?"

"I don't know."

"That's bullshit, Mikael, and you know it. It all makes sense now why you, me, and Eli all connected so fast. Why we felt like more than teammates." I glare at him. "Don't fucking glare at me, asshole. I know you sensed it, and I know what you're fighting with Charlotte and, on some level, I get it. I know you didn't have a great family; you haven't seen pack life. But I'm telling you, if you don't spend what little time we have with her now, you're going to regret it. I won't lie and say this isn't going to be hard. To be honest, I think we're going to have a brutal next two years, but I'd rather fight for this, figure it out, than to look back and realize I fucked up the best thing that ever happened to me."

"Really, the best thing?"

"Yeah, really. Your brother's an Omega, haven't you seen him with his pack?" I sigh and shake my head. Timothee left the moment he turned eighteen and never looked back. "That makes sense. You know my mom's an Omega. I came from pack life. It's a gift. Do you know how many Alphas find their scent match?" I shake my head again. "Less than four percent."

"Fuck."

"Yeah, fuck. What we have is rare, Mikael. Don't get in your head, and it's going to be hard. But she's worth it. We will figure this out—as a pack."

I nod my head, taking in all his words. Four percent. Four fucking percent of Alphas find their scent match. I've never felt special in my entire life. Never by my family or in hockey. I'm good, but I have to work hard to be that way. He claps my shoulder and walks out of the room.

"Charlotte wants to grab a few things before we go back to the cabin." I nod and go back to the kitchen. Charlotte and Eli pass me. Charlotte arches an eyebrow at me, but I just continue walking to thank her mother for the meal, so we can get out of here. I have a lot to process.

"Thank you for the meal, Kathy."

She smiles. I can see the resemblance to her daughter. It's her height, hair color, and eyes.

"Thank you for coming. Can I ask you for something?" I nod and look at the older woman. "Please go easy on her. She's been through a lot, hasn't really had a chance to experience the world. But she has felt a good amount of heartbreak in her life. My Charlie is special, and I know fate gave her scent matches for a reason. So go easy on her, and on yourself."

I nod, and I feel at a loss for words. "Thank you again for dinner."

"Any time, sweetheart." She pats my arm as she goes to package up the leftovers for us to take back to the cabin. I can't help but feel undeserving of all this kindness and understanding.

I want to disappear.

CHARLOTTE

Chapter Twenty

"What do you need?" Eli asks as I grab five massive T.J. Maxx tote bags. They don't look at me like I'm crazy, though I feel a little like it right now.

"Definitely my comforter, the two blue pillows, and the one with the flip sequins." Anders is packing my shit up with Eli as I point to things. I know I'm off-kilter when I tell them to take some of my macramé off the walls and pack it up. Not so subtly, I throw some cute bras and panties into the bag, as well as some fuzzy socks and a few changes of clothes and my favorite hygiene products. I shove my journal in my nightstand and sigh.

"Baby, you know you live right down the street?" I frown at Eli, and Anders smacks his chest.

"It's fine, Charlotte. Is there anything else you want to bring?"

"I think that should be fine. We can always come back." Eli looks curiously over the amount of things I'm making them bring back to his cabin. He looks concerned, and I'm sure Anders thinks he's slick, but I hear him whisper.

"I'll explain later, man."

At least I don't need to. Anders knows far more about Omegas than Eli does, and it shows in a lot of ways. But I kind of like how clueless Eli is and that I'm the only Omega he will ever experience. I know I'm the first Omega Anders has slept with, and I preen at that realization too.

Mikael, I have no clue. If only he would talk to me. He seemed different tonight at dinner though. We haven't really spoken since the kitchen incident. I'm actually pretty shocked he even came tonight. It means a lot to me. I'm not sure if this is his version of an olive branch, but I'll take it.

"Alright, let's get you warm and cozy back at the cabin," Eli says, and I smile at him. That sounds perfect.

The guys all say goodbye to my mother and walk outside to the car. Hank's snout is nudging my leg, and crippling guilt hits me. He's coming to the cabin with me.

"Mom, can you help me get Hank's stuff together?

"Honey, you feeling alright?" She touches my face and squints at me.

"I'm fine. He's just giving me puppy dog eyes, and I miss him, and I want more time with him."

"You're sure?"

"I'm sure. Thanks for having them over for dinner."

"Please." She shrugs as she packs up his food. "Like I wouldn't take the opportunity to meet your scent matches. I just wish your dad was here."

"Me too." I sigh, knowing that hockey talk would have taken over
the entire dinner, but I would have given anything in the world for
it.

She hands me Hank's leash and things and kisses the side of my
head. "Make sure you check in, yeah?"

"I will."

She pats Hank's head. "Be a good boy."

I walk Hank outside, and Anders opens the door, not even questioning me about bringing Hank.

"The dog too?" I hear Eli say from the front, but he doesn't
directly ask me about it, so I ignore him.

Hank sits in the middle between Anders and me as we head back
to the cabin. Mikael doesn't say a word, and I don't push. The ball
is in his court.

To put it quite simply, Eli's room is now my room. I'm not really
sure what came over me, but now it feels right in the cabin. Now
that Eli's bed is covered in my pillows and blankets, it's like I've scent
marked this room as me. I didn't know I had this possessive streak
in me, but here we are.

Warm arms wrap around my waist. "Everything better now?"
Anders asks.

"Much better."

"If you need anything else to feel comfortable here, just let us know."

I lace my fingers with his around my waist and hum. "You know, some blackout curtains would be nice. That way it doesn't get so bright in here in the morning."

"I'll tell Eli to order some." He kisses the side of my face.

"We're going to go lift for a while. Do you want to come?"

"No, I think I'll take Hank for a walk."

"Stay close to the house."

I nod and roll over in his arms. He bends down and places a kiss on my lips. Kissing Anders is like having a warm blanket wrapped around me. I feel safe with him. I groan as we break apart, wanting it to go further, but Hank is nudging my leg.

"Keep our girl safe," he says to Hank, and I grin.

I get on all my cold weather gear and put on my boots and take Hank outside. For the most part, he's a good boy, and I know he won't run off. The biggest worry about him is eating shit he's not supposed to.

"Come on, boy, you want to go play outside?" His tail wags, and I slide open the backdoor, and we walk toward the lake. It's not snowing today, but everything is still covered in white from the last couple of days. As we approach the lake, I see the back of someone's head. The dark tendrils of hair peeking out from his wool cap lets me know that it's Mikael.

Hank runs to him, and Mikael pets his ears and massive head.

"You're not weight training?" I ask, not sitting on the bench unless he asks me to. He shakes his head and sips the thermos in his hand.

He scoots over, and I take that as a good enough invitation. The bench is cold, but I do my very best to not complain.

"No, I need to clear my head." He sips again and holds out the thermos to me. It's stupid that I'm excited to put my lips where his have been, but I take it in my hand and sip. It's hot chocolate and Baileys. I hum as the chocolatey goodness slides down my throat.

"Penny for your thoughts?"

He groans and leans forward. His elbows resting on his knees as he takes a moment to collect himself. "I don't want to fight this anymore, but I don't know if I can let you in," he says softly, and I appreciate his vulnerability.

"You can talk to me."

"I don't know how to do relationships. I've never seen a good one. The idea of this being long distance sounds fucking awful. But I know deep down you're mine—ours. I don't want to fight it anymore."

"So don't."

He looks over at me. He looks vulnerable and almost like he's irritated by the fact that he's opening up.

"I feel like you only want me because I'm your scent match, or we're forced into this. I don't want you to feel like you have to be with me too. Eli and Anders treat you right."

"You could treat me the same, you know?"

"I don't know how."

"You think I know what I'm doing?" I ask him, arching an eyebrow in his direction.

"I mean with how quickly you whipped Eli and Anders, yeah, I think you know what you're doing."

I shake my head and give him a small smile. "This is the first relationship I've been in too. I don't know what I'm doing either. I just know that I've never wanted anything more. It may be that we're scent matches. But is that the worst thing in the world? For the universe to bring us together like this?"

He shakes his head and looks away from me. "How are we supposed to play hockey with you hours away from us?" He rubs the side of his face and looks back at me. "I...I don't know how I'll do with you so far away and trying to focus. Hockey is all I've ever wanted, and now..."

"Now what?" I ask.

"There's something else that I want just as much, and I can't help but feel like it's got to be one or the other. Hockey has always been how I measured myself, the one thing I've worked hard at and know that I'm fucking good at it. With this, with being someone's Alpha? I have no fucking clue."

"But you want to try?" I ask softly. It's a bit of an internal struggle that I see on his face. He's trying to follow his head and his heart at the same time. Maybe it's my Omega nature, but I want his heart to win. For him to finally give in completely and admit that he wants this, that he wants me. That I'm worth it. Maybe Mikael and I both think that way. I'm not sure why I vocalize it, but I do. "I think you're worth it."

His dark gaze meets mine, his thick eyebrows furrowed as he looks at me. "What?"

"I think you're worth it. All three of you. I don't care if there's distance and time and that it's all so fucking complicated that sometimes when I think about the future I can't breathe. I know that it will be worth it. You're worth it, Mikael."

His face turns from confused to soft, gentler than I've ever seen his face, as he leans closer. He's so close that the air from his breath is touching my face. "You're worth it too," he says softly, and my breath hitches from his confession. Just as much as Mikael is giving in right now, so am I. The way he's looking at me like he wants to devour me and make me promises, I'm ready to do the same for him. He doesn't move to kiss me though, and I tilt my head in confusion.

"Mikael?" I touch his hand, and he groans, looking down at Hank, who is sitting between his legs, and then looking over at me.

"Don't break me," he says softly before he leans over and cups my chin with his gloved fingers. His gaze flickers between my eyes and lips before he leans in and kisses me. It's chaste and delicate, honestly the polar opposite of how things have felt between us before today, and I bask in the softness. His hand glides to the nape of my neck as his kiss intensifies, and it lights my body on fire almost in a literal sense. It's freezing outside, but I feel like I've been sitting by a furnace.

Mikael pulls back, and I pant, ready to straddle him on this cold bench. His brows are furrowed as he looks at me. "Charlotte?" I moan when he says my name and grip the collar of his jacket, then pull him down aggressively toward my lips. He takes what I give him, his tongue matching against mine, his lips soft and cold. He tastes like hot chocolate, and I can't get enough. I want him to touch me more. Tell me that I'm his—theirs—again. Tell me how he was stupid for fighting this. The evidence is clear as we touch each other. It might be fate, stupid biology, but the proof is in this kiss. We're meant for each other.

"Please," I whimper as he parts from me again.

"Charlotte, are you okay?"

"Please, Alpha, I need you." So bad, I need him to take me, knot me, bite me, prove to me that I'm his. He owes me that much. I need his claim more than I've ever needed anything.

He pulls off his glove and feels my face. "Fuck. Come on, Hank," he says before he picks me up and throws me over his shoulder. The caveman treatment just makes me more excited, my perfume thick even in the cold air. "Goddamn," Mikael mutters a string of curses but doesn't tell me his plans. As long as it ends up with me on my back or knees, I'll be a happy Omega.

Mikael lets Hank in, who trails wet paw prints on the floor, and he curses before carrying me to Eli's room. God, it smells good in here, especially now that Mikael's smoky scent is in the mix. It makes me moan.

He puts me gently on the bed and leans down on his knees. Is he going to go down on me? Because that would definitely be an approved action. He doesn't though, he just unlaces my boots and sits them in the corner before coming back to remove my hat. He pats down my blonde hair and looks at me delicately.

"It's going to be okay. I'm going to get Anders and Eli."

I grab his wrist and tug him closer to me. "No."

"Charlotte."

"No," I tell him, unzipping his jacket. He does the rest of the work of tossing it on the floor. He takes his boots off with his feet, as I use every ounce of strength to drag him on top of me on the bed. The confusing Alpha goes to pull away again, and I shake my head. "No."

"Charlotte, *mon sucre d'érable.*" I moan at his use of French, having no clue what it means, but the way he says it; I know it's fucking good. "You're going into heat. I have no fucking clue what I'm doing. We just kissed. I need to get Anders and Eli."

"No." I tug him down, a fist in his soft, dark hair and another around the collar of his Henley. "I need you, Alpha." More than anything. He started this, him finally giving in, I know that. Now that all of my scent matches have given into me, it's started my heat. Timing in my life has never been right, but at this moment, it feels so fucking right.

"What do you need, *mon doux?* Fuck, you smell good."

"I taste better."

He groans, taking his hands off of me and blowing onto them to make them warmer, before sitting up on his knees and rolling down my leggings. I'm a helpful Omega as I lift my feet and help him take them off. I'm even more helpful as I roll up my long sleeve T-shirt to my neck and slide the cups of my bra down, so my tits are exposed.

"Fuck," Mikael hisses, leaning forward and sucking on a nipple while he cups my other breast. His cool skin feels nice, and I hold his head against my chest. I take in his scent and glow under his undivided attention.

He continues licking and sucking on my nipple, driving me crazy as his hand slides down my torso and cups my pussy. He squeezes me in a possessive way, like he's letting me know my pussy belongs to him. I groan, and he laughs against my chest.

"You like that? You like me showing you that you belong to me?" So contradictory to his words a few days ago, but I moan. I can't help it when my hips flex against his palm—I need more. He kisses down my abdomen before rolling down my panties and kissing the bare skin above my clit. "This cunt belongs to me now, *mon sucre d'érable*. I'm going to make you feel so good. You're going to be a good Omega and take what I give you."

I whine and nod my head, willing to meet any terms he sets for me. At the first swipe of his tongue, my back is arched off the bed, and one hand is tangled in his hair as the other kneads my breast. "Yes, Alpha. So good," I praise him, and he hums around my pussy.

"So fucking sweet," he says around my slick cunt before licking and sucking on me again. When he puts two fingers inside of me and I feel how much slick is dripping from my core, I groan. "Fuck, Charlotte, all this for me?"

I nod and hum, tugging his hair and putting his mouth back on my pussy. He laughs but continues showing my clit complete devotion as he fingers me. His long fingers touch the perfect spot as his lips suck on my clit. I shudder and grind my hips against his face as I come undone. Not wanting to miss a moment, I watch as he makes me come. A keening noise leaves my lips as my thighs shake, and my head feels light. He keeps licking and fingering me as he watches me.

Only as soon as I crest over my peak does he stop. His lips and chin are covered in my release as he sits up and wipes his face on the inside of my thigh before climbing up my body and touching my chin. "So good for me. Taste how sweet you are," he says when his lips meet mine. I do taste sweet, but I need more—I need to be full. I whine against his lips, and he leans back. "What do you need?"

"Your knot."

His eyes are wide, but he nods and uses one hand to remove his pants. I tug at the hem of his shirt, which he helps me remove. God, he looks so fucking good naked. I don't stop myself from licking and sucking on his collarbone. He groans, his grip tight on my hip as I mark him as mine and show him just how good he is for me.

"Tell me if I'm doing something wrong," he says, and I nod, knowing that he couldn't ever do anything wrong. He's my scent match—he's mine. Mikael's thumb rubs against my clit softly until I get so frustrated that I reach between us and grip his cock, feeling his knot. That's a nice knot. Mikael must like my reaction because he gives me a handsome grin as I line him up against my pussy, and he pushes forward.

Both of us moan as he enters me fully. His weight presses down on me, and his forearms bracket my face as he toys with my hair.

"You feel so good, *mon doux.*"

"Knot me, I need it."

He nods, his hair sweaty and sticking to his face as he thrusts into me. He's not gentle, and I love it. I eat up every pump of his hips and moan. I'm so close to coming again, and when he thrusts hard, pushing his knot deep inside of me, I nearly scream the word Alpha.

He moans against my throat, his tongue and lips sucking on my neck.

My body trembles, wanting his teeth biting down on my waiting throat. But I feel so deliciously full I'm able to think past it. He pants against my throat as he keeps thrusting into me as much as he can.

"That's it, Omega. Take my knot so fucking good. Built for this cock. Good girl." His words of praise extend my orgasm as I shake below him. My head feels light and fuzzy as he moans into my neck, and I feel his cum filling me. It's only then that I feel slightly less needy, knowing that he marked me in the most primal way possible. I hold him tightly against my chest. He tries really hard not to put his weight on me, but I want it.

"Alpha," I moan as we're locked together.

"What do you need?"

"You."

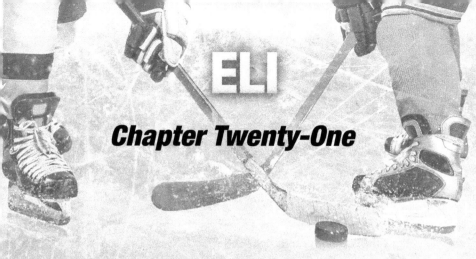

"So she's kind of taken over my room," I say to Anders. "It's an Omega thing."

"What do you mean?"

"Jesus, your parents really never sent you to any fucking classes, did they?" I shake my head no. Now I've just got another thing to add to my list when I eventually go to therapy. "Omegas are comfort creatures. Very particular about how things feel, smell, and taste. Charlotte clearly felt uncomfortable sleeping here before. So bringing all of her own things, her scented things, and mixing them with ours helps. I also think the dog just brings her a lot of comfort."

"So just give her whatever she wants?"

"Basically, yeah." He laughs, and I do too. That's something I can do.

We're finishing our set when Mikael comes running down the basement stairs. He smells more like Charlotte than himself and only has a towel wrapped around his waist. Anders laughs. "About fucking time."

"About that, uh, she's in heat," Mikael says.

"What?" I ask, panic trickling out of me in waves. I'm learning the fucking basics of taking care of an Omega, and now I'm going to need to get one through heat.

"Okay. Everyone, calm down," Anders says. "I'm going to call her mom and let her know, so she doesn't worry and picks up Hank. Eli, go make sure we have plenty of food first. If not, get some delivered to the house. Mikael, go around the house and collect every single fucking blanket we have, and bring some waters and Gatorade to the nest."

Mikael and I blink at him, and he groans. "Um... now."

We're brought out of our daze as we all do our jobs. I worry about leaving Charlotte alone, but we need to get everything in order. I'm so used to being the one in charge, but right now Anders is the only one who seems to have a single fucking clue as to what we need to do. I take stock of the pantry and make a list of what we'll need. Then I order everything on Instacart and submit the order, stating to not knock on the door and just send a notification when it's here. I put a huge tip on the order so that it gets done quickly.

There's a knock on the door, and I groan, quickly answering it. I need to get up to the bedroom and be with Charlotte. As I swing the door open, Charlotte's mom, Kathy, is smiling back at me.

"Hello, dear."

"Hi, Kathy," I say in a panicked tone. She grabs my forearm. "You alright, Eli?"

"This is probably really messed up to say to you as Charlotte's mom, but I have no clue what I'm doing. I'm going to fuck it up." She laughs, and I wince. "Sorry for my language, ma'am."

"It's okay. Just follow your instincts. I trust you three to take good care of Charlotte. You can all call me if you need anything, okay? I'd go up and see her, but I know she will only want her Alphas in the nest right now."

I nod my head and blink at her. Did she come over to specifically give me a pep talk? "I'm here to get Hank."

"Right," I say as the massive beast comes rambling down the hallway and stands at Kathy's side.

"Just make her comfortable and treat her like you already do," Kathy says again. She leans forward and gives me a hug. "You're a good man, Eli. She trusts you, and so do I."

This woman is more motherly than my mom's right fingernail and I appreciate her pep talk.

"Thanks, Kathy. I promise we'll take care of her."

"I know you will. Come on, Hank."

The dog looks back into the house, like he knows Charlotte is here somewhere, but follows Kathy nonetheless. I take a few deep breaths; I can do this.

The lights are off in my bedroom, but the sun peeks through the blinds, and I look in the room. Mikael is sitting on the bed looking exacerbated and Anders is knocking on the bathroom door.

"Charlotte, sweetheart, just tell us what you need."

"Too bright," she says through the door. Her voice sounds like she's been crying. I groan and leave the room to grab the staple gun from the garage along with the black, thick comforter from Mikael's room.

When I get back, both of my teammates are in the same position. "Help me," I tell Mikael, and he stands as I have him hold one side of the comforter against the window and I hold the other. I staple along the top of the window, making the most busted curtain possible, but it blocks all the light. The room is pitch-fucking-black. "Go grab the clear Christmas lights from the front door," I tell Mikael. He nods and goes to take them down in just his underwear. It takes him a few minutes. But once he's back, we use the staple gun to pattern the lights into a heart on the wall. My parents are going to fucking kill me for doing so much damage to the walls.

"*Kulta*, Eli blocked the sun and got you pretty lights. Will you come out?" Anders asks her softly, a voice that is specifically saved for Charlotte.

She cracks the door and peaks out, completely naked with her blonde hair in slight disarray. No care in the world or need to cover herself. I swallow thickly. I'm not ashamed of the fact that I'm nervous or that I don't know what I'm doing. I'm just going to try my best and hope that's enough. Mikael relaxes on the bed, and his posture isn't as stiff as she walks in the room. I wonder what shifted between them in the last few hours. Whatever it is, I'm happy about it.

Her gaze follows the stapled, fucked-up heart on the wall, and she smiles. She approaches me and cups my face.

"On the bed." I blink at her a few times. "Now," she demands.

"Charlotte, are you hungry?" Mikael asks, and she scowls at him and pushes my chest. I don't move, so she pushes again, and I finally give her what she wants. My back hits the cloud of blankets that she's piled onto my bed, and she climbs on top of me. My heart rate is beating a million beats per minute as she climbs on top of me. Her dripping pussy sits on my abs as she leans forward and licks me from my nipple to my jaw.

"Jesus Christ." My hands are tight on her hips. I worry I squeeze too hard, but she nips my neck playfully.

"Need you."

"What do you need, Char, baby?"

"Please, Alpha," she keens, and it goes straight to my dick. I didn't know begging would be a thing for me. But fuck, it sounds pretty coming from her plump, pink lips. I squeeze her ass again and look down, my stomach covered in slick, and I groan. Her scent is so thick in the room I feel like I'm in a haze.

"I want you to make a mess of me first, baby. Get that pussy nice and dripping for me." I rock her cunt along the ridges of my abdomen, her hands are firmly planted on my chest, and I watch her pupils dilate as she uses my body for her pleasure. "Marking me all up with that sweet scent, aren't you? Give me a taste."

I guess I expected her to use her finger to put some slick in my mouth, but she doesn't. She glides her whole body up mine and plants her pussy right on top of my mouth. This woman is a fucking queen, and I'm going to give her the treatment she deserves. Her hands are planted on the wall as she rides my face. She takes what she wants. I'm not even doing much, except sucking her clit when she lets me. More of her weight presses down on my face as she moans, and I feel her slick drip down the sides of my lips. I groan and fist my cock with one hand, stroking myself as she lets me devour her release.

Maybe there should be some shame that I know Mikael and Anders are watching this happen, but I feel none. She's not just mine, and I understand that. They will both have their moments with her, but right now it feels like Charlotte and I are in our own lust bubble. I'm surrounded by her scent, her warm skin, her delicate touches, and tantalizing moans. I want to bottle this moment up and keep it forever. It's like I never knew my purpose in life, but caught up in this woman, it feels like I found it.

She slides down my chest, kissing me frantically. No care in the world that I'm covered in her slick. "Please," she begs.

I gulp and nod my head. Fisting my cock, I wet the tip with her dripping pussy. Her hands are pressed against my chest again as she slides down my length, moaning the whole way down. She doesn't even give me a second to take it all in before her ass is perched against my thighs and my knot is fully inside her. It's not at its full size, but I buck up into her anyway.

It's like every nerve firing off in my body is telling me to claim her. That she's mine, and she just proved that, having me taste her and letting me put my knot in her.

I growl and flip us so that I'm on top, my hand clutching her jaw tightly. "Yes," she groans, nodding her head.

"Fucking mine," I growl, and she nods her head again. I fuck her hard, pushing my knot in and out of her entrance. She nearly screams every time as I push it inside of her. I don't think I've felt anything more pleasurable than this. The way her cunt clenches around me every time I pull out. I watch entranced as my cock comes out wetter than it did before as I fuck her.

Our scents are so intertwined. I don't know where she ends and I begin.

"Knot me," she begs, and I thrust so hard into her she screams, and her nails scrape down my back. I feel like an unleashed beast as I rut into her, wanting to fill her up with my cum and mark her mine in every way possible.

She's panting and trembling as I fuck her, pretty tears staining her face as she nods her head in approval. "Mark me."

"Yes," I growl, wrapping my hands around her shoulders and opening my mouth as my orgasm reaches me. I lean forward to take her neck between my teeth.

Two sets of hands pull me back, and I growl, anger radiating off of me as they pull me away from my Omega. The only thing holding me back is my knotted cock and the precious thing under me that I need to protect.

"RELEASE ME!" I growl.

"No, man. You can't mark her like this. You're in a rut," one of them says.

The Omega cries fat tears beneath me, not the pretty ones from earlier. I ignore the other two Alphas beside me and pull a hand free to cup her face.

"Please," she begs. I growl again, trying to release myself and give her what she wants, what I want. She's full of my cum, but she needs my bite. She needs me.

"Let go!"

"*Kulta*, Charlotte, look at me," the smaller of the Alphas requests of my Omega. "It's going to be okay. You're so good. You did so well. Look at you, perfect." She nods her head, and he continues. I decide that he's not so bad. "One day we're gonna mark you, but not like this, okay?"

She whines, and it makes my cock twitch, and she moans. A sense of calm and reality is fading back into me as I blink down at where Charlotte and I are connected.

"I'm sorry, Charlotte," I whisper, and Mikael releases his hold of me and sighs. "I didn't know that would happen."

"You don't want me?" she says in a soft voice. Anders is petting her hair, and he seems relieved that I'm back to myself. I sigh, lying down on top of her and wrapping my arms around her back.

"Suck on her neck," Anders tells me. I nod and do what he says. She sighs contentedly, and I groan as she wiggles with my knotted cock inside of her.

"Such a good Omega," Anders says to her, and I nod my head.

"Can I get anything?" Mikael says, clearly just as out of his depth as I am.

"A washcloth, some snacks, and water," Anders says gently. I hear the door click, and Charlotte starts crying again.

"He will be right back," Anders assures her, continuing to pet her hair. She eventually relaxes beneath me, her cunt releasing me and

my knot. The mess is both erotic and impressive as I lift up. She grabs
Anders by the wrist and tucks them both into a mound of pillows
and blankets so deep I can only see strands of their hair.

I sit in the lounge chair in the corner and catch my breath, trying
to rationalize my behavior. Mikael comes back into the room with
all the supplies and sighs.

"You okay?" he asks, and I shake my head. "I don't know what I'm
doing either, but I think you did a good job," he assures me. I give
him a forced half smile as he puts the food down. We eat in silence
as I sit here and think about how I'm going to behave the next time
she wants me.

Chapter Twenty-Two

I'm fucking tired. So exhausted and thankful that Charlotte is finally out and let me catch some sleep. Her heat has been going on for two days, and it doesn't seem like it's relenting any time soon. I feel like I can't sleep when she's awake. I need to be alert with Eli and Mikael to make sure neither of them go into a rut. When Eli went full blown feral Alpha, I was terrified. I didn't know it could be like that, and I'm at least thankful that we all are here to keep each other in check.

It's been an emotional rollercoaster to say the least. Not just making sure no one bonds before we talk about it, but how this experience has affected me. It's like the core of my being has been altered. There was a little Charlotte-sized puzzle piece missing inside of me that I didn't know existed. Once I realized she was my scent match, the piece was found, and now it's fully clicked into place. She's mine—ours. There's no denying it now, we're hers.

Seeing her in this state has been humbling and assured me of my Alpha designation in every way. I need to know that she's okay. That she isn't hurting. That she's fed, hydrated, and content. The idea of her in pain or being uncomfortable makes me feel unsettled. The worst moment was when she was crying when we pulled Eli away. It was clear that they both wanted it in that moment, but I know we would have all been left with regrets. Bonding should only happen when we're all sure, not in the middle of a surprise heat.

I make a mental note to get my mom in touch with Charlotte, and I smack my head for not thinking about it sooner. She would be the best person to talk to, to help her realize that what she's feeling and going through is normal. I've just wanted to keep Charlotte to myself, well, to us, a little longer. One day I'm bringing this girl to Finland, so she can see the magic, see where I come from, and meet my family.

I'm lucky I grew up with loving parents and siblings. I want that so badly for all of us, to have what I had growing up. But it seems like nothing about this relationship is going to be normal, and I need to grapple with a new idea of reality. Just because it wasn't what I originally envisioned for my future, doesn't make it wrong. It's just new and different.

It's a relief that Charlotte has an affectionate and loving mother. I'm glad that she has that when we leave. As I think about Kathy, I send her a text message to let her know that Charlotte is okay. The fact that she's trusted us with her daughter at this moment means everything, and I intend to prove that we can be good Alphas for her.

Kathy:
Charlotte is doing good. I think another day or two.

Thank you for letting me know, sweetie. If you boys need anything to eat, you just let me know.

Will do, thank you, Kathy.

Kathy:
Thanks for taking care of my girl.

I smile to myself and see how similar Kathy is to my mom. Maybe that's why I instantly liked her. They are both so loving and warm, and they love to feed you as their love language. I'm feeling wistful and realize I should probably try and get some more sleep.

There's a shuffle next to me, and I groan, Charlotte's scent picking up in the room, and I know she's waking up. We're all naked on the bed. I'm on the left-hand side, Mikael at the bottom, and Eli on the other side of Charlotte. We're going to need a bigger bed next time.

Next time... The concept is paralyzing, and I shake my head. I need to be present in the now.

"Charlotte?"

She moans, squeezing me around my waist and inhaling my scent at the base of my neck.

"Alpha. Need you." I don't know what it is. I'd never been into the designation thing, but when she calls me Alpha, it gets me instantly hard. She squints at me, and I wonder how her eyesight is right now. I took out her contacts for her a few nights ago. If that isn't devotion, I don't know what is.

"Let me take care of you, *Kulta*. What does my girl need?"

"Just you," she sighs, and if my heart doesn't fucking tumble out my chest and bleed for her on this wet and sweaty bed. I've tried to contain the laundry situation, but she's been growling at me and throwing blankets in the corner. I guess because they smell like all of us. I look around, and both Eli and Mikael are out cold. I know if they're a fraction of how exhausted I am, I should let them sleep.

"Let's go to the bathroom."

She whines, and I'm sure she thinks she's going to get her way, but not this time. I get off the bed and take her and the blanket she's holding with. Then I hold her against my chest and prop her up on the bathroom counter. Her pretty eyes are hazy with lust, and she licks her lips as she looks at my chest. "You're good for a man's confidence, Charlotte."

"Omega," she corrects me. I smirk. She seems to really like her designation right now. As she should, she's perfect the way she is.

"Have you been good, Omega?" I ask her, bracketing her hips with my hands gripping the countertop. She nods her head and drags her nails over my chest, making me shiver. "You see how hard you make me?" She looks down at my dripping, hard cock and licks her lips. "You want to watch me fuck you?" She nods her head again, her perfume nearly choking me in this small bathroom. "Turn around and stick that pretty ass out for me."

She obeys immediately, turning around, bending over the counter, and presenting her ass and dripping cunt to me. Knowing how much she liked me spanking her last time, I can't help myself as my hand strikes her left cheek. She whines and pushes her ass further.

"My good, little Omega loves a strong hand, doesn't she?"

"Please, Alpha."

"Such good manners too." *Smack*. I hit her ass again, and she moans. I was planning on fucking her right away, but as I watch her slick drip down her thighs, I get down on my knees and spread her ass to give me room to eat her cunt properly.

Her hand creeps up behind my head, gripping my hair and pushing me harder against her core. I take it all in, her scent, her wetness, and her eagerness for me. She moans as I lick and taste her, but I go slow, not letting her come. She whines, pushing my face harder against her cunt and ass, and I laugh before I stand behind her.

She scowls at me in the mirror, and I wipe my chin and grin at her. "You think I was going to miss seeing your face as I make you gush over my cock, Omega?" I laugh again and push her back slightly against the counter. Her hands push against the mirror, and her gaze alternates between her body and my own.

"I want you to watch how your Alpha fucks you." She licks her lips, and her eyes meet mine in the mirror.

"Knot, now."

I thrust into her with no warning, her hips pushing against the counter as she keens for me. Her tits bounce in the reflection in the mirror, her pouty lips parted in bliss as I fuck her how she wants me to. The scent of hazelnut and maple is so thick in the room, making me groan and want her to smell like me and carry her scent everywhere I go. I smack her ass, and the crack of her flesh has us both moaning.

"God, you're fucking perfect, *Kulta*. Made for me." I smack her ass again as my grip on her waist tightens, and she moans.

The door creaks open, and we both startle as a sleepy-faced Mikael opens the door. "Oh, fuck. Sorry," he says. Charlotte looks at him and whines, her hand reaching out to his. He's been quiet during the heat, always giving Charlotte what she needs, but we haven't had a moment to talk to each other. For the most part, it's been a bit of each of us taking turns with Charlotte. But the way she looks at him now, it seems like that's going to change.

"Please," she begs him. He nods his head and shuts the bathroom door behind him. "I need..." She shakes her head like she's confused and hits the mirror slightly.

"You want your Alpha to watch you take my knot?" She whimpers, and I change tactics, pulling out of her, which causes her to frown. I sit on the counter, my back to the mirror, and grab and hoist her to my lap. Her back is pressed against my chest as I spread her wide. Mikael's eyes are wide as he takes in our Omega and licks his lips. "See how he looks at you?" I ask her, and she moans.

I fist my cock and raise her ass up just enough that I can enter her. Her lush thighs feel like magic under my fingertips. She gasps as I push myself deeper inside of her warm cunt, and I catalog the sound to memory. My lips are on her neck, ravishing her sweet skin, and her hand tugs on mine to play with her clit. In this position, there aren't a ton of options for movement, so we're mostly rocking against each other. I can't help it when she gets close to my knot. I nibble at the tender flesh at the side of her throat, and she clenches around me.

I'm so focused on Charlotte I nearly forget about Mikael staring at us and jerking off. Charlotte removes her hand from her clit and basically gives Mikael a grabby hands gesture. He comes to her easily, no more of the resistance that he had earlier. Deep down I knew he would give in. I'm happy he at least got his head out of his ass to be here for this moment.

She crashes her lips against his while I continue kissing her throat and rocking into her pussy. Charlotte is whining, and I groan, knowing that she's close and so am I. With a firm grip on her hips, I push her down, making her take my knot. She moans against Mikael's mouth, and he devours the noise.

"That's it. Fuck, you feel good, Omega." I feel my knot swelling inside of her warm pussy, and my back arches, the back of my head hitting the mirror. Her pussy milks me for what feels like eternity. My thighs go numb from sitting on this counter, having her on my lap, and this earth-shattering orgasm. There's a slight mix of me and her dripping down my thighs, and she shivers on top of me.

I stroke her arms, and she pets Mikael's hair.

"More," she pleads with him.

"What do you need? Hmm? This pussy still needs attention?" She nods her head in response. A quiet rumble comes from Mikael's chest as he bends down onto his knees and pushes Charlotte's legs apart. As a team player, I help spread her for Mikael. No care in the word that he sees me locked inside of her. "Such a pretty, greedy pussy, isn't it?"

Charlotte gasps, and her head rests against my shoulder as Mikael licks and sucks her clit. She's shaking, her pussy clenching around my cock and knot as he brings her closer and closer to the edge. My knuckles are nearly white on her thighs, holding her open for Mikael.

"Yes. Uhh, fuck," Charlotte mutters.

"So good for your Alphas," I tell her, wishing I could hold her throat, but my hands are preoccupied with keeping her wide open as she continues dripping slick down my balls and thighs. I kiss her neck and can't help but groan every time she shifts or grips me in pleasure. Mikael is quiet, just eating her pussy and bringing her closer to her second orgasm. I know it hits her when she tries to close her thighs, which I have to forcibly keep open, and her grip on Mikael's hair becomes lethal.

She trembles on my lap and moans as she rides out her second orgasm. Mikael stands to his tall height and wipes her slick off onto his forearm. His dick is still hard as he stares down at our Omega.

He grins. A true grin. It's almost terrifying, only because I don't see it often. Then he leans forward and kisses Charlotte.

"So fucking sweet."

She shivers in my arms as my knot goes down and releases us. My stomach rumbles, and I groan in irritation. I try to think about the last time I ate, but as I watch Mikael hold out an arm for Charlotte to help her down, I realize I can leave them alone.

"I'm gonna eat. Want anything?" I ask them. Charlotte shakes her head and presses against Mikael.

"A sandwich would be awesome," Mikael says, and I nod my head, kiss the side of Charlotte's matted hair, and make my way downstairs.

I feel relief but wonder how Charlotte is going to feel when she comes to. Is she going to regret everything we've done? Will she feel uncomfortable? I doubt it. She seems pretty confident in her sexuality. I make a mental note to look up Omega behavior after heat, but I'll do that after I eat and catch up on some much needed sleep.

Chapter Twenty-Three

"Let's shower," I say to Charlotte as soon as Anders leaves. She frowns at me, and if I have to use my Alpha bark on her, I will. "*Mon doux,* you haven't showered all heat." She still looks pissed, with her ratty hair and her arms crossed against her chest. I can't help but think how adorable she looks.

Fucking great. Now I'm a goddamn sap. I knew this shit would happen. That I'd give in and be wrapped around her small, dainty finger. I turn on the shower spray and sigh as she looks at me with her eyes squinted. No doubt, I look fuzzy as hell right now, but she can't shower with glasses, and none of us are fucking brave enough to put new contacts in for her. Anders nearly gave up taking her contacts out, but when we Googled what could happen if you leave them in, he persevered. Thank fuck for Anders. I grab her hand and direct her into the shower. The warm water trails down her body, and she sighs and leans against me.

Instinctively, I wrap my arms around her and hold her tight. She smells like a mix of all of us and her natural scent. I do think her perfume is going down in potency though. So I wonder when her heat will be over. The fact that the three of us made it this far is honestly quite the accomplishment. Without Anders, I imagine she would have left here with at least one bond mark.

I move her under the spray and look at all the products in the shower, grabbing the conditioner to hopefully get some of these tangles out. Her eyes are closed as she steps out of the stream of water, and I lather her hair. She hums at my hands, rubbing her scalp, and I do my best to not tug on her hair.

"Fuck, there are a lot of knots."

She snorts, which makes me laugh.

"You in there, Charlotte? Making jokes about knots."

"Mmm," is all I get as a reply.

I sigh and work through her hair. "I don't know why I ever thought you would tear me and the guys apart. You made us closer in ways that I never imagined."

She snorts again, and I laugh, my legs feeling like Jello, and she's leaning a lot of her weight against me. "Let's sit on the bench." I expect her to follow, but she doesn't. She stands under the water, clearing all the conditioner out of her hair. I sit on the bench and hold my hands out for her. She squints but isn't uncoordinated as she reaches me. I expect her to sit on my lap, but she slowly brings her knees to the tile floor.

Her hands glide over my thighs as she looks up at me with half-lidded eyes.

"Charlotte, you don't have to do that right now."

"Want to. Mine," she says before she fists my cock with one hand and swirls her tongue over the weeping slit. I groan, and she moans, her soft breath against my length as she licks and explores me. She looks up again. "Mine," she says possessively, like she has to convince me. I guess I deserve that.

"Yours."

She gives me a satisfied smile before leaning forward and nearly swallowing my cock whole, her lips touching my knot and my length completely down her throat. I can't help it when I shift slightly, making her take me deeper. She doesn't gag, just hums around me. Her one hand now fondles my balls as she glides her lips up and down my length, her tongue giving special care to the view on the underside of my dick.

"Fuck, *mon sucre d'érable*. You want my cum? Hm? I want to see it on your tongue, *mon doux*."

Charlotte moans and picks up speed. Like me coming in her mouth is a reward. That only makes me come even sooner. I moan and fist her wet hair as I spill down her throat and tongue. She doesn't stop looking at me like I'm something fucking special as she's on her knees for me.

I realize how fucking unworthy I am in this moment. But it's bittersweet because I know I was right. She has a power over me unlike anything or anyone. Even on her knees, Charlotte holds all the power here. A scent match is an undeniable connection. I was a fucking idiot to think I could dodge fate.

She looks at me proudly and opens her mouth, showing me my cum on her tongue. I grip her chin and smile at her. "Good girl. Swallow for your Alpha." She swallows and smiles at me brightly, like I gave her a fucking gift. I lift her up on my lap and kiss her frantically.

I just hope that when she's out of heat, she wants me as badly as she does now and won't hold how big of an asshole I was against me. I wouldn't blame her, but I've already missed out on so much time. We have to go back to school the day after Christmas. Time is fading quickly.

I do my best to wash us both off quickly before shutting off the faucet and wrapping us both in towels. "Time for you to get some sleep," I tell her.

She frowns at me again, somehow yawning and rolling her eyes at the same time. I don't bother dressing her as I put her in the bed. Anders is passed out on the floor, and Eli is on the other side of the bed. I put her in the middle and crawl in next to her. I see the sandwich he made me, but at this point, I'm too fucking tired to even eat.

As soon as my wet hair hits the pillow, I'm out.

There's a hard smack on my chest, definitely not a Charlotte sized hand. "What?" I grumble.

"Get up, man," Eli says.

I blink my eyes open and closed, then look to my left—Charlotte is no longer there. Matter of fact, neither are most of the blankets and pillows.

"Where's Charlotte?" I ask groggily.

Eli points to the corner where we were tossing messy blankets and pillows. Charlotte has added every single pillow and blanket off the bed and floor that she could find. She's basically in a mountain of blankets and pillows. I can only see a few strands of blonde hair poking out.

"What is she doing?"

Eli shrugs his shoulders and pushes Anders' side with his foot to wake him up.

"The fuck?" Anders groans.

"Something's up with Charlotte," Eli replies, and that has Anders popping right up.

"What?"

"She's in the corner with all the blankets and pillows."

Anders' brows furrow, and he shakes the sleep away as he stands up, and we all approach where Charlotte is in the corner. Three big ass men who are all naked look terrified, like we're approaching a feral animal.

"Charlotte," Anders says in a soft voice.

"Go away," Charlotte says clear as day. We all look at each other and pale. If she's out of heat, shouldn't she be happy and content?

"Char, baby, is something wrong?"

There's a sniffle, and a rumble of purrs echo in the room. It's fucking pathetic and embarrassing, and I'll never admit that mine is probably the loudest.

There's another sniffle. "Everything's wrong," she says.

"Charlotte, can we come in, or can you come out and talk to us?" I ask.

"Talk about what? How I can't go back to school now? How I've gone through heat with my scent matches, and now we're going to be separated? Or about how I can't help but feel rejected even though I know it was best not to bond? Maybe we could talk about the worst thing, how I basically forced Mikael into being with me," she cries, and I can't help but snatch the blanket back and look at her watery eyes and tear-streaked cheeks. She has her glasses on and has to pull them up to wipe under her eyes.

"You didn't force me into anything, Charlotte. I wanted this. I was just done fighting it."

"You're sure?"

"I'm sure." She nods, but wraps her arms around herself. "As for the rest of the stuff, we'll figure it out."

"You can't just keep saying we'll figure it out. I'm an Omega. I need security. I find comfort in routines, scents, and familiarity. It feels like my life has been flipped upside down, and I don't have control of anything. Do you know how much I fucking hate crying? Yet, here I am, a fucking mess in front of all of you."

"Charlotte, you just went through a lot. Of course you're going to have strong emotions afterwards. It was your first heat," Anders reasons with her.

"I didn't even ask for your consent." She starts crying again, and Eli looks like he's about to shit himself, and Anders sighs.

"*Kulta*, if you think for one second none of us wanted that, you're out of your mind. It was the best time of my life."

She wipes her eyes. "It's time I won't get back. Time we were supposed to have together," she whispers to Anders.

Eli pets her hair. "We'll figure it out. With you not being able to go back on campus, maybe it will make things easier?" When he says it, I internally wince, thinking about our schedule and all the work we need to put in before the draft.

Charlotte takes a few deep breaths. "Tomorrow's Christmas."

We all grimace externally then. "We haven't had time to get anything," Eli says, rubbing the back of his neck, showing how uncomfortable he is.

Charlotte smiles. "I think I'd just like to get some pictures of us together before... you know."

Eli nods and smiles. "We can do that."

"Plus, my mom always makes Christmas dinner. We can have it there and come back here before you all leave Monday morning." She sighs. I can tell she's keeping herself together, not wanting to cry anymore.

"I think maybe we should clean up and get some rest before we see your mom," I say, and she blushes.

"I guess so."

"You need help out of this giant cum blanket?" I ask, and Charlotte laughs and covers her face. Anders and Eli both start laughing. It's nice to have some happiness in the air after that conversation, but uncertainty lingers in the back of my mind.

What the fuck are we going to do?

CHARLOTTE

Chapter Twenty-Four

C hristmas was nice, but it was obvious all of us were thinking about tomorrow. My mom's cooking was amazing, and she somehow made the guys all adorable knitted hats that match. They all agreed to put them on for a group picture. I automatically saved it as my screensaver.

It feels like tomorrow is the end. I know not really, but it's the end of this simple life we've had with each other. The future is so unknown, and all it's causing me is unbridled anxiety. I keep toning down my fight or flight instincts that tend to always lean toward flight.

Eli is petting Hank's ears, and Mikael and Anders are thanking my mom for having them over for Christmas. She didn't say anything to them, but I know her heart broke for them, the fact that they aren't close enough to their families to have Christmas with them. In Anders' case, it's a matter of distance, but it's clear that it's deeper than that for Eli and Mikael.

"Don't be strangers," my mom says, and the guys all smile.

"There's no chance of getting rid of us now," Eli says, and my mom squeezes his cheek.

"Good." His cheek is pink from embarrassment and my mom squeezing it, but he looks happy to have her approval. My mom wraps her arms around me and squeezes me tight. "I'll see you tomorrow, honey." I nod my head, and she pushes some rogue hairs behind my ears. I give Hank a few solid pats to the top of his head before heading out to Eli's truck.

It's lightly snowing, and there's a decent breeze in the air, making the weather seem like how I feel on the inside. Turbulent, unstable, and depressing.

The drive to the cabin is quiet, all of us in our own heads about what tomorrow means. They go back to school, and who knows what happens with me? I have to notify Mercy about my heat. The repercussions of hiding my status could make my previous scholarships void.

It's mean, but I wish they would have picked any other profession. Why couldn't they want to be accountants, engineers, or fucking gym teachers? Anything that would make this simple, that would keep us all in one place. My chest feels tight, and all I can think about is how I'm being abandoned. I'm the one being left behind. I'm the one with no intense passion, but I'm also going to be the one to suffer the most with this separation.

Anders' hand is on my palm, and he squeezes tightly. "Don't think too much about it."

"How can't I? We have tonight, and then when will I see you again?"

"Been thinking about that. We have some stretches at home for games, and I think that would be the best time for you to come to the house. We're off campus, and it's just the three of us," Eli says.

I nod my head, wondering why they aren't asking me to stay there full time. I guess that would be a pretty big step, but it's not like I've got anything else going for me.

"We've got to stay focused to get drafted," Mikael says quietly, and I nod again, wanting to cry. I feel like second best. He looks over at me from the front seat. "I want this, Charlotte," he assures.

"I know." My voice cracks, but I hold the emotion in. I wonder if I'll be competing against hockey for the rest of my life, and if it's something I could learn to live with. They're my scent matches. I'll do whatever I need to do to be with them.

Eli pulls into the garage and gets out of the car, then opens my door. He grabs me by the waist and tugs me close, whispering in my ear so only I can hear. "I'm going to figure this out for our pack. Just be patient with us, okay?" I nod and squeeze him tightly, wondering exactly how the fuck he's going to make this okay.

Our scents in the cabin are thick and oh-so satisfying. I inhale deeply and store the scent so deep into my memories that I will only correlate this smell with the happiest moments of my life. I walk across the living room and sit in the middle of the couch. Mikael on one side of me and Anders on the other, while Eli sits in the standalone chair.

We all look at each other, not wanting to talk about logistics. We could talk till we're blue in the face, but at the end of the day, they all want to play professionally. Until we have an idea if that is a reality and where, there's really no planning to be had.

Plus, the fact that we just had the biggest sex-fest of our lives, we're wrung out. I just want to be with them, have these moments that were lost because of my heat.

"Movie?" Mikael asks, and I smile and lean on his shoulder slightly. He purrs for me, and it genuinely helps calm my anxiety. He puts on some Leonardo DiCaprio movie, but all I can do is take turns staring at each of them.

Still leaning against Mikael, I sigh. "You're still sure about me?"

"Yes. I still don't know what I'm doing though." He squeezes my thigh, and I wonder why he lacks this confidence. Mikael always seems to think he's not good enough, and I don't know how I can make it more clear that all I want is honesty and effort.

"I won't ask you to give up hockey," I say to him, reassuring the question he'd asked me a week ago.

"Thank you," he says, leaning down and kissing my hair. "We're going to make this work, Charlotte."

They feel like famous last words.

We're all asleep on the couch when their alarm goes off. All three of their faces are sullen and I'm pretty sure like I'm on the verge of losing it. It's awkward watching them pack their bags and load up the truck while I sit at the island, waiting for them to drive me home for the last time.

"Are you sure you can't pack me too?" I ask Anders playfully. He grips my hips and swivels the stool to face him. His face is serious when he scans my features.

"I would, *Kulta*. You have no fucking idea. But Mikael was right. We have to focus. Not just on getting drafted, but for our team. Plus, between school and hockey, we don't have a lot of time at home. I'd rather you be home with your mom."

I nod my head and place my forehead in the middle of his chest. "We have to talk every night."

"You think I could go a day without talking to you? You're crazy."

I shake my head and then look back up at him. "And you'll plan for me to be in Boston a few times during the semester?" He nods, and I sigh. "I'll take what I can get."

He looks uncomfortable and rakes his hand through his dirty blond hair. "I want you to have everything."

"We're young, we're scent matches. We'll get through it." I probably say it more for myself than Anders because I have no idea how I'm going to get through it.

He cups my face and leans in and kisses me so sweetly. His lips are soft and delicate as he handles me with care and puts so much devotion behind the kiss I can't help but melt under his touch. His scent is thick and warm around me as he shows me just how much he's going to miss me.

"Stop hogging our girlfriend," Eli says. I can't help when I grin at the term. It's a little silly, seeing as we're scent matches. Girlfriend almost sounds trivial, but I'll take any and all titles.

"Make sure all the girls at BU know you have one of those," I say, pointing at all of them. They all nod like I'm being an idiot for even having to say anything.

Eli scoops me up in his arms, my legs dangling in the air as his arms support my weight, and he kisses me ravenously. Where Anders' kiss was sweet, this one is claiming, letting me know that I'm his and he is mine. I can't help but moan when his tongue enters my mouth in a needy sweep. He slowly puts me down, my front dragging against his all the way down. I'm pretty sure he's trying to get me worked up before he leaves. Eli sighs and kisses my cheek one more time before pulling back and giving space for Mikael.

Mikael doesn't jump on me like Eli or give me tender affection like Anders does. "This is for you," he says, holding out a large tote bag to me. "Open it later when you get home." I nod, and he leans forward, his fingers turning my face up to his. The kiss is chaste, but when he pulls back, and I look into his eyes, I know that if we do anything more, he wouldn't be able to leave.

The last thing I want to do is to be the reason why Mikael gives up his dream. I refuse to be that person. We're going to make this work. It might not be a normal pack dynamic for a while, but someday it will be, and that's what I'll hold on to. That soon, we'll all be together like this again.

It's a somber ride back to my house, but they all get out of the car to say goodbye. I will not cry... I will not fucking cry. Then the three of them wrap me up in a group hug where they are hugging too, and I fucking lose it, and the tears fall freely. The cold air makes crying even worse than it normally is, basically crystalizing the awful emotional intrusions streaming down my face. All three of them are touching me, telling me that they're happy this happened and we'll find a way. I hate that they've turned me into a crybaby. I just can't seem to stabilize my emotions around them. When I'm around them, I can let myself feel everything. It's somehow comforting and terrifying at the same time.

But right now, I feel hopeless, and if they don't leave soon, I'll make them promise me things I promised I would never ask of them. I kiss them each one more time.

"Call me when you get home?"

"Of course. Call us if you're not okay?" Anders says. *So you mean start calling you right now, because I'm not okay.* I nod my head, and he wraps his arms around me one more time before heading to the car. Eli does the same, kissing the top of my head and squeezing me tightly.

"Missing you already," he says, and I push his chest, irritated that I'm still crying. He kisses my head one more time, and Mikael takes over and wraps his arms around me.

"You're tough, Charlotte. Be my tough girl, alright?" I nod and sniff. Squeezing me tightly, he hands me my tote bag from earlier. He kisses my cold cheek and gets into the truck. They all wave before they drive off and I'm standing here in the cold snow by myself. I wipe my eyes in frustration and head into the house.

My mom is already there with outstretched arms, and I just collapse against her. Before I know it, we're snuggling on the couch. She just pets my hair and lets me cry. She doesn't give me words she can't promise; she doesn't tell me that it's going to be okay; she doesn't shush me. My mom just lets me get all this pent-up emotion out, and I'm thankful for it. Hank's big head is on my lap, being the additional emotional support I need. It takes about a half hour before I finally calm down.

"Do you want to talk about it, honey?"

I shake my head. I feel raw, tired, and I just want to crawl into my bed and sleep.

"Okay, I'm here when you are." I squeeze her tightly, grab the tote from the mudroom, and head to my bedroom. I put the tote on the chair and stare at it, wondering if I should open it now or later. I sigh and decide to open it now, my curiosity getting the best of me.

There's a letter on top, but beneath that are three hoodies and a blanket we used from my heat. These thoughtful fuckers. I sniffle as I use my thumb to open the manila envelope.

Charlotte,

This situation is fucked. I honestly don't have any other words to describe it. If you haven't noticed, I'm not great with words. But I think letters may help. My address in Boston is below. I was hoping that we could write to each other. I know we have our phones, but I wanted something special with you.

I know this is going to be hard. Probably the hardest thing any of us has done in our lives. I wish I could tell you that I could give up hockey, that we all could. I would give up anything else, Charlotte, I promise you that. Please be patient with me.

I've put a hoodie from each of us in the bag as well as a blanket that smells like all of us during your heat. If you ever need our scents, make sure you tell me, and we will ship you something.

On a lighter note, did you know I've never broken a bone? Pretty crazy, huh? Lost some teeth though, hoping I don't lose any more this season. I can't afford to lose another front tooth if I'm going to continue to be your most attractive Alpha.

—Thinking of you, Mikael.

I laugh and cry at the last line. The way that he's made light of the situation makes me feel more confident in what we had. I like his idea of letters; writing things can make it easier to express yourself sometimes. I grab the one red hoodie, knowing instantly that it's Elis. I wrap his pine scent around me and seal the rest of the items up, hoping to preserve the scents for when I need them.

Hank hops on the bed, and I wrap my arms around him. "This definitely isn't how I imagined winter break going," I tell him. He breathes loudly, and I know he gets it. I don't cry the rest of the night, and Hank doesn't leave my side.

CHARLOTTE

Chapter Twenty-Five

2 Months later

This has been the hardest two months of my life, but we've made it work. Their season ends in about a month anyway, so I'll get a little more of their time... at least, I hope.

It's been a ridiculous amount of texts, letters, obscene FaceTime calls, and lots of coordination. But this is the first time I'm going to get to see them since Christmas. I'm not a huge fan of driving, but the weather looks clear, and I just need to see them so badly.

They've all done such a good job of keeping in contact and letting me know how much they want this to work. I've honestly been most impressed with Mikael. I thought maybe he would send me one or two letters, and that would be it. But we exchange letters every week, even though we talk on the phone almost every day.

I've fallen even deeper these last few weeks, not being blinded by my lust for each of them. I've been able to genuinely get to know them, and I love what I see. Anders is just so kind, giving, and in touch with my needs. Eli is so funny and seems to need the most attention out of my Alphas, but I don't mind giving that to him.

Mikael is still the quietest. He really opens up in his letters the most, not when we're all on the phone together.

I will say, one of the best things about this separation are the pictures they send me. My spank bank is stacked. They even help each other take photos sometimes. I have one of Mikael wiping his face with his jersey and showing his delicious abs. I may or may not have killed my vibrators batteries staring at that masterpiece.

We've made the best of it, but it's been hard. Especially since I had to leave Mercy University. They told me that if I agreed to go on dates with a few alumni, they might be able to waive my online fees. They're a bunch of classist fuckers. I'm glad that I didn't go back, but it was too short notice to sign up online with another school. I'm thinking that maybe I can sign up next year. It will give me something to do while the guys are working.

The longer we're apart, the more okay I am with the idea of living with each of them separately during the year, and then all of us living together in the off season. I just know we can make this work. It's not going to be easy, but I'd rather have one of them at a time than none at all. If this is the sacrifice I have to make so they all have their dream and I have them, I can do it.

"Honey, you sure you're okay driving all that way?" Mom asks as I pack the last of my things—all of their hoodies to re-up their scents, clothes, lingerie, and all my bath products.

"Yeah, it's only a few hours. I'll be alright."

"I just don't like you driving that far."

"I promise I'll be super careful. I need to see them so badly."

"I know you do, sweetie. They miss you just as much. You know I have my weekly catch up texts with them." I grin and nod, loving how much my mom loves my Alphas and they love her. She wraps her arms around me. I will say, getting this time with my mom has been invaluable. We've cooked, gone to bingo, did a pottery class, and even an indoor chocolate festival. People always say things happen for a reason, and I wonder if I met my guys when I needed to and had my heat while they were here so I could have this time with my mom. Especially if I'll be moving away next year. Mom and I have talked about it. She's happy for me. I'm just trying to figure out if I leave Hank with her or take him with me. I don't like the idea of my mom being alone, but he's a lot of work.

Speaking of the devil. He jumps on my bed and sniffs the hoodies. Seems my Alphas have left an impression on the big guy as well.

"Don't worry, buddy, you'll see them soon."

"I've been thinking," Mom says.

"Yeah?"

"Why don't I move to where you and your Alphas decide to spend the off season? That way, I'll always be close."

I blink at her and smile. "I'd love that." She smiles and kisses the top of my head.

"You tell those boys I say hello and am working on matching scarves for all of them." I laugh and nod my head.

"I will." I kiss Hank on the head and toss my bag over my shoulder and start up my mom's van, smiling as I head to Boston.

My GPS has me in front of a nice townhome. Only issue is parallel parking.

Fuck me upside-down.

I quickly call Eli. I don't know why I feel like he will be the best at parallel parking, but it's just my best guess.

"Hey, baby. You almost here?"

"I'm out front. Can you park my van? People are honking at me."

"Be right there."

"Get out of the fuckin' road!" some asshole yells behind me. So I give him the finger out of the window and put my emergency flashers on.

"Calm the fuck down, asshole!" Eli yells as he comes to the driver's side. His grin is massive as he opens the door and looks at me. "Hey, Char baby."

"Hey." I don't know why I feel so shy all of the sudden.

"Slide over." I do as he says as he moves the van into the tight spot like he's a professional driver. The guy behind us honks and gives us the finger as he drives past. "Come here," he says, and immediately, I'm on his lap with my hands on his neck. His hands grip my ass as he kneads the flesh like he's making sure I'm real. I kiss every freckle on his face before taking his mouth against mine.

"I missed you." My voice is raspy, and all I want to do is fuck him hard and fast in this car.

"Baby, it's three in the afternoon. Let's take this inside, yeah?"

"Are you sure you don't want me right now?" I tease him, scratching the back of his neck with my nails and making him shiver.

"Damn. I missed you, baby." He tugs me close, and his lips are on mine again, exactly where I want him.

I groan and keep kissing him. His pine scent makes me realize how diluted his scent is on his hoodie I sometimes sleep in.

Good god. "You smell so good."

"So do you," he groans, kneading my ass again, grinding against me. I've humped a lot of objects around my room to get off on lately, but none of them come close to this. We could just both finish like this, completely clothed and rubbing against one another. Eli is basically panting when he looks out the window and sees what looks like two of his classmates on the sidewalk balking at us. "Let's get inside, so I can show you just how much I missed you."

"Fine. Grab my stuff?" We could just give them a show. I quite like the idea of them telling everyone they know that they saw Eli Beckford—BU superstar—in the front seat with his Omega/girlfriend/scent match. Maybe I need to leave a hickey on his neck so everyone knows what's up. I smile as Eli kisses me one more time before getting out of the van. Yeah, I'm going to leave marks on him tonight.

"Of course."

I pop the trunk, and Eli laughs but collects all of my bags. It looks like I'm moving in, not like I'm here for just three days. Thankfully, he now knows what to expect when I pack things. He doesn't even scoff at the amount of stuff I packed, just grabs it all in one trip. I shut the trunk behind him.

"Game day tomorrow?"

"Yup!"

"I'm excited to see you guys play a real game."

"Me too." He leans forward and places a kiss on my lips while still managing to hold all my shit. Suddenly, two arms wrap around me, and I squeak as I'm thrown over a shoulder. Once I see his ass, I know it's Anders.

"Missed you, *Kulta*." He smacks my ass for good measure, and I can't help the laugh that escapes me. Fuck, I missed them so much. And I've missed Anders' spankings more than I care to imagine. There's really not much you can do to simulate spanking at home. Really, nothing beats their hands actually on me. You can FaceTime, text, talk as much as you want, but physically being with someone just can't be topped.

"Missed you too, but put me down," I say, pinching his ass.

He laughs and carefully slides me down his body before cupping my face and kissing me so hard I nearly see stars. "You look beautiful."

I grin and tug on his shirt and kiss him again. "You all gonna show me your place or what?"

"You can see my room, Charlotte," a deep voice says from the doorframe, and I basically fling myself into his giant body. He catches me, his campfire scent so soothing, I hum. "Hey," he whispers in my hair, and I smile as I wrap my arms around his neck and hold him tightly. Still trying to be so cool, it's not like he doesn't tell me all the things he misses about me in his letters. In extremely graphic detail, might I add.

"Hey. You gonna show me around, or take me to your room?" I suck hard on his neck, and he groans.

"My room." He carries me in his arms as I continue kissing his neck, no longer giving a single fuck what their house looks like.

Anders and Eli follow. After my heat and the obscene things we've done on the phone with each other these past weeks, I don't think there's any shame here. And well, I've been a patient girl, and I want all my Alphas at the same time. Call me greedy all you want, but I'm seriously a little knot deprived.

A door shuts loudly, and it takes me out of my haze as I look up at Mikael. "What do you want, Charlotte?" His tone is deep and promises so many naughty things.

"All of you at once." Something we haven't done before, but I'm ready. I've done some butt stuff before, but I'm ready in more ways than one for one of them to do that to me now.

"I think we can do that." My jacket is ripped off of me, and my sweater is pulled over my head, my hair hitting my back as hands wrap around my waist and unbutton my jeans from behind. Mikael pulls the cup of my bra down to expose my breasts. "Need to show our needy little Omega how much we missed her." I moan, and my head falls back, hitting Anders' chest. He kisses the top of my head, and I feel bad that Eli is being left out.

So I tug him by his pants to bring him closer to me and squeeze his hard cock. "Fuck."

Anders has my pants at my calves as he cups my pussy, my underwear the only thing separating us. "So wet for your Alphas already, aren't you?"

"Mmm."

"How do you want to do this?" Mikael asks. I don't know who he's talking to. I just know someone better fuck me soon.

"Let's get her nice and ready," Eli says, groaning as I hold his cock still. I like that plan and push Mikael onto the bed, unbutton his pants, and he eagerly helps me slide them down his legs.

"Take your shirt off." I need to see more of those abs I've been touching myself to lately. When he takes his shirt off, I can't help but groan. He's perfect. I lick from the V above his cock to his left nipple.

"Fuck, *mon sucre d'érable.*" I whine, loving his nickname for me. His maple sugar. That's damn right.

"That's right, yours. Now fuck me."

His boxers are down in a flash, and he's nudging the head of his cock along my already slick entrance. I groan as he fills me up, having missed this so much. How our scents intertwine and how his flesh feels against mine. "You want all of us?" I nod frantically, and he grins before pulling me down for a kiss. His cock leisurely thrusts in and out of me, his thick knot teasing me with each thrust, but not going inside.

Anders moves so that he's naked and on his knees on the mattress. I lick my lips and fist his cock before leaning forward and taking him into my mouth. I hum around his impressive length and can't help it when I see Mikael watching. His mouth parts as he groans from the sensation of fucking me and watching me give head to his best friend.

Suddenly, Eli's hands are on my hips as he spreads my ass. "You're sure, baby?" I nod and hum around Anders' cock. Eli collects slick between my thighs and uses it as lubricant to tease my asshole. Everything is happening in such a slow way, like every one of my nerves is just begging for more. Mikael fucks me slow, Eli toys with me, and I suck Anders like I have all the time in the world.

Mikael groans beneath me. "We gotta switch, or I'm gonna come."

Anders nudges his shoulder, and Eli grabs me around my chest and pulls me up against him. "Gonna make a mess of you, Omega," he whispers in my ear, and I shiver.

"Promise?"

He nips my neck, and I nearly come on the spot. Images of him actually putting his bond mark there are now a new fantasy. Anders lies down, and I crawl on top of him and put his cock inside of me. Eli ups the anti by slowly fucking me with one and then two fingers, my slick lubricating both of my Alphas.

Mikael is now where Anders was on his knees, his cock dripping with my slick from earlier. "Taste how sweet you are, *mon doux.*" I greedily take him into my mouth and taste my sticky maple flavor over his length. "So fucking good." I feel nearly feral for my Alphas at this moment. If I hadn't experienced my heat already, I would think it was happening again. My all-consuming need for them is cataclysmic, and I just never want to stop touching them.

"Damn," Anders groans beneath me. I'm a panting, sweating, wet mess as I suck Mikael and ride Anders. Eli is nearly torturing me, I don't know how many fingers are inside of me, but the stretch feels amazing.

"That's it. You want me, Char?" I nod my head, and I hear the clicking of a lid. Eli dribbles lube along the crack of my ass and his dick. I groan and momentarily stop sucking Mikael's cock as Eli pushes inside of me.

"Fuck," I groan, my nails digging into Anders' chest. He hisses, but looks at me like I'm a fucking goddess rather than the wanton woman I feel like.

"Goddamn, baby. You look so good taking all of us," Eli praises me from behind. His hands are tight on my hips. Anders is holding my ribcage, and Mikael has my hair wrapped around his fist.

Eli thrusts slow while Anders doesn't move. It's so deliciously intense I'm not even sure what noises are leaving my mouth as they fuck me together. I lazily stroke Mikael's cock while I get myself together enough to put him in my mouth. All of our scents are mingled together, and the way Eli has me bent over, my clit rubbing against Anders' pubic hair, I'm so close.

Anders must notice as he fucks into me from the bottom, making me shout and shatter as the friction against my clit and the over-whelming fullness hits me. I can feel my pussy spasm around both Eli and Anders, and my hand is just basically tugging on Mikael at this point. All three Alphas groan, but I'm too lost in my pleasure to even notice what's going on with them. My body shakes, and I feel like I'm spasming everywhere as I come. After my vision clears and

I can feel my body again, I look up at Mikael and lick the tip of his cock before taking him deeper down my throat.

Eli moans behind me and slaps my ass before squeezing the cheek tightly. "Gonna come," he mumbles. His pace quickens, and I moan around Mikael's cock as he takes what he needs. His grip on me is brutal as he moans and stutters, finishing inside of me. He pulls out, and I wince as Mikael pulls me by the hair and kisses my lips, tasting himself before getting off the bed and taking Eli's place.

I ride Anders like my life depends on it while we wait. He cups my jaw and kisses me with no care in the world. "So fucking good," he says to me. "Our perfect little Omega." I moan, and there's another lid clicking as Mikael enters me where Eli was. This time Mikael and Anders enter me in intervals so that I'm never empty. I pant against Anders' neck, taking everything that they give me, loving their hands on my body and all of our scents together. I need them to all come in me, on me, bite me, and claim me as theirs.

"Please," I hum against Anders' throat.

"Fuck," Mikael grumbles behind me. I feel him fill me up with his cum as he finishes, and he pulls out. His teeth are on my ass cheek where he gives me a light bite before I feel his fingers pushing against my ass, making sure that he and Eli stay inside of me. I groan at the sensation. The level of possession he has for me in that moment has me nearly ready to come again.

"I'll always give you what you need, *Kulta*," Anders says, pushing his swollen knot inside of my pussy, making me scream and gush around his cock. The pleasure is so intense I swear my face goes numb and my hearing goes out.

He wraps his arms around my back and shoulders as he ruts into me and whispers the sweetest words of praise in my ear. "This sweet pussy belongs to us. You're ours, my beautiful fucking perfect girl."

I'm sure I'm moaning loudly right into his ear, but he doesn't care as he fucks me through my orgasm, filling me with his cum. I feel drained, thoroughly fucked and scent marked by my Alphas.

I groan as my high comes down, and I look down at Anders' face, his smile radiant when I kiss his cheeks.

"I'm hungry," I grumble, and all three of them laugh around me.

"We'll get you something as soon as my knot goes down," Anders promises.

"God, I missed this," I say. Of course, I missed his knot—dearly. Me and Anders' knot are very close. But I just missed being close to all of them in this sense. Talking every day is nice, but being able to feel, touch, and smell. It's everything.

"Us too," Anders says, kissing the side of my head and stroking my back as we wait for his knot to go down.

Chapter Twenty-Six

After getting fucked within an inch of my life, the guys fed me. They're on some very interesting meal prep diet, so I'm glad they made me a delicious sandwich and chicken noodle soup. They have to be up early for pre-game workouts, so we're not going to stay up too late—tomorrow will hopefully be another story. Hopefully they aren't too tuckered out from the game.

I sit on Anders' lap in the living room while Mikael and Eli shower in their respective bathrooms. I push his blond hair back and kiss his forehead.

"You feeling good about tomorrow?"

"Yeah, Providence is sucking ass this year," he says, and I smile.

"So only what, a month left in the season?"

"Yeah, and then we can hire an agent and go into the draft since we're all still twenty." I nod my head, knowing that we've talked through it before, but it's still confusing.

"And then?"

"Then in July, we'll all know where we're going, and we can plan. The best-case scenario would be for all of us to be on the same coast at least." I nod my head in agreement. My biggest fear is that they will all be spread out. "Eli is going to likely be a first or second draft pick. I'm lucky if I get fifth or sixth. The teams right now who need goalies aren't the best." He shrugs but continues. "Mikael is the wild card. He might not get drafted, but he will definitely get picked up by a feeder team if he doesn't." I nod and sigh. It's all so confusing, and I'd just like some idea of how our lives would look in the next coming months. But I need to be patient. I promised that I would understand their passion, that I would never ask them to change their goals because of me, and I plan on sticking to that promise.

"Are you nervous?"

He squeezes my waist. "Just a little stressed about managing all of this. The draft alone is fucking terrifying, let alone not knowing where we will all end up."

"But we have a plan." He kisses the side of my hair.

"It might be a loose one, but we have a plan."

"I'd rather have one of you at a time than none of you."

"Same. Oh, that reminds me. My mom sent you something." I gape at him.

"Your mom sent me something from Finland?" He nods and smiles, pulling out a medium-sized shipping box.

"You can look at it later, but she's excited to meet you. I was thinking maybe after our first season we could all go out there and meet them."

"I've never even left the country. I'd love that." He grins and gives me a kiss.

"Your mom has been so kind to me, my mom would like to return the favor." I furrow my brows and look at his perfectly handsome face. "Me and Kathy talk, and she might mail us baked goods from time to time." I smile, thinking about how my mom hasn't told me any of this, but loving the fact she seems to like my scent matches.

"We got pretty lucky with our moms," I say tenderly, feeling sad for Eli and Mikael.

"We will just have to share with Eli and Mikael."

"I like that idea." I smile and kiss his temple.

"Just as long as I'm still Kathy's favorite." I laugh and push against his shoulder. I can't help the yawn that takes over. "Let's get to bed. Big day tomorrow." He carries me to Mikael's room, and I rumble with pleasure. I love the fact that he knew I would want to sleep where all of our scents are. I kiss his face a million times before I fall asleep with an Alpha on each side of me and Mikael's head on my stomach. This is the life.

The guys left early for all of their pre-game stuff, and I drove to the stadium and got my ticket from will call. The stadium is chilly, but the atmosphere is alive with excitement, and I can tell the fans are pumped for the game. My seat is right by the glass, and I can't help but feel a little special. There is a group of girls to my right, and the two seats to my left are empty for now.

I wait patiently for the festivities to begin, and I can't help but overhear the girls next to me. "Supposedly, they have an Omega. No way is it going to work," one of the girls scoffs.

"How the fuck do you have an Omega when you're all traveling for different teams? They should just cut their losses and fuck me instead." The girls laugh, and I swallow thickly, knowing they are talking about my guys. There's just no way they are talking about someone else.

"It was my two-year plan to fuck Mikael Martel. I don't plan on giving up either."

"Good luck with that. Eli would be the easier target."

I've had enough. I clear my throat absurdly loud, and the girls all look over at me. "You okay, sweetie?" the one who looks a little too drunk for a Thursday at 2 p.m. asks.

"Just watching my Alphas play hockey," I say with a grin on my face, trying to take the high road. They scoff but lower their voices and talk to themselves. I turn and find an extremely uptight couple glaring at me as they take their seats next to me.

The woman is wearing a tailored pea coat, and her red hair is half up with the rest in loose curls. "You must be Charlotte?" she says in a fake friendly voice. I swallow thickly and nod my head. None of the guys told me to expect to sit next to someone who knew about me.

"I am."

"We're Eli's parents."

"Oh, nice to meet you." I hold out my hand. His mother looks at it, and then looks back up. His father is a very plain man. He looks rich but bland as he ignores me and sits down.

"Jean and Edward Beckford. Pleasure," Jean says, sitting down. "So you were able to make a game?" Her voice is so snide and rude. But it's Eli's mom, so I do my best to be overly friendly.

"Yes, I live in Vermont, so it's not easy to make all the games. Plus, they needed time to focus."

"How do you plan on letting them focus if they're all worried about you at home when they're playing professionally?" Edward chimes in, not even looking at me but staring at the ice before us.

"We're going to make it work."

"So naïve, just like Eli. Never thinking things through. So emotional, that boy." I really want to punch Eli's mom in the tit.

"We're scent matches."

"And?" His mom gives me a glare.

"You might be a Beta and not understand the relevance, but it's the equivalent of having a soulmate."

Jean scoffs and looks at her perfectly manicured nails. "Convenient, is how it sounds. A poor Omega from nowhere Vermont finding three Alphas headed for the NHL and getting a free ride."

I gape at the incredibly rude and offensive woman. "I would love for them to be anything other than hockey players."

"I'm sure. Hockey is the only thing Eli has excelled at. While we may not understand it, we understand his potential for success. Perhaps we could come to an arrangement?"

"An arrangement?" I ask, baffled.

"What would it cost for you to break up with Eli? I don't really care about the others."

I blink at her, and I can barely close my mouth.

"Nothing, there's nothing you could give me to leave Eli."

Jean hands me a rectangular folded piece of paper, and I open it. It's a check for one hundred and fifty thousand dollars. "Perhaps that number might change your mind?"

"It doesn't. Are you two going to move seats, or do I need to?"

"Very well. If you won't see reason, perhaps Eli will."

"Perhaps," I say, ripping the check in half and handing it off to her. It's then a buzzer sounds, and the teams take the ice. My eyes immediately catch Eli's, who looks furious as he sees his parents looking down on me as they leave their seats. I watch him skate over to Anders and Mikael, who all look pissed. I give them a watery smile and a thumbs up to ease their nerves. Eli shakes his head in frustration but skates off as they do their warm-up.

I wrap my arms around myself and focus on the hot goalie stretches that Anders does. I've missed watching him do his splits and the hot humping thing on the ice. I really hope they're not too tired to fool around some more tonight.

The announcer shouts at the starting lineup, which is all of my guys. I do my best to shrug off the encounter with the bitches next to me and Eli's parents as I cheer as loudly as possible for each of them.

The game is intense. Far more violent and fast than the one I watched a few months ago. I watch how Eli commands the ice. It's obvious why he's the captain. He's the one everyone on the front line looks for to make the shot, and he just steals the show. Mikael knocks multiple people onto their ass, and I probably shouldn't like watching that as much as I do, but it's kind of hot.

I get so excited every time Anders stops a goal, and I love the smile he gives me when my voice carries over the ice. By the time the first period is over, it's still 0-0. I'm hoping that I get to see a win. It would suck to have to go home with them after a major loss.

When they come out for period two, it seems like their coach has lit a serious fire under their asses. Everyone skates faster, the hits are harder, and the communication improves. The opposing team ices, and Mikael and some guy are in a faceoff—that Mikael wins. The other player hits him with his stick, and Mikael pushes him up against the glass. He doesn't hit him, just manhandles him a bit. I know a relative amount about the rules, but I'm not sure why they are both sent over to the bad boy box. Mikael, his coach, and other team members look pissed by the call. He squirts water into his mouth and spits it out.

That... that should be illegal, and I feel like it awakens something in me.

Both teams are down a player, and Eli takes that opportunity. He passes back to a defender, who passes to Eli's right wing, who passes to him. Like a bullet train, Eli reels back and knocks the absolute fuck out of the puck, then sirens blare that he made a goal. I'm jumping up and down and screaming before I can even think about it. All his teammates hug him, slap his ass with sticks, and grab his mask. I definitely don't miss his grin in my direction before he skates over to the bench.

"Lucky bitch," the girl next to me hisses.

Yup, that's me.

The guys won their game, not by much. It was a close game, and I can't help but feel like I was a distraction. It was like Eli, Mikael, and Anders kept gazing over at me. I'm not sure if it's because Eli's parents were there, or if they were just worried about me.

I try not to overthink it as I drive back to their townhouse. Relief hits me when there are two spots together, and I'm able to manage parking the van myself. I only have to back up two times. It should probably feel weirder than it is to just unlock their front door and walk right in, but it doesn't. But now I just have to wait for them to get home, and I don't know what to do with myself. The box from Anders' mom is in the corner, so I decide to spend some time opening that.

With a knife from the kitchen, I open the box. There's pink tissue paper and a gold envelope on top with my name in cursive on top. I use my thumb to open the letter, and I'm so fucking thankful I decided to open this today. Especially after that horrific encounter with Eli's parents.

Charlotte,

It is our pleasure to know our son has found his scent match. He makes us so proud every day, and we worry about him being so far away from his family. To know that he has you is the sincerest blessing. I have some Finnish treats and items in the box along with some pictures of Anders as a boy. We hope that we will be able to meet you soon.

Thank you for bringing so much brightness to Anders' life. With love,

Eevi, Kal, Askseli, and Eino

I read the note a few more times, realizing the startling differences between Eli's and Anders' parents. Smiling, I fold the note back up and put it in the envelope as I dig into the rest of the box. There are a few pairs of the most comfortable looking socks I've ever seen in my life, as well as a colorful knitted hat. There's something called Salmiakki in a black-and-white checkered box. I open it and take one of the black squares out. As soon as I chew on it, I have instant regrets.

"What the fuck is that?" I say, spitting it into my hand and throwing it in the trash. I eye the rest of the snacks suspiciously. There's a pink wrapper that says 'Geisha' on it, and I take my chances, peeling back the wrapper and taking a bite. I hum as the chocolate washes out the taste of whatever the fuck it was that I just ate.

Lastly, there's a small box on the bottom, and I open it and flip through the photos of baby Anders. There are multiple pictures with him and his dads, mom, and siblings. It makes a lot of sense now why Anders was so quick to accept me and want me. This life he had with his family is what he wants for himself. His parents aren't scent matches, but it's clear that their bond is something special.

My favorite picture is one where he's riding a sled with his two dads and smiling going down a hill. I never gave much thought to my future, honestly too scared to worry about the future. I've always been a present time person. Because if I worry too much about what tomorrow will bring, I won't be able to enjoy myself. But as I look through these pictures, showing a happy pack and family, I realize that it's something I want. I've already made up my mind about Anders, Eli, and Mikael. Well, maybe the universe made that decision for me. But they're mine, and while I try not to think too far ahead, it's at this moment that I wonder if I want too much.

Luckily, I'm not left with my thoughts for too long as the guys nearly rush into the house. Their hair is still wet from their post game shower.

"Are you alright? What did they say to you?" Eli says, staring at me like he's shocked I'm still here.

I shrug my shoulders and take another bite of chocolate. "They asked me to leave you alone."

"They did fucking what?" Eli says.

"You're really surprised?" Mikael says, coming to sit next to me on the floor. I hand him the nasty candy that he eyes suspiciously.

"They handed me a check. I ripped it up." Anders grins, and Eli looks like he's seen a ghost.

"I'm so sorry, Charlotte. I had no idea they were coming. They never come to my games."

"Probably saw your post from yesterday," Mikael says, putting one of the black squares in his mouth. As soon as he bites down, he sputters and spits it out in his hand. "What the fuck is this?"

"It's from Anders' mom," I reply, which has Anders smiling and holding his hand out. I hand him the box, and I watch as he puts three in his mouth at once and hums.

"Mmm, missed Salmiakki."

"I don't know how you eat that."

"It's an acquired taste. We had it all the time as kids," Anders replies. Mikael and I look at him like he's crazy. When I glance over at

Eli, he is still clearly having a moment about me meeting his parents and them being such assholes.

I tug him down by his sleeve, and he sits down on the floor with me. "Do you care what your parents want?" I ask him softly.

"No," Eli says, but I don't believe him. I rub his back gently, trying to bring him some comfort.

"We're a pack of four people. Surely we can't all have normal parents."

Mikael scoffs next to me and takes the chocolate out of my box, then takes a bite.

"I just can't believe they tried to bribe you to leave me. Why?"

"I think they're worried I'm going to be a distraction." What I don't say is I can see where they are coming from. I worry about being a nuisance too. I want them to have it all, but I need my Alphas probably just as much as they need hockey—if not more.

"You're not," Eli says softly. "Without you, the three of us would be a mess. You're not a distraction. Never think that."

He leans forward and gives me a kiss while rummaging through my box.

"Hey, get your own Finnish candy, or eat the stuff that Anders has."

"Not sharing," Anders replies, and Mikael shudders, remembering the taste of the supposed treat.

"Good, please keep that atrocity to yourself," Mikael replies.

"So what's the game plan for tonight?" I ask with a smirk on my face. I'm not willing to let Eli's parents ruin what little time I have with them in person. I have a bet with myself to see how many times

I can get knotted before I have to drive home. And let's just say we've barely made a dent.

"How does truth or dare sound, *Kulta*?"

I grin at my hot goalie Alpha and take my shirt off, knowing we won't last more than a round or two.

"Mikael, truth or dare?" I ask.

"Dare."

I grin, knowing that the evening is saved, and I still have today and tomorrow left with my guys.

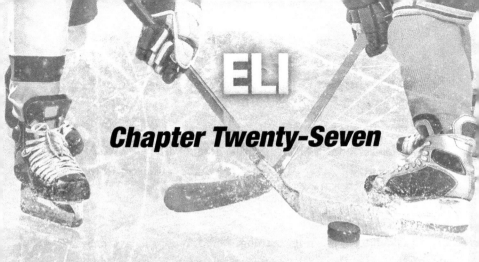

ELI

Chapter Twenty-Seven

3 Months later

"You're sure you're okay with us going?" I ask her as I walk back home from the convenience store.

"Yes! Go, have fun. This is a big deal," Charlotte says on Face-Time, looking even more beautiful than ever. We've seen her four more times in person since the game my parents intruded on. I had serious words with my parents, but they acted like they did nothing wrong. At least I know that Charlotte isn't about to bail on us. Not that I thought she ever would. We're scent matches. We may not be bonded, but as soon as we know where we're each going and have a plan, I'm going to change that immediately. I need my mark on that girl as much as I need to fucking breathe.

"I just feel bad. I feel like you should be there." I want her to celebrate with us, but our agent said that it was boring and no one else brings their girlfriend.

"Your agent is paying for you guys to go. It's only a few days. We can plan our own celebration as soon as you get back."

"Jake said it's a big deal for us to go, even though none of us can legally drink." She rolls her eyes, and I laugh. We all got pretty lucky meeting the deadline. We all turn twenty-one in the next coming months.

"It will be fun. I'm so excited for you all. Do you have any hopes?"

"I'd be lying if I said I didn't want to be a Bruin. But as long as I can play and have my girl, that's all I want."

"Such a sap," she jokes. "Piper is home for the summer before she transfers to Yale anyway. We're going to have some girl time."

"She still with that guy from tubing?"

Charlotte coughs and smiles. "No. Piper, my little heartbreaker. He got a job in Raleigh, and Piper doesn't do long distance." She winces, and I shake it off.

"It would be different if he were her scent match."

She smiles into the phone and nods. "That's true. Speaking of which, I'm gonna need some more scents."

"You want our hockey gear after we've been sweating all day?"

"Don't tempt me," she jokes.

"Alright, I got to head to the airport. Be good."

"Me, be good? You're the one going to Vegas. You be good."

"Always, Char baby." She grins and makes kissing noises over the phone and hangs up.

As soon as I'm back at the townhouse, the guys are all packed up, and the car is ready to go. "Ready to go, fuckers?"

"Are we sure we should go?" Anders asks.

"Jake said it was a big deal." We all landed the same agent, hoping that would help us with our goals to be near each other and figure out how we're all going to be the Alphas that Charlotte needs.

Mikael and Anders nod as we get in the car and make our way to Logan, something telling me I should have pushed harder for Charlotte to come with us. But I'm sure it's just my nerves over the draft and nothing more.

"Boys!" Jake Lawson, our agent, grins and spreads his arms, grabbing each of our shoulders as he meets us at the airport. "Things are looking good. Real good." He tugs me off on my own. Mikael and Anders walk behind us. "It sounds like the Lightnings want you real bad. It sounds like franchise potential. I know you wanted the North East. But to be a major part of a franchise is everything."

"You're right. What about Anders and Mikael?"

"Not sure yet. We will need to see where the cards fall."

"Thanks, Jake."

"That's why you guys hired me. I'm only going to work to get you the best." I nod as he walks us out of the airport to a luxury SUV that takes us to our hotel.

Vegas is unlike anywhere I've been before, and we all take in the lights, the people, and chaos around us. The hotel we're staying at is in the heart of everything, and we take our time exploring the casino floor and restaurants before heading up to our suite.

The suite is huge, and we all get our own bed, not that we would have minded sharing. But it's opulent and has a ridiculous view of the strip.

"This is insane," Mikael says as he riffles through the room.

"The hotel, or the fact that the draft is tonight?" Anders says.

"Both."

"It's fucking terrifying," I say.

"You're going to be first or second round. What are you terrified of?"

I glare at Mikael, and he shrugs. It's not like we all haven't had this conversation till we're blue in the face.

"Let's get ready."

"I'm going to FaceTime Charlotte before we leave," Mikael says, and I grin, wanting to show her the hotel room. She answers, and it looks like she's at her favorite coffee place with Piper, who smiles and waves in the background.

Mikael gives her a tour, and Charlotte *oohs* and *ahs* at everything as Mikael pans around the room. "Fancy," she whistles.

"We should have dragged you here with us," Mikael says, and I nod my head in agreement.

"It's okay, really. This is a big deal for you guys. You should celebrate." Mikael furrows his brows, and Charlotte *tsks* at him. "Stop it. You're going to be in the NHL, Mikael. I have a good feeling."

Mikael smiles down at the camera. The change I've seen in him has been unreal. He's still an asshole, but something about finally accepting Charlotte has softened him. I know for me, Charlotte's attention is like crack, and I think Mikael is the same. When you're used to getting affection like crumbs, when you meet someone like Charlotte, it's like winning the lottery and experiencing intimacy for the first time.

"I know. I promise either way we'll celebrate."

"I still have a good feeling. Just make sure you check in with me tomorrow. I want to hear all about it."

Anders steals the phone and tells her how pretty she is and how much we miss her before the phone is handed to me.

"We'll give you all the gory details about Vegas," I promise her, and she smiles, sipping her iced coffee. Fuck, I can't wait to live with her all the time. I groan internally. It won't be all the time, but we're all making sacrifices to make this pack work, Charlotte most of all. So whatever we can do to make her happy given the situation, I'll do it without complaint.

"Good. Have fun, but not too much. I can't wait to hear all about it tomorrow."

"Lo—Yeah, tomorrow." I smile, and she smiles back, and we hang up.

"Seriously, you almost told her you love her for the first time over the phone," Anders says, tossing a pillow at my face.

"Oh, shut up. Not like either of you have said it."

Mikael opens the door to Jake, who gives us a beaming grin and takes in the phones in our hands.

"Oh, come on, guys, it's Vegas. It's the draft. You won't be needing these." He takes all of our phones and shuts them into the safe in the closet. "Now let's get this show on the road."

Mikael, Anders, and I share a look, knowing that today is going to shape the rest of our lives.

My heart is beating out of my chest. It's been hours of the draft going on, and my name was called long ago, but it's the seventh round, and Mikael Martel gets called for the Montreal Canadiens.

Fuck. Fuck.

I'm going to the Tampa Bay Lightning, Anders to the San Jose Sharks, and Mikael to the Montreal Canadiens. This is the worst case scenario, as far as geography goes.

Anders looks over to me, and so does Mikael.

"Really, Canada?" Mikael scoffs.

"Does Charlotte have a passport?" Anders asks.

"I don't know," I mumble. This is supposed to be the best night of my life. I was a first-round draft for Tampa Bay. I'm living out all my wildest dreams, but it feels tainted. "Fuck." I toss my water bottle across the room.

"Why the long faces?" Jake asks as he comes into the room. "You all just made it into the mother fucking NHL. It's time to celebrate."

Mikael nods. "He's right, Eli. We've worked hard for this. We can figure everything out later."

I shrug my shoulders, wanting to call Charlotte and talk to her, but remember that Jake took our phones before we left tonight. "Come on, boys, you just got the biggest news of your lives. It's time to learn how to celebrate like a true athlete."

I grimace, but could really use the night to clear my head and try not to panic about the future. Jake takes us to a club where they don't even check IDs. We're behind a red velvet rope sitting on a circular couch as a waitress starts doling out shots. The liquor warms my bloodstream, and the future seems to feel less chaotic the more I drink. It appears Anders and Mikael are having the same euphoria as we keep tipping back cocktails and try to celebrate making it into the NHL.

The night and day after feel like a blur, but I'm thankful that Jake always makes sure there's a drink in my hand.

2 days later.

"Ugh, fuck. Close the curtains," I grumble.

"Our flight is in two hours," Anders says. He looks like shit. We all look like shit.

"What do you mean in two hours? Our flight's tomorrow?"

He's trying to open the safe and is cursing. "What's the fucking code?" The thing keeps beeping, this horrible droning sound, and I cover my head with a pillow, wanting the noise to stop and for the sun to stop blinding me. I've never drank this much for so long in my life. I feel like and smell like death.

There's a knock on the door, and Anders flips it open harder than he needs to as Jake strolls in, tossing us each a packet of Tylenol and Gatorade. "You boys are gonna need to work on your partying. Anyway, chop chop. We need to get to the airport."

"We need our fucking phones!" Anders complains, and Jake laughs, getting down on his haunches, and enters the code. The safe whirls and opens, and Anders tosses us each our phones.

"What the fuck?" I grumble. I have at least fifteen missed calls between an unknown number and Charlotte's number. "Do you have all these missed calls?" I ask, holding up my phone. Anders and Mikael nod their heads. "I'll try calling her back first."

I call the number, and it rings once before going to voicemail. "You call her," I direct to both Anders and Mikael. Mikael calls first and nearly tosses his phone on the bed. "It rang once and went to voicemail, and her voicemail is full."

Anders dials out and gets the same thing.

"What the fuck?"

"Girl troubles?" Jake says.

"Jake, if you don't want to get punched in the fucking face, I suggest you leave," I growl. He throws his hands up in mock surrender and leaves.

"Do you think she was just worried about not hearing from us?" Anders asks, scrubbing his face.

"We fucked up. We fucked up bad."

"It can't be that bad," Mikael says.

I scoff and try to call the unknown number that called me multiple times.

"Hello," the voice on the other side says, and their voice is vaguely familiar.

"This is Eli. Is Charlotte there?"

"Now you call back? Fuck you." She hangs up, and I stare at the phone.

"What the fuck?" I bellow and dial the number again. She surprisingly, and thankfully, answers the phone.

"Listen here, you selfish piece of shit, I get you were living out your dream in Vegas. But Charlotte needed you."

"Needed me?"

"Yeah, needed, as in doesn't anymore. I'm not sure if she will change her mind. But you don't deserve her. And until she reaches out to you, you need to leave her the fuck alone and let her heal. Until you can be the Alphas she deserves, stay the fuck away." The line goes dead, and I stare at the phone for what feels like forever. Mikael and Anders both look solemn next to me.

"Let me try calling her mom," Anders says, dialing Kathy. He shakes his head as the phone continues to ring. "No answer."

"We have to go to Vermont." What other option is there? Charlotte isn't this dramatic. Something must have happened. She wouldn't just give up on us like this.

They both nod their heads, and we're packing up our shit, tossing it all into bags haphazardly as we attempt to make our flight. We'll drive to her house after we land, explain ourselves and why we were out of contact for so many days.

"This seems a little dramatic for not hearing from us for a few days," Mikael says, and I nod my head. Fear weighs heavily on my stomach, and I think of all the possible awful scenarios. What would have Charlotte that upset that she would dodge our calls and have her best friend tell us to go fuck ourselves?

All of us get the same notification at the same time while we're waiting for our car to pick us up. My stomach falls completely when I read the email.

Fuck.

CHARLOTTE

Chapter Twenty-Eight

3 days ago

After I get back home from my date with Piper, I feel so much lighter. We got coffee, went shopping, and saw a movie. I didn't realize how much I needed time with my best friend. She really thinks I can do this, that I can make my pack work. This long distance stuff will be hard, but I think being with one of them at a time will make it easier.

Plus, Piper said if they ever have long stretches of games, I can always come and stay with her. It sounds like I'm going to be doing a lot of flying. The idea is a little scary, all of this is still really scary. But I'm trying to keep a positive attitude for myself and for the guys. I want them to enjoy this huge accomplishment and not worry about the future. They deserve it. And that's another reason I wanted them to go alone. So that they can really celebrate what a big deal this is without me there freaking out about logistics.

When I put my key in the door, I already hear Hank barking on the other side. My eyebrows are furrowed as I walk over the threshold. I walk in to find my mom on the floor, clutching her fist against her chest as Hank licks her face in between barks.

"Mom!" I'm down on my knees next to her in a second, feeling her face and noticing how sweaty and warm she is.

"Hospital," she rasps out.

"Come on, let's get you in the car."

I'm able to get her on her feet and wrap her arm around my shoulder. She's heavy, but the adrenaline is fueling me. Hank is barking, and I make a note to call Piper and have her let Hank out. My mom is gasping for breath, and I have tears streaming down my face as I get her into the passenger side door. "It's going to be okay, Mom."

Her fist is clenched against her chest as she breathes heavily and I put my seat belt on before flooring it and heading to the hospital. I call 9-1-1 as I'm driving, frantic and crying.

"9-1-1, what is your emergency?"

"My... my mom is having a heart attack, I think. We're on our way to the hospital."

"How far out are you?" There's a fucking red light, and I stop the car and bang my hand on the steering wheel in frustration.

"Maybe ten minutes." My mom gasps next to me, and I cry even harder on the phone.

"Okay, are you the one driving the car, ma'am?"

"Yes."

"I need you to pay attention to the road. Do you know where you are, so I can get you an escort to the hospital?" The light turns green, and I floor it as I look around for a street sign.

"I... I don't—"

The clash of metal on metal is severe, the pressure on my right arm intense and the impact on my face is starling. It smells like motor oil, metal, and powder. I gasp for air as I look around and blink, realizing that a car just hit us on my side of the car. As I look to my right, I see that my mom's airbag also activated. I nudge her arm.

"Mom." I shake her arm hard, but she doesn't move. "Mom," my voice cracks as I try to get her attention. I wince as I remove the seatbelt from my chest and lean over the console to check for a pulse.

Nothing.

"Mom," I gasp out, looking at her pale face that is bruised from impact. "No." I lean against her chest and cry. My arm and face hurt, but nothing compares to this. It's summer, but her skin is cold. Someone needs to do compressions. Something.

I unbuckle her seatbelt and wince at the pain in my shoulder. "We've got to get you out. Get help. Help!" I shout as I try to get her ready to be extracted. They'll be able to help. She just needs CPR. "Help!"

"Are you okay?" a voice asks from the side. I don't have the energy to answer as I clutch against my mother's shirt and cry. I hold onto her tightly, like maybe if I hold her close enough to me, she'll wake up. "Oh, fuck. Get EMS and police over here!" the voice yells.

I don't let go of her though. It wasn't supposed to be like this. We were supposed to have more time. She's my mom. I take in her face that looks so much like mine, and I can barely see with my contacts and tears. "Mom, what am I gonna do?"

There's a jarring metal noise, and I cover my ears.

"Miss, we need to get you out of the vehicle."

I shake my head. "I can't leave her. She needs me. She needs compressions or something."

"The car is leaking fluid. It's not safe for you to stay in the vehicle, and your right arm looks dislocated."

"But she's my mom."

"I know. We're going to take care of her. I just need you to trust me, okay?" The fireman holds out his hand through the passenger side door. I have to climb over my mom. I kiss her cheek one last time before the firefighter scoops me up into his arms and puts me into the back of the ambulance.

As I look back at the car, I notice they aren't getting my mom a defibrillator or a standard stretcher. They're bringing out a body bag. I can't really gather my thoughts as I see that. I should have called an ambulance from the beginning. I should have been paying better attention as I was driving. This feels like my fault.

"We're going to give you some Dilaudid for the pain and to help calm you down. We've got you."

They're hooking me up to IVs and taking my vitals as I stare at the obtrusively bright ceiling. I don't remember the ride to the hospital or the hours that follow. I feel numb. I don't know if it's the drugs, my brain helping me handle this trauma, or just me.

At this moment, I wish I could just sleep. I want to sleep and wake up to have this all be a horrible dream.

"Sweetheart, is there anyone we can call for you?"

"My Alphas," I say on a sob.

They nod, and the paramedic hands them my bag. I give them the names, and the calls go to voicemail. I'm hurt, but I know they are at the draft. More than likely, they don't have their phones with them. "Can you call my best friend, Piper?"

Piper answers on the first ring, and I sob uncontrollably. One of the EMTs explains the situation, and Piper agrees to meet us at the hospital.

I know that Piper is here in the room as my eyes start to close. "We gave her something to sedate her. We've stitched up her face and relocated her shoulder. Her elbow is sprained. Does she have a good network to help her get through this?"

"She has me," Piper says.

"I would suggest therapy and going to high grade suppressants. With her blood work, I would suspect she's only a month or two away from her next heat. High grade suppressants can have some negative effects, but it would postpone her heat."

"What are the effects?"

"Depression, no libido, there can be weight gain, and headaches."

I groan and turn to lie on my good side. I don't care what they give me, I just don't want to feel like this anymore.

"Yes, let's start her on the suppressants."

"I need confirmation from Miss Hodges since she no longer has a next of kin." Piper scoffs, and I groan.

"Whatever she says."

"Alright. I'll have the nurse come in shortly."

"Thank you," Piper says before coming behind me on the hospital bed and cuddling me from behind.

"Have they called back yet?" I ask.

"Just get some rest, Charles," she says as she pets my hair and back. Just like my mom used to. I fall asleep in pain and with a tear-streaked face.

Piper checked me out of the hospital, and we're at my house. Hank is whining, his giant head on my lap. I feel so disassociated as I look around the living room, knowing she'll never sit on the couch with me again, or cook another dinner in her kitchen.

"Have they called back yet?" I ask Piper.

It's been two days. The fact that they haven't called back has a sinking feeling in my heart. What if something terrible happened to them too?

"Can I have my phone?" Piper reluctantly hands it to me. I look at their social media and nothing has been posted. So I click over to their agent's, Jake Lawson. His first picture is of him and the guys holding up the teams they've been drafted to. I sigh and click on his stories.

That's what ends me.

I click through and see videos, clips, and pictures of Jake and my Alphas partying. They were partying while I watched my mother die. Not only that, but there are tons of beautiful women around them in every picture. They went on a two-day bender while I laid in the hospital.

I could understand maybe a day of not answering me, but after dozens of calls, nothing? Betas had their tits basically in their face, and they were celebrating while I was at the lowest of lows. There's a part of me that is trying to be understanding, but as I click through each story, my anger and frustration grow. Pictures of Eli dancing on a table, Anders singing karaoke, a girl's elbow over Mikael's shoulder. I toss the phone back to Piper and put my head between my knees.

It's time to leave before I get left again. This won't work. This is how it will always be, me alone and hurt and them out living their best lives as hockey superstars. We were so fucking stupid. I was so goddamn stupid. Everyone leaves me, and it's best that I end this now before it gets even worse.

"Block their numbers," I say to Piper.

"Charlotte, you're in shock. This is a lot. Are you sure?"

"Yeah. I'm going to take a shower."

The warm spray hits my skin as I slump down onto the floor, my knees bent and my arms wrapped around my legs. I don't cry, I don't think I have it left in me. My mom is gone.

She's fucking gone, and it's my fault. If I would have called an ambulance, maybe this wouldn't have happened. If I would have taken care of her, made sure she saw the specialists more frequently... She depended on me, and I let her down.

Why did I drive her? Why did I think that would get her to the hospital quicker? I wasn't in my right mind, and I wasn't paying attention. The guilt felt consuming before the suppressants, but I can feel it releasing me.

It's almost like I feel nothing, like I've detached myself from my reality. It's better this way, not feeling anything. Because if I truly let it sink in—that I'm the reason she's gone—I'm not really sure how I'd be able to live with myself.

It's probably why they haven't answered my calls. I'm not worth it, and I'll never be worth it. I'll never be more important than hockey. And I shouldn't be. Surely if I couldn't help my mother when she needed me the most, there's no way I could be a strong enough Omega for a pack of professional athletes.

I deserve this hurt. It feels like cosmic justice in the most fucked up way, and it's up to me to take the penance. I wasn't there for my mom, they weren't there for me. We might have been scent matches, but it's clear as day that now... now we're nothing.

The warm water continues to hit my skin, but I don't feel anything. All I feel is like a deep void of a person.

I have nothing left. I'll need to continue to take care of myself to some extent. But not for me, for Hank and Piper, the only people who are truly there for me, that still need me here. I can do this, even if I'm never the same, they still need me. And that will have to be enough.

The acceptance of everything I've lost flows through me as I realize what I have to do. Somehow I manage to bathe myself, even with my fucked up arm. I dry myself and get dressed, then sit on my bed and stare at the wall. The macrame that I never put back up lies on the floor, and the pink wall is empty. It feels metaphorical, but I'm too fucked up to put the pieces together.

"Come to New Haven with me," Piper says, sitting on my bed.

"Okay," I say back. "As long as Hank can come." The choice is clear, what else can I do? Sit here and wither away? Going somewhere where they can't find me, not that they would want to, makes the most sense.

"I'll have to find out about my renter's pet policy, but we'll make it work."

"When?"

"When do you want to leave?" she asks. I look around my room. At the pink walls my mom painted when I was five, at the height chart in the corner, and the chandelier that my dad let me pick out at Home Depot.

"Tonight."

"Alright, pack your stuff up, and let's go."

I sit down on my bed, and I do what's best. I write a letter, well, an email. They didn't have the time or need to call me back, so I don't feel guilty over the blunt and brutal nature of the email.

New message   • • •

To   Anders, Eli, Mikael

Anders, Eli, and Mikael,

It's over. I've blocked your numbers. I can't do this anymore. Timing has never been on my side. Maybe if we met at a different time or if circumstances were different, it would have worked. I need to be by myself, and I can't do that moving state to state with each of you. I need to be with someone who can be there for me, so that's what I'm doing. Please don't try to reach out, it would be too painful right now.

I'm being taken care of, and this is what I want.

Congrats on the draft.

—Charlotte.

📎 🖼 ☺ 🔍   Send

I send the email and pack up the rest of my feelings. No tears fall, my heart doesn't hurt. I don't hurt, I just am. I'm okay floating through life like this, as long as I don't have to feel the inevitable pain once this all hits me.

Running is what I do best, and there's no looking back now.

MIKAEL

Chapter Twenty-Nine

4 months later...

"Good game, Martel," Johannson says as he claps my shoulder, making my hand shift. A few drops of whiskey spill over the glass and onto my fingers.

"You too." He walks away, and here I am again, at this bar—alone.

I'm in the NHL, playing with the best of the best, and here I am after a huge win, sulking. I like my team, the people on it. Fuck, I even like the location. But this place, it's missing something.

I, of course, know that thing is a five-foot nothing blonde who walked away with no second fucking thoughts. Anders and Eli are doing everything to win her back, and I'm grateful for their initiative and what it's done for me. Personally, I think we should cut our losses and move on. The one fucking thing I asked her not to do was break me—and she did it. She did it fucking flawlessly, might I add. Not only did she make me fall for her, become addicted to her scent and taste, but she made me love her. I never told her, of course, and I'm thankful for it now. She didn't deserve it.

She's blocked our numbers and all of our social media accounts. Eli and Anders get tidbits of information from her friend, Piper, but she keeps her lips pretty sealed. We've tried reaching out to Kathy with no luck. Anders and Eli are positive that we don't know the whole story, and they're completely okay with just waiting for their moment. I've asked multiple times what exactly that moment is though.

This is exactly why I wanted to fucking wait and not do anything during winter break. The stakes were way too fucking high. Thank fuck we can all at least continue to play at a high level and stay focused. In the end, I guess I got what I wanted, to be in the NHL and become a better hockey player. Somehow it still doesn't feel like enough.

A blonde Beta woman sits at the bar stool next to me. She's wearing a jersey for our team. I lean back, and I'm not surprised by the teammate she is repping. I shake my head and lean back over the bar. My forearms rest on the clean bar top as I stare into the whiskey glass, wondering when this empty feeling will go away and why this whiskey doesn't seem to be helping.

"Oh my god. You're sin bin Martel," she says, and I grimace, hating the nickname I've been coined in only a few months.

"That's me," I say in a shitty tone, sitting back and taking another sip of whiskey.

"Great game tonight. That fight with Petrov was something else."

It was, wasn't it? I fucking hate that guy, hoping I get to smash his pretty little face up against the glass in the near future. I don't reply to the eager woman, but she keeps on going.

"So can I get you a drink?" I look over at her, and she just looks like a woman. I don't find anyone attractive anymore. Part of me wanted to find as many Betas as possible and fuck the living daylights out of them. But I can't. I don't want them.

I want pancakes and maple syrup. I want sass and that tight Omega cunt she got me addicted to. I sigh and throw back the rest of my whiskey, knowing that sitting here isn't going to help shit. Plus, if I don't get home soon, I know they will come here looking for me.

"No, thanks."

"Can I get you anything else?" she says, placing her manicured hand over my forearm. All it does is make me miss Charlotte's nails dragging down my back as I fucked and knotted her senseless. Don't even get me started on how much I miss knotting. I even bought an Omega jelly masturbator. Unhappy to report that it's nothing like the real thing, and you will be gravely disappointed.

"No, thank you. Have a nice night."

She scoffs, but turns around and scans the room, likely looking for her next target. I wish her luck. A year ago, I would have had her in the closest bathroom stall and taken what I wanted. But the one thing I want is the one thing that was taken away from me. Ironic, isn't it? When we met, all I wanted was my hockey career, but now that I have it, all I seem to want is Charlotte. Or the idea of Charlotte. I'm angry with her for leaving, and I don't know what I would do if she were actually in front of me.

I'm nothing but predictable as I pull out my phone, waiting for my ride to get here. She's blocked all of us on her social media accounts and her number. But I still try to pull up her information anyway—as suspected, nothing.

My phone buzzes, and it's Anders. I snooze the call immediately. I feel like they treat me like I'm going to go off in the deep end, when I know that I'm not. The ice has been my outlet. Feeling pissed off? Punch someone without my gloves on, so it hurts the both of us. Feeling sad? Drink a whiskey alone and think about what could have been. I think I'm handling things very maturely, and they can fuck right off.

The October air feels cool on my skin as I look around at the busy street. Everyone looks so fucking happy.

Well, fuck them.

My ride gets here, and I get into the backseat. Proud of myself for not having that much whiskey. Practice tomorrow is going to fucking blow. *Stop thinking about her, and focus on the game in three days.*

I will myself to push her out of my mind, knowing damn well I'll be thinking of flashbacks of fucking her while I stroke myself tonight.

I hate feeling like this, and I hate Charlotte even more for making me feel this way. *Fuck scent matches.*

"This you, pal?" the driver says, breaking me out of my self-loathing.

"Yeah, thanks." I get out of the car and look at the house, something else I hate. With almost impossible deft, I'm able to make my way through the front door and to my bedroom, not wanting to wake up my teammates or be asked a million questions. The purple journal on my nightstand glares at me, and I pick it up and write in it, just like I do every day.

My handwriting is shit, but I get out what I need to say before I go to sleep and start the vicious cycle again.

CHARLOTTE

Chapter Thirty

I actually have a reason to get dressed today—so that's something. I stare at myself in the mirror, noting that my face is fuller, and my eyes aren't as sunken in as they used to be. While I may look relatively healthy again, I still feel like the shell of the person I used to be. I don't enjoy things like I used to, not that I do much of anything. Avoidance has seemed like the best way to handle everything. If I don't think about it, it won't hurt me. But in the end, I'm no longer who I was.

Piper's taken care of me in so many ways that I feel like a burden. I live here in Connecticut with her. We're right outside of the campus, so luckily, everything is walkable. She pays the rent, buys most of the food, makes sure I see the sun now and then. But I can't keep using her like this. If I'm going to be staying here, I need to contribute. I've thought about selling my mom's house, but I just can't bring myself to do it, not yet.

If I don't find work soon though, I'll be forced to. I still need to pay the property tax on the house. I turned everything else off utility-wise for now, but I pay the neighbor to come and check on the place once a week. Mom stopped paying her life insurance apparently. When I looked at the timestamp, it was back in December—when I met *them*.

I shake my head and look back at myself in the mirror. With a steady hand, I apply some mascara, and I sigh, not allowing myself to go there. To think about *them*. I've gone as far as having Piper block their information from my search bars and social media. Any reminder would be too painful, a reminder of what I lost, what I ran from.

Before I can meet John, my possible new boss, I have therapy. I scoff, but pull on my jacket and put my purse over my shoulder. The jangle of Hank's collar alerts me he's awake. I feel a little judged by my dog as he looks at me in confusion.

"Yes, Hank. I'm leaving the house."

I lean over and kiss his head. Hank and Piper are the only two I can count on, and Hank isn't even a person. I scratch behind his ears as I walk the eight blocks to my therapist's office.

I low-key hate Janet. Every time she pushes the tissue box close to me in our sessions, I want to smack her hand away. She makes me feel judged and that I'm not grieving in a healthy way—her words, not mine. But, if I want to stay on my suppressants—which I absolutely fucking do—then I have to meet with Janet every week. The suppressants make me feel numb and subdued, but I like the feeling. It's better than the alternative, that's for fucking sure.

I haven't cried since that last day at my mom's house with Piper. I've done my best to not think about the accident, about my mom, or about *them*. Janet thinks I'm dissociating and that the suppressants are making my depression worse.

Well, Janet, wouldn't you be fucking depressed too if you were the reason your mom's dead, and you left your scent matches in the same week? Janet is a Beta, and I know it's not fair to use it against her, but she really just doesn't fucking get it. I swear to god, if she tries to make me talk about *them* again, I'm going to walk out. Surely my insurance will cover a new therapist for me.

The bell to the door dings as I walk into Healing Hands—what a stupid fucking name. Gabi is the receptionist, and we have an unspoken agreement that I just walk in and sit down, and she checks me in. She doesn't ask me about my day or the weather; she just does her job, and I sit down in the lobby like I'm supposed to.

The back door opens, and Janet isn't smiling as widely as she usually does. I'm not sure if I like this version more or less. Part of the reason I don't like Janet is because of how happy-go-lucky she is. But something feels off about the way her back is ramrod straight and how her smile seems forced.

"Charlotte, how are you today?" she asks.

"Fine." The standard answer of people who are not fucking fine.

"Take a seat." She holds her arm out to the tan loveseat and I sit down as she takes her office chair across from me. She folds her legs and taps a pen on the clipboard and paper in front of her.

"What is it, Janet?" I ask, tired of waiting for her to spit out whatever it is she wants to talk about.

"Your current dosage is no longer covered by your new insurance."

My mom's lapsed, and I had to go on state insurance two weeks ago. "What do you mean it's not covered?"

"You've been on Klidya for too long anyway. I think we can see this as a blessing in disguise."

I scoff and glare at her. "I need them. How much is it out of pocket?"

She shakes her head and pushes the box of tissues closer to me. "It was going to be both mine and your primary's recommendation to wean you off anyway. It's not healthy to be on this high of a dose, let alone with your current SSRI. I think you will start feeling a lot better moving over to this new dosage."

She scribbles on the pad next to her and hands it to me. "I know that this isn't what you wanted to hear today, Charlotte. But you knew this was going to come eventually. Do you want to talk about how you're feeling or discuss what this means for the future?"

"Does it mean I'm going to go into heat?"

"This new prescription we're putting you on should still help keep your heat at bay, but your hormones will want more from you. Your perfume will go back to its full strength. I would expect some mood swings changing from the dosage and brand. You will stay on the Zoloft to help with the depression. But eventually, the goal is no suppressants."

I've really pushed that reality so far back into my mind. Hearing her say it makes me shudder and clinch my thighs with my fingers.

"I think we should talk about your scent matches," Janet says. My fear of getting off suppressants is stalled by the thought of talking about them.

"I don't want to."

"Why? Because talking about them makes you feel what?" Janet pushes.

Regret, hate, anger, love, loss, fear... How do I say that it makes me feel too much at once? I'm not even sure what the biggest emotion is.

"There's no point in talking about them. They aren't out there waiting for me, Janet. And they shouldn't be. I don't want them."

Janet taps her pen on that fucking clipboard again. "I don't believe you. I think you still want them but don't feel like you deserve them."

"Because you know everything?" I say back, so fed up with Janet's bullshit today.

"Because every time I ask you to talk about them, I see the pain written over your face, Charlotte. You're an Omega, and you have needs. What happened to you was traumatic, but if you keep living your life blaming yourself and not allowing yourself good things, you'll be left with nothing."

"I ran because I knew they couldn't give me what I needed. Because I would always come second. They weren't there, and I was so mad. In that moment, I made a decision, and I have to stick with it."

"It's okay to change your mind and ask for forgiveness."

"They're all in different states now, and I have them blocked on all platforms."

"Maybe unblock them and see what happens?"

I shake my head at her, not wanting to face the consequences of my actions. "I'll think about it," I lie, wanting Janet to leave me alone.

"Here's your new prescription. Reach out to me on the portal if you have any issues."

I nod my head and take the new prescription, feeling worse than I did when I left the house in the morning. I'm really thinking about calling it a day, going back to bed, and trying again tomorrow when my phone buzzes in my purse. I tug it out and see a text from John, the owner of CT Promotions. We were supposed to meet at his office in thirty minutes, but it seems there's been a change of plans.

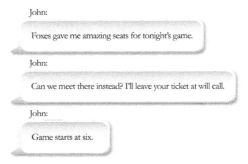

John:

Foxes gave me amazing seats for tonight's game.

John:

Can we meet there instead? I'll leave your ticket at will call.

John:

Game starts at six.

I groan, not wanting to step foot in a hockey stadium. I look up the game, but I'm immediately blocked with my search. Piper really blocked everything related to the guys and hockey. I sigh and reply to John, reminding myself how badly I need this fucking job.

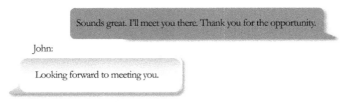

Sounds great. I'll meet you there. Thank you for the opportunity.

John:

Looking forward to meeting you.

I find it odd that a potential boss wants me to meet him at a hockey game, but I'm guessing the Foxes are one of his biggest clients. CT

Promotions is looking for work-from-home employees to help with putting in purchase orders and track shipments to clients. It's by no means my dream job, but I didn't finish college, and I certainly have no hands-on experience in accounting. It's a starter position and one of the few I was able to find that would allow me to work from home and is okay with my designation.

I walk back home, stopping at the pharmacy and getting my new prescription. I'm thankful that I can at least take a nap before the game. The walk home has me thinking about everything Janet said. If I did unblock them, would they reach out to me? Or are they living their best lives as professional athletes? It makes my stomach sink to think about them out there fucking other girls, but I am the one who ended things. It's not like I want them back anyway. Hockey comes first, not their Omega. I'm sure one day I will find Alphas who put me first—but they won't be my scent matches.

My head hurts, and I wonder if changing suppressants will help with the headaches. At least that will be one positive. As soon as I turn the knob to the front door, Hank is greeting me with his cold nose. I let him walk around the fenced-in front yard, and he handles his business before coming back inside. I feel guilty when I look down at him. I used to take him outside all the time, but lately, I barely ever have the energy to leave the house.

"I'm going to work on being better, for you, Hank," I promise him, petting his head as he follows me to the bedroom. I take my new suppressant and undress from my clothes except my underwear and climb into bed. Hank follows. This is the first time I feel like unleashing some of the pent up emotion. I sigh and bottle it all back up again. Now is not the time to fall apart.

There's a light knock on my door, and I startle awake, holding on tightly to Hank's fur.

"Charlotte," Piper's soft voice says from the hallway.

"Yeah?"

"How did the job interview go?"

"Oh, fuck." I pull up my phone, and it's six, right when the game is supposed to start. "Shit. shit. Shit." Piper opens the door, not phased that I'm nearly naked as I rush to get dressed and ready for the evening.

"Charles, what's going on?"

"Change of plans. I was supposed to meet him at six."

"Shit, I'm supposed to meet with my study group, but if you need a ride?"

"That's okay, I'll get a BetaRide." Plus, I can't ask Piper to do one more thing for me. I feel like she basically has a bonded Omega with none of the benefits.

"You're sure?"

"Yeah. Seriously, it's fine."

"Okay, what time will you be home?"

"Probably before ten."

"Ten?" Of course she's shocked. I haven't done anything outside the house since we moved here. I don't know why I lie to her about the hockey game, but I do. I guess I worry that she will baby me or think I'm doing something wrong.

"Yes, it's not a big deal."

"You're sure this John guy is okay? It's a little odd to not have a formal interview anywhere."

"It will be fine. I'll text you later to let you know how it's going. Go to the study group."

She eyes me suspiciously but nods, letting me get off a little easy this time. I sigh with relief when she leaves my room. I grab my phone and order the car as I brush through my hair and apply new makeup. I make sure to wear a pad and as many deodorizers I have. Suppressants aren't something that builds up in your system. It's more like a birth control pill, working as taken. With these new pills, I'm not sure how I will react.

I do a cautionary once over in the mirror. Eh, it will do. I grab my purse and wait outside until my driver pulls up. I check the license plate with the app and get in. The driver is likely a college student as he takes me the five miles to the stadium. My heart is beating out of my chest the entire ride there.

Will call was easy enough to get my tickets. The first period is already nearly half way done as I find section 112. I look down at my ticket and see row A. *What the fuck?*

One of the attendants puts out a hand as I go to walk by. "Wait for a stoppage of game," he says dryly, and I nod my head. I'm glad I wore my fuzzy pullover today. It's pretty cold in the stadium. I can see the game behind the attendant, and I swallow thickly. I want to run, turn back, and go home. But I need this job. I need this job more than I hate hockey at the moment. A play is called, and the attendant lets me walk down the stairs to row A. They aren't even normal stadium seats, they are folded chairs with the Foxes logo embroidered on the backs. I look at my ticket and see that I'm seat 7. I kindly scooch past the other people seated in the row, and that's when I see John stand up and smile.

He's tall and lean, probably in his mid-forties. He's got bright blue eyes and short salt and pepper hair.

"Charlotte, so glad you could make it," he says while holding out his hand, which I shake.

"Sorry I'm late."

"No worries. Traffic can be a mess on game days. So many people are complaining about the expansion team because of the new traffic." I hum in agreement, and he continues. "Not me though. The Foxes are now my biggest promotional and print client that I have. They had an opening for these seats. That's why I had the last minute change."

"Thank you for inviting me," I say politely and think back to Piper and how strange it is that he has invited me here tonight instead of a formal interview.

"Icing!" John shouts, getting up on his feet, and he bangs on the glass in front of us. So does the man next to me. I'm so confused by the behavior, but I just keep my legs folded, and my hands buried in my thighs, planting a fake smile on my face like I enjoy being here.

"Sorry. So the position," he says, sitting down. He makes eye contact and gives me a warm smile. "It would be work from home, except one day a week for meetings and team building." I nod my head, thinking that is a reasonable request. "I'm looking for someone who can enter purchase orders and track shipments for clients, and really just handle the complete process for my sales managers. I want them out there selling and having a good back end staff to handle the desk work."

"I'm very organized, and I'm a fast learner. I can learn your systems quickly, and I'm really open to however many hours you need me to work."

He smiles and puts his arm around the back of my chair. It's not creepy, maybe more so to just stretch out his arm as he smiles. "That's exactly what I'm looking for. I do have something to ask." I nod my head, and he smiles again. "Will you need time to take off for your heats?"

I swallow thickly and shake my head no. "Um, no. Not right now anyway." I'm like 95% sure he can't ask me that question, but I need this job, so I ignore the comment.

He nods his head and licks his lips. Suddenly there's a loud bang right in front of us. It startles me. John doesn't move his arm, and when I look up, deep brown eyes that I'm so familiar with stare back at me.

Mikael has a player pinned against the glass as they both fight for the puck. Another one of his teammates comes to help, and Mikael glares at me as he holds the player against the glass. I swallow, feeling raw and exposed. I'm not sure if I even blink as I stare back. Mikael's gaze leaves mine as he looks at John, who finally removes his arm from my chair to bang on the glass and cheer on the roughness happening on the ice.

The other player is let free, but Mikael continues to stare at John. Mikael swings and hits the glass where John's hand currently is. The men and women around me cheer as Mikael skates backwards back to the bench, his eyes darting between me and John the entire time.

"Holy fucking shit! Did you all see that? Sin bin Martel!" John shouts. Some of the men clap him on the shoulder. I'm in a daze, riddled in shock. Mikael got traded to the Foxes? I guess I wouldn't know. I have everything blocked. Did he know I was living in Connecticut?

I watch as he hoists one leg over the barrier and takes a seat on the bench. I'm so laser focused on him that it takes me a moment to notice the man with the reddish-brown beard sitting next to him. Now there are two sets of eyes on me, and I look between them. They look at me, and then back at John. Eli's features aren't as aggressive as Mikael's, but I guess that's always been the case.

Eli doesn't break eye contact as he ushers someone toward him with his gloved hand. The woman is pretty with light brown hair in a high ponytail, and she's dressed business casual. She looks up in our direction and nods her head. I swallow thickly, wanting—no—needing to escape. My throat feels tight, and my heart is pounding out of my chest, but I can't look away. I just stare at them across the ice, and I can't help but wonder what they're thinking. Do they miss me? Are they angry with me? Do they hate me? As much as I don't want to be, I'm still angry with them. I look down at my shoes and blink a few times, trying to process.

Why the fuck are Eli and Mikael on the same team? They all got drafted to three completely different teams from what I remember. I turn to John, who is completely entranced in the game, and I remember him mentioning the Foxes are a brand new team. He called them an expansion team. How did Eli and Mikael find themselves in the same state as me? Is it purely coincidental?

The buzzer for the end of the period blows, and I wonder how I can escape but still ensure a job with John. Maybe a stomach ache? Or my roommate slipped and fell and needs me?

I look up and watch as the rest of the team heads over to the bench. Mikael and Eli are both still staring in my direction. As soon as the goalie reaches them, they spin him around, and his bright blue eyes meet mine. *Anders.*

Anders doesn't glare like Mikael, or stare at me in shock like Eli. He just smirks and shakes his head. That's until he sees John. Anders glares at the older gentlemen next to me, and I shrink into my seat.

Maybe it's a good thing. They all clearly think I'm on a date with John. Maybe if they think I've moved on, they will leave me alone. The three of them glance my way one more time before they walk back to the locker room with the rest of their team.

"John, I think I might need to head out."

He smiles and puts his arm around the back of my chair. "You just got here. Let's get some snacks. We still have two more periods to go. Plus, I'd like to talk to you more about the position while we have the time."

I swallow and nod my head. *You need this job, Charlotte. Don't let seeing them ruin this for you. As soon as the game is over, you can escape. There's no way they can follow you. They will be in the locker room.* I go to respond to John as the woman I saw Eli speaking to approaches us.

"Congratulations, you two, you have been randomly selected to come to the locker room after the game and meet the team."

John stands up and does a little jump, and the surrounding men look jealous but in awe at the same time. "You're serious?" he asks.

"Yes, you can buy merchandise to be signed at the kiosk. And you will have twenty minutes with the team. I will come collect you before the third period is over."

"Oh, John, you should bring one of the fans with you instead of me."

"Nonsense. Let's go to the kiosk." The woman smiles at us and then shakes her head.

"I will need to take a picture of your ID for security purposes."

I furrow my brows, and John takes out his license, so I do the same. She takes a picture of both of our IDs and gives us a smile before handing John her card with her number on it, in case she is late getting to us.

"I think this is a sign that the job is yours," John says, and my cheeks heat. Fuck.

"Seriously?"

"Seriously. Let's go get something for them to sign." John seems like a pretty decent guy to work for. My options are limited with not finishing school, and it seems like there may be an opportunity for advancement. However, there's no way that I'm stepping foot in that locker room. I'll go along with John until the time to go in comes, and I'll figure out my escape plan.

John puts a hand on my shoulder and directs me through the crowd to where all the merchandise is being sold. As far as sports gear goes, they actually have some pretty cute options. John refuses to let me walk away without choosing something. So I pick the navy hoodie with the embroidered fox logo with the word Foxes underneath.

Before we head back to our seats, John gets a beer, and I get a seltzer with my newly twenty-one-year-old status. Maybe some alcohol will give me an idea of how the fuck I'm going to get out of this and still get this job.

The buzzer for the next period starts. I have to sit through the rest of the game wanting to disappear. I have three sets of eyes that continually glance over at me. Luckily, they are winning by a lot, and I don't seem to be the distraction that I was when I came to their last game.

John gets us another drink during the third period, and I feel a little buzzed. Not enough to make a fool of myself, but it does help with my nerves. Throughout the game, John takes time to tell me about himself and the company. He doesn't ask me a lot of questions, and I'm grateful.

At this moment, I don't think I could form a coherent sentence. Not as I watch them skate on the ice and think about our history. I shake my head. I'll always be second best to hockey. There's no competing with a passion like that. There's no way they will be faithful to me on the road. I'm nothing but a distraction. And the root of it all is I don't deserve to be happy.

My heart sinks at the three-minute mark of the last period when the woman I now know as Lori comes to collect us to go to the locker room.

I spent too much time drinking and daydreaming to think of my escape route. John puts a hand on my lower back, which makes me grimace as he directs me to follow Lori to the locker room.

Chapter Thirty-One

The entire game is a blur of clashing bodies, terrible calls, and staring at Charlotte. Out of all of us, I probably keep my cool the best. Mikael is extra violent on the ice tonight, and Eli is making stupid mistakes. Mikael is angry at Charlotte and says that he doesn't want her back after she ended things. Eli had lost all hope and thought that this plan was stupid, and it wouldn't pan out the way that I wanted to.

Meanwhile, I've never lost faith. I'm not sure what made Charlotte disappear. Trust me, I've tried begging Piper for answers, and I've even tried calling Charlotte's mom, with no response. I know whatever spooked her, it was only a matter of time before we would win her back.

So I hatched a crazy fucking plan, and it's worked. Our agent, Jake, wasn't happy, and even though Mikael might be bitter and Eli was feeling hopeless, they agreed. Eli probably lost the most out of all of us to make this happen. He was going to be the Lightning's next big franchise player. Not that he might not be for the Foxes, but as the first pack contract in the NHL, our combined paycheck is less than what Eli was going to be making on the Lightning.

Mikael was just happy to stick together and not go back to Canada. The fact that we could somehow manage to all be on the same team was a near impossibility. But it seems like we continue to beat the odds every time. By making the NHL, having a scent match, and now playing together. Our timeline is a little fucked up now. We were hoping that maybe after we got a little more comfortable on the team, we would be able to win her back. Eli put a PI on retainer, seeing as Piper wouldn't tell us exactly where they were living. But it just so happens that the expansion team in Connecticut was also in the same town as the college we knew Piper would be going to.

The Foxes needed a goalie desperately, seeing as the goalie that they took from the Penguins suffered a serious injury right before the season started. So we had Jake talk with our respective teams and see if we could negotiate a pack contract for us all to play together and be in one place. The contract is good for three years, and we get a combined pack salary. They can't trade us individually, they have to trade us as a pack. It seemed like the only solution for us to play hockey and have our Omega. Honestly, if I had to choose, I would leave hockey to win her back if she asked me to.

Not having her these past few months has been torture. I miss talking to her, holding her, hearing her laugh. I know deep down that she's not okay and has probably been hurt by whatever she's going through. It cuts that she ran. I know we fucked up in Vegas. But I still just don't understand why, why she didn't just talk to us and tell us she was upset. It just doesn't add up. Charlotte was adamant about making this work, that you don't run away from your scent match, but she did.

Eli was smart in having Lori tell Charlotte and that old dude she's with that we're inviting them to the locker room. Mikael, of course, automatically assumed that Charlotte was on a date, but I know Charlotte. She didn't look comfortable with that man at all. He's pretty big, but I don't think he's an Alpha. One thing I know about Charlotte is if she was going to date again, which I don't think she is, it would be with an Alpha.

We're in the locker room, Coach Persson giving us feedback and kudos for the game. It was a shutout, and I feel pride swell in my chest that this is the game Charlotte got to see. Most of my gear is off, including my jersey, chest pads, and skates. My chest is bare, and my legs are still covered as I sit on the bench. My heart is racing from the adrenaline of the game and the thought that I'm going to be near Charlotte again.

Mikael and Eli are whisper-arguing next to me.

"You fucking invited her to the locker room with that old fucker. What were you thinking?"

"I was thinking that our scent match is here, and we need to talk to her and figure out what's going on with her. Why did she leave us, and how can we fix it?"

"Fuck that. She's clearly moved on. She left us, Eli. It's time to move on."

I scoff at Mikael's words. Why is he so fucking stubborn?

"Don't be a fucking idiot, Mikael. You and I know she wouldn't leave without a reason."

"She didn't even do it to our face. Give us a chance to talk? She just vanished. What makes you think she wants to talk to you?" Mikael sneers.

"She sat through the game, didn't she?" Mikael glares at me, and Eli smiles, clearly liking my train of thought.

"You two stay here. I'll go see if Lori has brought them down." I glance around the locker room. "Everyone put your dick away. We're about to have company." A bunch of my teammates scoff, but they do as I say, protecting their modesty. Lori passes through the locker room and points her thumb toward the hallway.

"They're right outside. Seems like she's trying to get out of the situation."

I grunt and nod my head at Lori as I softly open the door and hear their conversation. Charlotte's back is against the brick wall as the older man has an arm against the wall, looking down at her.

"Come on, Charlotte. I'm looking for a team player for this position. Don't you want to prove to me how good you can be as an employee?"

"I'm sorry, John. I appreciate the opportunity, but I just can't go in there."

"Aw, come on, Charlotte. I thought Omegas were supposed to be obedient." His fingers touch a lock of her hair, and I lose it. I march up to the man and push him so hard he falls on his ass.

"Don't touch her," I say, pointing down at the man.

His hands are up in surrender as he sputters, "Sorry. I must have had too many beers. All I wanted was for her to come into the locker room with me." Yeah, sure, that's all this fucker wanted.

"Then go into the locker room by yourself. Leave Charlotte the fuck alone."

He nods, getting to his feet and skittering to the locker room. I turn to Charlotte and instinctively go to touch her face. She shrinks away and shakes her head.

"It's okay, *Kulta*. I'm here now."

She shakes her head, and her fists are balled against her sides.

"You're here now?" She laughs sarcastically, definitely not in a funny way as she puts more space between us. "You're here now?"

"He was hitting on you and trying to make you do something you didn't want to do."

"He was going to be my boss!"

I furrow my brows and shake my head at her, wondering how she is supposed to manage finishing up school and holding a job. "Well then, I did you a favor. That asshole is a scumbag."

"I needed that job, A—" She stops herself from saying my name.

"What do you need, Charlotte? I'll give you whatever you need. Please, can we just talk?"

"What do I need?" she says with a venom I've never heard from her before. She scoffs and walks away from me. I grab her by the arm and spin her. "What do I need!" she shouts as she spins around, her blonde hair whipping me in the face.

"What I needed were my Alphas by my side when I was grieving over my dead mother. But they were out partying with their new agent. I saw all the pictures on your agent's Instagram story. While I watched my mom die next to me, you three were surrounded by women and celebrating a future without me. What I needed was this fucking job, because I'm broke and didn't go back to school and Piper pays for everything. What I need is for you three to leave me the fuck alone, because it will never work."

My mouth drops, and my heart sinks. "Charlotte." I'm at a loss for words. Her mom? "Kathy?"

I swear I hear a sob start in her throat, but she quickly swallows it down. "Leave me alone. I'm not your Omega anymore." She turns away from me, and I don't stop her as she walks through the tunnel and leaves the stadium. This is worse than I ever thought it could be. The person in front of me didn't seem like my Charlotte, my *Kulta*.

I knew deep down that something bad had to have happened for her to run away, but I never expected that it would have been this bad. Never could have imagined that having our phones locked in a safe could cause this much damage in our lives. She's been suffering with this for so long.

My ass is on the floor before I know it, my fingers tangled in my hair and my face on my knees as I try to compute everything that she just said. She feels like we abandoned her in the worst moment of her life. Charlotte's biggest fear is being abandoned, and we did it when the most important person in her life was lost. *Fuck.*

Eli is shaking my forearm, and Mikael is next to him, staring down at me in the hallway when I'm out of my daze. "Where is she?" Eli asks hopefully.

I look back up at both of them, wondering if they can see the forming tears in my eyes. "It's worse than we could have ever imagined." Mikael's brows are furrowed, and Eli looks at me in fear as I tell them everything Charlotte said.

All I know is that I need to find a way to take that hurt look off of her face. A way to make this better. I don't care what has to be done. Charlotte is mine, and I'm not letting her go or letting her hurt for another minute.

"We need a plan," Eli says, and I nod my head. Mikael stands, dusting off his pants.

"Leave her alone, that's what she asked for."

Eli and I both gape at him. "Did you not just hear what she said? Her mom fucking died."

"She doesn't want us. How can she make that any more fucking clear to you two? I'm devastated to hear about Kathy. But when Charlotte could have leaned on us, she left. Everyone fucking leaves. God, you two are so fucking naïve. I'll see you back at home."

"Jesus Christ, how did we get stuck with the most stubborn Alpha and Omega?" Eli asks.

"How are we going to fix this, Eli?"

He sighs and leans his head back against the wall. "I don't know, but I did get her address."

"How?"

"Told Lori to tell them we needed their IDs to come down to the locker room." He holds up his phone and shows me the address.

"We missed her birthday," I say sadly when I see the date. Not that she didn't miss ours too.

"I think we just need to show her that even though she ran, we did everything we could to be better for her."

I nod my head, liking this plan. "Let's give her a few days to cool off."

"Probably a good idea," Eli says, even though all I can think about is driving over there right now and standing outside of her door until she lets me in.

"We'll figure it out," I say. It feels like déjà vu to all the times we promised each other that we would make this relationship work after we were drafted. And it feels like the odds are stacked further against us this time.

CHARLOTTE

Chapter Thirty-Two

My ride home feels like a blur as I finally open the townhouse door, throwing my purse inside and letting Hank out front to do his business. I sit on the front steps and wrap my arms around my body. The cold late-October air cools my skin, and I sigh.

Hazelnuts.

His scent. I didn't realize how much I missed it, how all-consuming it was to be around Anders. The look on his face when I word vomited everything. The way his face fell when I told him about my mom. When his hand wrapped around my arm, I felt the warmth, and I craved it.

That's the problem with scent matches. They make you need them; you become addicted to them, and then, when you need them the most, they aren't there. But the look on his face was one of sadness, not anger or irritation with me. Anders has always been the most in tune with my needs, and he let me go tonight. He let me shout at him and be cruel to him, and he didn't push me. Anders didn't force me to stay; he didn't chase after me and beg me to come back. I don't know what's worse, Anders giving me what I want or the fact that the deep-rooted Omega part of me wanted him to chase me.

I can still scent him on me. It's thick and heavy, like I'm swimming in a hazelnut latte. I should wash it off, but I don't. Instead I let Hank inside and sit by the fridge with a bag of shredded Monterey jack cheese, cookie dough, and a can of Pringles. I rotate between the three and hope that maybe salmonella will take me out before I have to actually process my feelings.

Being numb was so convenient. I shut down the feelings of regret over walking away. It was easier to be angry at them and push them away, avoid them, the emotions that are tangled up in them, and how I'm dealing—or not dealing with my mother's death. It's easier to shove it down, to protect myself from these feelings. I know if I let myself feel everything, if I process everything that's happened, I don't know if I'll be able to pick myself up again.

I give Hank a fist full of cheese before trickling a handful into my mouth. That's how Piper finds me. In our dark kitchen, on the floor, stuffing my face with junk and petting Hank.

"Uh, Charles. Interview didn't go well?"

I scoff, shoving a hefty piece of uncooked cookie dough into my mouth and wondering about my chances of getting sick off of it. "No, it didn't."

Piper sits down on the floor next to me, petting Hank and slowly taking my method of expiration away from me. "You know this is the bake or eat kind, right?"

"Well, that takes away part of the fun." Piper's eyebrows furrow, and she looks at me in confusion. I can hear a purr start in her chest, and I scoff.

"Piper, just stop. You're not my Alpha. No one is. You don't have to take care of me."

"I'm your best friend, and you're on the floor eating junk and looking sad. Sue me for caring and making sure that you're okay, Charlie. For fuck's sake, it's not like I don't have my own shit going on." That's when it hits me that I'm being such a bitch. I'm pushing away the one person who has put up with my shit continually and always makes sure that I'm okay.

"Pipes, I'm sorry. I saw them tonight."

"What?" Her eyes are wide, and she bites her fingernails. It's one of Piper's biggest tells. I always know if she's nervous or lying when she bites her nails. "Yeah, John asked me to meet him at the Foxes' game." Her biting stops, and her cheeks are covered in a red blush. "Piper, did you know?"

"What do you mean?" she asks in a small voice.

"Did you know they were all in Connecticut?"

"Listen, let me explain." I'm on my feet and walking to my bedroom when she grabs my arm and spins me in the hallway. "I knew you telling them to fuck off after your mom was a mistake. That you would regret it. But I knew you needed time. So, yeah, I keep them up-to-date. Well, Anders and Eli. I let them know that you're okay and when I think you would be ready to reconcile."

"You've been texting them?"

"I don't tell them anything personal, Charlie. Just that you're sad and not coping well and you wouldn't be ready to accept them. They told me they were working on a pack trade to come and play for the New Haven Foxes. They weren't going to try anything until later in the season and after you've gone to therapy longer."

I gape at her and pull my arm away. "You told them I'm in therapy?"

"No, Charlie. I just told them that you're not in a good place. I didn't even tell them about your mom. Just that you're not in a good place and that until they are the Alphas you deserve, you aren't ready to see them."

"That wasn't your place, Piper," I say her name with a little more disdain than she deserves.

"I know it wasn't. But fuck, Charles. I've watched you spiral for months. You're the shell of the person you used to be. Your mom wouldn't have wanted that for you. She loved the guys and wanted you to be happy when she was gone."

"Don't bring her up," I say in a small voice. I'm on the edge of tears, almost letting everything flood me to the point I can't breathe. I push it down, deep down, to where it doesn't hurt.

"It's true. Why do you think she canceled her insurance? She knew you were going to be taken care of. Your mom would hate it, knowing that you used her death to run away from your scent matches."

I've had enough at that point. I don't say another word to my best friend. Sometimes growing up is knowing when to walk away before you say something you can't take back. I slam my door behind me and lock it for good measure. I crack the window on the side wall and light my weed pen, smoking just enough to help me sleep through the night.

Part of me knows that Piper's right. But who does she think she is, taking care of me like that or making decisions for me? She's told them what a mess I am, and that they need to leave me alone. It's what I wanted. I wanted to leave them in the past, because they weren't there for me and I would never be first.

I sound like a fucking broken record. It might be the weed or the events of today when I come to the conclusion that I pushed them away because I don't want to be happy. I don't deserve to be happy when she's not here, and it feels like it's all my fault.

Piper is busy with school stuff today, and I'm happy about it. More time for me to stew alone at home. I spend a good two hours looking for job listings online, narrowing down my searches by Omega friendly work environment, work from home, and HS diploma. I'm twenty-five credits short of getting my bachelor's degree, but many dollars short of being able to afford even online school.

There's this overwhelming presence around me telling me what a failure I am all the time, and it keeps me from wanting to do anything about it. I let my mom down. I'm not a good Omega, I'm not a good enough dog mom, and I'm a dropout with no job for my best friend to support me.

Sometimes I wonder what the point of all of this is. I wish my mom were here to give me one of her warm hugs and her advice. My mom had the best advice on the planet. I would do anything just to talk to her one more time.

I feel melancholy as my phone vibrates.

Piper:

Don't forget, tonight is Halloween. Candy is in the pantry.

I'll set it out.

Piper:

Okay, turning my phone off. Big test tomorrow.

Things feel tense, no, things are tense, and I know I only have myself to blame. I grab the popcorn bowl and fill it up with the candy from the pantry and sit it on the bench by our front door while I brush my hair and maybe put some makeup on. Maybe seeing trick-or-treaters will help my mood.

I go with black sweatpants and a long black T-shirt. Piper has some old cat ears in her bedroom, and I'm about to go find them when I hear a gurgling noise from the living room.

"Piper?" I shout as I walk down the hallway to the living room. On the floor is a panting and groaning Hank. I get down on my knees and stroke his fur. "Hank, what's wrong, baby?"

His tongue is hanging out of his mouth and when I press my hand against his chest, his heart rate is through the roof.

"Do you need to go outside?" I ask. Usually, the word outside has him up in a flash. But he doesn't move. I try to move him myself, but he doesn't budge. I look around the room and don't see anything, until he hacks up what looks like a fully wrapped Hershey bar. "Oh, fuck. No, no, no."

I grab my phone and call Piper. It immediately goes to voicemail. "Fuck." I call the vet next, and the receptionist answers on the third call.

"Sound Veterinary Clinic, this is MaryJane, how can I assist you today?"

"My dog, Hank Hodges. He ate chocolate, and he won't get up. He's panting, and his heart rate is super fast."

"Do you know how much he ate?"

I look over at the wrappers. "Probably a few pieces, including the wrappers."

"Can you bring him in immediately?" she asks. I can tell she's trying to stay calm for me. I nod, and she asks me the question again.

"I'll figure it out. I'll get him there."

"Okay, I'll make sure he gets right in with the doctor as soon as he gets here."

"Thank you." I hang up the phone and kneel over Hank, petting his fur and trying to figure out how the fuck I'm going to get him to the vet. It feels like I'm ready to blow. I hold it back. I want to cry so badly, but if I do, I'll never get Hank out of here, and I'll never stop crying.

The doorbell rings, and I groan, forgetting about trick-or-treating. But when I open the door, it's the biggest relief I've felt in weeks.

ELI

Chapter Thirty-Three

"This isn't a good idea," Anders says.

"What, like she's going to make a scene in front of a bunch of trick-or-treaters?"

"You didn't see her face, Eli. I'm not sure she's ready."

"If she won't listen to me, then fine. But I've got to try."

"Alright, but I don't want to hear you bitch about the fact that she turned you away."

I roll my eyes. Anders was all team Let's Win Charlotte Back ASAP, to now being like, let's give her as much space as she needs. Fuck that. I let Charlotte get away from me once, and I'm ready to make things right. Our Omega, our girl, is fucking hurting, and she needs to stop being so stubborn and let us in.

Her townhouse is right outside of Yale. It's a nice street, and I'm glad that Piper found them decent living arrangements. She would be much happier at our house though. It's perfect for her, we made sure of it.

There's no decoration for Halloween on the property, and I wonder if they just didn't have time or if neither of them is in the spirit this year. There are a couple of children wandering down the street collecting candy, and I wonder if I should wait until a group goes up to Charlotte's house. Not wanting to wait a second longer, I unhitch the gate and walk to the front door and ring the doorbell. It doesn't take long for her to answer.

"Thank fuck you're here. Do you have a car?" She's frantic and tugs me by the cuff of my long sleeve shirt.

"Char." She winces at my nickname but says nothing. "What's going on?"

She hiccoughs, and she looks like she's ready to cry, but she shakes her head and brings me into their small living room. It's then that I see Hank lying on the floor. It's immediately clear that he's not okay by the way he is panting and whining.

"He..." Charlotte composes herself again. "He ate some of the Halloween chocolate and the wrappers. I don't have a car or a way to get him to the vet."

I can't help it as my chest purrs, and I touch Charlotte's shoulder. She doesn't back away from the touch, and I consider that a win. "My car's out front. Grab your stuff, and I'll carry Hank out." Charlotte hurries to get her belongings while I scoop Hank up bridal style, keeping him close to my chest as Charlotte opens the front door.

"Keys are in my pocket. Can you open the back door?" Charlotte doesn't even think twice as she digs into my pocket, unlocks the car, and opens the back door. I lay a blanket down for Hank as I put him on the seat and gently shut the door. I open the passenger's side door for Charlotte, and she gets in as I round the vehicle and get in.

"Which vet?"

"Sound Vet Clinic." I put it into my phone, and we're only ten minutes away. The car ride is silent, and I watch as Charlotte eyes Hank in the backseat every few minutes.

"I'm so fucking stupid. I just left the candy out there. I'm so fucking careless."

"Hey." I touch her shoulder, and she lets me. She doesn't cry, and it's a little jarring to see her so upset without outwardly showing it. "You're not stupid. Mistakes happen."

"I can't do anything right."

"Char, we're going to be at the vet in a few minutes. Hank will be fine."

"He's all I have."

I want to slam on my brakes and tell her that isn't true. She broke my heart, but I'm still here, and I'd do whatever she asked of me. Especially now that I know more of the story, a lot of my anger has vanished. All I want is my girl back and happy again. "He's definitely not all you have, but I promise he'll be okay."

She doesn't say anything, choosing silence for the rest of the ride.

As soon as we get to the clinic, I take the closest parking spot, and we both get out, and I take Hank into my arms. He seems worse than when we originally put him in.

"Baby, I'm so sorry," Charlotte says to Hank, stroking his ears back as she talks with the receptionist.

"Good thing I've been lifting, buddy. You better be good because I promised her you would be. So do me a solid, yeah?" Hank groans in my arms as the receptionist takes us back to a room. She instructs me to put Hank on the floor as the vet comes in.

"Alright, this isn't going to be pretty. If Mom and Dad can go wait out in the lobby," the vet says. Charlotte doesn't correct her, just kisses Hank's head one more time before we go and sit out in the lobby. Charlotte is silent, her knee bouncing up and down as she waits. I feel hopeless again, like I don't know the first thing about what an Omega needs when I look at her now.

She looks sad and defeated. She's put on a little more weight, and she wears it deliciously. I feel like a complete creep for looking at her like this when we're at the vet's office.

Charlotte makes a whimpering noise, and I put my hand on her back. She stills, but doesn't tell me to stop touching her. I keep quiet, knowing that if I speak, I might ruin it, or she might push me away. I just rub her back and physically show her that I'm here and not going anywhere. It must be an hour after we've brought Hank in that the receptionist finally calls Charlotte to come back to the room.

I keep my hand on her back, and she doesn't tell me to stop. Hank is sleeping on the ground, his chest rising and falling, and I let out a relieved breath.

"Hank is going to be fine. We had to give him some activated charcoal to induce vomiting to get some of the chocolate out of his system. I didn't notice any tremors or seizures, but because of the amount of chocolate consumed, we would like to keep him overnight to monitor him."

Charlotte nods but doesn't speak, so I do for her.

"Okay, thank you so much."

"MaryJane can go over the details with you up front." I pet Hank's head, and Charlotte gets down on her knees and strokes his fur and kisses his face. I can hear her whispering apologies to him, and it makes my heart sink. She finally stands, and we make our way up to the front desk where MaryJane hands her some forms. "You will need to sign here, here, and here, for giving us permission for emergency treatment." Charlotte signs. "This last form is the bill. With the overnight stay, it's going to be eight hundred and fifty dollars."

Charlotte rubs her forehead with the back of her hand and sighs. "Do you do finance options?" she asks quietly.

"Put it on this card," I say, sliding my Amex over to MaryJane. Charlotte looks at me with a frown on her face but says nothing. MaryJane smiles and nods, swiping my card and giving it back.

"Hank should be ready for pickup at 10 a.m."

Charlotte nods and walks out the door. I follow her, and she gets in the passenger's side without letting me open her door. The drive back to her house is quiet and awkward. I just want my Charlotte back. She's not yelling at me or telling me to go fuck myself, so I'll take what I can get.

Once I'm parked in front of her house, she turns to me. "You shouldn't have paid for that."

"It's not a big deal. I wanted to."

"Hank isn't your responsibility."

"No, but you are." It slips out before I have a second to even think about what I wanted to say.

"I'm not. I thought I made that clear."

"I'm not going anywhere, Charlotte. You can push me away, tell me you hate me, tell me that this will never work. But all we've done since you left was find a way to get you back."

"Why would you want me now?" she says. It's the first time I see tears in her eyes.

"Charlotte, what are you talking about, baby?" She shakes her head, and it looks like she's trying to stifle her emotions again. I reach out and tuck a piece of hair behind her ear. "We will always want you. Please let us in, let us help you."

"I don't deserve it," she mumbles, and that's when the floodgates open. Big fat tears roll down her face. She tries to wipe them off before I can see them. "Hank almost died today because I was careless. My mom died because I was careless. I ran away from you because I was fucking careless. And now..." She sniffles and sucks in her sobs. "Now I don't even know who I am. Who would want to be with me? I don't even like to be with me."

I've had enough as I unbuckle her seatbelt and tug on her. She resists slightly but finally gives way as I tug her to my chest. My purrs are so deep and intense that it rattles both of our chests as I stroke her back. Her tears wet my shirt as she lets it all out. It's like she's been an active volcano about to erupt for some time, and now it's finally all spilling over.

"I'll always care for you, Charlotte. I'll always want you."

She shakes her head and continues crying horrific sobs, so much worse than that one day in the nest.

"I need to go inside."

"You shouldn't be alone right now."

"Please, Eli." Her voice is soft and pleading.

"I'll come by after the morning skate tomorrow to come pick up Hank." She doesn't argue with me, and I take that as a win. She let me help her, take care of her, and she confided in me. Charlotte is in a lot more pain than I realized. It fucking breaks me to see her like this. "After tomorrow, do you think we could talk?"

"Can I think about it?" I nod, pushing her hair out of her face. Her scent is faint, but fuck, it does something to me. I've missed everything about her, but now more than ever, all I want is to see her happy. I want my teasing, smartass Charlotte back. I thought I put in a lot of work to be a worthy Alpha before now, but now it's time to get serious.

I walk Charlotte to her door. I want to hug her tight, but I don't push my luck. "Tomorrow," she whispers, the faintest of smirks on her face.

"Tomorrow," I reply. She wipes a tear from her face and shuts the door. Every Alpha instinct inside of me is begging me to knock down the door and take her into my arms until everything is better. Knowing that isn't what she wants, or at least is what she's outwardly telling me she doesn't want, I leave, sending a text to Piper before I go.

> Hank ate chocolate, took him to the vet. He's going to be fine.

> Charlotte is at home crying. Can you check on her and let me know that she is okay?

I don't get a text back, so I do what any rational Alpha would do. I sit in my car outside of her house until I hear back.

CHARLOTTE

Chapter Thirty-Four

I don't stop crying; it floods out of me like a dam as I walk through the house and go to my bedroom. My shirt now smells like fresh pine needles. I'm so fucking weak as I take it off and collect my shirt from the hockey game that smells like Anders. I crumple them under my head like a pillow and bawl my eyes out. It's the hardest, most cathartic cry I've had in my life. I know I sound like a dying animal, and I'm at least happy that Piper and Hank aren't here to witness it.

All the feelings of the past few months pour out of me. How much I miss my mom, and how much anger I have about how she died, how I didn't get to say goodbye, and how I blame myself. I know that I haven't been thinking rationally since that day, and it makes my heart hurt. The sobs won't stop. I'm not even sure if fresh tears are coming out of my eyes or if my face is just wet from all the crying. I soak the two shirts below me, and then I cry even harder because their scents aren't as strong.

Eli held me tonight even though I ran away. Even though I said horrible things to Anders. He still showed me so much compassion and kindness. I'm not mad about the Vegas trip anymore, I know that. It hurt in the moment, knowing that they were oblivious to my pain. But rationally, I know it wasn't malicious intent. It was three men who just got drafted into the NHL celebrating, like I told them to. The reality of the fact that I've been suffering these last four months, and more than likely they have too hits me, and it's my fault.

Everything feels like my fault lately, and it's hard to really take a deeper look at myself. I was so afraid of being abandoned by them that I was the one who ran away and caused my biggest fear to come to light. Piper was right, my mom would be so disappointed in me right now. She would be so upset that I used her death to push away the three people who were meant for me. My scent matches. Part of me wonders how much of my disassociation and actions were a factor of the high grade suppressants I was on. Now that I'm on a significantly lower dose, I'm feeling everything, and it fucking hurts. It hurts to think about my mom and *them*.

I don't know all the details, but clearly whatever strings they had to pull to be on the same team couldn't have been easy. I push the shirts against my face, trying to scent them just a little better. But there's nothing left. I've washed away their scents, and I feel devastated. It's the first time I've let myself truly feel the weight of the last few months, and it's so heavy I feel like it might crush me. But it feels like I can breathe for the first time in months, realizing what I've done and how I feel. Maybe the absence of them made it easier for me to rationalize staying away for so long. But seeing Anders, Eli, and Mikael. Having Anders touch my arm and protect me and having Eli take care of me today... To scent them again?

I'm so fucking stupid.

It seems like Eli and Anders might forgive me and take me back, but there's no guarantee, especially when it comes to Mikael.

I wipe my face and put a shirt and sweater back on. I'm not sure what compels me to go back outside, but I didn't hear Eli leave. When I walk outside, his SUV is still there. The lights are off, and the windows are tinted. I inhale deeply and knock on the driver's side window. He doesn't roll it down, he just opens the door instead.

"You okay? What do you need?" Ah, fuck, I cry again. He gets out of the SUV, and his hands are on my upper arms. "Charlotte, what do you need?"

"Can you come inside?"

He nods his head, rubbing my arms one more time before he shuts his car door and locks it, then he follows me back into the house. I don't know what to say, where to start. So I don't. I just lead him to my bedroom and lie on the bed. He follows me, and we both lie on top of the covers and stare at each other. His green eyes are full of concern, and I breathe a few deep breaths before I speak. His thick pine scent in my room feels so right, and all I can think about is how much I've denied myself, denied all of us, in my grief.

"I haven't cried in about four months. I think everything with Hank made everything come up to the surface."

He nods, his hand on top of mine in the center of the bed. "I really fucked up, Eli." I can't help the horrific noise that escapes out of me. My fucking heart hurts, but as Eli pulls me against his chest, the rumble of his purr soothes me.

"I... I don't even know where to start."

"You don't have to say anything tonight, baby," he says softly. His chest rumbling affectionately as he strokes my back.

"I don't know how to make this better, how to make me better."

"You're not broken." That makes me sob even more.

"I am, Eli. I'm so fucking broken I can barely get by day to day. Sometimes I don't even get out of bed or brush my teeth. Sometimes I wish that I could just be sedated until these feelings go away. And right now, I feel like I've ruined everything and deserve to be this way."

He pushes my face closer to his chest. There isn't a part of us that isn't touching. "Charlotte, I don't know what to say that would help. I just want you to know that I'm here. I'm not going anywhere."

"Why are you being so nice?"

He kisses the top of my head, and I shiver. "You're my Omega, Charlotte. That never stopped. I knew something bad must have happened for you to disappear on us. I'm so fucking sorry about Kathy. She was the kind of mom I always wished I had."

I sniffle at the mention of my mom's name. "It was worse when I saw the Instagram stories and none of you had answered the phone."

He backs away from me slightly on the bed, giving us about a foot of space as he looks at me, his brow furrowed in confusion. "The what?"

"When we couldn't reach you, I looked at your agent's Instagram. There were pictures of you all partying, and Betas were all around you in the pictures. That, on top of your parents and so many other people telling me that this would never work out, I guess I just thought it would be easier to end it there. I was already on the suppressants and felt so numb, I thought I was protecting myself."

"Fuck," he grumbles, pulling me closer to his chest again. "I didn't know there were pictures. You have to know that we would never cheat on you. None of us have touched anyone else since we last saw each other. You're it for us. But I can see how seeing those pictures would hurt you. I'm so fucking sorry, baby." I cry softly at his acknowledgement of what they did as being hurtful. Even if what I did was worse, I wasn't in a state of mind to see rationally. I don't even know if I am now. "I would do anything for you. I wish that we could have been there for you. I hate knowing you've been hurting all this time."

"It really hurts." And it does. It feels like I've cut my heart out and presented it to Eli on my bed. Hearing someone say my mom's name, thinking about that night and the past couple of months, it hurts deeply. It's like I was in a cloud of fog that suddenly cleared, and I can see my life for what it truly is. A complete fucking mess that feels like it's my own doing. I could have had this—this sweet Alpha wrapping his arms around me and comforting me this whole time. I suffered alone. Why? Because of guilt? Because I was so afraid they would hurt me that I hurt myself instead?

I want this pain to go away. I don't want to feel it. Part of me wishes I could get back on the high dosage suppressants, but another part of me knows that I need to sit in this pain and reflection. The only way I'm going to heal and move forward is to truly feel the weight of everything. I cry softly with all these thoughts raging in my mind.

Eli pets my hair, his scent is heavy in the room, and I wonder if he's projecting because of my distress. I don't deserve him, but at this moment the only thing making me feel somewhat like everything will be okay is his presence. I push myself so close to his chest that all I can smell is pine. He pets my hair and whispers softly to me, "Get some rest, Charlotte. I've got you."

"Stop, or you're going to make me start sobbing again."

"If that's what you need," he says and just like that, I'm crying again. I hate this so much, but at some point I must cry myself to sleep.

"Char, baby," a soft voice says. It's definitely a dream. There's no way Eli's in my bed. I must still be sleeping. "I've got to go to morning skate. I'll be back later to help you pick up Hank."

Yesterday and last night come flooding back to me, and I blink my eyes open, which sting like a motherfucker. I wince, and two giant hands are on my cheeks. "What's wrong?"

"Slept with my contacts on, fuck." I roll my eyes and blink a few times before I give up and have to take them out. Eli is a blur in front of me, which just adds to the theory that this isn't real. "Just you, this afternoon?"

"Yeah, just me. I won't bring Anders or Mikael." I nod, not knowing if that's what I truly want. All I know for certain is I wish Eli wasn't leaving me right now.

"What time is it?"

"Five-thirty. Go back to bed, baby."

I'm groggy as I lie back down but hold on to his hand. "You'll be back?"

"I'll be back." He kisses my hair before leaving, and I can't help the feeling of being empty all over again. At least I'm not fucking crying again.

He's been gone for about ten minutes, and I wish Hank's giant body was on the bed with me. It's then that the mattress dips. I smell her before she says anything. Piper smells like citrus, and while I'm not drawn to it, it's comforting to me.

My friend spoons me from behind, holding me close. "You okay, Charles?"

"Hank," I say in a pathetic voice.

"Eli told me everything. Can't say I was shocked to see him."

"I'm sorry," I say. We've been friends for so long that she knows what I mean. I'm sorry for yelling at her and treating her like I did the other day. She knows me better than anyone else. She was only looking out for me, and I'm starting to see where she's coming from.

"I just want you to be happy."

"I'm not sure how to do that anymore," I say with a sigh.

"Just take it day by day. How did it make you feel to be around one of them again?"

I clear my throat and really think about it. "Like I've been asleep for the last four months and I finally just woke up again."

She nods her head behind me. "I'm always going to be here for you, no matter what. But I saw the look on Eli's face this morning.

It was like he would rather eat his own hand than leave you. Maybe give them a chance, and maybe bring them to therapy with you."

I scoff, thinking about Janet and how we have an appointment today. "Janet would love that."

"No offense, but I've never seen you hate someone like you hate Janet. Why?"

"She's a nosy bitch."

Piper laughs behind me. "Maybe you should stop thinking of Janet as someone who is out to get you and someone who's there to help you and maybe, just maybe, she'll be able to help you through this."

"Ew, when did you get so pragmatic?"

"Ugh, it must be medical school." She laughs, and I do the same. Some of the weight that was piling on my chest falls off piece by piece. This is the easiest conversation Piper and I have had in months.

"Thank you for being my person, Piper."

"Always," she says, giving me a tight squeeze. I don't know how I got the most amazing best friend in the world, or my scent matches. But they're all right. I need to figure out what's going on with me emotionally and with my brain chemistry after being on high dose suppressants for so long. This is me making the changes I need to make. I can't keep living in this dark void. My parents wouldn't want it, and neither do I.

CHARLOTTE

Chapter Thirty-Five

J anet sits across from me, and it's like I see her with clear eyes. I'm not sure why I felt so adversarial to her, but when I look at her now, I think about what Piper said. I'm supposed to be here for help. Janet isn't judging me. She's trying to figure out how to help me. I go through everything that happened last night, and Janet listens carefully.

"Can we go back to the part where you mentioned everything crashing down and feeling like a veil is being ripped off?" Janet asks.

I nod and take a deep breath. If I want to be better, I need to be vulnerable. "It's like everything feels brighter. I feel more, and I can't shut my thoughts or emotions off like I used to on the higher dosage. I still don't feel great, and to be honest, feeling all of this shit sucks. But I feel more like myself again."

Janet writes everything down and looks at me with compassion in her eyes. "I'm going to be sending this to the FDA. Depression is one of the biggest symptoms with this medication, but to the extent you were at, even with an antidepressant, is concerning. I wouldn't recommend this high of a dosage to my patients." I nod and understand where she's coming from, but I also know the state that I was in when my mother passed. This was the best alternative for me. I needed to pause my heat. Hell, I needed to pause my whole life. It just shouldn't have gone on for this long, and I hope the effects aren't detrimental.

"With how you're feeling, I'm not worried about any long-term side effects. I just want to manage your depression and make sure we get you to a place where you feel like yourself again."

I have a new appreciation for Janet, and it's the first time I feel like I can ask for advice. "I'm not sure how to talk to them."

"Your scent matches?" I nod, and she smiles. "Eli seemed more than happy to be with you the other night and take care of you. It doesn't seem like he blames you, and he even took responsibility for their actions and how that made you feel. It sounds like he would love to reconcile and be there for you as long as you would let him."

I nod and know that Anders would feel the same way. But Mikael is never easy, and I don't expect him to be on this either. He asked me not to break him. I remember it like it was yesterday, and I can't help but feel like I did. Janet looks at me like she knows my mind is churning, and if there's any place to let this out, I should do it now.

"I'm afraid to let them back in," I whisper.

"Because you're afraid of giving them the power to hurt you?" I nod, and Janet gives me a gentle smile.

"That's what love is all about, unfortunately. Giving the other person or people the power to hurt you. But it's a risk worth taking, especially in your case. I know that it's not fair that you go into heat or have the physical and emotional needs that you have. But you need Alphas, and the universe gave you scent matches for a reason."

"Because I'm fucking difficult." I didn't mean to say it out loud, but I do.

"It's refreshing to get to see your personality come through finally."

I smile at Janet. She looks like she's seen a ghost, and I guess I've never smiled at the poor woman before.

"Thanks for today, Janet."

"Of course, my homework for you is to list out your fears, but to also list out all your hopes for the future."

I nod and shake her hand before leaving the office. Just like that, it feels like another chunk of weight has been taken off of my chest.

Eli does as he promised and comes to get Hank with me. The big lug seems to be completely fine, and the relief that floods me is visceral. Eli seems a little off from this morning as he drives Hank and I back to the house.

"Eli, is everything okay?"

"Yeah, baby, everything's fine."

"You don't sound fine."

His green eyes glance at me before they are back on the road again. "Anders and Mikael might have gotten into it at practice, but I don't want you to worry about it."

I bite on my thumbnail and think about the time on the lake last winter. "Because of me?"

"I shouldn't have said anything. I'm sorry, don't worry about them. You know how they get." The only reason they would fight is because they disagree, just like last time, and my heart sinks knowing that Anders wants to be with me and that Mikael doesn't.

I feel like crying again, and it pisses me off. Is this going to be me now? Crying over every single fucking thing that reminds me of the past or hurts my feelings. Maybe it's not such a bad thing. I mean, clearly bottling everything up hasn't done fuck all.

A large hand clamps down on my thigh and shocks me back to the present. "Hey, I don't want you worrying about anything, okay?"

"Thank you for always being so good to me."

"You're my girl, of course I'm good to you." He scoffs like I'm being stupid, and it makes me smile.

"Do you have to go back to work after you drop us off?"

He sighs and nods his head. "Yeah, I have to be back at the rink in about an hour."

"Do..." Courage, Charlotte. Get some of your spine back. "Do you think that we could maybe do dinner or something soon?"

Eli beams while he holds the wheel. "I'd love that."

"Maybe even all of us?"

His grin falls. "Anders and I for sure."

History does seem to repeat itself. I sigh and nod my head, proud of myself for taking this step.

Hank is happy to be home as he trots around the house like he owns the place. He nudges Eli's leg in thanks for paying his vet bill, adding a ridiculous amount of slobber to his pants, before he goes into my bedroom to lay on my bed.

"Guess sleeping at the vet wasn't that great," I say, feeling awkward now. I want to fast forward and be as comfortable with Eli as I was in the past, but I know that it won't be so easy.

"So do you think you could maybe unblock my number, so I could text you?" he asks, his cheeks heating, and mine do the same in embarrassment. I nod my head and pull out my phone, then unblock all three of them in my contacts.

Eli smiles and leans over and kisses the side of my head. "Can I text you tonight?"

I smile and feel like I did when we just met and this was all fresh and new. "I'd like that." He nods and awkwardly stands there. What do we do at this stage? To break the tension, I wrap my arms around his waist and squeeze him tightly.

"Thanks for everything with Hank. I'll talk to you tonight." He strokes my back lazily, and I can't believe I've gone without his touch for so long. I feel addicted all over again to his scent, his touch, his everything. I need more Eli time.

He kisses the top of my head one more time before turning and heading back to work.

Eli does text me later in the night, but I feel restless and needy. How I went from acting like they didn't exist to now feeling sad about not having Eli in my bed is jarring. Hank lies on my bed with me, and I pet his head as we watch *Hell's Kitchen* together. Hank is a big

Gordon Ramsey fan, and I hate to admit it, but I get it. What is it about fantasizing about the mean ones who are only nice to you? Yes, I have problems.

There's a soft tap at my window, like a small pebble hitting the glass. It even garners Hank's attention as his face perks up and glances toward the window. I get out of bed and squint out the window to see a very tense Anders pacing back and forth in my front yard. I crack the window open, the November air cold, and I shiver.

"Anders?"

"Hey," he says softly.

"How long have you been out here?"

"A while."

I shake my head and look at him. Guilt is heavy in my stomach when I think about how I yelled at him the other day.

"I'll meet you at the front door." We're no longer sneaking into my mother's house. We can act like civilized adults and use the front door. He nods, and I walk down the hallway to the front. I look down at myself and scoff at what I'm wearing, but don't change as I answer the front door.

God, he looks good. A few dark blond tendrils of hair peek out of his beanie, and he's wearing black sweatpants and a tight hoodie that clings to his chest. There's a small, red bag in his hand, and he holds it to his side as he stands outside.

"Do you want to come in?" He nods and follows me to the living room. As soon as he sits on the couch, Hanks drools all over Anders' crotch in greeting. I try to pull him off, but Anders just smiles and pets him like an old friend he missed, which I guess is true.

"He missed you," I say softly, and Anders rubs the spot behind his ears that Hank likes. Anders' blue eyes meet mine, and he smirks.

"I missed him too. Glad to see he's doing okay."

"I was lucky that Eli came by."

"You know I wanted to come by sooner but didn't know if you wanted me to or not."

I wrap my arms around my legs and rest my chin on my knees. "I haven't been myself lately."

"Eli told me everything. I hope that's okay." I nod. When we were all together, we all told each other everything. We're a pack, and that's just how things go.

"I had a therapy appointment today, and I think I realized just how badly the high dosage suppressants messed me up. It doesn't excuse anything, but I just wanted you to know that I'm not on them anymore, and I'm trying to get back to that Charlotte you all liked."

"I don't care if you've changed. I don't care if you'll never be the same again. You're mine, and I'll do whatever it takes to prove it to you. What happened to Kathy..." He shakes his head back and forth, and I can see the pain in his eyes as he thinks about my mother. I feel it too. "...Your mom was special. I don't know if you knew, but we talked often. She became important to me, and I'm so fucking sorry to hear what happened and that you were there. I got you something."

He holds out the bag next to him and hands it to me. "If it's too imposing, then I can take it back. I just kept thinking about Kathy, and I can't imagine how much you miss her, so I thought I could give you a piece of her."

I furrow my brow, wondering what he has in the bag as he hands it over to me. Once I open it, it's a big black dog stuffed animal. Maybe not as fluffy as Hank is, but still adorable nonetheless. I must look confused as Anders gives me a small smile and squeezes the dog's ear between his two fingers.

My mom's voice starts and my eyes well with tears automatically.

"Anders, sweetie, it's Kathy. I wanted to give you a call and let you know that Charlotte started her drive to Boston. I know she'll be too excited to call me when she gets there. Can you make sure to give me a call to let me know she's safe? We gotta make sure our precious girl is cared for. You kids have fun. Love you."

I tap on the ear three more times, just wanting to hear my mom's voice over and over again. The "love you' at the end of the message clenches my heart every time. I can't think about how many times I've missed her voice and just wanted to hear from her.

Looking up at Anders, his eyes are watery as well. I can see that he truly did care about my mother as much as he said he does. It's comforting to be around people who understand your grief in the person you lost. My mom was special, and to know that Anders knew that as well means everything to me.

I'm silently crying as Anders leans forward, his big hands cupping my jaw as his calloused thumbs wipe the tears falling down my face. The emotion lately has been high, and while I feel sadness over hearing my mom's voice, happiness outweighs it. Being able to hear her voice brings me joy, not hurt like I thought it would. Remembering her won't always bring me hurt, and it's Anders who is helping me realize that.

"I don't know how to say thank you, Anders."

"You don't need to thank me, Charlotte."

His eyes are boring into mine as I shake my head in disagreement. "No, I do. This means so much to me. I thought remembering her and thinking about her would make me feel sad, but hearing her voice again makes me think about all of the amazing conversations I ever had with her. I needed this."

We're in this position for a while, but it's not as uncomfortable as it should be with how much time has separated us. It's soothing, and I feel my heart rate slow and my tears dry up. This man doesn't blame me for anything that happened, he's only looking for ways on how he can fix it. I suppose it's a very Anders type thing to want to do. When I look into his light eyes, all I see is honesty. Maybe I'm a sap and giving in way too fucking easy, but I want his comfort. I want what he wants to give.

I clear my throat. "Maybe I shouldn't have shut you out." Guilt has been consuming me, and I don't know what else to say after his sentimental gesture. He shakes his head, his hands not leaving my face. I can tell he disagrees and that guilt is heavy on his conscience as well.

"Charlotte, we should have done more. You're an Omega, and you were in limbo the entire time we were together. We didn't offer you any security, and Eli told me about the pictures in Vegas. We weren't there when you were at your lowest, and it will always be my biggest regret."

His hands haven't left my face, and his scent is heady and comforting. I haven't had a hazelnut latte in months because it was too painful. Scenting him is like being welcomed back home.

"How exactly did you all find yourself on the same team?" I ask. I've been curious about it since I saw them the other night. And I want to change the subject from being so heavy.

"The Foxes were struggling as an expansion team. They needed a goalie and a stronger offense. So Eli made Jake propose the first ever pack contract, and it worked."

"You knew I was in Connecticut?" He nods his head.

"I've checked in with Piper every week or so, and she told us that you were with her and that you were safe. So, begrudgingly, Jake made the trade happen, and we're all here."

"You were planning on getting me back?"

"It was never a question of if, just when. If I would have known things were so bad, I would have tried sooner. We haven't been the same without you."

He wipes away a rogue tear from my face, and I look at him. This beautiful man doesn't blame me for my behavior, rational or not, who also seems to be grieving after knowing what happened to my mom.

"Does your mom hate me now?" I ask in a soft voice. While I might not have spoken to Eevi as much as Anders talked to my mom, I was excited to meet her in person and have another Omega to relate to.

Anders scoffs and shakes his head. "I got an earful of what idiots we were for going to Vegas in the first place and how not giving you any assurances probably upset your Omega nature."

I let out a puff of breath. At least I have someone I can take off of my apology tour. I thank all the stars in the sky that Anders has an Omega mother, and he seems to get it more than anybody. His thumbs rub gentle circles under my cheekbones, and I breathe in his scent and groan. Falling for Anders was so easy, and when I look deep into myself, my love for them hasn't changed. Even if we never said the words, even though we didn't bond, Anders Larsen owns a piece of my soul and always has. Even when I was a shell of a person, it was his, but now looking at him, I know there's no running away.

"Kiss me," I say softly, and he doesn't hesitate, crashing his lips against mine. The kiss is just as I remember. It's passionate and explorative, but possessive all the same. Anders' full lips feel plush and so right against mine. I take his beanie off and lace my fingers in his hair. I missed the texture and the softness.

"I missed you, *Kulta*," he says, breaking away from the kiss and touching my face so delicately, like I might disappear. I need this, a moment of reprieve from all of this emotional heaviness. I just want to feel good and free and be with someone I know I can trust.

"I promise I'm not going anywhere." And I mean it. Not being with them just brought me more hurt than anything. Having their scents again, their touches, it's everything. Maybe we needed this time to realize what we all had. Maybe I needed this time to come to this conclusion. No, I'm not magically okay, but being with them is making it better. "Can you stay the night?" Anders nods his head and stands up, picking me up in his arms, and I instinctively lock my legs around him. My ankles meet right above his perfect ass.

My hands are in his hair again as he holds my thighs and carries me to the bedroom. I don't know how I forgot how easy being with Anders is. It's like muscle memory being together again. He places me on the bed gently before tearing off his hoodie and shirt. He leaves the sweatpants on. Somehow his chest is even more toned than I remember. It sends a pang of a reminder about my own body, and I suddenly feel self-conscious.

Not only am I not the same girl mentally they were with before, but I've gained some weight since we were last together. It's not that I'm ashamed of my body. If anything, my boobs are bigger and my stomach isn't as flat, but I like how I look. I just don't know how they will feel about it. The fact is, I'm a different Charlotte altogether, and I can't help but feel insecure that they might not like what they see. I put the blanket over me, and Anders furrows his brows.

"What's wrong?"

"I... I just don't look like I used to," I say.

"You look pretty fucking good to me." His hand is on my hip as he drags my body closer to his. His thumb digs into the skin of my hip. "Always so soft and sweet, *Kulta*." He leans forward, and my hands land on his chest as he takes a deep inhale at my collarbone. "Do you know how many times I've touched myself thinking about you? How sexy, beautiful, and perfect to me you are. Don't ever hide yourself from me."

"Okay," I say breathlessly as Anders licks a trail from my shoulder to that delicious spot behind my ear. It's the first in a long time

I've actually felt turned on. My perfume fills the room, and Anders groans. It's at that moment I panic.

Chapter Thirty-Six

C harlotte feels so fucking good under my hands. I don't know what she's nervous about. She looks fucking unreal. My fantasies didn't do her justice. Her tits are bigger, and I want to suck on them for hours, and her hips are softer than I remember. I want to spend all night showing her how much I missed her, how much nothing has changed for me, and how sorry I am for not being the Alpha she deserved.

Somehow this all got fucked up and twisted, but we're all in the process of correcting our wrongs. I know my *Kulta*, my sweet Omega, is not alright. It's clear in the way she speaks and reacts. She's still grieving and working through a lot of things, and I need to be that person she can depend on.

I didn't know how she would take the gift I got her, if she would feel like I intruded on her grief. But I wanted to do something to show her that I care and, more than anything, grieve for Kathy too. If I would have known the whole story, I would have dropped everything to be with her. The fact that she was alone in what was the hardest time of her life weighs heavily on me. I should have been there for her, instead I disappointed her, I disappointed Kathy. She trusted us with her daughter, the most precious thing in her life, and we fucked up. As soon as Charlotte dropped the bombshell on me, I made a vow to myself to make up for my indiscretions, and I don't want a single day to go by where Charlotte feels alone or hurt. I will make it right.

She's mine, and I'm willing to do everything and anything to prove to her we can be the Alphas she needs and deserves. Of course, it's proving difficult with Mikael, but I didn't expect anything less. He took Charlotte leaving harder than all of us, and he's a stubborn asshole. He also doesn't have the same value of family like Charlotte and I do, so there's no way he understands how heavy this pain is. But I plan on making him see it clearly, how we're the Alphas. If Charlotte feels betrayed or like she's not being put first, that's on us, not Charlotte.

I know for a fact though, if he was holding Charlotte like I am now, he would give in right away. Her maple and fresh pancake scent fills the room. It makes my cock hard, and I groan.

After I'm done telling her how much I missed her body, she sighs and says, "Okay." But I can see the panic in her eyes, like I would lie to her about how attractive she is. Tonight has been emotional, and I can tell we're both going through the motions of working through pain. As badly as every nerve ending inside of me is craving her scent and touch, I'm fine just being here with her. I want to give her whatever she needs.

"We don't have to do anything, Charlotte. I'm just happy to be able to hold and kiss you again."

Her expression softens, and she smiles. "Can we take it slow?"

I nod and bring my lips back to her neck, tasting her skin and a getting direct hit of her scent. "My Omega can have whatever she wants."

"I'm still yours?" she asks unsure.

"You never stopped being mine, and I never stopped being yours."

Her cheeks are pink as I lift my head and look up at her. "I wouldn't blame you all if there was someone else when I left."

I pull back and glare at her. "There was no one for any of us. You never stopped being ours. I don't want anyone else. None of us do." It's not a lie. Mikael might try to act like he doesn't want this again, but he's a fucking liar. He doesn't look at other women, and hasn't tried sleeping with anyone else. As usual, the stubborn asshole will realize he's being an idiot, eventually.

"I, um..." She looks down at me. I've never seen Charlotte look so shy, especially when it comes to something physical. "I haven't really done anything in a long time."

I'm confused as I look down at her, and a growl rumbles in my throat, wondering if there was someone else for her. "No, not like that. I just haven't even really been touching myself. This is the first time I've been turned on in a really long time." Her voice is soft and shy, like she's embarrassed. I can't help the masculine pride that floods me at her confession. "The suppressants I was on really messed me up. I want to be me again," she says, and I lean forward and kiss her tenderly. I want her to know that I want her in any shape or form, but above all, I want her happiness.

"What can I do?"

She licks her lips and looks at me softly. Her blonde hair in a bun at the top of her head bounces when she slides up. "Maybe... It could be like that night when I snuck you into my mom's house?" I like this idea, but I like the idea of tasting her more. I've missed her taste, her slick, how wet she gets for me.

"Can I go down on you?" I make a note to ask her what she wants from now on, not taking charge like I used to. I need to tread carefully with Charlotte, so I don't spook her. "You don't have to touch me tonight. I just need to show you how much I've missed you."

She bites her bottom lip and nods. I know the smile on my face must be ridiculous as Charlotte lies back, and I'm back to kissing her neck. "Fucking missed this scent. How wet my girl gets for me, how good she is for her Alpha." My words have her moaning and I haven't even touched her pussy yet. "I couldn't even eat pancakes with syrup because it made me think about eating your sweet, little cunt." She wiggles under my body, her nails gently sliding over my chest as I lean forward and kiss her again. It's messy, sloppy, and wild. Like both of us are throwing everything into the kiss, our regrets, frustrations, and missed time with each other.

"Anders," she sighs, and it goes straight to my dick. I didn't come over here to do anything physical, but I can't help myself.

I work my way down her body, doing like I wanted to earlier and kissing her breasts through the fabric of her tank top, the wetness of my mouth making the material see-through and her pink nipples presented to me. I hum as I kiss her chest and take in the feel and weight of her breasts. "So fucking perfect," I say between alternating from one side to another. Her fingers are laced in my hair, and her nails are gently scratching my scalp, making me groan. I look up at her, not wanting the shirt between us anymore. She knows what I'm going to ask and nods her head before the words even come out. My thumbs pull the material from her stomach and push it up to her chin. Her tits bounce as she helps me move the offensive material.

I kiss her stomach before moving back to her chest. I use both of my hands to push her tits together, licking, sucking, and kissing each one. Charlotte keens beneath me, her thigh pushing against my hard cock, and she pushes her chest closer to my face.

"Mmm, still so greedy for your Alpha's touch, that hasn't changed." That has her moaning. It's clear she needs to be reminded of how special she is, and I make a note to do it as often as possible.

"Please," she begs as I take my sweet time giving her breasts all the attention. I always loved when she begged.

"What do you need, *Kulta*?" I drag my hand from her left side over her stomach until I'm cupping her pussy from the outside of her shorts—which are completely drenched. "You need my mouth on this needy pussy? Is that what you need, little Omega?"

"Yes, Anders, please."

"Always so sweet," I praise her as my kisses go lower and lower. My tongue swipes out each time to reverently taste her skin. I fucking missed this—missed her—so much.

Charlotte lifts her hips eagerly as I slide her shorts off her thighs and calves and toss them onto the floor. Her scent of arousal is magnetizing and sweet, and all I want is to give her pleasure and remind her of how precious she is to me. I take my time though, kissing her thigh and licking the trail of slick back to her needy pussy.

"Please. God. Anders, don't tease."

I smile against her thigh and put my face where she wants me, *where I want me.* I swipe my tongue through her wetness and moan. Nothing, absolutely fucking nothing, is as good as tasting your scent match. Not being able to contain myself, I push down my sweatpants and cover my hand with her slick before bringing it down to my cock. I stroke myself lazily as I reacquaint myself with my scent match's pussy.

She's so fucking wet that her slick trails down my fingers as I fuck her, and I know my chin is wet from sucking on her clit. Her hips thrust against my face, and I take a moment to look up at her. She isn't looking at my face, but watching me touch myself as I eat her out. It makes me want to please her even more.

I suck on her clit hard, and she whimpers, her eyes shutting as she throws her head back against the pillows, but she continues to rub against my face. Her pussy is clenching against my two fingers, and I know she's close; so am I, watching her writhe for me, her hand in my hair, that she likes watching me touch myself. But her sweet taste on my tongue is what has me on the edge. She moans loudly as I flick my tongue over her clit at a rapid pace and curl my fingers inside of her warm, needy heat.

"Oh, Alpha. Right there." I groan against her and keep up the same motions. My fist is tight on my cock, and my knot is heavy as I stroke myself. When her thighs shake and her back arches off the bed, that's when I finish, spurting cum over her sheets while she uses me and comes on my face.

We're both panting when I rise up on my elbows and climb on top of her.

"Fuck," she says breathlessly. With no thought, I kiss her with her taste on my tongue, but she doesn't care. She's always liked that.

My hands are in her messy bun cradling her face when I look at her, and it's the most at ease I've seen her all night. I kiss her forehead before leaning mine against hers.

"No more fighting this?" I ask, needing to make sure that she isn't going to run off again.

She shakes her head. "No, no more fighting."

I don't care that the bed is a mess or that we're both covered in slick and there's a cum puddle somewhere on the bed.

"We have a string of away games coming up." She swallows but nods. I can tell she's nervous, and I make a mental note to contact her as much as I can while we're away. "Once we get back, maybe you can come over, and we can make you dinner." A small laugh escapes her, and she covers her mouth. "What?" I ask, poking her side.

"What is it exactly that you all will be cooking?" I grin back at her, loving seeing this playful side of her again.

"Okay, more like ordering food and having it brought to the house."

"I'd like that," she says, leaning over and kissing me. It's a relief to have her make a move first, and I sigh contentedly.

"You're still going to stay the night?" she asks sheepishly.

"Of course I am." I tug her close to me, my chest rumbling, and Charlotte burrows against me. "Nothing could make me leave this bed right now."

"Me either."

It feels like tonight was a step in the right direction, but when it comes to Charlotte, with this pack, nothing is ever truly easy.

W e're completely and absolutely sucking ass on the ice. This is our third game away, and it's embarrassing. I know why we're losing, and that's what pisses me off even more. Anders and Eli have their heads so spun up with Charlotte they can't even stay focused.

I told them they were stupid for letting her back in, for giving her that power, seeing how easily she could crush all of us like that. Fucking idiots, it's like slamming your finger in a car door and doing it again to see what happens.

Anders has let stupid goals slip in, and Eli is a mess on the ice, tripping over teammates and not making the shots that he's known for. Coach is pissed, I'm pissed, the entire team is pissed. It's not like we expect to go to the cup or anything; we're an expansion team, and the growing pains are real. But playing like shit because you're thinking about an Omega who dropped you the second life got hard is bullshit.

I heard what Anders said about Kathy, and I feel awful that we weren't there and what Charlotte went through. But she didn't trust us. We weren't worth keeping in her life when things got the toughest. I told her not to break me, and she fucking did. I love Anders and Eli, but it's clear the only person I can truly depend on is myself. My family wasn't shit, and this pack is a farce I'm not falling into again. I won't ditch Anders and Eli, but I sure as fuck am not going to squander this chance I was given. That means not messing up this pack contract and not letting Charlotte back into our lives.

I'm hoping they don't get too deep and this all implodes before it even starts. We can't have a repeat of four months ago. Of us trying to navigate our new careers while being heartbroken and fucking pathetic for months on end. I'd never really given a shit about my designation, but as of late, I wish whole-fucking-heartedly that I was a Beta and didn't have to deal with this bullshit.

While I've always had an issue with my temper, it feels like it's bubbling over the surface during this game. I'm pissed at everyone, and the only way I can think to make it better is to show up on the ice and do what I do best. This is the last game away until we're back in Connecticut, and it's close. The Hurricanes are only up by one point, and we have ten minutes left in the game. There's a line change, and I'm back on the ice, ready to unleash everything to help myself feel better.

Anders glares at me from his helmet, and as badly as I want to give him the finger right now, I ignore the bastard. We've gotten into it more times than I'd like to admit, Eli in the middle trying to defuse the situation. But at the end of the day, Anders is pack, and he's my goalie. If anyone fucks with him, they fuck with all of us.

So the minute Alexeyev from the Hurricanes knocks him over, his back hitting the post hard enough to unlatch it from the ice, it's fucking on.

I'm on him in a flash, pushing him against the glass. We've each got a fistful of each other's jersey as we hit each other. There's a clash of players on the sides of us and refs waiting patiently for when to jump in. Before I know it, my helmet is off, and I feel the full force of Alexeyev's gloved fist hitting my face. I welcome the pain and return it tenfold by flicking off my glove and hitting his skin. I'm glad I took my partial out, even though I look like an idiot as Alexeyev hits me right in the teeth. I bite the inside of my cheek.

It spurs me on, and I hit him in his already busted nose twice with my fist. My knuckles are burning from the sensation. It's then we're tugged apart, someone grabbing the back of my jersey as I glide backwards on my skates.

"You fucking bitch weasel!" I can't help but laugh at the Russian's insult, knowing blood is dripping down my chin.

"What are you going to do? I think I did your nose a favor."

"Come say to my face, pussy chicken!" I wipe the blood off my chin and grin at Alexeyev. I'm in a much happier place after fucking up his nose and hearing his terrible comebacks. I'm immediately taken to the sin bin for my actions, but so is he. Luckily, no one else on the team got involved, so each team just plays down a player while we wait out the five minutes. It appears that my genius plan of picking a fight with the Hurricanes team doofus helps, as Eli ends the penalty and scores a goal. It's not a pretty one, but it puts us on an even playing field, nonetheless.

I put on my big boy pants as I leave the box and head to the bench, preparing myself for the verbal lashing I might get from the coach. I'm surprised when I get a clasp on the shoulder and a water bottle tossed my way.

"That's how you protect your goalie, son," he says as he goes down the line and gives tidbits of advice and tells others how shitty they are playing. I'll take what I can get, and I can at least be grateful that he isn't standing behind me anymore. Why do all hockey coaches chew gum like deranged, anxious animals?

With five minutes left on the clock, I'm waiting to be rotated back into play, but it doesn't come, and I watch as Alexeyev scores against Anders. I want to crack my stick in half, but hold it all in. When Alexeyev skates by, he gives me a shit-eating grin, and I note to fuck up his nose the next time we meet on the ice.

The clock keeps winding further down, and my actions are all for naught as we lose our third away game in a row. Being superstitious as fuck, I know the causes of the loss and need to find a way to make it end.

We're back at the house in Connecticut and to say I've been pissy is an understatement. After all the travel and the fact that we have a home game tomorrow, I'm in a goddamn mood. It gets even worse when Eli drops the bombshell on me. I'm tired and sore, and all I want to do is lay in bed or maybe spend some time in the hot tub.

"Charlotte's coming over for dinner tonight," Eli announces. Anders clearly already knew as he nods his head in agreement. I just can't with them, so I don't argue. I'm too exhausted. I throw my hands in the air and just walk away.

Great, outstanding. Now our whole house is going to smell like her, and I won't be able to escape it. Anders and Eli will be cooing over her downstairs and letting her get away with everything. It's not that I'm fucking heartless, but there's no accountability. If she hadn't run away, I would have taken my stock of the blame for Vegas and being unreachable, but right now I don't see anything from her end. She hasn't reached out to me, and I haven't reached out to her either. Maybe she's realized Eli and Anders are the ones she truly wants, and I'm the scent match she doesn't want to be stuck with.

I've only seen her through the plexi glass of the last game, and that's as close as I want to get. I need... I don't know what I need. But I know it's not her sweet scent, or all of the things that made me want her in the first place. I don't want to be reminded of her. I just don't know what I want...

I stay in my room all night until I hear her feminine laughter downstairs, and I can't take it anymore and decide to take a shower to drown out the noise. The temperature is nearly scalding as the water beats against my back. My dark hair hangs over my eyes as I breathe in and out. They're just letting her back into their lives like it was nothing. Like these last four months haven't been hell. It pisses me off; she pisses me off.

Her sweet scent, her pretty face, her long blonde hair, her snark. It all... *fuck*. I scrub my face roughly, the water losing some of the heat, and I decide to get out. I'm hungry, but no fucking way am I going downstairs. I scrub a towel over my hair and wrap it around my waist, then go back into my bedroom.

What I don't expect to see is a teary-eyed Charlotte standing in my room looking at the few things I have scattered on my nightstand. I don't see the purple notebook, so I let out a sigh of relief. As much as I don't want her back, I wouldn't want her reading the entries. It was definitely not meant for her eyes and more of an outlet for my feelings. I sigh in relief as she picks up the news article I had framed that features some of my best hits this season.

Her eyes move from the page she's on, and she looks at me cautiously.

"You got what you always wanted."

I scowl at her, not liking this game. Not her throwing my own words back into my face before we came together. Before she abandoned us.

"Are you happy, Mikael?"

I'm shouting no in my head, but refuse to give her the satisfaction. She looks pretty tonight, wearing a deep maroon dress and tights. The dress hugs her figure, and she looks great. I lick my lips and shake my head. "Yes, I'm happy."

She glares at me and puts the article down. Her big purse is clutched under her arm, and her hands go to fidget with the straps.

"Do you think we could talk?" she asks softly.

"What's there to talk about, Charlotte? I know the whole story from your boyfriends. There's nothing left to say."

She furrows her brows and puts her hands on her hips, like I'm the one being difficult.

"It's not that simple, and you know it."

"I know you went through something horrible, and I'm sorry for that. But you ran, Charlotte. You didn't give us a chance to explain or trust us enough to let us take care of you. You fucking ran, not giving a single fuck about what it would do to us."

"I was going through a lot," she says, her tone matching mine in anger now. Her eyes look like they are going to water, and my stomach sinks. If I make her cry, I know she'll leave, but I don't know how I'll sleep at night. But my anger weighs heavier than how Charlotte is projecting right now.

She treated me like trash, like I could be thrown away. It's what I grew up knowing, and Charlotte only proved me right. This would never work, and it wasn't worth putting my heart on the line.

"You should have at least let us contact you to know what happened. You completely ditched us. Didn't believe in us. We weren't worth it to you. I wasn't worth it to you." I say the last part softly, because deep down I know Eli and Anders are better than me, and I'm what dragged this stupid fucking pack down before it could even start.

"That's not it." She shakes her head like I'm the one not making sense.

"Then what is it, Charlotte?"

"Ugh! Why are you always like this?" She walks closer to me and puts her hands against my chest. Her scent is thick and annoyingly enticing. Part of me wants her to rake her nails down my chest, and the other wants her touch to burn me. I wrap my hands around her wrists, pushing her away or tugging her closer, I'm not sure.

"What? Calling you out on your shit? Being honest with you? We would have done anything for you, Charlotte. Do you know what it felt like to not know if you were okay? Not knowing what we had done wrong, or what you were going through? It was torture."

She tries to move from my grasp, but I don't let her, not done saying my piece.

"I could hardly function, worrying about you. But everyone said to give you space, you'll come back around. You never did. You were the first time I gave in, the first time I put everything aside and took a gamble, and you ran from me."

She shoves at me again. "You weren't there, you don't understand."

"Cause you wouldn't let me!" I yell back.

"You're so fucking stubborn. I'm trying to talk to you."

"You want to talk? Let's talk about how we lost three away games because Anders and Eli are all caught up in your fucking web again, or how our house is going to smell like you all week and none of us will be able to think straight. Or how when we see you again after months of silence, it's with some old fucking man sitting front row at a Foxes' game?"

She glares at me, and I can see her temper rising, ready to meet mine. It's a lot like that night she threw that snowball at the back of my head. "Or we could talk about how hard-headed you are and will never listen to what I'm saying to you." She pokes me in my chest, and I'm getting pissed.

"Don't push me, Charlotte."

"Or what?" she says, poking me again. I don't know what takes over me, but suddenly my towel is on the ground and Charlotte's back is pressed against the wall.

It's like all thoughts leave my brain as I inhale deeply against her neck. Her scent brings back some of my favorite memories that now feel so fucking tainted I can't stand it. My grip on her hips is tight as she breathes heavily against me. She doesn't tell me to stop, she's not yelling at me.

Of course this is what she wants; she wants me so fucking frenzied for her that I can't control my dick, so I'll give in. Well, fuck that, I'm not opening my heart up to her again. I don't think I could take it.

I wish my sensibility took over before I decide to lick her skin, humming at the flavor. But that's when she speaks, and my head starts thinking instead of my dick.

"I missed you, Mikael. I'm going to convince you to give this another chance." I grunt as I remove my hands like her skin is burning me and step away from her. She looks over my naked body and licks her lips and shakes her head. She's still breathing hard even though we separated. Her face looks pleading as she looks at me and shakes her head. "You need to know that I wasn't in the right state of mind when everything happened. No one was innocent in that. But I'm trying now, and it's your actions that could fuck this all up." She takes a breath, and her back is to me as she walks away. "I lost my mom, Mikael, in front of me, and all you're thinking about is how you think I left you."

She parts with those words, and I let them sink in. They sink into the depth of my soul until they rattle around in my brain. Have I been completely selfish in thinking about myself? Have I even tried putting myself into Charlotte's shoes even though I never had a parent like Kathy? If my parents died, I'm not even sure I would cry. But Charlotte? She's different; her situation is different.

I'm thinking about how much I'm fucking this up—again. I lie down on the bed and groan, rubbing my hands over my face. Like I have for the last four months, I decide to put it in the journal. I need to write down how I'm feeling in order to process tonight and how I can talk to Charlotte after.

Am I really being the unreasonable one? Even if I don't want to give this another shot, am I being a complete prick to Charlotte?

I open the nightstand and riffle around for the purple journal. That's when my heart sinks when I realize the reason why it's not here. Charlotte took it.

I race downstairs to a ferocious looking Anders and Eli as I look around for Charlotte.

"What did you do now?" Anders asks.

"Where's Charlotte?"

"She left, had Piper come pick her up. We were having a great time before she went upstairs," Eli says. His arms are crossed over his chest, and he looks pissed.

I don't tell them that things are about to get fifty times worse as I spin on my heels and go upstairs, trying to remember the contents of each page.

I told Piper to pick me up before I went up to Mikael's room, knowing that it wouldn't be easy. I didn't think that he would completely disregard me the way he did though. He was cold and compassionless. Even if Eli and Anders harbor some resentment toward how I left, they at least have an understanding of why I did what I did. And how their actions resulted in me leaving.

But it seems like Mikael only sees how I hurt him, not the cause of the effect. I know he's stubborn, but this is a little much. He's being hurtful, like *Sorry your mom died, but you fucking hurt my feelings.*

I had to leave before I said things I can't take back. I still care for Mikael and crave his scent, but the ball is in his court. I'm not going to actively pursue someone who is so hurtful with no remorse.

And I might have stolen his notebook to understand him better. Our preferred way to communicate was through writing, and when I opened the purple spiral notebook and saw the first words were dear Charlotte, I took it. I wasn't thinking, just saw my name and took his damn notebook.

I know he's going to be mad, and part of me feels extremely guilty for taking it. He told me he read my journal before he agreed to be with me, and maybe this is me hoping the same thing will happen. That this tiny purple journal will give me the insight I need to bring us back together. I had already taken the journal, and Piper was already here, so I stole it. It sits in my purse like I just stole a Fabergè egg. I clutch it against my chest, both curious and scared of the contents.

The look on Anders' and Eli's faces when I left made my chest clench. But I had to get out of there. Being so close to Mikael like that with no resolution and sitting downstairs with them just didn't feel right. It felt like ignoring our problems, and by now we've learned that it doesn't work well when we just ignore feelings and don't work together as a unit.

Piper looks tired as I look at her from the corner of my eye.

"Everything okay, Piper?"

She smiles and nods. "Just a little stressed about midterms." I nod and think about how much Piper is always there for me, and I decide to push further.

"You know if something is bothering you, you can always tell me."

Piper glances over at me before paying attention to the road. "I'm not sure if I'm built for this, Charles."

"For what, med school?" She nods and sighs.

"I'm so used to being effortlessly good at things, but this shit is fucking hard. I'm not the best, and it seems like others are catching on so much quicker than me."

"What would you do instead?" I ask, gauging her reaction. My best friend has talked about being a surgeon since she was in elementary school.

"Uh, I have no idea."

"You were meant to be a surgeon, Piper. You're one of the smartest, caring, and driven people I know. Don't let not being the best be a reason to put yourself down."

She smiles and nods at me. "See, Charles. This is why I keep you around."

I smile back, feeling like I'm finally holding up my end of this friendship.

"How was the date?" she asks.

"Okay."

She grunts in acknowledgement. "Things were never easy with him. I wouldn't expect that to change now." Piper doesn't dislike Mikael, but he is the one she knows the least. It seems like a common theme. Mikael is not an easy person to know and guards his feelings. I sigh and nod my head, clenching my purse close to my chest. Fear and curiosity are heavy in my stomach when I think about what I'm going to find out about my difficult packmate.

The journal stares at me. I have it sitting on my nightstand, and I've debated for at least two hours on if I should read it or not. Part of me expected Mikael to show up banging on my door, asking for it back. But he doesn't come, and my curiosity about how Mikael's brain works overrules the side of me that thinks I should respect his privacy. With delicate fingers, I flip the first page.

July 18th

Dear Charlotte,

What the actual fuck? An email? You broke up with us in an email! Anders and Eli assure me that you will come around. That something must have happened to make you walk away. We've had months to talk about the draft and what was going to happen. Why wouldn't you speak up and tell us what's bothering you? Why the fuck did you leave? I'm hoping you come to your senses soon because I'm fucking losing it. The only bright spot about going back to Canada was that you would be there with

~~Please~~ Please un-fucking-block our numbers,

and speak to us. For fuck's sake,

Mikael

August 15th

Dear Charlotte,

I hate you today. And I know that hate is a strong word, but right now all I can feel is hate. ~~Because you were the first person~~ Because you were the first person I let in, and you fucking ruined it.

Am I that big of a piece of shit that you won't even tell me what I did wrong?

Hate,

Mikael

August **25**

Charlotte,
You're really just going to fucking never talk
to us again? After all this declaration of
being scent matches and how you don't run
away from your scent matches.

You know I wanted you to come to Canada?
So we could pick out an apartment, and I
could finally tell you that I loved you?
I wanted to get a fucking ground-floor
apartment, so Hank wouldn't have to take
the elevator. I had it all planned out.

~~I'm glad I didn't say it now.~~ That I was waiting.

I'm glad I didn't say it now. That I was waiting.

Why would I tell you I love you when
you clearly don't give a shit about me?

Mikael

September 13th

I'm starting to hate this fucking journal and how pathetic it makes me.

I met a girl at a bar tonight, and I wanted to fuck her so badly, just to get you out of my system.

I couldn't, and ~~it's your fault~~ it's your fault.

If you're going to leave me, you should at least let me live.

Mikael

September 30th

Do you even care that Anders and Eli did everything possible to get us traded to the Foxes?

You don't deserve their devotion. I hope they come to their senses soon.

Mikael

October 19th

I HATE THAT I SAW YOU TODAY.

Hate that I was mad about seeing you
next to that old man.

Hate that you made Anders cry

and Eli has his hopes up.

I wish you would leave.

Mikael

November 3rd

I want you out of my head.

I want you away from Anders and Eli.

~~This is too much~~

This is too much, and I don't want to
feel like this anymore.

When you look at me ~~xxxxxxxxx~~

I feel like I'm a worthless piece of shit,

and that's your fault.

Mikael

I close the journal on a sob, half of the writing now skewed with tears. I throw the offensive purple notebook on the floor, and Hank immediately is in my face, licking my tears. There's so much to unpack in his letters to me.

There's so much hurtful anger in his words, and there's a part of me that hates Mikael back for making me feel this way. There's no sympathy in how he treats me, and after reading his thoughts, all I feel is even worse after my encounter. I wonder how it's possible to love someone but still want to hurt them so badly. Because that's what Mikael is doing to me, and currently I don't think I would take him back if he simply apologized.

I know deep down he never wanted me to read this journal, and I've only done this to myself by stealing it and reading it, but fuck. There's only so much I can take. I'm still trying to heal, grieve, and come to terms with possibly reconciling with them.

At this moment, that's only true for Anders and Eli. I think back to my conversation with Piper at the coffee shop. *If they aren't willing to make it work, they aren't worthy of you.*

The fact is, the man that Mikael is right now is not worthy of me, and I'll be damned after everything I've been through. I will not let a man make me feel the way he did tonight.

Hank nudges me with his big head, and I pet him, which somehow always brings me comfort. It doesn't hurt that my clothes smell like the three of them. Even if I feel my own level of hate for Mikael right now, my body doesn't get the message about his scent.

I inhale the collar of my dress and sigh, wondering why one fucking thing in my life can't be simple. I'm still angry when I decide to add my own entries beneath his. I grab my purple pen, and my slanted font is a stark contrast to his angry scribbled writing. I think back on these dates he has on his letters and think about my mindset during that time. It's not a pretty reflection.

July 18th

Dear Mikael,

Piper had to drag me into the shower today because I couldn't do it myself.

This might hurt you, but none of you have been on my mind this past week.

I feel nothing.

I spend most of my time sleeping, wishing I would wake up from this nightmare.

Not everything is about you,

Charlotte

August 15th

Dear Mikael,

I hate myself today, like I do every day.
I wear guilt like it's a badge of honor.

What could I have done differently?
What could you have done differently?
What if you answered your phone?
What if I called an ambulance instead?

I put all of our things in a box.

Piper said it's sunny out, and she wants
me to go on a walk with her. I just
want to lie in bed and feel nothing.

No one hates me as much as I do,

Charlotte

August 25th

Mikael,

I had plans for us too.

Big plans.

But nothing seems like it's worth
planning without my mom here.
Not when hockey will always come
first, when I can't trust my own
scent matches to be there for me.

I'm better off alone.

and you probably will be too.

Charlotte

September 13th

I want to forget that I have scent
matches every day.

I wish we never met.

If we never met, then I wouldn't know
what I left behind.

Truth is, if you really wanted me, you
could have tried harder.

We're better off without each other.

Charlotte

September 30th

I don't deserve anything.

Charlotte

October 19th

I hate that I saw you all today.
It was easier to forget, to think of you
as this imaginary concept that wasn't real.
        But you are real.

And the looks you all gave me shattered me.

I wasn't prepared to see any of you and
what emotions that would bring back for
me. I've only been off my high grade
suppressants for one day, but I don't like
how I feel. I don't like feeling at all.

I'd rather stay numb and forget all of you.

Why can't this be easy?

Why is none of this ever easy for me?

        Charlotte

November 3rd

I wish you could see what I went
through and have more compassion for
my situation. I didn't leave to hurt
you all. I left because I was broken.
I haven't been a functioning human for
the last four months. You've still been
functioning, doing what you love with
your best friends by your side.

I can understand why you're hurting,
but don't you care about how broken I am?

I plan on being a better Omega
for Anders and Eli. But at this point,
I'm wondering if we forced being
together, and maybe our being scent
matches is a fluke. I'm ready to let
you go if that's what you want. Just
know that I deserve more than an
Alpha who lacks empathy and
understanding.

You hurt me too.

Charlotte

I sit there looking at my letters, tears still streaming down my face. I'm truly not enjoying that I'm a crier nowadays. But I guess it's better than letting your life pass by as you don't live. I debate tossing the notebook and just letting the emotions I bore be tossed away. But then I think about how much hurt I feel, and I do something brash. I print out the postage and grab an old amazon poly mailer. Once the label is tapped on the front, I walk it out to the mailbox and raise the flag for pick up.

There's still probably about four hours before the mailman picks it up, so I can change my mind at any time. But I don't. I think it's about time that Mikael gets the reality check that he isn't the only person in this fucked up pack with feelings.

ELI

Chapter Thirty-Nine

Two more away games, more time away from Charlotte. I knew this was going to be hard back when we started our relationship but damn. I wonder when Anders and I should mention that one specific part of our contract that includes her. I know that it's too soon now. Everything is about healing and getting closer. Not that Mikael is helping at all. There's always so much tension between the two of them. Anders and I have agreed to let them try to make it work before we meddle. The last thing I want to do is leave Mikael behind, but as much as I hate to say it, Charlotte comes first.

I feel like I've done a good job of being there for Charlotte and showing her how much I need her in my life. But I want to do more. Charlotte always said I needed more fun in my life, and now I feel like we've switched. Sometimes when we talk on the phone or I see her face, I can still see sadness written in her expression, and I just want to make her heart feel lighter.

I have a big stupid grin on my face when she texts me back, and a part of me is eager to have her to myself. That's when Anders walks into the room with the biggest pout on his face.

"You already asked her on a date tomorrow?"

"Yeah." He nods, and I feel guilty as fuck, so I sigh. "You can join us."

"You're sure?" he asks, though I can tell he really wants to come. The season is brutal, and our free time is limited, so I would feel like an asshole for hoarding Charlotte to myself.

"Yeah, you can come too."

He squeezes me by the neck and kisses the side of my head like I'm a child who did something he's proud of. "Thanks, man."

"Yeah, yeah, yeah. Just don't be a cock block."

He gasps and clutches his chest. "I would never. So where are we going?"

"Fall festival."

Anders points at me and smirks. "Girls love fall festivals."

"That's the plan."

"Looks like you're trying to come for my spot as the Omega whisperer. Don't think I don't see you, Eli." I roll my eyes and turn back to my laptop, making sure I plan the perfect date for tomorrow. Anders has been so much happier lately. Honestly, we all have. Mikael might be in denial again, but he isn't drinking as much or doing reckless shit. I think he doesn't even realize how much knowing Charlotte is safe has calmed his Alpha nature.

It pained me to smell anything that reminded me of Charlotte's scent, but now it brings me the same comfort it used to. I need this to work so badly. Those months without her have made me realize just how much we're destined to belong to each other. And I'll be fucking damned if anything gets in the way of Charlotte being mine.

My palms are sweating, and it's embarrassing as hell as I knock on Charlotte's door. She opens the door, her blonde hair blown back by a light gust of wind. I barely have a moment to take in her smile. A smile that I haven't seen in forever. It's one of genuine excitement. I have to look away only because Hank's huge fucking head is in my crotch.

"Hey, boy." I pet his head and push him out of my crotch as he leaves a trail of slobber and sits next to Charlotte.

"Good boy, Hank." She gives me a sheepish look and smiles when she sees Anders waving from the car because we couldn't find parking. "Hank's just excited to get out of the house."

I nod and note that I think Charlotte is feeling the same way. She's wearing a Foxes branded hoodie, and I can't help but grin. That's got to be a good sign.

"You sure you're gonna be warm enough?" I ask her. It's nice enough for early November, but I know how she can get.

"Yeah, I'll be good," she assures me by squeezing my forearm and giving me a smile. I'm so gone for this girl, and I hope that today is everything she needs.

"Alright, let's head out."

I take Hank's leash in one hand and hers in the other as we walk to the car. I open the passenger door for her to get in, and she shakes her head at me. "Eli, you sit up front. No way will you be comfortable in the backseat."

I don't listen and hoist her by the waist, putting her in the passenger's seat and buckling her seat belt. I snag a kiss to the side of her head before shutting the door. She gives me a mock pout, but immediately leans over and gives Anders a kiss. I hate that I'm jealous of that kiss, mostly because we haven't kissed yet. I know everything will come with time, but I just want her so badly. Even though I know it's impossible, I wish I could rewind time, and we could go back to a time when we were so comfortable and free with each other. *Patience, Eli. Patience.*

"Alright, Hank, you be a good boy today. No vet trips or making Charlotte cry and I will give you all the snacks you want. Okay, boy?" He tilts his head, his eyes blocked slightly from his dark, shaggy hair. He tilts his head in what I'm assuming is agreement as I open the door, and he jumps in the backseat. As soon as he's in, there is slobber along the interior and the window.

"Oh, um, you might want to put the window down," Charlotte says from the front, covering her mouth from laughing at how her dog has completely taken ownership of the backseat.

Anders laughs. Asshole joined my date, and he is somehow the one sitting cushy in the front seat with his hand on our Omega's thigh. Clearly I didn't think this arrangement through.

"So are you going to tell me where we're going?"

"Gonna have to be patient," I say, leaning forward and tugging lightly on a piece of her long blonde hair. It's even longer than I remember, and that's when my thoughts turn dirty, and I shut them down immediately.

"Fine, be sneaky. But you didn't tell me this one was coming." She points over at Anders, and he shrugs.

"I might have sulked, and Eli was gracious enough to let me tag along."

She leans over the center console and gives me a small smile. "Your generosity will be rewarded." That has me grinning right back.

"Then it was worth it to bring his needy ass along with us."

Anders laughs and shakes his head. I watch as his hand flexes over Charlotte's thigh, and I'm back to regretting not driving.

The rest of the drive is light, and Charlotte seems the happiest I've seen her so far. The corn maze and festival are only about twenty minutes away, so we get there quickly. Which I'm thankful for. Hank has taken turns sitting on my lap with his massive body, drooling on me, licking my face, and I know he's farted a few times for sure.

"We're here," Anders says from up front, parking in the grass and hay covered parking spots.

"A fall festival?" Charlotte says with a smile.

"Thought it would be fun."

"Can we get pumpkins and carve them?"

"We can do whatever you want, baby."

She beams at me, and her old pet name just feels so right. God, I need to kiss her, but I'll wait until Charlotte is ready.

I get Hank out of the SUV, and he sniffs around at the hay and dirt. His tail that serves as a weapon wags as he leads the way to the front gate. Since Anders imposed on the date, he decides to pay, but at this point all of our money is combined except my inheritance. So really, we are paying for the date.

"What are these?" Charlotte says as Anders holds out her wrist and wraps a plastic orange band with pumpkins on it.

"Gives you access to anything on the farm and a pumpkin at the end of the hayride." She nods her head as he puts it on. I hold out my hand, and Anders rolls his eyes as he puts on my wrist band too, which makes Charlotte laugh, so he doesn't give me any shit.

"You guys should prepare yourself," Charlotte says, and Anders and I both look confused. "We will be stopped every five feet for someone to pet Hank, talk about how giant he is, or ask questions about him."

I shrug, and so does Anders, both of us thinking she is exaggerating. Charlotte shakes her head, but holds the leash, and as soon as we turn to head over to get cider donuts and hot chocolate, a woman and two children stop us.

"My goodness, he's huge. What breed is he?"

"Newfoundland," Charlotte replies with a soft smile. "He's friendly."

The little girls and mom pet his head, and Hank is loving the attention as he drools over the strangers and accepts their affections.

"I think he's been overdue for an event like this. Hank is a bit of an attention whore," Charlotte says, laughing. I take Hank's leash and put her hand in mine. Her head leans in against my biceps, and I can't help but think how good she feels pressed against me. How much time was missed with my Omega, and how I can make up for that lost time.

We wait in line. Apparently these donuts are something special as I watch people walk away with a box of a dozen. The whole time, Charlotte's hand is in mine, and Anders has his arm around her shoulder. It's so natural for us to be like this, but I can't help but think about the broody brunet missing from the situation. Sometimes I find myself pitying Mikael. Other times I want to punch him in the gut for being such an idiot. I push my feelings aside for our missing pack member as we finally reach the front of the line.

Charlotte had no problem taking charge of the order. "Can we get a dozen apple cider donuts, three hot chocolates, and one bottled water please?" The tender nods and we stand off to the side and wait for our treats. Anders plays with her hair while I rub her knuckles with my thumb, and I swear I watch Charlotte glow under our affection. Seems like Hank isn't the only one who missed a little attention. I can't help it when I lean over and kiss the side of her hair. She smells so fucking good, and I'm lucky that we're interrupted by them calling our order number or else I might have thrown her over my shoulder and said fuck the fall festival.

There's a spot with hay bales covered in blankets as we go and sit to eat our donuts and sip our hot chocolate. People come up and pet Hank, cooing over his cuteness the whole time.

Charlotte hums as she inhales her donut. "These are so fucking good." I nod my head, and so does Anders. She's got a bit of granulated sugar on the side of her lip, and I use my thumb to swipe it up and suck the sugar off my thumb. Doesn't compare to how sweet Charlotte tastes, but it will do. She flushes as she tracks the tip of my tongue, licking the pad of my thumb and she clears her throat.

"What's next?"

"There's the hayride, corn maze, face painting, potato sack race, and musical baked goods."

"What the hell is musical baked goods?" Charlotte asks, and I can tell Anders is just as confused by the idea.

"Come on." I drag Charlotte by the hand, Hank on the leash, and Anders following us as we go to play the stupid game.

We wait in line and watch as people do musical chairs. Each chair is numbered, and they draw from a hat. If your number is called, you get the baked good of your choice.

"What the fuck, this isn't even competitive?" Charlotte asks, and a woman balks at her language next to us. Charlotte doesn't apologize, and I smile.

"We could always make it more interesting," Anders says, and I shake my head at these heathens who are my packmates. Or will be, when the time is right.

"First one to win gets to pick what we do tonight," Charlotte says, and Anders and I grin at each other. I didn't want to push anything, but I was hoping she would want the date to go further than the festival.

"Deal," I say, shaking her hand, and Anders follows. If I would have made the rules, it would have been for touching, so I'm glad that Charlotte came up with the idea. Maybe I can still hope that her plans involve touching.

We're lucky that we're in the next group, and we all play a few rounds, none of us getting called. Until the fifth round when, lucky me, my number gets called. I give both Anders and Charlotte a shit-eating grin as I head to the baked goods table. Not being a sore loser, I let Charlotte pick the baked goods as we head over to the hayride.

"Know what you're going to have us do this afternoon?" Charlotte asks.

"I have some ideas," I say, smiling before kissing the side of her head. I smell her perfume, and I couldn't remove the smile from my face if I tried.

Hank was very confused about the hayride, and it was a combined effort between Anders and I to get him up and situated on the ride.

We're near the back of the ride as the conductor is trying to shove two more people on the ride. "Get together real close, folks."

I take the opportunity with enthusiasm and pick up Charlotte, then put her on my lap. She doesn't try to get up and just wiggles closer. I may have miscalculated because now I'm hard, and we're at a family-friendly fall festival. She leans against me, her back pressed against my chest as she sighs.

"Thank you, Eli. Today was what I needed."

"Anything for you," I reply, and I fucking mean it. I band my hand around her waist, and I feel like I am a true champion for not coming in my pants as the hayride seems to hit every bump, pushing Charlotte's ass further against my crotch.

CHARLOTTE

Chapter Forty

My cheeks hurt from smiling so much. It feels nice to be happy. There isn't an undercurrent of guilt that comes along with how I'm enjoying myself with Eli, Anders, and Hank. I know if my mom could see me right now, this is what she would have wanted. Not the shell of the girl who never left the house, didn't laugh or smile. She would want me to be me, and the truth is I am my best self with Anders and Eli. I hate to admit it, but Mikael makes me better too. But right now I'm ignoring him and all his attempts at reaching out with letters. I'm scared, scared that he's put the nail in the coffin of our relationship. I'm mad, stewing over his diary entries, but what if the letters are ending things for real? What if this is the end? What if those letters are worse than what I read?

I shake my head and bring myself back to the present. Sitting on Eli's lap, his thighs are even bigger and stronger than I remember. His erection is digging into my ass, but I act like I don't notice it. I may exaggerate every single bump that the trailer hits. His grip is firm on my hips, and I smile over at Anders, who is looking at me like I'm his reason for living. He reaches out and places his hand on my thigh. No one on the hayride balks. Pack life is common, maybe not with Betas, but in a general sense, people are very comfortable with polyamorous relationships.

"Have you thought about what you would like to do after?" Anders asks. I know what I want, and I'm assuming they want the same thing too. Closeness, in whatever form. They just genuinely want to spend time with me, and damn if that doesn't make me feel some kind of way.

I nod and put my one hand over his. The other is on Hank's head, who is currently panting heavily and enjoying the fresh air.

"Maybe we could go back to my place, get some dinner, and carve these pumpkins we're about to pick out?"

Anders smiles, and I feel Eli squeeze my hips. "That sounds perfect," Anders says, and I blush. Maybe I let Anders off too easily, seeing as we have already been intimate, but I can't help it. Something about him puts me at ease, and I know he was being completely truthful with me when he told me how he felt. While Eli and I are in a good place, I haven't so much as kissed him, but after today... Well, after the last few months, I think he deserves it. I know I sure as hell need it.

I'd be lying if I said that my appetite for my Alphas wasn't growing day by day. It's becoming slightly concerning, but not surprising. I'm on a lower suppressant, and our pheromones were built for each other. It's what's meant to happen.

The hayride stops in the middle of the pumpkin patch, and we're the last ones to get off, having sat so close to the tractor's end. Anders holds out a hand to help me down, and then Eli has to help Hank get down the hayride steps.

"What are you going to carve into yours?" I ask Eli.

"A fox, obviously."

I roll my eyes. "Obviously."

"What about you?"

"Mmm, not sure. I think I'll need the pumpkin to speak to me first."

Anders, decisive as ever, picks out his pumpkin immediately and holds it under his arm. He holds Hank's leash as Eli and I look around. Eli picks the most hideous warty pumpkin with green splotches, and I finally settle on a mammoth of a pumpkin, in which I make Eli carry.

"You just don't do small do you, Char baby?" Eli says, and I grin.

I think about the two large men in front of me.

Eli taps the farmer, who drives the tractor on the shoulder. "Would you mind taking a picture of us?" The farmer nods and holds Eli's phone. He puts my giant pumpkin on the ground. Eli's arm is around my shoulders, and Anders is around my waist as Hank sits at our feet. The moment feels profound and sweet.

But like always, there's a deep-rooted negative feeling in the back of my head about how a man with dark eyes, a bad attitude, and a campfire scent should be in the photo too.

It's a mess of pumpkin guts and seeds all over the kitchen counter by the time we're done. Eli carves a surprisingly on point fox into his pumpkin, and Anders does a spider. I carved mine to have a giant face and put Ander's pumpkin inside of its mouth.

"Hope you weren't planning on bringing your pumpkin home," I tell him.

"I'll just have to visit it here."

I smirk at him as I toss the pumpkin remains in the trash and wash my hands.

The front door slams, and I turn around to Piper waving the disturbing pink-colored envelope.

"The daily depression mail has arrived. Are you going to open it this time?" she asks, not taking the time to realize we have guests. As soon as she looks up and sees Eli and Anders, her cheeks flush, and she hides the pink envelope under the mail.

"You can just put it on the table, and no."

I have a week's worth of pink envelopes. All addressed to me from Mikael. I know that I should probably open them and see what he has to say. But I'm feeling petty and pissed.

Anders and Eli both act like they are busy searching for pumpkin seeds on the table. That's when I get suspicious. "Did you know he's been writing letters?" I ask them.

"He might have said something," Eli says.

"Did he mention what I read?"

"Not specifics," Eli says.

"Mmm. Well, I'm not sure a simple letter is good enough."

Neither of the guys says anything, and I'm glad. I feel bad that they are constantly in the middle, it's not fair to them.

Piper gives me a look from the corner of the room, and I already know what she wants to say. She doesn't have to vocalize it, she already has. She scolded me for stealing what was clearly Mikael's private journal and taking things he said while he was upset to heart. She also mentioned over and over how letters were always our thing, and to give him a chance. Maybe if I read it, I would feel better.

I will give Mikael credit. He has been sending one every day. Perhaps I'm the chicken shit for not finding the courage to open it just yet. He may have also sent some text messages that I have left unread. I'm not sure why the idea of getting under his skin gives me a high. Maybe it's because he is a permanent resident under mine.

"Well, I won't bother you. I was just stopping by to eat and grab some of my study guides before heading to the library," Piper says, and I nod.

"We have pizza coming if you'd like to stay. Should be here soon," Anders says.

Piper groans and nods her head. "That sounds amazing, if you don't mind."

"Of course not," Anders says confidently. It's clear that his respect for Piper is pretty high, as it should be. She picked me off the floor and didn't let me spiral too hard, even with everything on her plate. If it weren't for Piper, we probably wouldn't all be in this kitchen right now. I don't even want to think about where I would be without her.

"Oh, Charles, can you help me with something?" Piper says as she walks to her room. I sigh and follow her as she shuts the door behind me.

"You better fuck their brains out tonight."

I blink rapidly at Piper. She looks tired, and I know she's been studying and working so hard. I wish I could do more. But this is definitely not what I thought she would be pulling me into her room to discuss.

"What?"

"Please fuck them for the both of us." I clearly give her a curious look. "Ew, gross. I don't want your man. But I'm not getting any, and you have two guys who are basically drooling over you in our kitchen. Please fuck them. Get all this tension out of your sweet little system, and then tell me all about it."

I stare at her and blink a few more times. Not knowing what to say.

"And for the love of god, open that poor man's letters."

"Piper—"

"No. Listen to me." She grabs me by the shoulders and looks me in the eye. The look on her face is serious and cautious at the same time. "Now is your chance. They've made the logistics of this relationship possible. Please, Charlotte, don't make yourself suffer for another minute. Be with your scent matches, be happy. You deserve it."

I sniffle and wipe my nose. "Why do you have to be so fucking sweet? Don't you know I'm a crier now? You can't say that kind of shit."

"I mean it. Go fuck those hockey players, get your bite marks, babies, whatever makes you happy. It's what I want for you, and you know it's what your parents wanted."

I shove at her shoulder, so over the dramatics. "Fine, I'll fuck their brains out, you happy?"

She arches an eyebrow. "And you'll read the letters?"

I roll my eyes. "Maybe."

"I'll take it," Piper says, and we walk back into the kitchen where a grinning Anders and Eli stand. *I wonder how much they heard.*

Am I hiding in the bathroom right now? Yes, yes, I am. I feel more nervous tonight than I did that night of the hot tub when I knew we would all be together for the first time. Why am I so fucking nervous all the sudden?

There's a light knock at the door, and I sigh and crack it open, looking up to see a smiling Eli.

"You hiding in here?"

I groan and open the door for him to fully come into the bathroom.

"I'm nervous," I admit.

His eyebrows furrow as he looks down at me. God, he looks so handsome. The NHL has filled him out. He was already big before, but now he looks stronger. I even like the stubble along his jawline.

"Baby, we don't have to do anything you don't want to." Of course he says the sweet thing, and I know neither of them would pressure me to be intimate.

"I want to. I guess I'm just scared it won't be the same as before, or that... I don't know." It's hard to explain exactly how I'm feeling. "I just don't want to disappoint you."

He steps closer to me to where he's fully in my space now. His hands are on my hips as he lifts me to sit on the vanity counter. He's still taller than me at this height. It's just not as severe. I expect him to be all cute and adorable and give me the same speech he and Anders did before that they will want me in any state or form. But he doesn't. His hands cup my jaw, and he just goes for it and takes the kiss from me.

He doesn't hold back as his lips touch mine. His thumbs press against my cheekbones as his fingertips dig into the back of my neck and head. My hands automatically grip his shirt and pull him closer to me. With Eli's lips on mine, all my worries and fears about being intimate slowly dissipate. I can feel how much he craves me in his kiss. Eli isn't hesitant at all as he demands access to my mouth, both of our lips parting as I taste him for the first time in months.

Both of us moan against one another as the kiss deepens. Our scents fully suffocate the small half bathroom. I can feel myself getting wetter with anticipation the more he kisses me. One of his hands leaves my face and trails down my body where he squeezes my hip and drags my body to the vanity edge, pushing me against his firm, muscular chest. He holds me close as he kisses me, not asking for anything more. I'm flooded with emotion by how content Eli and Anders are to just be with me. They would be happy to kiss me forever. I've always been afraid of not being wanted or good enough. But to them, I am, and I plan on never letting this feeling go again.

Eli needs to know just how much I need and miss him too.

"Eli," I whisper as I break the kiss, and he immediately starts trailing kisses along my jawline and throat.

"God, you're so fucking beautiful." He continues kissing the tender spots that he knows I like, and I have to collect myself.

"Eli." He finally straightens and looks at me. I can tell he's nervous that I'm stopping things. But I know, without a shadow of a doubt, that if I told him I wasn't ready, he would be content and hold me all night. "Let's get Anders and go to my bed."

His bright green eyes bore into mine, and his hands are back on my jaw. I don't want to be coddled by him, and he must sense it as he grins and picks me up by my waist, tossing me over his shoulder. He swings the bathroom door open and barks the order to his packmate. "Anders, bedroom, now."

I'm upside down and pushing myself up from Eli's perfect ass when I see the beaming grin on Anders' face. The last thought I have before Eli tosses me on the bed is that I deserve to be happy, and I'm not going to overthink this.

Chapter Forty-One

*D*on't overthink, I chant in my head. But as Eli's thighs bracket my hips as he gets on top of me on the bed, I begin to overthink everything.

What if the suppressants make me not able to get as wet as I need to?

What if I taste different?

I haven't been knotted in forever. What if it hurts?

What if Eli wishes I looked like I did when we first met?

"Hey," he says in a gentle voice, leaning down and kissing the side of my head. "I want you, I want this. You look fucking beautiful and perfect, and you smell so goddamn good I might come in my pants."

That lightens the mood, and I smile. They're my scent matches. They're the loves of my life. Why am I freaking out?

"I think we need to get that little brain to shut off," he says, pointing at my head. The mattress dips as Anders sits next to us, and I lick my lips.

"You know she can't think straight when she's getting eaten out," Anders says to Eli, who snaps his fingers and points at Anders.

"Good point."

He doesn't hesitate or ask, just unbuttons my jeans and starts rolling them down along with my panties. As soon as he has them down to my ankles and I'm helping him kick them off, he groans. A deep inhale sounds through the room as he grips my hips and pushes my leg back. Anders and him have an unspoken agreement as Anders holds my leg back and Eli trails kisses up my thigh.

Eli is toying with me, making me anticipate his every move as Anders uses his free hand to roll up my top. I did wear a fairly attractive purple lace bra tonight. Maybe I had high hopes or knew I would be getting undressed tonight. He leans forward and licks and sucks my breast through the fabric.

I forgot how all-consuming it is to have multiple Alphas' attention on you. Both of their lips leave wet hot kisses, making my skin prickle. I can't help but to wiggle at their ministrations. Each of my hands goes into the back of their heads and tangle with their hair. Anders sucks on my nipple through the fabric, and my back arches off of the mattress. I attempt to shut my legs, but Anders and Eli both hold my thighs flat on the bed.

Eli's teeth grace the inside of my thigh. He's so close to my pussy his chin grazes my clit slightly. I moan as his sharp canine drags along the tender flesh. At least I'm in the right state of mind to not beg him to bite me, but I wouldn't mind. If anything, it would lock us together for life with no need for me to feel this sense of panic anymore.

Eli must notice my thoughts and worries coming back to my head as he leans forward and swipes his tongue from my entrance to my clit. He swirls the tip of his tongue against the sensitive bundle of nerves, and I shudder. Eli and Anders work together to drive me crazy and remove all negative thinking from my mind.

It works almost too good. Four hands on me, two mouths. The overwhelming scent of maple, pine, and hazelnut in the room has me nearly coming. But when Eli puts two fingers inside of me, curling them, touching just the perfect spot while still sucking on my clit, I know I'm close. It's when Anders sucks on my nipple so hard I nearly black out that sends me over the edge. My thighs are shaking under their firm grip. My fingers nearly pull out their hair as my back arches and my body trembles. I can hear how wet I am as Eli continues fingering me throughout my orgasm. I'm a panting mess as he finally gives me some reprieve, and I'm lying here, blinking up at the ceiling.

"I think you fucked the negative thoughts out of me," I say in between breaths. I watch as Eli and Anders undress like their clothes are on fire, and Eli is back on his knees between my legs.

"Not yet, baby," Eli says, gripping his cock and thrusting into me. I groan at the full sensation of his cock entering me. His hands are on my hips as he slowly thrusts, his gaze fully locked on where we meet. The look of complete awe and hunger in his eyes has me shivering. He looks at me like I'm his everything. I bask in it. He leans forward, kissing me softly before pulling back again to watch himself fuck me.

It takes me a moment until I look over to my left and watch as Anders strokes his weeping cock while he watches. One of his hands grip his knot while the other grips his cock loosely, his fist going up and down the length of him. He flicks his wrist at the tip and drags his pre-cum down his length to his knot. It makes my mouth water, and I lick my lips as I watch him. Anders' gaze connects with mine, then down to where my breasts bounce, until he finally stares at where Eli and I are connected. It's then that he speeds up how fast he's jerking off. I moan as I watch, and Eli groans above me.

Eli's hand moves from my hip and drags it down to my oversensitive clit. He rubs firm but rhythmic circles while he fucks in and out of me. I can't believe I thought I would have a problem getting wet. Every time Eli fucks in and out of me, I can feel my wetness gliding down my ass and thighs.

I hold out my hand to Anders, who immediately shuffles forward. I take his cock in my hand and take over for him, jerking him off over my chest. Both Anders and Eli can't help but watch what I'm doing and groan in unison.

"Fuck, *Kulta*. Are you going to let me come on those pretty tits?"

I nod my head, my heady Omega nature wanting for nothing more than this Alpha to mark me as his in every way possible. I want to leave this room and have everyone know that they belong to me based on my scent alone.

"Gonna knot you, baby," Eli says. A trail of sweat drips down his temple as he grips my hips firmly and thrusts hard. I nearly scream as he pushes his thick knot into my pussy. God, I missed this fullness. "Missed this sweet, tight pussy so much."

My movements are unsteady and shaky as I touch Anders' dick. Eli's knot inflates to completion, and Anders uses his hand to play with my clit as Eli ruts into me. As my second orgasm starts to hit, I can't help but squeeze Anders tighter, making him groan and thrust into my fist. At the same time, my body starts to go static from my release. I feel Anders' warm cum drip on my chest.

I can't help the obscene moans leaving my lips. "Your knot is so fucking good," I tell Eli. He moans under my praise. His eyes trail from my face to where Anders' cum lies on my chest. My lips are parted as I whimper, the overstimulation almost being too much.

Anders groans next to me as he puts two fingers in his cum and brings it to my mouth. I eagerly take them between my lips and suck, tasting his essence. His pupils are blown as he watches on with rapture.

Eli must be watching too, as his grip on me tightens and his hips stutter. His warm cum fills my pussy as he ruts into me. "So perfect, little Omega."

My cheeks heat and I nod. I need them close. Well, Eli is as close as he can possibly be, since he's knotted in my pussy. But he leans forward, keeping his body weight off of me and not lying down in Anders' cum. Eli gives Anders a look, and he rolls his eyes, grabbing a shirt and wiping off my chest. I pout slightly, but his scent is still there, so I don't complain. With my chest clean, Eli rests his head on my shoulder, and Anders lies down next to me. I pet his hair lazily as we lie there in silence.

Negative thoughts don't flood me like they used to. I don't feel consumed with guilt for missing out on this these past months. I feel content for the first time in a long time, and I just want it to last.

After a quick clean up, it only seemed fair that Anders got his turn, and so I was knotted yet again. I didn't realize just how much I missed that feeling of being full. We were all wrung out from our rounds of debauchery, but a light snore wakes me up.

The three of us on a queen bed is comical and inefficient. I smile at their large sleeping forms on my bed as I make my way to the bathroom. A stack of pink envelopes stops me in my tracks as I look down at them and groan internally. I don't know why I do it, maybe because how nearly whole I felt tonight, but not complete? Or maybe it's Piper's words to me from earlier tonight. For whatever reason, I take the stack of letters and bring them with me into the bathroom.

I sit down and stare at them for a long moment, contemplating putting them back. I don't know just what to expect in the contents and if it would make things better or worse.

I sigh and apparently get some courage as I open up the first letter. It's short and to the point.

Charlotte,

That journal wasn't meant for you to see. Can you let me explain? I sent you three texts today too.

Mikael

I roll my eyes at the bluntness and open the next one.

Charlotte,

I've read all your responses on the journal entries, and I don't know what to say. Coming to terms with the fact that I might be a selfish asshole is a little daunting. I'm trying to put aside my feelings and put myself in your shoes. Can we talk?

Mikael

Still not really an apology, but I never know what to expect from Mikael.

Charlotte,

I never said that I was sorry, truly sorry about what happened to Kathy. I don't know what it's like to have a mom who actually cares about you the way yours did. I also don't know what exactly happened, but I want to know, I want to understand. I feel like shit about how I handled things and spoke to you. But I still need to know why you didn't trust us to take care of you and help you through this. These last few months of not really knowing how you were doing... I think it broke me.

Mikael

Charlotte,

I've tried calling you five times and
have left a ton of text messages.
Will you please talk to me?
        Mikael

Charlotte,

I can't take your dog to the vet, and I'm not
thoughtful enough like Anders to get you a
fucking Build-A-Bear. But I do care more than
I think I even realized. Will you please talk to
me? I feel like I'm shouting into the void and all
I want is some clarity. Can we please talk?

P.S. I will keep sending letters every fucking day.

-Thinking of you, Mikael

I can't help the smile that takes over as I read the letters. I read them in Mikael's tone, and I can't help it, I feel a little guilty for having held on to the letters for so long without reading them. I still feel a little angry after having read them, if I'm being honest. It's clear that what Mikael and I have to work through is going to take more than pen and paper. More than a simple phone call or text message. We need time and space to talk in person, I need to hear him say he's sorry, and as much as I hate to admit it, I have things to be sorry for as well. We're a pack, and we always will be. I'm hopeful that Mikael is ready to finally accept his place in this pack and truly put in the effort to build us back together.

As I make my way back to the bed, Anders holds out a hand and draws me back to the bed. I'm basically on top of him.

"You alright?"

I nod and kiss his bare chest. "Better than I've been in a long time."

He clears his throat and kisses the top of my head.

"We have a game against the Lightning in two days. Do you think you could come? I know it would mean a lot to Eli." I bet it would mean a lot to Mikeal as well; maybe this could be our moment.

I smile against his pec. "I'd love to come. See if you guys have improved any."

He pinches my side, and I yelp, which wakes up Eli, who attempts to tug me against his body.

"We going again then?" he asks groggily. I laugh and nod my head, unable to get enough of these two.

Have I been checking the mail religiously like a pathetic asshole? Yeah. I slam the lid to the mailbox far harder than I need to. I'm not sure what I expected after how I spoke to her, how I made the situation about myself. The moment I saw her feminine writing in my journal and read what she wrote, my stomach sank. There was realization that I'd been so fucking selfish in my own insecurities while she was suffering in her own way. After I read her letters to me, I made it my mission to earn her forgiveness, even if she doesn't want anything to do with me. In all honesty, I wouldn't blame her if she wanted to be done with me. What do I bring to this pack anyway? Regardless, even though I'm not worthy of her, of Anders and Eli, I'm willing to do anything to be a part of this pack.

I sulk back into the house. "Still no letter?" Eli asks. I want to reply with obviously fucking not. My hands are empty. So instead I just shake my head. "If it makes you feel any better, I can tell she misses you."

"Yeah?" I sit down on the couch. We're all getting our shit together to head to the stadium for the game today. I haven't been able to gauge just how Eli feels about it. The Lightning was going to give him everything, but he gave it away so he could have a pack, and so that he could have Charlotte. In many ways, Eli is the type of man I want to be.

"I can just tell, ya know. She misses you, even if she's pissed at you, rightfully so." I don't say shit back, because he's right. Charlotte has every reason to hate me right now. There's a part of me that's so deeply insecure I wonder if she only misses me because of my scent and nothing else. "Maybe you need to figure out a way to get her attention."

"I've been writing letters, texting, and calling. She ignores them all."

"But she hasn't blocked your number?" My brows furrow as I look at Eli.

"No, she hasn't."

"Then you've still got a chance. Figure out a way to make it happen."

I nod my head and devise a plan as we drive to Navy Federal Stadium.

"Don't let Petrov get the puck. Martel, hit that motherfucker into the ice," our captain, Alexi Babanin, says to me. The man has been playing hockey for almost as long as I've been alive. I don't think this is anywhere near his last season. Somehow the old fucker just keeps getting goals and taking hits like a goddamn mack truck. He's just as tall as me and probably has me beat when it comes to bulk. He's currently missing his front tooth, and his dark hair is graying at the corners. He's thirty-seven, but it's clear a pro career has been hard on his body.

"You got it, cap."

"Becky tells me your lady friend is coming tonight," he says in his thick Russian accent. It makes Eli's nickname even funnier.

"Yeah," I say solemnly.

"Do not wait. Look at me. Old man, no Omega. All I have is hockey. Do not fuck it up."

"She won't talk to me. I've tried everything." I know I sound like a little bitch, but thankfully Alexi takes pity on me. He half hits, half smacks my shoulder with his gloved hand.

"When I was young, I had this pretty little thing. He was sweet, my Gregor." He looks off to the distance like he is reminiscing about this lost love, and I'm not stupid enough to take him out of whatever he is thinking about. He shakes his head at the memory and smiles. "He always hated it the most when I was hurt on the ice. Always 'poor baby,' I will take care of you when I bled. Like he was the Alpha and I the Omega." He shakes his head and smiles at the memory. "Omegas, at the end of the day, don't want their Alphas hurting."

"Okay?"

"Fuck, *rebenok*. Get a little boo boo or something, and she will come running to make sure you are okay."

"Babanin, you're a fucking genius."

He raises his arms in surrender. "I have been trying to tell everyone this for years." His face then gets serious. "Don't do anything until the last period and only if we are winning."

I shake my head in agreement. There's a lot that I would do for Charlotte, but I'm not about to put my team in a bad place just to get her attention. If we aren't doing well, I'll come up with something else.

I'm about to walk away when Alexi stops me. "Does she have any Omega friends?"

I shrug. "Maybe. Are you ready to settle down?"

"Why not? Pack contracts are apparently a thing now." He laughs as he walks away. I always thought Alexi was a few brain cells short, but apparently not. He's spent most of his career in Dallas, but was plucked to the Foxes during the expansion draft. At first he was pissed, but it seems like he's finally found his place on the team.

We're all dressed and ready for pre-game skate when Anders stands next to me, his gaze super focused.

"Where is she sitting?" I ask quietly so just he can hear.

"Her and Piper should be section 101 row D, I think."

I nod my head, happy that she's not here by herself. If anyone is going to make sure she's okay, it would be Piper.

"Maybe she can sit in the box next time."

I can't see the smile behind his goalie mask, but I know it's there. "Glad to see you finally care."

"I've always cared," I say it solemnly, feeling like a piece of shit that none of them realize how much I truly care about them. I need to do better.

"Good to see you showing it."

I look down at my skates, the blade of my stick hitting the toe of my skate. "I'm going to do better." Anders' shoulder hits mine, rocking me to the side.

"That's all we ever wanted, man."

I clear my throat. "Alright, great, enough feelings. Let's go out there and kick some ass."

Alexi makes some crazy caterwauling noise as he comes to the front of the tunnel. "Let us light these motherfuckers up!" he says as the horn blares, and we skate on the ice to stretch and prepare for the game.

My gaze automatically goes to section 101. Her blonde hair is wavy and tucked behind her ears, and she's smiling. A true beaming smile I never thought I'd see again. At that moment, my plan is clear.

CHARLOTTE

Chapter Forty-Three

The stadium is loud and lively as the guys hit the ice. The sheer amount of excitement and enthusiasm has me grinning. It feels nothing like the last time I was here. When I came here with John—I grimace thinking about the perv—I felt suffocated and wanted nothing more than to escape. But now I can feel the excitement zip through me like an electric shock. I want to be here and, more than anything, I want to watch my guys do what they do best.

Anders is the easiest to spot, looking like Gumby as he skates on the ice. His helmet is fun. It's dark blue like their uniforms with two gnarly looking foxes on each side. I can see some tendrils of blond hair peeking from the base of his helmet. He immediately starts doing his ice humping work outs, and I pretty much need to fan myself.

"Shit, Charles, you better chill out or else we might have a riot in here." I blush and shrug my shoulders.

"Do you not see him doing splits and basically humping the ice?"

"Yes, I see it. Hey, who is number eight?"

I squint and try to remember the players that the guys told me. When I see the C patch on his sleeve, I shake my head. "That's the captain, Alexi Bandnin."

"That ass," Piper whistles.

"He could be your father."

"I would definitely call him daddy if he wanted." I shove her, and she laughs. "What can I say? I've got a penchant for older men."

"Yeah, we know."

She furrows her brow, and I sigh. "Your celebrity crushes are Jeffrey Dean Morgan, Denzel Washington, and Mads Mikkelsen." I grimace at the last one.

"Bitch, have you not seen Hannibal?"

"Yes, and that's what makes it weirder."

She rolls her eyes but watches number eight as he skates. "You know I could use a distraction."

"Can't you fuck an age appropriate nerd in one of your classes?"

Piper grimaces and shakes her head. "You would think that as medical professionals they could find the clit. You would think wrong."

"Gross."

"Gross, indeed," she agrees and I go back to eye fucking my guys on the ice. They are taking turns shooting on Anders, and damn, is he limber. His legs bend incredibly fast to stop pucks with his leg pads. Eli doesn't have his helmet on, and his reddish brown hair gives him away. He must feel me staring as he gives me a boyish grin as he hits the puck that goes right past Anders' waist and into the goal.

I just know that if Anders didn't have his mitt in one hand and his stick in the other that he would be giving Eli the finger. Mikael shoots, and Anders blocks it. They bump their cute little gloved fists, and then that dark stare is on me, and my heart sinks. He isn't growly or giving me a death glare. His expression is soft and almost... pleading with me?

"Have you read his letters yet?" Piper asks, and I nod my head.

"Yeah."

"Making him suffer?"

"Yeah," I say regretfully.

"Fair enough. He was always my least favorite." I smack her lightly on the arm.

"You can't have favorites in a pack."

"You can't have favorites in your own pack. Doesn't mean I can't have favorites in your pack. For me, it's Anders, Eli, then Mikael."

"Yeah, well, one day when you have a pack, I'm going to rank them, and you aren't going to like it."

"Don't hold your breath because you're going to be waiting a long time."

"Whatever." I shoo her with my hand as I watch them continue to warm up.

"How much longer are you going to make him agonize over all his life's decisions?"

"I'm hoping we can talk tonight."

"Good. You want a beer?" She nudges my shoulder, and I can tell she's happy that I'm finally going to have my pack together again, maybe almost as happy as me.

"Seltzer please."

"Of course, the precious Omega doesn't want a beer," she jokes and squeezes my arm gently as she squeezes past our row to go get the drinks. I can now openly stare at each of them and damn, do they look good. They look even bigger on the ice with their padding. All of their asses look even bigger, and I kinda like it. Something is wrong with me.

The buzzer sounds, and the announcements are made for the starting lineups. We do the national anthem, which I always thought was weird as fuck for sports games. The woman who sings is on point though, hitting each note.

Just like that, the game starts, and it's like bats out of hell skating rapidly on the ice. I'm not sure if the game itself is fascinating, or if I just like watching them do something that they are so passionate about. My relationship with hockey always seems to be a roller-coaster. There are times when I hate and blame it for most of my problems. But right now I get it. Watching them play at this level. Hockey and I aren't in a competition, but it is something that they love, and it's clear in the way that they play.

It still shocks me to see Eli and Mikael so graceful on the ice. Not only that, but how truly fast they can skate. I'm not even paying attention to plays, I just can't help tracking my guys on the ice.

Piper comes back with my drink, and I thank her and sip slowly.

When I glance over, Piper is wearing a jersey she wasn't wearing before.

"Where did you get that?"

"Just bought it, you like?" I roll my eyes as I see the number eight on the back.

"Sure, Pipes."

"Oh, you're just jealous because you don't have a jersey."

"I can't just wear one. That would be fucked up." She taps her chin and nods.

"We'll have to suture you something together."

"It's called sewing."

"Same fucking thing." She stands up suddenly and cheers. "Your man just scored."

"Shit." I'm on my feet and clapping and cheering with the rest of the fans in an instant. His grin is clear even from where I'm sitting, and he glances at me before his team swarms him. Including Mikael. My heart swells at their affection for each other when I sit down. It just makes it even more clear that I'm done making him suffer—done with both of our suffering.

Suddenly the seat next to me has a resident. He looks familiar, but I can't place him. He looks me up and down like he knows me as he takes his seat.

"So you're Charlotte."

Piper gives him a glare, and I can tell she is completely zoned into the conversation.

"And you are?"

He holds out his hand. "I'm Jake. Eli, Anders, and Mikael's agent."

"Ah, right?" I hold out my hand and shake the Beta's hand. I swallow back the metallic tang of fury I feel for this asshole.

"Guess I owe you for getting them traded and the way they are handling Tampa right now."

"Hmm." I don't know what to say.

"It's important they stay focused and don't get distracted."

"Are you saying I'm a distraction?"

He looks me up and down again. It's not like he's checking me out, but almost like he doesn't see the appeal.

"Of course not." He sits back down and doesn't speak to me the rest of the game, but to the man to his left.

"What a fucking prick," Piper mumbles next to me, and I nod my head in agreement and wonder if I should say something to the guys. I don't want to put a wedge between them and their agent, but the way he spoke to me was not okay.

I ignore Jake to my left and try to enjoy the remainder of the game.

To put it plainly, the Foxes are beating the Lightning's ass. It's five to one, and there's only ten minutes left in the game. Not that a comeback couldn't happen, but with how intensely our team is playing, I don't think they stand a chance. All three of them are on the ice again, and I'm laser focused on each of them.

The opposing team has gotten a little dirty with their moves since they are at such a deficit. One of them gets a break away and is immediately headed toward Anders. Mikael draws him to the right side of the ice and pushes him against the glass. Fans are banging on the glass and cheering him on as he attempts to get the puck from the other player. It's a mix of Mikael pushing him into the plexiglass and the other player elbowing him.

It's then that the elbow hits Mikael square in the face, knocking off his helmet. I'm on my feet immediately and watch as a thick trail of blood drips from his face onto the ice. He doesn't need assistance and skates back to his bench. I watch on, expecting him to sit down and have his nose or mouth inspected. But they send him back to the locker room. The announcement is loud over the speakers. "Number sixty-seven, Mikael Martel is being sent back for medical attention. We're waiting to hear about the severity."

I'm on my feet, and Jake scoffs behind me. "It's hockey. He's going to get hurt. I'm sure he's fine."

"Fuck you," I spit, and Piper is standing.

"What do you need, Charlotte?"

"I've gotta make sure he's okay." My heart is beating out of my chest and more than anything, I wish we had a bond right now, so I would have a grasp on his emotions. If we were bonded, I would know for sure if he was okay. It makes my chest hurt thinking about him being in pain or hurting.

"Okay, I don't think they will let you see him, Charles."

"They better let me see him. You." I point to Jake. "Get me in to see him, now."

"Sorry, sweetheart, no can do."

"Take me to the locker room, and I won't tell them that you called me sweetheart or a distraction. I'm sure by now you know how they can be when people hurt my feelings." Jake blanches but weighs his options.

"Fine, let's go."

He walks so damn slowly I'm about to push him, but he has a lanyard with a barcode on it and takes me down to the locker room level. Security scans it and gives me a curious yet expectant look. He puts a hand on Jake's shoulder but waves me in. "Mr. Martel said she was allowed back, but no one else."

Jake rolls his eyes but walks back to his seat, and I press the door open. Mikael is sitting in front of his locker on the bench holding a cloth to his lip. I can't help it. I'm in front of him in a second, grabbing his wrists.

"Are you okay? Do you need to go to the hospital?"

He drops the rag, and his lip is barely bleeding. "I'm fine."

I gape at him and look at his lip that is just slightly swollen and cracked.

"Then why didn't you stay on the bench?" I push his shoulder.

"I had to get your attention somehow."

Irritated, I turn around and go to walk away, pissed that he would trick me into thinking he was hurt. There's a firm grip on my wrist, and I'm spun around. He hasn't taken his skates off yet and is so tall and menacing as he looks down at me.

"I can't go back to the game now that I've gone for medical attention." His grip doesn't leave my wrist. "I just wanted you to talk to me. I wanted to talk to you." I tug my wrist away, but he doesn't let me leave. "I'm sorry," he says softly.

"For what?" I ask.

"Can we sit?"

I huff slightly but sit next to him. He's only taken off his gloves and helmet. He looks larger than life like this. And I hate how much I like it.

He grabs my hand, and I let him. He stares down at my knuckles as he toys with them. His touch feels so fucking good. Damn, do I hope this apology is good.

"I'm sorry for only thinking about myself and how I felt and not giving you a chance to explain. I'm really fucking sorry for my journal entries and how they hurt you."

"They did hurt," I say softly, and he squeezes my hand. I take a deep breath. "I'm sorry for taking the journal." He shakes his head and squeezes my hand again, then shocks me with his next sentence.

"I'm glad you did. I think we needed it. I was angry, frustrated that you left, just like everyone else. Mad that you didn't give us an explanation and disappeared. I know Eli and Anders care about me, but you were mine, and I was yours. I've never felt so intensely for someone in my life, and you leaving just made what everyone always said about me feel true. That I was a piece of shit and not worth it. I went back to my old self, and I put that blame on you instead of thinking about what you went through, only how I felt. I want to do better."

My eyes are watery, and I nod my head. "I watched her die."

He grabs me and puts me on his lap. He feels huge with his pads still on, and I wrap my arms around him. His campfire scent is so thick after sweating during the game.

"I'm sorry, *mon doux.*" I can't help but give a tear-filled smile at his use of the term of endearment and hold him tighter. "I'm going to be a better Alpha. I'll prove that I should be a part of this pack, if you're willing to forgive me. I want to be here for you. Whenever you're ready I'm ready to listen to everything. I'm sorry I wasn't listening before, I was being selfish."

I lean back, looking at his face, and I can see the honesty there. "I'm sorry for leaving you, Mikael. I was just in such a bad place."

"You promise if anything happens again, we will stick together? No more running?"

"No more running."

Mikael looks up at the left corner where the game is streaming, and he looks back at me and grins before taking a fist full of my hair and crashing my lips against his.

Chapter Forty-Four

I check the feed of the game in the left-hand corner of the room. Eight minutes, which will probably turn into twenty. Charlotte on my lap feels perfect. Why I was so hard on her and myself doesn't seem to make sense as her blue eyes connect with mine. I can't hold back anymore. I grip her soft hair at the base of her head and bring her lips to mine.

She tastes sweeter than I remember, her soft lips pressed against mine. It hurts, but I welcome the pain as she kisses me back with just as much intensity as I'm giving. I shuffle her on my lap, wishing I didn't have all this gear on. She perfumes, and I groan. The idea of my teammates scenting her makes me growl, and she gasps as she parts from the kiss. I place her down next to me, quickly ripping off my jersey, shoulder pads, and elbow pads, and tossing them into the locker.

"Mikael, what are you doing?"

I grab her hand and drag her to the showers, stopping by each stall and turning on the hot water. The steam billows into the air, and the fans automatically turn on.

"Like I'd let anyone smell what's fucking mine."

She moans, and I grab her by the thighs and ass, hefting her so that her back is pressed against the brick wall. She moans when I knead her ass.

"I fucking need you, *mon sucre d'érable.*"

"Who do I belong to?" she asks breathlessly.

"You're mine. So fucking mine."

"That's all I ever wanted," she says, her lips next to mine as I capture her mouth again, putting everything behind the kiss. My apologies, my insecurities, how much I need and want her. Showing her that we're fate, we were meant for each other and I'm never leaving.

Her teeth drag along the busted part of my lip, and I groan.

"Don't ever pretend to be hurt again."

"Never."

"Don't push me away."

I shake my head, wanting to kiss her again.

"You'll be mine, for real this time?"

"Always belonged to you, *mon doux.* Never stopped belonging to you. Never stopped loving you."

She gasps, her weight still supported by the wall and my hands.

"You've never said it before. None of us have said it before."

"We were fucking stupid, Charlotte. You should have known every day that I love you—that we love you. I'm going to be a good Alpha to you." I squeeze her ass because I don't have a free hand to touch her face. "Let me love you, okay?"

Her hands cup my jaw, her thumbs rubbing soft circles on my cheekbones. Her blue eyes shine as she smiles. "Okay, only if you let me love you too."

I smile. "That's all I need."

"Good, because I love you too, Mikael."

My lips are on her again, and I can't describe the all-consuming feeling of trust and care in this moment. I've never told someone I love them before. It's like it's been reserved for Charlotte this whole time. Like we had to go through all this horrible shit, be broken down into traumatic little fragments, so that we could be pieced together into something stronger and imperfectly beautiful.

We had to break for me to understand what she deserves, what my pack deserves. We're not complete without each other. This pack is built on a lot of hurt, but a lot of love too.

"I love you," I say breathlessly between kisses. It feels like so much weight and internal struggle has been taken off my shoulders to finally be able to say it. To communicate fully how much she means to me. How much being a pack together is more important than anything.

"I need you, Mikael," she says, grinding against me, but between the layers, I feel nothing.

"Gonna need to be fast."

"I don't care. Give me what's mine," she says in a demanding tone. I can't help but grin, missing this side of her so fucking much.

"You want my cock, *mon sucre d'érable?*"

"I want fucking everything."

I groan and put her on her feet, so I can slide down my pants, and the velcro is so damn loud as I push my breezers down as fast as I can. I go to take my shin guards off, but Charlotte is already grabbing me by the neck to bring me down for more kisses. Not being able to resist or wanting to strain my neck, I want to put her in the same position we were in.

"My leggings," she says, and I look down at her dress and leggings, then lick my lips.

"Fuck 'em." I lift her dress past her hips and grip the hem at her crotch, ripping a hole. The noise is satisfying as I pick her back up and push her against the wall. My hand goes between us as I feel how wet her panties are. "Still always so wet for your Alpha, aren't you?"

"Always," she pants as I push the material to the side and stroke my thumb against her clit a few times.

"Fuck, how am I supposed to make this quick? I want to devour you, *mon sucre d'érable.* I missed you and this pussy." I accentuate the statement by strumming her clit softly. "So fucking much."

"Please, Mikael."

"Only if you promise we get to take this slower later. I want to taste you and knot you so many fucking times you can't walk the next day."

She moans at my words and nods her head.

"You're sleeping in my bed tonight."

"Yes! Please, please, Mikael."

"Always so sweet when you beg."

I fist my cock and push forward into her tight pussy, leaning forward and moaning against her neck as she takes all of me. Her wetness surrounds me, and I sigh, remembering how she's always ready to go. Her scent fills the space, but the steam helps circulate it out of the room. I groan as she perfumes, and I feel her slick dripping down my shaft and onto my balls.

My grip is tight on her thighs and ass holding her up, knowing I'm leaving finger tip shaped bruises in their wake. She feels so goddamn soft I never want this to end. Her hands are tangled in my semi-damp hair, and I wish more than anything that her dress was off and that I could watch her tits bounce while I fuck her. *Later.*

"Are you going to come for me?" It's nearly a growl against her ear.

"Are you going to come inside of me?" she replies, and I moan, pushing into her harder and faster. I almost feel bad about her back hitting the wall. But when she moans after each thrust, I forgive myself.

"Going to fill this tight, wet pussy up, little Omega. Mark you as mine."

"Yes, yes, yes. Mikael." She's gripping my hair so tightly that I know she's getting close, the small flutters of her pussy making me shudder. I have to hold back from pushing my knot inside of her, even though it's all I want.

"Fuck, you drive me crazy."

Her teeth graze my neck, and I shiver, gripping her ass as I thrust into her as hard as I can without giving her my knot—it's torture.

"Mikael," she nearly shouts as she shakes under my grip, her cunt squeezing the life out of me as I try to keep my motions rhythmic. My orgasm reaches me, and I fill her up with my cum. I'm panting into her neck, and her arms are wrapped around my shoulders and her legs around my waist as she holds on for dear life.

I pull back to look at her face, and all I see is lightness, complete happiness written in her expression. She makes me smile more than anyone ever has. I can't help the stupid grin that takes over my face as I lean forward and kiss her.

"God, I missed you."

"I missed you too, my maple sugar."

She grimaces. "It's only cute in French, never again."

I laugh and squeeze her hips one more time.

"Game's almost over. I'm going to have Jake take you to the main office to wait for us." She has a slight reaction to Jake's name, and I make a note to ask her about it later. "I've got to shower your scent off, and then we can go home."

"Where you're going to shower me with knots?"

"And snacks if you're a good girl."

Her cheeks heat, and I kiss the side of her head. I put her down on the ground and grab a towel to clean her up to the best of my ability. It's part of the reason I can't let her go back to the stadium. It's more than the fact I don't want anyone scenting my Omega. But it's also a safety precaution for her.

She makes a disgusted sound. "Can I take these panties off?"

I groan, but nod my head as she takes her leggings and panties off. I plan on zipping them up in my bag. But knowing her pussy is bare under her dress both turns me on and brings out such a dark, possessive side of me that I didn't even know existed.

I look over at Anders' locker and know he will be pissed, but once he knows what happened, he will agree with me. I dig through his locker and grab his boxer briefs.

"Put these on," I tell her, and she shrugs and grabs them, sliding them on.

"These aren't going to stay on." I roll my eyes, get to my knees, and tie a knot at the top of the elastic. "This looks stupid."

"Good thing you're just going to the office and shouldn't see anyone then."

"Yeah, good thing." She kisses the center of my chest, and I kiss the top of her head. "Don't keep me waiting."

"Wouldn't dare," I reply. Hearing the final buzzer. I grab her biceps and take her to the door where Jim from security waits. "Jim, Jake should be taking Charlotte to the office. Can you make sure she gets there okay?"

"Sure thing, Mr. Martel." I give him a nod and kiss the side of Charlotte's head one more time.

"See you in a bit." She smiles at me, and I haven't been more excited to celebrate a win in my life.

Chapter Forty-Five

It's been a glorious but also long as fuck week. Mikael and I have made up, but we only had one night together before they had to go on a long trip on the road. I will give the guys credit though. The communication while they're gone has been everything I've needed to feel settled. Not to mention the flowers, chocolate-covered strawberries, and leggings and panties that have been sent to the house.

They call me every night, and I speak to each of them. Tonight's no different as I hold the phone out from my face. Anders' head is bracketed by pillows as he speaks to me. "You should move in," he says abruptly.

"What?" I say as I stop chewing my tasty cake and look back at the screen.

"Move into the house, so we can have as much time together as possible. I think we all know where this is headed. Then you don't have to worry about paying Piper anything, and you can finish school if you want."

"That's a lot, Anders."

"Is it though? You're our scent match. We're going to be together. Why fuck around?"

"Did you tell her yet?" I hear Eli say in the background, and Anders gives him a shitty look.

"Tell me what?" I ask, and Anders sighs.

"There's something about the pack contract we haven't told you." My eyebrows rise, and I'm internally freaking out about what they haven't told me. "Once we have a bonded Omega, they are permitted to travel with the team."

"What?" I'm shocked and intrigued at the same time.

"It's part of the pay cut we take to pay for our future Omega's expenses. It would be a ninety-day period to make sure it doesn't interfere with the team, but I can't imagine that it would."

"You would want that? Wouldn't it be a distraction?"

"*Kulta*, not having you with me is the biggest distraction of all. You could take classes while we were on the road."

I shrug and sigh. "I'm not even sure I really care about a degree anymore."

Eli's face pops into the corner. "You know I'm loaded, and we make a shit ton of money doing this, right? You don't have to work. If you wanted something to do, you could always sell your macrame."

I blush, loving that he remembered. "It's been a while since I've made anything."

"You could bring all your crafting shit on plane rides, and then ride my dick after a win," Eli says, and I burst out laughing.

"Well, there's one issue with this plan."

"What's that?" they say in unison.

"We're not bonded, you idiots," Mikael's voice says, though I can't see him on the screen.

"Well, that's easy to fix," Eli says.

My mouth gapes at how casually he says it, like we haven't been to hell and back to be where we are today. I haven't even gotten an 'I love you' from him or Anders, which is confusing. I know it's there, it's always been there, just never spoken.

"We're ready to change that whenever you are, *Kulta*."

"Maybe we can talk some more about it once you guys are home?"

The phone goes blurry as it's snatched out of Anders' hand, and now all I see is Mikael's beautiful face. "You're coming to our game on Saturday?" I nod my head. "Jake has box seats this time, so you don't have to sit next to anyone else."

"I'll be there. I'll wear my Foxes hoodie."

"Fuck no, you won't. I'll send you a jersey."

"If she's wearing anyone's number, it's mine," Eli says from somewhere in the room.

"Maybe I should just get an Alexi jersey."

"Don't fucking test me, Charlotte," Mikael says, and I laugh.

"Send me one of each of yours. I have an idea."

Mikael nods and leans in close to the phone and says super quietly. "Love you, night."

When the phone is handed back to Anders, his mouth is open as he stares at Mikael. It takes him a moment for his shock to subside as he looks back to the phone and then over at Mikael.

"Night, baby, see you in a few days," Eli says, and I send him an air kiss, and Anders looks back at the phone.

"Seriously?" he says in disbelief, no doubt irritated that Mikael was the first to say it.

"Snooze you lose, asshole," Mikael says, and I laugh.

"Maybe you can tell me how you feel when you get home Friday?" I suggest to Anders, and he nods his head.

"Next time, I'm taking my phone into the bathroom and getting you to play with your tits instead." I laugh again, and he shakes his head. "Night, *Kulta*."

"Night, Anders."

I snuggle next to Hank and feel lighter than I've ever felt. They want me to move in and bond with me. Part of me is still scared, but the other part of me yearns for the security of their bite marks.

I may or may not dream of bonding with the three of them that night.

It's game day, and I'm excited to be wearing my hideous yet adorable jersey. I had Piper help me Hodge-Podge it together, ripping off the number but adding all of their last names. So I'm repping Beckford, Martel, and Larsen on my back. Piper has a big test to study for, so she couldn't come. But at least I'm in a box, so I don't have to worry about anyone else's scents.

Which, for some reason, feels extra terrible today. I must be starting my period soon. Janet reduced my suppressants to an even lower dose after I told her how everything was going with the guys. Is it stupid to be excited about your therapist being happy for you? Probably, but I don't give a shit. She called me her most improved patient, and now I want a poster to tape to my wall.

She told me it's unlikely that I'll go into heat unless something triggers it, but to be vigilant. I scheduled an appointment with my physician to do blood work in a few days, so hopefully I have an idea of when it will start. It might be soon, but I'm done waiting for life to make choices for me. I was hoping maybe they would want to possibly bond during my heat. After all my research, it sounds like it's so much more pleasurable during heat, and it can help immensely with pain.

I grab my side as a slight cramp hits and take a seat. I feel a little out of place, not knowing anyone else in the box. So I just stay put and wait for the game to start. That's when a familiar smelling Beta sits next to me. I swear he smells like recycled paper. It's fucking weird, and he smells even worse today.

"Still around I see?"

"Dude, what is your deal?"

He glances at me up and down. His brows furrow, and he looks out to the ice. "Eli Beckford could be the next Sidney Crosby. I'm not going to let an Omega bring him down."

"Well, I don't know who the fuck that is, so he must not be that great."

"Jesus Christ. I thought taking their phones away and posting that night would help speed shit up, but here you are. Still pathetic and waiting for them to pay attention to you. Did they tell you about all the girls they fucked that weekend?"

"You're lying." I know he's full of shit. They would never do that, drunk or not. If they're anything like me, they are probably repulsed by anyone's scent. His words still hit me hard, no matter how not based in reality they are.

"Am I?"

"You know I'm going to tell them everything you're saying to me, right? Like you're being really stupid right now."

"We're just talking about their future, and you took it out of context. It's like Mikael always said. Hockey before everything. Isn't that right?"

"Not anymore."

"Aren't you worried about all the nights they spend away from you, and what they're doing? I had to get Mikael that penicillin shot that one time." He acts like he's typing on his phone, and I look around the box. There aren't many people here, and I'm feeling really off. I look down at my drink. It's fizzy and my head hurts.

"Stop it." I just want this creep to leave me alone, so I can enjoy the game. As soon as I'm with the guys, I'm going to tell them everything Jake said. This guy is not someone they should be working with.

"Getting worked up?" he asks. "All you Omegas are the same. Pinning over Alphas, never giving Betas a chance. All you are is a distraction and leeches on society. I'm not letting you distract Eli and fuck up what I've worked so hard for." I'm not sure how to reply. I feel weird, worse than I did this morning, and my tongue feels heavy.

I fan my face; it's getting hot in here. There's a pang in my abdomen, and I wince. An evil smile takes over Jake's face. "Let's see how you feel when they aren't there for you again." He grabs me by the arm, and I grab my middle. A petite woman with a brown bob looks at us with curiosity.

"Honey, are you okay?" I blink at her and clutch my head. What is going on?

"I'm taking her to the med bay and letting the guys know," Jake says, and I whimper as he drags me down the elevator. The pain is excruciating. I don't remember it hurting this much. It's probably because Mikael took care of me right away. "Omegas are seriously the most useless fucking members of society. Magical pussy really isn't worth the headache." I'm glad that he at least seems repulsed by me and I'm not in a more dangerous situation. I think I might read that wrong as Jake grins. "I don't think they will want used goods, and you seem to be a spiteful little thing. How will you possibly be able to forgive them for leaving you alone again?" He drags me down the hall and uses his ID to open a door. He shoves me in so hard that I fall onto the floor. I just stay there curling into a ball. "Fucking pathetic. Don't worry, someone will find you soon enough. Just might not be your precious pack."

"Why?"

"I'm a fixer. I'm here to make sure my clients have long, lucrative careers, and they can't do that with you."

"They'll never forgive you."

"And they'll never believe you if they find you with another Alpha during your heat."

I grab for my back pocket to take out my phone, and he rips my forearm roughly, taking the device from me. My last life line is in his hands as he grins at me ferally and walks out of the room.

He slams the door, and I hear him drag a chair or something against the door handle. I wait a few moments and attempt to open it. The cramps are nearly debilitating, and fear is laced all throughout me. How am I going to get out of this? Nothing he's saying warrants what he's doing, and I know I'm dealing with a psychopath. It sounds like he's going to send other Alphas down here. I can't let that happen. I look throughout the room, and it looks like a physical therapy facility.

My skin is so hot, and my tears feel cool as they run down my face. I drag one of the tables and place it in front of the door. I grab my stomach as pain lances through me. My mind is getting more and more unclear every second, but I know that I have to barricade myself in here. I grab another table, putting it in front of the door. Next is a peddle bike, and luckily it has wheels on the bottom. I toss shit in front of the door haphazardly, just hoping it's enough that someone can't open the door. I toss a few chairs for good measure and make sure everything is locked into place.

They won't know until the game is over. It's going to be hours before they come and find me. That is, if no one else finds me in the meantime. I weep ugly, fat tears as I remove my clothes, wanting the aching itch of the material to go away and cool down my skin.

What if this gets taken away from me too? I just need them. I need them so badly.

In my haziness, all I can do is finger myself, which brings me no relief. It's a pathetic attempt to remove the pain, but it's all I have.

I have no one; I have nothing.

T he only negative thing about Charlotte being in the box is that I can't see her while I play. The game goes smoothly. Mikael only goes to the sin bin twice. I only let the Penguins get two goals in, and Eli is just one goal short of a hat trick. We're going away with a win as the buzzer sounds, and all I want to do is take all this gear off and get to our girl.

Fuck post-game interviews, the coaches pep talk, I just want Charlotte in my arms. I'm still bitter that Mikael told her he loves her first. It's my fault for not saying it after this time, but I have got to say it tonight, or I might explode. She needs to know how I feel. We need to move this pack forward with bond marks, sharing a house, being together every moment that we possibly can.

I sent off a quick text to Charlotte letting her know that we're running behind.

> Meet you in the box soon, Kulta. Half hour tops.

But we've gotta deal with this bureaucratic bullshit first. I get an obscene amount of stick pats to the ass as we skate back to the locker room. We tap gloves to the fans holding out their hands. Eli looks the most exhausted out of all of us as we sit on the bench.

Jake comes into the locker room with a beaming smile on his face. "Great game, boys. Eli, I've got a deal with Nike lined up for next week."

Eli sips his water and nods his head. I inhale, and Jake smells different. He honestly smells like bleach. I shake off the intrusive scent and take off all my layers of gear.

"Larsen, Beckford, Babinin, and Martel, you're on deck for the press tonight."

"Fuck," Mikael and Eli hiss in unison.

"Jake, can you let Charlotte know to wait up for us?"

"Oh, I think she left," he says.

"She what?"

"Something about needing to go take care of something?"

"Was she feeling alright?" Mikael asks.

"Seemed fine to me, except she did mention someone named Carter?"

"Who?" Eli asks with a growl.

"If I see her, I'll let her know, but you guys are needed for the press."

"What the fuck?" Eli says next to me.

"Let's get this figured out, and then we can go find her."

We sit for the press for about a half hour. I hate having to sit in, but as the goalie, it happens often. Same for Eli and Alexi as our top scorers. Mikael is only here because he had some serious hits tonight. In all honesty, he's not great with press. So Coach only asks him to do it when it's absolutely necessary.

We're finally free to go find Charlotte when a woman I recognize as Hoczel's wife comes up to us. "There you guys are."

"What's up?" Eli asks.

"The girl who was here tonight for your game."

"Charlotte," Mikael finishes.

"Yeah, that guy." She points to Jake. "Had her leave the box before the start of the game, and she didn't look okay. I just wanted to make sure she was doing okay."

"He what?" I growl, and she retreats. My voice softens. "I'm sorry. I didn't mean to raise my voice at you. She didn't look okay?"

"Like she wasn't feeling well."

"Thank you," I say as Mikael, Eli, and I approach Jake. I grab him by the lapel of his suit jacket and drag him into the empty side hallway.

"Where the fuck is she?" I ask. Eli and Mikael bracket me. Mikael cracks his knuckles, and Eli holds his hand on Jake's shoulder.

"Guys, what's going on?"

"Where the fuck is Charlotte?"

"I told you she left." I can't ask him another question because Mikael punches him right in the kidney. I have to hold his body weight up as he tries to catch his breath from the hit. "Guys, I was trying to protect you. This whole pack deal is cute and all, but it won't last. If you all want to make it, you've got to ditch the cunt."

This time I'm the one to hit him right in the nose. "Never fucking talk about her like that again. Where is she?"

He sputters. I know that hit to the kidney is still aching, and he's holding his bloody nose. "Unless you want me to fucking kill you right here and now, you will tell me where she is."

"PT room," he gasps out.

"Jim!" Eli says. Our favorite security guard turns the corner. "Lock him in the drunk tank, and call the police."

"Got it, you guys okay?"

"Will be," Eli replies. I let the fucker drop to the floor as we all sprint to the PT room. There are two Alphas I don't recognize trying to push in the door.

"I'm telling you, man, I smell an Omega in heat. We've just got to get the door open."

"Fuck, it smells good. Don't even care what they look like."

"You fuckers lost?" Mikael barks, immediately resorting to violence as he shoves them away. They don't stand a chance against Mikael, let alone the three of us. Both of the disgusting assholes back away, their hands up in surrender. I can't help but notice the chair that's been tossed on the floor.

"You better get the fuck out of here," Eli growls, and the two dick heads finally get the idea and skitter away.

I push on the door, and there is a significant amount of resistance. Mikael and Eli both use their shoulders to help me push the door. There's still resistance, but it budges slightly. As soon as I hear the whimper on the other side of the door, it's like I'm overcome by a beast. Adrenaline courses through my veins as the three of us shove against the door, making just enough room for us to squeeze through one by one.

The first thing I see are the piles of shit she put in front of the door. A training bike, multiple chairs, and massage tables. But the next thing I see shatters me into a million tiny pieces. Charlotte is shivering wide-eyed in the ice bath in the middle of the room. Her pupils are blown, but it's clear she recognizes me.

"A-A-Anders?"

I'm grabbing an arm full of towels and am on my knees next to her in a second. Her forehead feels hot, but her arms are freezing cold. "We're here, *Kulta*. We're here. Did anyone hurt you?"

She shakes her head no. "J-J-Jake."

I push her hair away from her face and nod. "He's taken care of."

Eli is picking her up by her underarms and holding her close to his chest as I wrap the towels around her.

"I-I-I was so hot."

"It's okay, baby. We're going to take you to your nest," Eli says.

"I'm going to kill that motherfucker," Mikael says, throwing a chair across the room that has Charlotte whimpering. I can see the guilt written on his face as he pets her back. "I'm sorry, Charlotte. We're going to take you to your nest."

"My...my...nest?"

"Yeah, baby. Your nest. Should we call Piper and have her drop off some of your things?"

"O-Okay."

"How the fuck are we going to get her out of here?" Mikael asks.

"I'll go get the car and bring it to the side entrance. Mikael, make sure everything is clear in the hallway. Call some extra security if you need to." Mikael nods, and Eli hands over Charlotte to me. She's naked, freezing, and wet. I hold her close, and she shivers, taking in my scent.

"We'll be right back, baby," Eli says, kissing her hair. Mikael does the same as they begin to take care of everything to get Charlotte out of here safely.

She shivers in my arms and whimpers.

"We're going to take care of you, *Kulta*. It's okay." I pet her hair softly.

"I was...so...so...scared."

"Fuck." I squeeze her tightly. "I'm never letting you out of my sight again."

"You're...you're...here, that's all that matters."

I can tell she keeps teetering on the edge of her heat. She's still with me, and it's probably poor timing, but I don't give a fuck.

"I'm always going to be here for you, *Kulta*. I love you; you're my Omega."

She pulls back. Her lips are her normal shade, and I touch her cheek, which is still too hot.

"I love y-you too. I want...I want the bonds."

"Charlotte, this is too much. You don't have to make that decision now."

She cups my face and looks me in my eye with a serious look, like her mind is at war with itself. It's clear she's held back her heat as much as she can.

"You would deny me?"

I shake my head. "Never."

"I'm...I'm telling you I want it. Please, Anders."

"Okay, we will bond."

She whimpers and folds in on herself slightly. My chest is rumbling with such a loud purr I can hardly hear her words. "Alpha, it hurts."

I clutch her close to my chest, knowing I've got to get her the fuck out of this stadium before we can do anything. "I'm going to make it better. So fucking brave and smart, such a good Omega." She whines and leans further into me.

"Please, Alpha." She pulls my hand to her core.

"Jesus." She's soaking wet, even after spending time in the ice bath. Her skin is already getting warmer. If she wasn't in heat, it would probably take her an hour at least to get back to a normal temperature. "Charlotte, we've got to wait till we get to your nest."

Tears trail down her face as she takes what I said as rejection. I cup her face, holding eye contact with her glazed over glance. "Charlotte Hodges, I'm going to take you home to your nest and fuck you so good you can't think, and then I'm going to bite you right here." I point to the right side of her neck. "I'm going to mark you as my Omega forever. You want that, don't you?"

She blinks at me a few times and nods.

"Good girl. Just have to wait a few more minutes."

She whines and grinds on my thigh but doesn't complain. Her scent is rich and thick, and all I want to do is bottle it up and kill anyone who might smell it in the room later.

Mikael comes storming into the room. "We've got to be quick."

I stand, holding Charlotte with one arm. More naked skin than I realize must be showing as Mikael swears and rips his shirt off, using it to cover her lower half.

Mikael has a hand on my shoulder the whole time as we speed walk through the long windowless hallways, making our way to the side entrance for players only. Jim is holding the door open for us as we rush out and are greeted by the sight of Eli's SUV. It's like I haven't been breathing for the last twenty minutes as Mikael opens the door for us. I slide in with Charlotte in my lap, and Mikael takes the seat next to me.

"She okay?" Eli asks as he steps on the gas. The tires make a horrific screeching noise as he speeds out of the parking lot.

"She wants to bond."

"What?" Eli and Mikael say at the same time.

"She said she wants it."

"She's going into heat. She doesn't know what she wants."

Charlotte's head pops up and looks at Mikael, grabbing him by the throat and bringing his lips to hers. "Mark me," she says next to his lips.

"Okay, maybe she does know what she wants. But we should talk about it more," Eli says.

"No," Charlotte says, kissing Mikael harder. She's still naked on my lap. My pants are soaked in a combination of her slick and when she was wet from the ice bath.

Her scent in the vehicle is thick and heavy as she rubs herself on me and continues kissing Mikael. She moans against his mouth, and one of her hands fists my shirt as she uses my body to grind against.

"Shit," I hiss as I grip her hips and grind her pussy against my pants even more. Eli clears his throat from the front seat.

"I called Piper. She's dropping off some of her stuff and some food. She's also helping file charges against Jake while we're...um...busy."

Charlotte whimpers when Eli says his name, and I want to take all this hurt away from her. She's been through more than any person ever should. She's been healing, and I have no idea if what Jake has done will set her back. I'm just so thankful she was smart to barricade herself in the room. It makes rage zip through my body when I think of what could have happened to her if we hadn't gotten there when we did.

Maybe I should wait until her heat is over to bond, but she said she wants it and deep down, I'm selfish when it comes to Charlotte. I need to be connected to her to know that she's okay, or I'll never sleep again.

Charlotte's deft fingers are unbuckling my belt and tugging on my pants. Mikael is shirtless next to us, watching with devotion. "Alpha. Now."

"Don't you want to wait till we get to your nest?"

She shakes her head, and I don't resist as she tugs down my pants and boxers. She doesn't say anything else; she just lines me up with her entrance and slides all the way down to my pelvis, taking my cock and my growing knot at the same time. My hands are tangled in her hair as she grinds herself on me, taking what she needs.

"Is that what you needed, *Kulta?*" She nods, and her lips part. "Use me, sweet Omega. Take whatever you need."

"More," she whispers. I'm not exactly sure what else I can give her. Until Mikael's hand is squeezing her ass and collecting slick that's dripping on my thighs, then pushing it to her asshole.

"This is what you need, *mon sucre d'érable?*" She whimpers as he pushes a finger inside of her asshole. "Our girl loves being fucking full of her Alphas, doesn't she?"

She nods as she bounces on my cock and takes the new sensation of Mikael's fingers. He adds another, and her pussy was already tight, but my vision is nearly going out with how good she feels now.

"This is fucking bullshit," I hear Eli mumble from the front seat. I'm so glad I'm not the one driving.

Mikael adds another finger, and Charlotte throws her head back, hitting the headrest of Eli's seat. She doesn't wince, just buckles as her pussy spasms around my cock. The grip so tight, along with Mikael filling her, I lose it, filling her with my cum.

"Mmm. Alphas. Mine," she says, leaning forward and passing out on my shoulder while I'm still locked inside of her.

Mikael slowly removes his fingers, wiping them on his discarded shirt on the floor and sighs as he leans back in his seat. "Someone should call Coach. You know, since we don't have an agent."

"Fuck," Eli hisses from the front seat and shakes his head. "I'll send a text when we get home. It's in our contract. Twice a year, no matter what the timing, we won't be available during heats."

I wince, feeling like shit. Our backup goalie isn't up to par, and we have a game in four days against the Predators, who are dominating right now. Mikael must see my reaction and shakes his head.

"It's one game, Anders. We'll figure it out." I nod, squeezing Charlotte harder. I'd give up ever playing a game for her. It's clear as day now. She's the main priority here, and I plan on showing her that every single day.

She rubs her face on my shoulder again, like she's uncomfortable. "I'm not taking her contacts out this time."

"You sure as fuck are," Eli says from the front seat, and I groan. The lengths we will go to for our Omega.

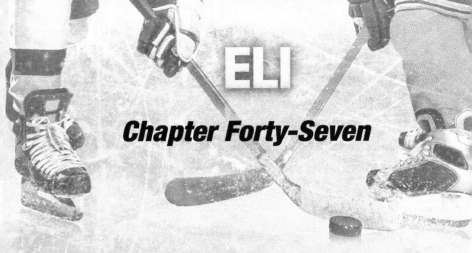

"Do you think she'll like it?" I ask Anders, and Mikael as we place her on the plush bed. This was the nest that Charlotte should have always had. It's in the basement of the house, so there's no light except the artificial ones we've added.

Twinkle lights line the ceiling, and it almost looks like it's snowing in the nest, or like we're surrounded by stars. They're dimmable, so we're prepared for whatever mood she's in. The amount of blankets in here is bonkers. There's a mix of waterproof blankets, soft ones we knew she would like, and larger ones dedicated to sleeping only, which is honestly super optimistic. Because whenever she wants to fuck, we're at her call, and it won't matter what blanket we're using. The bedding is all purple and plush, and I had macrame made to put on the walls to match what she had in her bedroom. There's a closet with a fridge and anything else we may need. I'm thankful that Piper is going to be dropping off food, taking care of Hank, and bringing some of Charlotte's comfort items.

"She will love it," Mikael says. When I look at him and see how he's looking at Charlotte, I rub my chest. It feels like we're about to be the pack we always should have been. Even if it took some of the worst things happening to get us here.

Charlotte maneuvers to her side, grabbing a pillow and putting it between her legs, whining as she wiggles and looks for relief. The doorbell rings, and Anders goes to answer it while I get down on the bed. I touch her cheeks and forehead. She's burning up.

"What do you need, baby?"

"It hurts," she says, not opening her eyes and moving her body on the pillow. She wasn't in this much pain last time, and I'm beside myself on what to do for her and how to make this better.

"Let me make it better, baby." I lie her flat on her back, and her legs spread open a combination of her slick and Anders' cum glistening against her soft skin.

"Please, Alpha."

I don't wait a second longer as I shrug my clothes off, tossing them in some corner of the room. Mikael gets on the bed next to us, stroking her hair and placing tender kisses along the column of her throat. Our purrs ricochet in the dark space.

I swipe the weeping tip of my cock between her wet lips and slowly glide into her. I groan with how wet, warm, and tight she is. Her calves lock behind my back, and her heels dig into my ass, urging me forward.

"Mmm," she moans, and I can feel the haziness taking over me. How badly I need to rut her, fill her up with my cum and mark her as mine.

"Baby...I'm not going to be able to control myself."

She hums and nods her head. I'm not sure how comfortable I feel with the consent given, but god dammit, I need her to be mine. To be able to feel her always, a reassurance that we will never be separated again. I look over at Mikael to gauge his feelings on it.

"Let's make her ours."

I'm not sure if he's saying this because Anders isn't here. When I look down at Charlotte, her hair is fanned around her face, her hands on her breasts, and her pink lips are parted as I lazily fuck her.

"Charlotte." She meets my gaze. "I'm going to rut you and mark you, baby."

She moans and nods her head. "Yes!"

Mikael licks his lips and stares down at Charlotte. "Should we do it at the same time?"

I look back at the door and wonder how pissed Anders is going to be, but my resolve is breaking moment by moment.

"You want to be full of your Alphas when you get your bonds, *mon sucre d'érable?*"

She nods her head frantically. And Mikael is taking off his pants and grabbing the lube. "Spin her around, so she's on top." I listen immediately, rolling around, so I'm on my back, and Charlotte is uncoordinatedly riding my cock, seeking out what feels right for her.

Her pussy flutters around my cock, and her nails are digging into my chest as she rides me. Her lips part, and her skin temperature cools slightly. Mikael is behind her, using a combination of her slick and lube to finger her ass.

She leans forward against me, her breasts pressed against my chest as I thrust into her. Mikael fingers her to get her prepared.

"Look at our Omega. Going to take both of your Alphas, aren't you?"

She nods against my chest, her grip on my throat and hair tight.

"Such a good girl," I tell her, and she whimpers on top of me. I can feel the moment Mikael is nudging his cock into her back entrance, and she bites down on my pec, making me groan. I can't help but grip her hair and bring her face to mine.

I swallow all her moans and screams with my mouth. I let Mikael situate himself and set the pace as I let Charlotte's warm pussy grip me like a vice. Our hands are frantic in each other's hair and on each other's faces.

When our lips part and she whispers the word Alpha. All my resolve is broken, and I can't help but thrust into her. My knot is filling her while Mikael is still in her ass. All three of us moan at the same time.

"Fuck," Mikael hisses, the indents of his fingers on Charlotte's hips leaving finger shaped bruises in his wake.

"Mine," I growl as I fuck into her, her tits bouncing with each thrust. Her cunt is gripping me, begging me to fill her up with my cum and make her mine. I watch as a vein pulsates at her throat, and my mouth waters over the thought of making her mine in every sense.

"Please," Charlotte begs.

I continue my thrusts, my hips snapping hard against her ass. My thighs hit Mikael's with each and every thrust inside of her.

"That's it, *mon doux,*" Mikael pants. He's leaned over to the point that his chest is pressed against Charlotte's back, and when he licks the side of her throat, it breaks my brain. My hips stutter, and my knot grows with each thrust. Mikael moans, and I growl, and Charlotte comes. Her body is shaking on top of me. Her thighs tremble, and her pussy grips my knot so tight I shudder.

"My Omega." She's too blissed out to hear my words, but she nods her head.

"Please. I'm good, Alpha."

"So fucking good," Mikael assures her. "I'm going to come." I'm just as close as I push into her the best I can, with my knot swelling to its full size. It's what pushes me over the edge, Mikael as well.

He pushes our Omega firmly against my chest. The left side of her throat is at my mouth and the right at his. I'm filling her with my cum and knotting her as I take the tender flesh between my teeth and bite down, the bond clicking into place immediately. I'm moaning, Charlotte's clutching my throat, and Mikael groans since he can't move, my knot holding us all in place.

I can immediately feel her contentment through the bond, all the love and devotion that flows freely through her. I can sense how worn out but relaxed her body feels at this moment. To the best of my ability, I push my love to her through the bond, how she's my everything and is the most important thing in my whole world.

I lick my bond mark, sealing and healing the bite as I look at the silver mark on her throat. "Love you, Char baby," I tell her, knowing that I don't need to say it out loud. I've been pushing it through the bond this whole time. But when I do say it, she moans lightly. We're still knotted together, and she pets my face and peppers my cheeks with kisses.

"Mine," she says, caressing my face with her thumbs. Her one hand leaves my face to touch her bond mark, and she sighs. Her hands are back on my face as she looks at me with so much devotion and care. It's easier to see how she's feeling during her heat and right now she's sated and so overjoyed I can see her eyes starting to water.

"No tears, baby." Though I think I'm saying it more for my benefit than hers.

She shakes her head. "Mine," she repeats in fascination as she lies flat on my chest, bringing a groaning Mikael with her. I don't even care about their weight, it feels safe, and I feel whole. My chest rumbles, and she buries her face into the crook of my neck.

Gazing over my shoulder, I see Mikael smiling at us, and maybe a slight tear rolls down my face, but I'd never admit it.

"You didn't mark her?" I ask him.

"Not yet. I wanted you to have that first. You and Anders deserve to mark her first."

I wrap my arms around Charlotte's shoulders, rubbing the tension out of her upper back, while Mikael massages her lower back.

There's a clearing of a throat behind us, and my cheeks heat. I feel like I got caught doing something bad, but the way that this bond feels, there's no way.

I expect a scolding, even though he is the one who brought up the fact that she gave permission when she was still lucid. But Anders always surprises me. He sits on the bed, putting a hand on Charlotte so that we're all touching her. "How does it feel?" he asks.

"Like nothing in my life has ever made sense until this moment," I say, truly meaning it. It's like any bullshit in life could come my way, but with this bond, with Charlotte and my pack by my side, I'm truly unstoppable.

"Proud of you," Anders says. He leans forward and kisses our Omega's shoulder. "*Kulta*?" he says, but Charlotte is already passed out against my chest. I know it won't last long, and I'm going to have to share her. But for now, I hoard her like a dragon does with jewels, holding her close to my chest and feeling her chest rise and fall with every breath.

As I hold my bonded in my arms, all I can think about is how fucking lucky I am and how I'm going to spend the rest of my life protecting this precious woman—our Omega.

Chapter Forty-Eight

I watched Eli bond with Charlotte, just stood and watched with complete awe. I'd be lying if I said that I didn't wish I was first, but it's easy to get over when I look at them together. She looks at him like all the bad shit from the last few months has been washed away with that one bite. It's truly an invaluable and miraculous thing to witness, and now all I want is to feel that same thing for myself.

Piper dropped off some of her favorite things and agreed to watch Hank during her heat. She took it pretty well when I told her that I was pretty sure Charlotte would be moving in with us after her heat was over. I'm indebted to the female Alpha who took care of our girl when we couldn't. If she ever needs help with anything, we will all be there.

The mattress on the floor of the nest is massive and fits us all comfortably. I can't help but laugh at how close Mikael and Eli are sleeping next to each other. Charlotte is in Eli's clutches, while I lay on the other side of her. She hasn't even stirred since Eli bonded her, and it's probably been the longest she's slept during her heat ever. We all got a full night's rest, and I feel guilty for wanting to wake her up and get my turn, so I'll wait. This heat seems different from her first.

She was in so much pain earlier. I hope that Eli's bond mark helped soothe that ache. With how much she's slept, I have to imagine it has.

But as I stare down at the bite mark on the side of her throat, all I want to do is decorate the other side of her neck with my own. I know how precious a bond is. I've witnessed it with my parents. We may be scent matches, and fate may have driven us together. But a bond mark is a choice that can't be taken back, and I crave it. That level of intimacy with someone is something that most people can only dream of. But here I am, lucky enough to have my dream girl and pack right next to me. I seriously am the luckiest fucker who ever lived.

Charlotte must be in tune with my thoughts as she blinks and stares at me for a moment. She licks her lips and huddles closer to me.

"What do you need, *Kulta*?" I ask her softly, attempting to not disturb Mikael and Eli, and maybe I'm a selfish asshole, but I want her all to myself at this moment. I push her messy hair behind her ears as she drags her hands down my chest.

"Hard," she says.

"You need it hard, Charlotte?" She nods her head and whimpers. I smirk at first, and that turns into a grin. "Are you going to present for your Alpha?"

She eagerly nods her head. She's already naked as she gets down on her knees and places her face on the mattress. Her hair splays to one side as her lips part, and she looks at me expectantly.

"So good for your Alpha, aren't you?" She nods and pushes her ass further up into the air, giving me the most delicious view of her cute asshole and dripping pussy. "You want me to fuck you rough and bite this sweet little neck?" I ask, dragging a finger exactly where I want to mark her. She moans, and her hands grab and clench around the sheets beneath us.

I want this moment to last, so I can ingrain it into my memory forever. My palm glides over her ass, squeezing the flesh before spanking her. Her whimper is like music to my ears as I do it again. I can't decide if Charlotte likes being spanked more during her heat or not. I think we'll need to collect a lot more statistical data to find out.

"I think I want this ass nice and pink before I fuck your needy pussy. What do you think, little Omega?"

She pants and nods as she keeps shoving her ass closer to me. I give her what she wants. At this point, with the cacophony of my hand hitting her ass over and over, Eli and Mikael wake up. Non-verbally, they must understand that I need this time alone with her, and they head upstairs to the kitchen to eat.

"Looks like I have you all to myself, *Kulta*."

Smack.

Smack.

Charlotte moans and whimpers, "Please, Alpha, please."

"What do you need more? My knot or my bite?"

She whines, and it has my dick weeping with need. I stroke her spine with my hand and take a look at her pink cheeks before spreading her and pushing my cock into her. I keep my knot just at her entrance, so I can fuck her hard before I give her everything she wants.

"Yes," she says as her grip tightens on the sheets, and her mouth parts with the most delicious moan.

Holding her hip with one hand, I smack her ass with the other, making her keen and moan. "Your Alpha always knows what you need, doesn't he?"

She nods and bites her lower lip. Her white teeth grazing on the tender pink flesh has me groaning, thinking about how I'm going to sink my teeth into her perfect skin and make her mine.

Needing her closer, and wanting her to come before I knot and mark her, I wrap an arm around her chest and bring her back to me. Her scent is so thick, and I feel like I'm drowning in rich maple syrup and pancakes. I kiss her throat, and her small hands wrap around my forearm, her blunt nails digging into my skin as I fuck her.

"Such a good girl for me. I think you need my knot."

"Please, Alpha," she whines.

I hold on to her chest tightly with one hand as the other slides down her abdomen and plays with her clit as I push all the way into her. My knot is gripped like a vise as I bottom out in her tight pussy. Both of us moan at the same time.

I want her gripping me so tightly I can't help but rut into her and finally mark her as mine. I use my fingers to strum her clit as I fuck in and out of her. My knot grows with each thrust. She whimpers and clutches at my arm as I give it to her just how she likes it.

"Please. Please. Please," she begs.

I lean over, licking the side of her throat and sucking on the spot I know I'm going to mark her. It's what sends her over the edge, her cunt fluttering and milking my cock. I groan against her throat as she shakes and moans in my arms. Charlotte's head is against my shoulder, and she just waits for me to do what I promised.

I'm like a beast unleashed as I fuck into her. Each thrust makes an audible sound of flesh on flesh. My knot swells to its largest size, and my mouth is on her neck as I fill her with my cum. Her scent is thick as I bite down, and she moans and whimpers. The pleasure I'm giving her cunt mixes with the pain of the bite. I feel the bond snap in place as my teeth are leaving her. Charlotte's feeling of pleasure, love, contentment, and the lingering confusion of her heat.

She pants in my arms, my knot locking us in this awkward position for the foreseeable future. I kiss and lick the mark, and each time I do, she funnels devotion down the bond.

"So good, *Kulta*. You did so good."

Her breathing is heavy, but she nods her head against my chest. "Mine," she whispers, and I smile. I've always been Charlotte's. From the first time I scented her, my future was solidified. She was going to be the most wonderful thing in my life.

"Love you," I tell her. She nods her head, and I can tell she's spent. Clearly taking this many bonds is tiring work, and I wonder what Mikael's plans are. Eli, well, I never have to wonder about Eli again. While his presence in the bond is nowhere as readable as Charlotte's, it's still there. I can feel his happiness and also his eagerness to get to our Omega.

Apparently he acts on that impulse as he walks back into the room with Mikael. One day, we will all know what's going on in that man's head. I'm just not sure if it will be during her heat or not. I don't think he is resisting this, but Mikael and Charlotte have always been on a different schedule than the rest of us.

"Baby, are you hungry?" Eli asks Charlotte, and she shakes her head no. "I brought your favorite." She eyes him as he sits down on the bed in front of us, holding a plate of fruit.

She shakes her head no and grinds on my dick, making me groan.

"Eat something, and you can have all your Alphas at the same time," Mikael suggests, and that has her perking up.

She parts her lips, and Eli pushes a raspberry between her lips. She rotates, keeping eye contact with Mikael and Eli. Knowing that I'm knotted and not going anywhere, I guess she's making sure we keep up with our promises.

"You need to drink something," Eli says, and she groans and tosses her head back against my shoulder in defiance.

"You two have no fucking tact," Mikael says, holding a glass of water and standing next to us. It makes him look even larger than he usually is. "Don't you want to be my good girl, *mon sucre d'érable?*"

Her blue eyes take in Mikael as she nods and sighs.

"Good, then open." He doesn't pour the water down her throat, however. He puts it in his own mouth and grabs her hair, tilting her head back, and she eagerly parts her lips as he transfers the water to her mouth. Charlotte shallows and hums.

"You need more?" he asks, and she grabs his thigh with one hand and eagerly nods her head. This ritual happens a few more times, and

I realize that Charlotte wants to be connected to us in any physical way possible, and the more unsanitary, the better.

My knot still hasn't released us, but Charlotte seems to be unsettled as she directs Eli to stand up next to Mikael.

"What do you need, baby?"

She doesn't say anything, just grabs the elastic of their boxer briefs and tugs on them. They both agree and slide their boxers off. Both of them are hard for our Omega. There was no doubt that they would be. With how needy she is and how thick her scent is during her heat, we're all ready to fuck her at a moment's notice.

"Charlotte?" Mikael questions.

She does a kegel around my cock, and I groan. My grip on her hip and chest tightens, she whimpers but takes Eli in one hand and Mikael in the other. She strokes them before bringing them close together and rotates on licking and sucking on the tips.

I move my hand to play with her clit more. She continues to squeeze on my length and knot while she continues exploring Eli and Mikael with her tongue.

"Charlotte, I don't think they are going to both fit."

She frowns at him and accepts his challenge as she puts both of their cocks in her mouth. She can't fit much more than the heads. But both Eli and Mikael groan as she does it. When she removes them from her mouth, she takes turns stroking one of them and sucking the other. She alternates in a fair order until Eli can't take it anymore.

"Gonna come, baby," he says, and she whines. I put more pressure on her clit as she takes him down her throat, moaning as he fucks into her mouth. Eli's hand is on the back of her head, guiding her and keeping the pace that he wants. Her hands grip his thighs as he uses our Omega and gives her what she wants. Mikael strokes himself and can't keep his gaze away from our Omega's face and what she's doing to our packmate.

Eli stutters and moans as he finishes, Charlotte moaning and swallowing everything he has to give. She holds on to one of his thighs as she goes back to licking and sucking Mikael's cock.

"How did we end up with such a good Omega?" Mikael says, and it spurs Charlotte on to suck him down harder and faster. I'm rubbing her clit in circular motions, and I know she's close. I feel close to coming again too.

"Going to be full of all your Alpha's cum, aren't you, *Kulta*? Such a good, needy Omega."

She shakes against my chest as her next orgasm hits her. Knowing that she's coming around my cock sets me off again as I fill her pussy for the second time. Mikael had to take over stroking himself, and he finishes on Charlotte's chest.

Charlotte pants and has involuntary shivers against my body as she comes down from her release.

"Are you okay, Charlotte?" I ask. She just moans and puts all her body weight against my chest. Having come twice, my knot releases us and the amount of slick and cum dripping out of her pussy is obscene and so fucking hot. I can't help but use two fingers to push it back into her. She makes a noise like it's too much and not enough at the same time.

Once I'm happy with how much of me is left in her, I remove my fingers. She holds out her hand, and we find ourselves sleeping in the nest together again. Our Omega sends just how much she loves us down the bond before she falls asleep unceremoniously.

CHARLOTTE

Chapter Forty-Nine

There's a heavy arm on my chest, and I groan and shift to my side. The person doesn't stir, and as I squint, I see dark hair over his eyes and know that it's Mikael. I wish I had my contacts or glasses on so I can look at the nest. I know from how I felt during my heat that it's perfect. It's such a deep feeling that your partners know you well enough to create such a perfect space right to your tastes.

What is even more significant is how they've peeled back all of my layers and love each one. I don't have to hide who I am or pretend that certain pieces of me aren't lovable. I couldn't hide even if I tried—now that I have two bonds—I feel them through the new connection. I do my best to not wake them, even though I'm not really sure how to hold back just how happy I feel. I seek them through the bond anyway.

Both of them are content and tired. I've no doubt run them ragged during my heat. Even though some parts of my heat are fuzzy, the part where we bonded is crystal clear. Unfortunately, so is the part about my heat being forced and exactly how much danger I was in.

The weight on my chest stiffens, and Mikael talks to me in a soft voice. "Charlotte?"

"Hey," I reply.

"What's wrong? Your scent."

I clear my throat. Everything is on the table with my Alphas, even if Mikael didn't with bond me during my heat, which hurts more than I'd like to admit. I open my mouth to speak, and I shut it. Mikael's hands grip my face, and he's close enough that I can see his face.

"I was just thinking about how I ended up in heat."

"I'm so fucking sorry, Charlotte."

I clear my throat. Thinking back to everything, I remember barricading myself into the room and Alphas I didn't know banging on the door and how helpless I felt. Someone the guys trusted had put me in such a dangerous position.

"It was Jake," I say, remembering that I mentioned his name, but not knowing if he had been dealt with.

"It's been taken care of. Never again, Charlotte. I wanted to fucking kill him. I'm never letting you be in a dangerous position like that."

"It wasn't your fault."

Mikael scoffs. "Trusting Jake was our fault. You're too precious to me—to us. You're everything, Charlotte. You've been through too much bad shit, and all I want to do is make it better."

I blink and squint at him.

"Why didn't you bond with me then?"

He shakes his head and stands up. "Come with me."

I grab his hand and shiver when the morning air hits my skin. He grabs a hoodie from the corner and puts it on me. The hem hits my knees, and I have to roll up the sleeves. When I sniff at the collar, I immediately scent it as Eli's.

Mikael rifles through another bag, grabbing my glasses case before taking them out and putting them on my face. I smile when I see his face clearly for the first time. He smiles back and kisses the corner of my mouth. With my hand in his, he walks me down to the kitchen. I've seen the guy's place before, but seeing it now feels different. They built me a nest. They had me in mind when they built this house. It's not massive, but it's big enough for all of us, plus some. The thought makes me smile, and I shake it out of my head.

Once we're in the kitchen, Mikael grabs me by the hips and puts me on the counter.

"Hungry?" I nod my head, and he digs in the fridge and pulls out some fruit and croissants. He tosses those in the microwave while he puts the fruit next to me. I'm hungrier than I realize as I start shoveling grapes in my mouth like a squirrel going into hibernation.

"How many days has it been?"

"Only four," he says. I nod and sigh.

"You guys missed a game?"

His hands are on my thighs under the hoodie, kneading my flesh as he kisses my cheek. "It was one game, Charlotte."

I furrow my brows. "I told you I would never make you choose."

He shakes his head. "I was an idiot. The choice is always you, *mon sucre d'érable*."

I clear my throat. The emotion of what he is saying to me is heavy and comforting at the same time. All I have ever wanted was for Mikael to fully commit to me, to not be on the fence, and to be one hundred percent sure about what we have.

"Why didn't you bond with me then?"

He nods his head. "I wanted to say a few things first and, well, I selfishly wanted to make sure you remembered it."

"I remember bonding with Eli and Anders," I assure him. I need to make sure they know that too. I might have been in heat, but that life-changing of an event made my mind clear.

"Good. I, um…" He takes a hand off my thigh and scratches the back of his neck. "I never grew up knowing what unconditional love looked like. I had a dad who was mean as hell and liked to use his fists to make a point and a mom who was so checked out that she didn't give a shit about me and my brother. Timothee cared about me to an extent, but left when he was eighteen and found a pack. I haven't heard from him in years. Eli and Anders were the only family I ever had that I truly felt like gave a shit about me, but I knew I could be replaced. They could go off to do amazing things, and I would be left behind. I'm always left behind. You're the first thing that has ever been mine in such a significant way. I want to break the cycle, Charlotte. I want to love you the way you deserve, and I want to accept the unconditional love you've always given me. One day, I want to have kids with you and make sure that they always feel loved. I want these things, and I know they're possible because of you and the guys."

My eyes are filled with tears, and I place my hands on his hips, drawing him closer to me so that he's between my legs. "I promise to protect your heart, Mikael."

His large palms are pressed against my cheeks, and his fingertips have the perfect amount of pressure on the back of my head. He leans forward, and his lips take mine. Mikael's kisses have always been consuming, and he takes what he wants. His tongue enters my mouth, showing me that I'm his. I melt under his touch as he finally lets go. Everything between Mikael and I is on the table. Our pain is shared, and we've both made the promise to love each other despite our flaws and what we've done to each other. This is a new slate. We're better people, more capable of loving each other after all we've been through.

His thumbs rub my cheekbones as he moans into my mouth. We've had a four-day sexfest, and this man is still hungry for me. He's promised his unconditional love to me and to protect me at all times. I need everything that Mikael gives, that my Alpha can provide. I need his bond mark like I need to breathe.

"Please, Mikael."

He nods, sliding me to the end of the counter. With this height, it's honestly perfect for him to be standing while he fucks me. He releases his hard cock from his boxers and pushes the hoodie up to my stomach.

"Look how hard you have me, *mon doux*. Addicted to this pussy," he says as he circles the tip of his cock at my entrance and pushes inside of me. His hands are back on my face, and he clanks my glasses, which he takes off and puts safely on the counter. "Love you," he says between kisses, and I pant and nod.

"Love you too, please bond me."

He's kissing me frantically now, he teases his knot every time he thrusts into me. I'm so needy for him, for this final bond to solidify our pack. One hand is tangled in his dark hair, and the other grips his biceps for dear life.

I groan as he pushes his knot inside of me. He breaks our kiss, so he can look down and see where we're joined. He moans as he watches me take his cock and knot. Seeing how turned on he is at watching us is what sends me over the edge. The stretch of his knot with how tender I am after my heat has me moaning and whimpering as my orgasm hits. Mikael fucks me through my release, whispering to me in French. I have no idea if it's dirty or sweet, but it sounds amazing. I'm a slick mess of an Omega when Mikael pulls back, his face close enough to mine that I can see his sharp features.

"Mine," he growls as his hips snap and his mouth is on my throat. He sucks the flesh at first, teasing me to the point that I'm gasping. He groans as he comes, and then his teeth are on the top of my throat, nearly underneath my ear. The sensation has me nearly coming again as Mikael slows his thrusts, kissing and licking our new bond mark.

It's at this moment that I truly understand who Mikael is. This man who shows such a confident, assured front is actually someone who just needs to be loved, and I plan to give that to him for the rest of my life. I shove how much I love and adore him down the bond, and he shows me his vulnerability as I sense his love, fear, and passion. I kiss his cheek and breathe heavily as we part and look at each other.

He tilts my face and gives my lips a soft, gentle kiss before he sighs.

"Fuck, that feels nice."

I grin. "Doesn't it?"

"I can even sense Eli and Anders. Not as strong as you, of course. But those dickheads are awake and hiding in the bedroom."

I laugh and wrap my arms around him, running my nails along his naked and perfect back. Mikael hums his approval and wraps his arms around me.

"What's next?"

"Well, you need to eat more, and we need to pick up your shit and Hank to move you in. We have practice tomorrow. But really, we have time to figure it all out, get used to living together and being a pack. It's whatever you want, Charlotte."

I sigh, feeling content but also spiraling a little at how much life has changed suddenly. It seems like a common theme in my life, but I've adapted so far.

He kisses the side of my head three times before kissing his bond mark. "Don't stress out. We've got you."

I clear my throat, needing to get it off my chest. I'm sure it's expected of me, and I do want to go to their games. But I'm not sure how exactly I'm supposed to go back to the stadium after what happened.

"What is it?" he asks, now that he can sense everything. I'm not sure if this is going to be awesome or annoying, having all of my Alphas in my head all the time.

"I'm not sure about going to the stadium again."

He nods and cups my face. "Jake is gone, likely going to do some serious jail time for maliciously putting an Omega in danger. He's fucking lucky we had to take care of you, or I would probably be in jail for killing him." I grip his arms tightly, glad that none of the guys seemingly have gotten in trouble. He shakes his head. "We were possessive and protecting our Omega. We won't be charged with anything. But I was thinking maybe we could hire personal security for when you're at the stadium."

I smile and nod. "Maybe Jim?"

He smiles back and nods. "Yeah, maybe."

He kisses his bond mark again as Anders and Eli come downstairs to the kitchen. Both of their hands touching my hair and kissing their bond marks. No fucking care in the world that their packmate's dick is knotted deep in me on our kitchen counter.

"Morning, *Kulta*."

"Morning." Anders kisses me softly as he scours the kitchen for food.

Eli is next with his kisses as he takes my lips. I feel his insecurity through the bond, and I smile as he kisses me. "Morning, baby." I grab him by the collar. Even though Mikael gets a front-row seat, I kiss him hard on the mouth.

"I love you too, Eli."

He grins and kisses me even harder. All his devotion pours into his kiss. "Love you too."

Mikael clears his throat as Eli gets a little handsy with me.

"Still knotted here," he says, squeezing my thighs for emphasis.

"Better learn how to share, Mr. Softy," Eli says.

Mikael rolls his eyes and pushes on Eli's shoulder. Eli kisses the side of my head one more time and parts with a shit-eating grin.

"Well, we have the rest of the day to do whatever you want. What does our sweet, little Omega want to do?" Eli asks.

I grin at them. "You guys still have *Catan*?"

"Our first day as a pack and you want to start it off with war?" Mikael asks, and I grin.

"You scared to lose?"

"No lap sits for resource trades," Eli says.

"No promises." Mikael's knot releases us, and as we look down, we both blush, realizing the counter needs to be cleaned up before anything. Mikael grabs a towel and begins to clean up while I look around the kitchen.

The three hottest Alphas I've ever seen are shirtless and eating breakfast in *our* kitchen. The road here might have been rough, but with this outcome, I can't dwell on the past. From here on out, everything is about our pack's happiness and what we can do to make this relationship as happy and as strong as it can be.

I scoff, thinking about how proud Janet is going to be when I tell her this at therapy. There's really only one thing left to do to help me feel completely ready to leave the trauma behind us. But this time is for us to enjoy our new bonds and move in together. When the time is right, I'll bring it up.

MIKAEL

Chapter Fifty

It's May, and we lost in the first round of the playoffs to the Senators. It was disappointing not going further into the season, but I can't deny having some extra time with our Omega is a bonus. The remainder of the season had its learning curves. Surprisingly, having Charlotte move in wasn't as big of an adjustment as I thought it would be. We're all so much happier having her in the house with us. I actually look forward to coming home after practice and enjoy any time off we have. Not to mention that we're eating like kings with Charlotte in the house.

I thought I loved Charlotte before we bonded, and even thought it couldn't get deeper after the bond, but I was wrong. I fall in love with our Omega just a tad bit more every day. She's the perfect fit into our pack, and she has helped my friendships with Eli and Anders grow to a level I never thought that they could. I mean, sure, fucking our Omega together requires a certain level of trust. But now that we're officially a pack. Pack Hodges, to be exact—though we all still have our last names for our jerseys. It's like I've finally found the strength to open up about my upbringing and let go of some of the anger that I've been holding onto. I'm such a lucky Alpha and man to have these people in my life.

That is my last thought before I'm whacked in the eye with a rogue hand. I wince and groan and turn on my side.

"Eli, you fuck, you smacked me."

"Mmm, subconscious me must have thought you deserved it."

I smack his face back, and he scoffs. "Dick."

"Takes one to know one."

There's a feminine groan in between us as she pulls the covers up to her nose and bundles herself up like a burrito.

"It's too early for this."

Hank disagrees as he hops up on the bed, walking across all of us and shoving his big ass between me and Charlotte.

"And how is my good boy this morning?"

"I'm a good boy," Eli says, and Charlotte shakes her head.

"Not when you wake me up this early with your bullshit."

"We need to get up anyway," I say, knowing that today is going to be a hard day, but it's something that Charlotte needs. Honestly, it's something that we all need. We packed up Charlotte's childhood home last night and are staying at Eli's cabin. He purchased it from his family, letting them know that it meant more to him than it would ever mean to them. They still haven't really come around to Charlotte, our lifestyle, or honestly anything. A bunch of stuck up assholes, if you ask me. But they did give Eli the cabin. It's kind of the staple of where our pack was formed, and it holds a lot of great memories.

It was a hard decision for Charlotte to sell her mother's house, but she decided that it was time. A lot of the décor is from the house, and we plan to use it in this cabin to give it the comfortable feel that Kathy always brought into her home.

Charlotte sighs and nods her head. She focuses on petting Hank's ears as he drools all over the comforter. I notice her squinting and hand her the glasses sitting on the bedside table.

"Thanks," she whispers.

"Thought anymore about LASIK?" I ask. She's brought it up a few times, but I can tell she's nervous. Shit, I'm nervous about the idea of my Omega needing any procedure done.

"Maybe I'll look into it during the season. Right now, I just want to enjoy the off season with you guys."

I nod and kiss her hair. I can't help but to pet Hank's head. The beast of a dog has grown on me, but it's clear he has favorites. Charlotte is his number one, with Eli being a close second. Hank may not be the brightest animal, but I think he knows Eli saved his life with that chocolate disaster a few months back.

Eli kisses her hair and sighs. "We don't have to do it today, baby. We're here for a few more days before Piper watches Hank and we go to Finland."

"I want to do it today," she says softly, and we agree. We work on showering and getting dressed. As we walk into the kitchen, Anders already has breakfast ready, and he gives our Omega an appraising look, making sure that she's doing okay and is able to handle today. We can all feel her through the bond. She is a little melancholic, some sadness, but some fondness as well.

Something you learn when you have a bond is the complexity of emotions. Not all standard 'bad' emotions are actually that bad. Being human is complex, and it's okay to not be happy all the time. If anything, it's important to let yourself feel everything so that you don't bottle up everything and explode at the worst time. At least this is what our therapist, Janet, tells us. Charlotte goes to her the most still, but we have had pack sessions as well as individual couple sessions.

Especially with Charlotte's past, we've come to learn that it's important for her to feel, process, and express her emotions to us. Just because we can feel her down the bond, doesn't mean that we should interfere or always have the immediate urge to make things better.

Today is a hard day, and how she is feeling makes sense. I fill up my Omega's plate first before making my own.

"Thanks for breakfast, Anders."

He nods as he sneaks Hank a piece of bacon before rounding the island and wrapping his arms around our bonded. He doesn't say anything, just holds her and rubs soothing circles on her back. It's odd, you would think in a pack there would be more jealousy, but in all honesty, we're a family, and our sole focus is Charlotte. Having Eli and Anders here to make sure all of Charlotte's needs are met is a gift. It doesn't hurt that we have no issue with sharing intimacy with Charlotte.

Are there nights where I wish I could steal her away for myself? Absolutely. But our girl is great at making sure we each get individual attention as well as time as a pack. She has her own bedroom, which we use when she wants to share the bed with more than one of us. When she needs alone time with any of us, she usually comes to our rooms. She said that it has to do with being drowned in our scents.

She rubs her face on his shirt, marking her Alpha, and I can't help but smile. She basically marks her territory anytime we leave the house. I love being with someone who is just as possessive of me as I am of them.

We eat in silence as we prepare for what we're about to do.

"Ready?" Eli asks, and she nods her head. I grab her light jacket, and she holds out her arms and puts it on. Anders is already in front of her and zipping it up.

"I'm ready," she says. She holds my hand with one hand and Anders with the other while Eli holds Hank's leash, and we go out to the new bench by the lakeside. The tree's leaves are coming back, and it's a stark contrast from how it looks in the winter. "Is this new?" Charlotte asks as she looks at the bench.

"We got it as a place where you could visit with her," I say as she looks at the plaque on the backrest.

In memory of
Katherine (Kathy) Hodges
Loving wife and mother
Forever missed

Charlotte sniffles and traces her finger over the plaque as she looks back at us with watery eyes. "Thank you," she says softly. The bench is huge, enough space for us all to sit as Charlotte takes the small portion of ashes out of her pocket. She stares down at them, and I watch as quiet tears track down her face.

"Do you want me to start, *Kulta*?" Anders asks her, and Charlotte nods. His hand is on her thigh as she quietly cries. "Kathy, I want to thank you for bringing Charlotte into this world and doing such an amazing job of caring for her. I wanted to let you know that you don't have to worry about her. We're going to take care of her, and we know how special she is. You always knew how special she was, and you were such a good mom. I didn't know you for a long time, but you always brought warmth with you everywhere you went. I can see that trait in Charlotte. While I wish you got to see where life heads for us, just know that we're doing our best. We'll come to this bench and check in with you now and then. We will miss you, Kathy."

Charlotte is in full-blown sobs and puts her face in Anders' arm as she rubs her back and soothes her. We wait as her breathing evens out. Eli nods and he goes next.

"I never had a great mom, but Kathy, damn, you were a good mom. You showed me more care in the few times we met than my own mother ever did. You trusted us with Charlotte when we probably didn't deserve it. I promise we'll take care of her, and I'll always remember your words. That I was a good man, and that you trusted me. I'll try to be a better man every day for you, Charlotte, and Hank." Charlotte laughs slightly when he adds Hank's name at the end. She wipes her eyes and looks at me.

I clear my throat and look out at the lake. "Kathy, you once told me that everything happens for a reason, and to be honest, I thought you were full of shit. That so many bad things have happened it would be cruel if everything happened for a reason. But looking back, maybe you're right. Bad things have to happen to make us who we are. In the wake of tragedy is where beauty thrives. I promise to be easy on myself and to put Charlotte first. I want to be a man that you're proud to see your daughter with. I hope you're looking down, and you like what you see. Thanks, Kathy."

Charlotte is crying into Anders' chest more, soaking his shirt as she sits up and wipes her tears. She takes a shuddering breath and starts, "Hey, Mom." She has to stop and compose herself for a second before she starts again. "Hey, Mom. I know you would be so mad at me for how long I held on to the guilt of what happened. I know now that it wasn't my fault, and there was nothing I could have done to change what happened. You always wanted me to be happy and for me to realize who I was, and I think I'm finally figuring that out. I want you to know that I'm doing okay—more than okay. I miss your hugs, but I have three Alphas who hug me more times in a day than I can count. I miss you telling me you love me every day, but I have three men who tell me it every waking chance. You were always worrying about me, and I think I can finally let you know that you don't have to. I'm going to be okay, and I'm happy. I still think about you every day, Dad too. I hope wherever you are that you're with him and you're both proud. I love you."

Each of us has a hand on her somewhere as she stands. She isn't sobbing, but tears still track down her face as she empties the bag, and Kathy's ashes are carried in the wind.

"She'll always be with us wherever we're here," I say softly, and she leans into my chest.

She nods, her small hand bunching my shirt as she calms herself down. I can feel down the bond her combination of emotions. There's a sense of sadness, but there's also relief and closure as well.

"I feel like a weight has been lifted off of me," Charlotte says.

"I'm glad," I reply.

"I just never really got to say goodbye, you know? Letting go of the guilt and finally being able to say goodbye makes it feel final, but it also feels like relief?"

Anders nods and kisses her forehead. "She'd be so proud of you, Charlotte."

She nods her head, and we sit down on the bench staring out at the lake, taking a moment to take in the scenery and what just happened.

I look over at my pack and my heart feels fuller than it ever has in my life. These people who chose to be a family. The amount of love on this bench is something I never expected in my life, and I'll do everything I can to protect it. A few months ago I would have said that we were one fucked up pack. Looking at us now, I would say that we're a pack that dreams are made of.

CHARLOTTE

Epilogue

6 months later

"Oh, damn," Piper says next to me as we stand in the background of the photoshoot going on. I roll my eyes as Alexi holds the foster kitten that was brought on set for the photoshoot. "Where do I buy this calendar?"

"Online. Why don't you just talk to him?" Piper rolls her eyes.

"I did, remember?"

I furrow my brows and shake my head. "When you all had your housewarming party, I was going to introduce myself, and I heard him talking to Mikael. He was going on and on about how he wanted an Omega and a pack. That—" She points at Alexi, who is in a suit and kissing the tabby cat on the cheek. "—is not the kind of man you just hook up with. He's looking for something serious."

"Well, you only have three more years of school."

She scoffs. "And then an internship and a residency. It's going to be a long time until I'm ready for someone like Alexi. Plus, he's what? Thirty-something. He's not sitting around and waiting for someone like me."

"If you say so, Piper."

"I need easy prey, like one of the rookies," she says, looking at the other men lining up waiting for their photo to be taken.

"Maybe Elias?" I suggest.

"Only if he puts in his fake teeth while we bang," she says, and I can't help but laugh and cover my mouth. It gets Alexi's attention from in front of the camera. He looks at my best friend and gives a grin. He's still missing his front tooth, and it's kind of adorable.

"He... he could fuck me with his front tooth missing," she says, and I can't help but laugh harder.

Suddenly I feel three pairs of eyes on me and I look over at my guys, Hank between them as they wait to get their picture taken first. They all smile at me. I can feel down the bond how happy they all are and just how much seeing me smile brings them joy.

"Oh, looks like your guys are up," Piper says, nudging me in the arm.

I look up and watch as they all sit on the floor with a drooling Hank in the middle of them. They're wearing suits, and they all look sexy as fuck. I mean, don't get me wrong, I love them in sweatpants, nothing, their jerseys. But seeing my guys in tailored suits, nothing gets me slicker than seeing that. They all smile and take turns interacting with Hank as the photographer takes picture after picture. Hank is loving the attention, and I swear the big oaf is smiling for the camera.

"Why don't you get your Omega in for one?" the photographer says. I could be someone who acts shy and says no thanks. But miss the chance to get a picture with them looking like this? Hell no. I nod my head, not caring that I'm wearing jeans and my homemade jersey that represent all of them. I get on the floor between Eli and Anders and pet Hank's head as the photographer takes pictures of us.

Once she's done, I watch as Mikael goes up to her. I can hear him clear as day. "I'll pay you on the side if you can get those photos expedited to me. I'll have Cheryl send you the info."

I grin and try to hide my satisfaction, but they all feel it down the bond. I get kisses to my head from each Alpha.

"Time to get ready for the game," Cheryl says, walking up to my guys. To say that I love their new agent would be a serious understatement. Cheryl is a no-nonsense female Alpha who already has an Omega and adores me. She doesn't smile at the guys, but smiles at me. "Charlotte, are you sitting in the box with me tonight?"

I nod. "Piper and I will both be in the box."

"Great." She looks back at the guys with a flat expression and points to Mikael. "No unwarranted penalties tonight." Points to Eli. "Score as much as you can, you've gotta keep up with Petrov for points." She looks over at Anders. "You just do your thing." She spins and walks away, likely heading to our box for the game that doesn't start for a few hours.

"I feel like Cheryl ranks us the same as Hank does," Mikael says, and I laugh.

"Well, I don't have a ranking system."

"You better not," he says as he grins and gives me a kiss. "See you tonight, *mon sucre d'érable.*" The nickname still makes me shiver as he leans down and gives me a kiss.

"However many goals I score tonight is how many times you're getting knotted tonight," Eli whispers, and Piper groans next to me. Eli doesn't care as he leans forward and gives me a gentle kiss.

Anders, my most patient Alpha, waits for his turn and grins when he has me all to himself. Piper, no longer wanting to hear any dirty talk, and the others go to the locker room. "Have you thought anymore about your next heat?"

I blush and shake my head. "Maybe not this next heat," I say. He grins and nods his head.

"We will just practice then."

"Lots of practice."

"Can't wait, *Kulta*."

I grin and tug on his suit lapels and crash his lips against mine. He smiles into the kiss, and I know that one day I'm going to give this man as many babies as he wants, but I'm just not ready yet.

"Get 'em, tiger," I whisper, and he laughs as he leans in for a kiss.

He kisses me one more time before he heads to the locker room with Anders and Eli.

"You all are like feral animals," Piper says, and I laugh, hooking her arm in mine.

"Let's go eat and drink on the Foxes' dime."

"Now you're talking."

Our neighbor is taking Hank home. She's been such a big help when we're on the road, and Hank loves her to pieces. I kiss his head and give him a pat for being the bestest boy before heading off with Piper.

The game is pretty anticlimactic, and this time when I sit in the box watching the game, I don't feel fear at all. All I feel is excitement. Now that I've traveled with the team and have become a staple, I've met so many more of the players' partners, and I actually feel like I belong. Jim always works box security when I'm here, and he's become part of our little hockey family as well. I make sure to invite him and his wife to dinner at least once a month.

The second period is over, and the kids come out to play a quick ten-minute game. "I fucking love Kits with Sticks!" Piper says next to me, and I nod my head. The kids look so small as they try to skate on the ice. They look so tiny in such a big stadium. About ten of the kids fall on top of each other when they all try to get to the puck. Some of them get up right away while others have a hard time getting back up. That's when one player gets a break away. The stadium and the box goes wild as we cheer for the small child. It takes them a while to get to the goal, but they swing back and take the shot, scoring a goal and ending the small scrimmage.

The child is taken to the Foxes' bench and interviewed by Opal, the commentator for the games. The child takes their helmet off and I smile to myself as I realize it's a little girl.

"Abby, how does it feel to have the winning goal of the game tonight?" Opal asks her.

"Um... great," she says.

"Do you have a favorite player on the Foxes?"

"Eli Beckford because he has a dog, and he scores lots of goals."

My ovaries explode on the spot, and I can feel my Alphas down the bond wondering what has me feeling this way. I try to shake it off, but can't help the grin that stays on my face the rest of the game.

The Foxes wind up winning, and Mikael only gets two penalties.

I wait patiently in the box for them to finish all their post game stuff. Piper goes home to study for her exams. I'm on my phone when they all walk into the box wearing their suits, looking delicious, and I'm all turned on again.

"Mmm, she seems happy to see us," Eli says.

"She seemed happy all game," Anders says.

"I think she could be happier," Mikael says.

"The only thing that would make me happier is if my Alphas took me home and kept their suits on while they fucked me and fed me fruit after."

The three of them grin. "That can definitely be arranged," Mikael says.

"Let's get our girl home," Eli says.

"Please," I ask breathlessly. God, they all look so damn good.

"Charlotte, you okay?" Mikael asks, and I push my thighs together.

I nod, and he groans.

"Your heat will never be on time, will it?"

Anders comes over and places the back of his hand on my forehead. "Let's get you home, *Kulta*."

"I still want you all to fuck me with your suits on."

"Okay, baby," Eli says with a grin.

With Anders behind, Mikael in front, and Eli holding my hand, we leave the stadium. I almost wish that I would have changed my mind for this heat. But when I find myself in the backseat riding Eli with his suit still on, just his cock out, I can't think about anything else.

All I can think about is how I have the best pack in the world and how everything in our future looks so bright. I want to experience the world with these three men. They've helped me overcome so many fears and shown me what it's like to truly live, and I can't thank them enough for it. Whatever tomorrow, or ten years, or fifty years for now holds, all I can think about is how fate brought us together on a frozen lake, but how love and determination will always keep us together.

Even if you are meant to be with someone, be it fate or a scent match, there's always work that has to go into a relationship. I'll never stop putting in the work or loving my Alphas with my whole heart. I know now that I'm worth it. I'm someone worth loving, and I'm going to spend the rest of my life showing Eli, Anders, and Mikael that I love them just as hard as they love me.

The road to happiness isn't always pretty, but damn if the destination isn't beautiful.

CHARLOTTE

Bonus Epilogue

5 years later...

"Let me hold her, *Kulta*, you're going to hurt yourself." I groan as I hand Katie to Anders. He holds our squirming three-year-old against the plexiglass, and my hands go to my back. The weight of our massive twins has been weighing on me lately. I think in my head about how I only have two months left to go and sigh.

Anders leans forward and kisses my hair before holding Katie up so she can watch her other daddies skate. She looks adorable in her dark blue Foxes dress and her blonde hair in pigtails. She has noise-canceling headphones on that she keeps trying to rip off every five seconds. She squeals as Mikael skates by, stops before her and kisses the plexiglass. She kisses her daddy through the glass and squeals as she grabs the headphones off her head and tosses them to the ground.

"Ah, ah, Katie," Anders says as he picks up the headphones.

"Don't want, Daddy?" she asks, looking for Mikael. He grins and waves a gloved hand at her, and she bounces up and down. I can tell she's looking around for Eli, who skates hard and fast to the glass. He blows me a kiss before giving our daughter a grin.

We didn't need a DNA test to know who Katie's biological dad is. She has Eli's bright green eyes and freckles. Though she has my light blonde hair.

Eli fist bumps her through the glass, and she wiggles all around in Anders' arms. "Daddy, come back!" she yells. Anders, Eli, and Mikael are all Daddy, and I happen to think Katie knows exactly what she's doing. She says the word, and they all come running.

"*Kulta*, are you okay?" he asks, and I groan.

"Can we sit?"

"Let's watch daddies from the box, okay, sweetie?" Anders says to Katie, kissing her head. She nods, knowing her friends will be in the box.

Anders holds Katie on his hip, and he holds my hand. He's very patient with me with each step I have to take to get to the main floor, so we can get to the box.

While I can sometimes see the longing look that Anders has when we come to these games, the look he gives me, my pregnant belly, and our daughter is so much deeper. He had a groin injury two years ago and decided to call his career then. As much as I supported either decision he made, he said being a father meant more to him than playing hockey. And damn, is he the best. I don't know how I could handle Katie and being this pregnant on my own. It also grants Anders and I a lot of time together. Which I know is hard for Mikael and Eli, but I know that they both have long careers ahead of them. The only thing that has changed since having Katie is that I don't attend any away games. It's just too much with a toddler, and now it's even harder with how huge I am.

Eli and Mikael have stayed on the Foxes. They still have a pack contract. They can be traded, but it would need to be to the same team, but thankfully they've—we've—become a staple for the franchise. More pack contracts are coming up in professional sports, and it should be interesting to see how it plays out.

"Ugh," I huff as I climb the last four steps. "I'm as big as a fu—" I look over at Katie and sigh. "I'm as big as a house."

"A very beautiful, sexy, perfect house. Like one that would be on *Million Dollar Listing*," Anders says, and I roll my eyes. He grabs my arm and leans in so only I can hear. "*Kulta*, if you don't think I don't want to ravish you while you're carrying my children, you're fucking crazy."

I groan but nod. He holds my hand as we walk to the box and take our seats. Katie is running around like a wild woman as she hangs out with the other toddlers who were brought by the other teammates' parents.

Anders rubs my neck as we sit, and the game starts.

"Dadddyyyyy," Katie runs up to Anders and basically flings herself onto his lap.

"Yes?"

"Can I has pretzels, please?"

Both of us can't help but grin at her. "That was such nice manners, of course you can." Katie beams as Anders picks her up. "Do you want anything?" he asks, and I nod. He doesn't even ask what

I want, he already knows my favorites and, well, I'm really hungry growing these two little monsters inside of me.

I'm rubbing my belly when Piper comes up to the side of me and takes the seat to my left. "How are my little nieces or nephews doing in there?"

"Killing me slowly," I joke, and she squeezes my arm.

"How's everything with you?" I ask, seeing the sadness written on her face, and she shakes her head. I can tell that she wants to cry, and it's my turn to be the strong one in this friendship. "Piper, if you ever need anything, you let us know."

"My first year of residency wasn't supposed to be like this."

"I know, Piper. It wasn't." She wipes her eyes, and when Katie comes running to her aunt with two fistfuls of soft pretzels, Piper smiles at her niece.

"Auntie P!" she says, climbing into her lap. Piper holds Katie like she's a lifeline and squeezes her tightly. Like my toddler will make all of her problems fade away, sometimes I feel like that too.

"So is this Alexi's last season?" Anders asks, and Piper scoffs.

"How would I know?" Anders and I both roll our eyes but don't push her any further. She's going through enough right now. Falling in love with her patient while she's supposed to be learning how to become the surgeon she wants to be. And who knows where she and Alexi stand. The fact that she's at the game as his guest speaks volumes though.

"Enough about me. When are we finding out what you're having?"

"When they're born," Anders says, and Piper scoffs.

"I'm ready to start shopping now. You're really being an unreasonable best friend, Charles."

"Oh, I forgot that me lugging around two growing humans was about you," I joke.

"Clearly," she says as she kisses Katie's head. "What about you, Katie? Do you want a brother and sister?"

"Sisters," she says.

"Good choice," Piper says, squeezing her tighter. "Are you guys staying for the after party?" I shake my head no. I'm already exhausted being here. "I don't have work tomorrow. If you'd like, I could take Katie for the night. I'm not feeling much up to the party either."

Katie bounces up and down on her lap and nods her head. "That would be awesome. Do you still have the car seat in your car?"

"Of course I do. A good aunt needs to be ready to take away her perfect little niece at a moment's notice."

"I love Auntie P," Katie says. Making Piper grin.

"This is why I'm always going to be the cool aunt instead of the mom, so you just keep popping them out for me, Charlotte."

I groan and glare at my best friend, who just smiles. If spending time with Katie gets her mind off things, then so be it.

We watch the game, and it never gets old watching them on the ice. I do worry about them getting hurt, but I've learned to manage my emotions. Nothing is more distracting for them than if my emotions are all over the place when they are playing a game. It's taken a lot of practice, but as long as I remain calm when something happens, they will be okay. I think it helps that I have Anders with me now, so they know someone is always there for me.

Eli has only gotten better the longer he spends in the NHL. Now that there are rumors of Alexi retiring, it's likely he is going to become their franchise player, which means that he and Mikael are going to have a long run on the ice together.

One of the babies is kicking me on the side, and I grab Anders' hand unconsciously and put it there. All the guys are obsessed with me being pregnant in more ways than one. I'm sure it's some possessive Alpha thing. Can't say I hate it, especially with how needy I am when pregnant.

Anders smiles and rubs my stomach as he kisses my hair.

"Going to take care of you tonight," he whispers in my ear, and I can't help how turned on I am. Mikael and Eli feel it too as I see them look up at the box but continue the game. Sometimes I think Anders likes fucking with them on the ice. There was that one time Piper had Katie, and he fingered me in the bathroom. Eli and Mikael were pretty pissed after the game, but since they still won, Anders and I felt no guilt.

I try to tone down exactly how much I would love to have this pressure taken off my back and a good orgasm so the guys can focus. I know I'm not doing a good job when they make stupid little mistakes on the ice, and it doesn't help that Anders keeps rubbing his hand on my thigh.

Katie yawns and leans against Piper.

"I think I'll take her home now," Piper says.

"Do you want us to tell Alexi?"

"No," Piper says. I lean forward and kiss Katie's hair. Anders grabs our daughter and smothers her with kisses.

"Be good for Auntie P. We'll see you in the morning."

"Okay, Daddy." Katie kisses Anders' cheek and holds out her arms for me. She wraps her small arms around my neck, and I can feel her twist my hair between her fingers. "Love you, Mommy and my babies," she says, patting my belly.

"Love you." I kiss her cheeks a million times as she giggles, and Piper puts her on her hip, and they wave as they leave the box and head to the garage.

"I wasn't joking about the ravaging."

"Oh, you didn't say you were going to ravage. What does that include?"

His thumb is rubbing circles on my thigh, and he squeezes the flesh now and then as he releases the tension in the muscle.

"So many massages that you're nice and relaxed." I groan, wanting that so bad. "Then I'm going to taste how sweet my Omega is until you're a shaking, wet mess. Then all of your Alphas are going to make you feel so good."

I'm nearly panting like a wanton hussy when I look at the monitor. "There's still a whole period left."

"Should we go home early and get you all ready for when your Alphas get home?"

"They'll kill us,' I say, knowing just how crazy it will drive them if they know we're fooling around while they're still playing their game.

"Maybe irritated, but when they have you to look forward to, they'll get over it." I rub my thighs together and look over at Anders.

God, I love him so much. He just always gets me, always knows what I need. He's only gotten better at it as time passes.

"Let's go."

He stands up, holding his arms out for me. I grab his wrists as he easily helps me get out of the seat. His hand is at my neck, rubbing gently as we do our best to sneak out of the box.

I groan as he rubs my neck in the elevator, and he grabs me, so I can feel how hard he is at my back. "I'm going to make such a mess of you tonight, *Kulta*."

Oh, I fucking love his promises.

I thought that maybe Anders was joking about all the massages and once we got home, he would just push me up against the wall and fuck me until I couldn't think. I should know better; Anders is a man of his word. He had me change into my robe and has my back propped up against the headboard of the bed as he rubs my ankles and feet.

"Honestly, I think I could come from just this."

He laughs and shakes his head. "My ego is already big enough."

"This is true." I laugh as his talented hands relieve the tension in the arches of my feet and my swollen ankles.

I thought that maybe I would feel self-conscious when pregnant and that I wouldn't like my changing body. But having three men who worship every inch of me, it's impossible to feel that way. I'm growing humans, and it's not an easy task. My body is going to change. I see it as a gift, not a curse. It also doesn't hurt that all three of my partners still take every opportunity to seduce me, even if I do feel like the size of a house.

"What else hurts?" he asks, and I shuffle sitting down.

"It's just a lot of pressure."

"Scoot up."

I do as he says and leave room for him behind me. Anders undresses except for his underwear, and god, he still looks so good. He might not be as cut as he was when he was playing for the Foxes, but the man still has a body that could put Greek statues to shame.

He climbs behind me, his hands under my stomach as he lifts up and relieves some of the pressure. I sigh in contentment and rest my head on his shoulder. He kisses the side of my head, and I smile, feeling so lucky to have this.

"Feel good?"

"Mmm. Thank you."

"I'd do anything for you." He leans forward and kisses his bond mark. "So lucky to have you, our pack, our children. We're so fortunate."

"We are."

"This house, Katie, the pack. I just—" I hear Anders getting choked up, and I grab his arm. He shakes his head. "I'm just really fucking happy."

"You don't miss hockey?"

"I'll always miss the thrill of playing pro, but nothing compares to this," he says, kissing my neck. He's still holding the pressure off of me as he kisses my neck. I can feel his honesty and love for me down the bond, and I feel so loved and content at this moment. Anders doesn't push any further. Just kisses and rotates from rubbing my back, neck, taking pressure off of my stomach.

"I'm feeling quite spoiled."

"Good." He takes his bond mark and lightly takes the flesh between his teeth. The feeling making me wetter and needier for him and my pack all at once.

He must feel my impatience through our bond as he laughs. "Just waiting for our pack to get here."

"It's been a while since it's been all of us."

"Mmm, I love watching you and having all of us together."

It is a euphoric feeling, the way they are all connected through me and when I can touch them all at once. I never really put much thought into how it would feel being the center of a pack, but I love it. I flourish under their attention and care more than I'd like to admit sometimes.

"They're probably going to be so ready and eager for you when they get home. What do you need, hmm? You want sweet?" he says, kissing my neck tenderly. "You need messy?" He licks the side of my neck, making me whimper. "Whatever our girl wants."

Suddenly the door swings open to suit-wearing Mikael and Eli. *My favorite.*

"You two are in fucking trouble," Eli says, ripping his blazer off and losing his tie. He starts scolding us as he undresses. "Do you know how much it sucks having a boner with a jockstrap on? It's fucking mean."

I can't help the laugh that squeaks out of me. Mikael is still undressing, but he looks just as irritated.

"We're out there trying to finish the game up, and all we feel is how horny our Omega is. And don't think I didn't feel your smugness, asshole." Mikael tosses his tie at Anders and scoffs as he crawls on the bed.

Anders parts my robe, exposing my breasts and playing with them from behind me. They're fucking huge, and both of them stop bitching as they watch Anders toy with me, rubbing my nipples between two fingers, which makes me moan. Perfume thickens in the room.

"She needed a massage. You can't blame me for giving our Omega what she needs." I hold back a laugh. Anders can be a sneaky, little shit when he wants to be.

"Are you hurting?" Eli asks sweetly. He truly is fucking adorable. I shake my head and hold my hand out for him.

"Anders took care of that, but he didn't take care of everything."

I spread my legs and place his hands on my pussy. He groans as he feels how wet I am. Leaning forward, he kisses my lips as he slides two fingers inside of me. Anders is still toying with my tits, and I feel like this is all I need to come.

Suddenly, another pair of lips are on my neck, and I shiver. The feeling of having all of my Alphas touch me is unlike anything else. I feel like royalty, and that I'm their sole devotion. All three of them see my pleasure as a prize. The thought is all-consuming alongside their touches. I moan as Eli picks up his pace, Mikael sucks on his bond mark, and Anders is rubbing the tips of my nipples with his thumb.

It's all it takes to set me off as I gush over Eli's fingers and put most of my weight on Anders' chest.

"So good, but we're not done with you yet," Anders whispers in my ear, and I moan, willing and ready for what they have to give. With my current situation, we have to get a little creative, especially with the three of us.

I usually love being on top, but it's too much with all that I have going on. "Lie down on your side," Mikael instructs, and Anders helps as I lie down. Anders lines himself up with my entrance and pushes in. He helps me spread my legs wide, so my other mates can watch as he fucks me. Eli groans, and his hand is back on my clit. I whimper and hold my hand out for Mikael.

"You want my cock?" he asks, and I nod.

Immediately, he is holding onto the headboard as he lines his cock up with my mouth. He thrusts in and out of my mouth, taking what he needs. I look to my left and see that Eli is toying with my clit at the same time that he strokes himself.

That all three of them love me like this and still find me beautiful and irresistible is everything.

"You look so fucking pretty taking my cock down your throat," Mikael says.

I whimper around his length and can't help moaning against him as Anders fucks me, and Eli only brings my pleasure to the next level. It doesn't take long for Mikael to finish down my throat. I swallow his cum dutifully and hungrily like I can never get enough of him. He leans down and kisses me with no care of his taste on my tongue.

Anders groans behind me, his hips stuttering, and I can tell it's taking everything in him not to knot me. His grip on my thigh is bruising, and I love the feel as he fills me up with his cum, kissing my bond mark as he does. I can feel all his emotions, and it nearly has me falling over the edge.

When he pulls out, I whimper, and Eli tsks, "Like we'd ever leave you hanging, baby. Hands and knees like a good girl."

Anders and Mikael help me get into position, and I moan, loving how much he likes it when he looks at me like this. "Love when you present for your Alphas," he says before pushing all the way into me. I can feel the stretch of his knot, and it has me nearly screaming in ecstasy. He rubs down my spine and sighs. "You good, Char baby?"

"So good. Please, Eli."

He holds onto my hips, fucking me and giving me that stretch that I so desperately needed. I can't focus on anything else besides how good he's giving it to me. And when I look up to see Anders and Mikael stroking themselves as they watch, I lose it, almost falling on my face as my orgasm hits me. My thighs shake, my vision fuzzing. It's such a cathartic orgasm it takes me a moment to realize that Eli is following me in bliss as his knot reaches its full size, and we're both in post-orgasmic bliss.

What we didn't think about is how much it would suck to be knotted in this position. Mikael scoots beneath me, so he can help hold me up, so I'm not putting any weight on my stomach.

"Hey," he says, grinning like the menace he always is.

"Hey."

"How are the babies doing?"

"Is this appropriate conversation when our packmate is balls deep?"

Mikael laughs and puts his face against my neck. "I don't know. Do we really care about being appropriate?"

"They're fine."

"I think they're girls. I think we're going to have a hockey team full of girls who look just like their mom."

I smack his chest as my eyes well up with tears. "You know how emotional I am right now. You can't say adorable shit like that right now."

"If we have three Katies, we're going to have our hands full."

I laugh and nod. Eli is rubbing my lower back so firmly it has me making absurd noises of pleasure.

"They're ours, so they will be perfect no matter what," Eli says. I smile, loving seeing how good of parents Eli and Mikael have become when they didn't have good examples has been one of the biggest joys since becoming a parent.

"I'm just ready for them to get here."

"Just not too soon," Eli says. He, out of all of my mates, is probably the biggest worry wart when it comes to my pregnancies, and I love him for it.

"Not too soon," I whisper, kissing the side of Mikael's face. "You both played great tonight."

"Mmm, you didn't even watch the third," Mikael says.

"Can you blame me?"

"No."

It's then that Eli's knot releases us, both of us moaning as he pulls out and a mixture of me, him, and Anders drips out of me.

"God, that will never get old," he says. I roll my eyes as they help me up and walk me to the bathroom where Anders is waiting with the bathtub filled with bubbles and candles glow in the small space.

"Have I told you all how much I love you?" I say as I hold their hands and sink into the warm tub.

I don't think it's possible for life to get any better than this.

7 years later...

"Andrea, Linc, and Katie, we've got to go!" I shout up the stairs.

"Coming!" I hear Andrea shout as she runs down the stairs like a goddamn rhino. I'm holding Jamie on my hip as I make sure I have all of their bags packed.

"Here, I'll hold him, baby," Eli says as he takes Jamie in his arms, and I go upstairs to see what is taking everyone so long.

Katie is dressed and ready heading downstairs, but Linc is nowhere to be found. "Linc!" I say as I open his door, finding him huddled in his quiet spot of his room. It's only for him, when he's feeling overwhelmed or overstimulated.

"Linc, honey. We've got to go to practice."

"I don't think I want to go," he says.

"Is something bothering you? Did something happen last practice?" He shakes his head no and fiddles with the Rubik's cube in his hand. "You can always talk to me, Linc," I say softly.

"All the boys and girls are bigger than me on the team. I fall down all the time and my dads are professional hockey players. I'll never be as good as them or even my sisters!"

"Honey, you don't have to play hockey."

He looks up and blinks like this is a revelation. "I don't?"

"Of course not, Linc. Just because your dads played hockey and your sisters like hockey doesn't mean you have to. I want you to pursue what makes you happy."

He looks at me contemplatively and shrugs.

"Is there something you wanted to try?"

"I really just like skating."

I grin at him. "Is it okay if I come into your quiet spot?" He nods, and I sit on the giant beanbag with him. "Want to know something?" He nods his head. "I loved ice skating. I only took a few classes. But I loved it. If you think you would rather do that than hockey, the rink has classes. Would that make you happy?"

"You mean it? I don't have to play."

"No, sweetie, you don't have to play."

He wraps his arms around me and squeezes. Linc reminds me the most of myself and I wouldn't be surprised if he designates as an Omega one day. I hold my son and hope that he knows he can always talk to me the way I did to my mom.

There's a clearing of a throat, and I see Anders standing at the door. He smiles as he sees me hold our son. "We ready to go?"

"Linc decided that he wants to try ice skating instead of hockey."

Anders smiles at his son. "That sounds great. We'll talk to the program manager when we get to the rink."

Linc stands up and hugs his dad before heading downstairs. Anders wraps me in his arms and plants a fast and hard kiss on my mouth, taking my breath away.

"What's that for?"

"Watching you be such a good mom does something to me."

I smile and take his hand as we walk downstairs. Eli has our toddler on his hip as Mikael helps the girls with their gear. We just take Linc's skates. It's rare that we can all go to their practice like this, but I know the girls are excited. Especially Katie. Now that she's on the U12 team, she's excited to show her dads what she can do.

All three of my men are on the ice as I hold Jamie on my lap. He plays with his octopus toy as each of them takes turns between Katie's and Andrea's teams. Linc is meeting with his new skating instructor to discuss what he needs to practice off the ice.

I kiss Jamie's dark hair and squeeze him tight, thinking about all my kids growing up. Jamie was a surprise, but a welcome one. He's the only child that didn't get blond hair and light eyes. Of course Mikael's genes would conquer mine. Jamie is giving gimme hands to the ice, and that's when Mikael comes to the waist-high wall.

"Do you want to skate, bug?" he asks, and Jamie squeals and wiggles in my arms.

"Are you sure?" I ask, holding him tight.

"I can skate holding the both of you, *mon doux*."

I roll my eyes but hand Jamie to his father. They are basically carbon copies of each other. Mikael leans forward and plants a kiss on my lips.

Eli skates over to the wall, kisses Jamie, and then me. "Did you see Katie's slap shot?" he says proudly, and I nod. "Go get your skates on, baby."

"That's okay, go have fun."

"Linc is coming on the ice next. Go get your skates on."

I sigh and nod my head, grabbing my skates and putting them on quickly. Never in my wildest dreams would have thought that over a decade ago when I laced up my skates and went to skate on the frozen lake, I would find the loves of my life.

But when I skate onto the ice now, seeing all my family in one place, I can't help but get choked up at how beautiful it is to see us doing the same thing that brought us together. There might have been fractures on the ice along the way, but everything is smooth skating from here on out.

I skate on the ice to smiling faces and know that if my mom and dad are looking down at me now, it's with beaming smiles on their faces and pride in their hearts.

Life isn't always perfect, but man, it feels pretty perfect right now.

Afterword

I want to thank you so much for reading One Pucked Up Pack. This book was a serious emotional labor for me. I've had this idea for nearly a year and I'm so glad that I finally got it on paper. I'm sorry if you cried, but if it helps, I cried while writing the bench scene, so you're not alone.

I love this pack so much and I feel like Charlotte and Mikael are some of the best characters I've written to date. Like Charlotte, I can't rank the guys, but that doesn't mean that you can't.

And if you would like to see what happens in Piper's story Don't Puck With My Heart you can pre-order that now. It is set for February 2024, but the date may be moved up.

Also By Sarah Blue

Coming soon:

Don't Puck With My Heart

Why Choose Omegaverse Hockey Romance coming February 2024

Piper was supposed to become a surgeon, not fall in love with an Omega with a bad heart.

What I already have out:
Heat Haven Universe

Heat Haven

Omega's Obsession

Protector's Promise

Too Tempting

Heat Haven Holidays

Vera and the Vegas V duet

Want to take a walk on the paranormal side?

Charming Your Dad – Out now!
"Fuck his dad, become his stepmom and give him a son he actually loves."

Pre order Charming the Devil – Coming April 2023

Acknowledgments

Sam- If you read the dedication you know this book is dedicated to Sam. Without Sam, it's likely that this book would have never happened. Thank you for always cheering me on and pushing me to be a better author. I value your friendship so much and don't know where I would be without you.

Sandra- My other favorite and the designer of the cover as well as the hockey jerseys is Sandra. Thank you for always giving me feedback and being one of my biggest cheerleaders. I don't know what I would do if I didn't have you to bounce ideas off of - @s maldo.designs

Stephanie- The queen of hypens and someone who has become such a great friend. Thank you for your attention to detail and for being such a supporter of my work. I'm so happy we have each other and this cobined interest in fictional love interests. hyphens

Janey- Thank you for your feedback and love for Omegaverse.

Nikki - Thank you for beta reading and your words of encouragement for this series. You are so sweet and I love working with you so much.

Leisha – Your comments always make me laugh the hardest. Thank you for all your support and for pushing me to go further and keep writing, it means so much to me.

ARC readers – Thank you for all you do, and for supporting me throughout this author journey.

My Husband- I would like to let it be known that my husband did help with some of the hockey references in this book. He is the person who brought hockey into my life so without him you guys wouldn't have had this book.

Tom Wilson – Thank you for having an amazing ass and being such a point of inspiration.

Author Friends – Flora, Kass, Alisha, Anna, and so many more. Thank you for always being willing to answer questions and giving me the motivation to keep going. references

Content Creators – To anyone who posts an image, a comment, or a video about any of my books just know I absolutely adore you. The work that goes into creating content is one of passion and it really warms my heart that you liked my book enough to post about it. Thank you for your hard work and effort.

About the Author

Sarah Blue writes contemporary sweet omegaverse, erotic, why choose romances. She loves romance in nearly any genre. When she isn't writing you can find her nose buried in a book or lit up from her kindle. She loves the sweeter side of romance and creating interesting characters while adding adventure and spice. Writing strong female characters and male characters willing to show weakness is something that makes her gooey on the inside.

Sarah lives in Maryland with her husband, two sons, and two annoying cats. If she isn't reading or writing she is probably working on a craft project or scrolling on Tik Tok.

@sarahblueauthor for most socials. Website is authorsarahblue.com and reader group is 'Sarah Blue's Reader Group' on Facebook

Ingram Content Group UK Ltd.
Milton Keynes UK
UKHW021127180423
420361UK00015B/1170